Love makes you stupid.

THE ONYX COVENANT

ENEMIES TO LOVERS ROMANTASY

THE LUNATERRA CHRONICLES

MILA YOUNG

CONTENTS

DEDICATION

For the girl who thought she could outrun fate—
He's behind you. And he's smiling.

I Don't Even Care About You

MISSIO

Fear Becomes Wishes

Lily Kershaw

1 Last Bye

Kiran + Nivi

Atash

Hatef Mehraban

Cause You Trouble

Ghaliaa, Ryana Bailouni

Darker Things

Lily Kershaw

To Love So Gently

Nome Naku

Journey

Natasha Blume

**Listen to the Soundtrack on Spotify -
The Onyx Covenant playlist by Mila Young**

WELCOME TO THE ONYX COVENANT

Welcome to the Harvest Ritual—where power is inherited in blood, and weakness is hunted.

This isn't a world of mercy.

It's built on survival, dominance, and old-world brutality wrapped in tradition.

At the center of it all lies *The Harvest Ritual*—a brutal trial designed to cull the unworthy and crown the ruthless. Every territory must offer up their fiercest heirs. Only one will emerge victorious. The others? Forgotten, broken, or buried in the soil that demanded their sacrifice.

These regions are bound by an ancient pact controlled by *The Onyx Covenant*—a blood-forged agreement that no one defies without consequence. Once chosen, there's no escape from the ritual. Not for the heirs. Not for their rivals. Not even for those they used to love.

The Onyx Covenant follows Lyra Mooncrest and Theron Shadowmane—two former lovers turned enemies—thrown together in a deadly game of dominance, revenge, and survival.

Some themes you'll find in *The Onyx Covenant:*

✔ Enemies to Lovers

✔ Ritual Trials with Deadly Stakes

✔ Alpha Hero with a Vengeance

✔ Rejected Mates

✔ Ancient Magic

✔ Second Chance (But With Knives)

✔ Touch Her and You Die

✔ Epic Fantasy Vibes with a Steamy Core

Prepare yourself. The ritual is about to begin… And it always ends with sacrifice.

PROLOGUE

LYRA

Love makes you stupid. Not the sweet, tender kind they sing about in temple hymns—I mean the raw, reckless kind that burns through your veins and turns your brain to fucking ash. The kind that has me stalking through Wolfhaven at midnight, risking everything for a man who's my family's enemy.

The ancient stones of our settlement seem to judge me like accusing eyes as I slip between them, already hearing my father's angry words as if he's caught me...

Foolish girl. Priestess in training. Alpha's daughter. Only eighteen years old. Sneaking out for an Umbra wolf—our enemy!

I press my back against the cool temple wall, breath caught in my throat as a guard passes so close I could reach out and touch him. My heart hammers wildly—not from the fear of being caught, but from the excitement that still burns inside me to see *him* again.

The guard doesn't see me as he patrols the area.

When he rounds the corner, I dart across the central clearing, my white-blonde hair tucked in my hood. I keep to the shadows cast by the massive firepit that burns day and night. The flames dance high tonight, almost as if they're trying to reach Elios, the veiled moon that hangs half shrouded in wispy clouds. Her sister, Umbra, is nowhere to be seen, hiding behind the mountains as she often does this time of year.

Tonight marks three months since I first started seeing him. Of stealing away on moonless nights to rendezvous at our meeting spot.

Of course, if my father finds out, he might very well murder me... and yet, I go against him to see Theron another night. My stomach flutters, the anticipation driving me to move quicker.

I reach the edge of our territory, slipping through the gap in the lofty pines that mark our boundary. The river comes next—Silverthread, we call it—running between our territories. Eclipsia, my home, where the Elios wolves live, and the Tenebris territory, where the enemy Umbra wolves reside.

I pause at the bank, staring at the rippling water, my wolf vision cutting through the dark to reveal my reflection. The girl who looks back at me is almost a stranger—light hair falling loose from within my hood, framing a face marked with delicate silver lines across my brow, the ceremonial tattoos of a moon priestess in training. Pale lavender eyes remind me of my mother's. My gut twists at the thought of what my parents would do if they discovered what I'm about to do. What I have been doing.

But I won't panic now. He'll be waiting like he always does.

Ahead is a natural stone alcove where the water has carved away the bank over centuries, covered in shadows. The place where we kissed the second time we met.

I hurry over there, hopping over the stones to cross the shallow river, but he isn't there.

I pause, confused. In three months of secret catch-ups, Theron has never failed to be here first, waiting with that crooked smile that makes my heart skip. I sink down onto a smooth river stone, worry threading through my chest.

The day we met, his hunting arrow had whistled past my ear, embedding itself in the oak behind me as I'd been foraging for moonberries. He'd rushed to me, horrified at almost harming me, his gaze wide with concern. He was the most handsome man I had ever seen. Despite everything I'd been taught about the Umbra wolves, I'd found myself drowning in those eyes. And with that, our first kiss comes to mind...

My heart threatens to burst from my chest as I slip through the forest, each twig snap making me freeze at the thought of being caught. I've never done anything like this—sneaking out of my house past curfew. The punishment for disobedience would be severe, but something stronger than fear pulls me forward.

I reach the alcove by the shallow river. The small cave-like space is shrouded in shadows, private and hidden from prying eyes. Perfect for a meeting that should never happen.

Will he even come? The thought makes my stomach lurch. Perhaps I misunderstood him when we parted ways after our chance meeting when he almost speared me with his arrow. Perhaps this is all a cruel joke, and he never intended to meet me again.

Then I hear it—the soft, deliberate crunch of leaves. A tall figure emerges from the darkness, and my breath catches. Theron. Moonlight glints against his sharp features, the angles of his face softened by the gentle curve of his lips as they spread into a smile.

"You came," he says, his deep voice sending a shiver down my arms.

"I shouldn't have," I answer, but I take a step toward him anyway.

Something electric passes between us. One moment, I'm standing three feet away, and the next, I'm in his arms, drawn to him like a tide to shore. His scent envelops me—pine, amber, and winter frost.

His hand reaches up to cup my brow, his thumb tracing the silver lines of my tattoo. "I haven't stopped thinking about you," he confesses, his gaze searching mine. "Not for a single moment."

"This is madness," I whisper, even as I lean into his touch. "An Elios and an Umbra..."

"Do you feel it, too?" he asks, his voice rough with emotion. "The energy between us?"

Before I can answer, his lips find mine. The world tilts on its axis. His kiss is gentle at first, questioning, but when I respond—rising on my toes to press closer—it transforms into something hungry, desperate. My fingers tangle in his dark hair, anchoring myself as my knees go weak. Heat blooms everywhere on my body, spreading like an inferno through my veins.

When he finally pulls back, his breath comes in quick gasps that match my own.

"I've been counting the hours until I can see you again," he murmurs against my lips.

My heart hammers wildly. "You know this is wrong," I say, though I make no move to step away.

A dangerous smile curves his mouth, sending another thrill through me. "I know," he admits, his hand sliding to the nape of my neck. "But it's not going to stop me. Not when you taste like everything I've ever wanted."

"My family would disown me if they knew I was here with you," I whisper, even as my fingers trace the strong line of his jaw.

"And mine would challenge me to combat for dishonoring our bloodline," he counters, pressing a kiss to my palm. "Yet here I stand, unable to stay away."

"What are we doing, Theron?" I ask, vulnerability threading through my voice.

He pulls me even closer, his forehead resting against mine. "Something brave," he whispers. "Something true." Then his lips find mine again, and I'm lost in the perfect rightness of his embrace, knowing that after tonight, nothing will ever be the same.

"Five minutes," I tell myself, trying to calm the rapid beating of my heart. I'll give him five minutes, then I'll go looking.

Five minutes stretch into ten. Ten into thirty. Thirty into an hour. My worry deepens with each passing moment.

I pick up a stone and roll it between my palms, feeling its smooth contours.

Where are you, Theron?

His words from our last meeting echo in my mind.

Lyra, if I'm ever not here waiting for you, there's only one reason—something's happened to me. I would crawl through fire before I'd miss a chance to see you.

Something coils tight in my chest—not doubt, but fear. A cold certainty that something is wrong. Not with us, but with him.

The Umbra wolves know only possession, not love. They take. They consume. They destroy. My mother's warnings ring in my ears.

But Theron is different. The way he looks at me when we're alone, as though I'm something precious. The gentleness in his touch. The stories he tells me about his family, his dreams of uniting our packs.

Gods, I know this is wrong. He's my enemy by birth, the son of our pack's greatest adversary, yet I'm utterly captivated by him. Every logical part of me knows I should walk away, return to my pack, and forget these forbidden meetings, but my heart knows better.

Worry gnaws at me as I rise to my feet. What if he's been hurt? What if his father discovered our meetings?

"I have to find him," I mutter, straightening my shoulders with determination. Something's happened, and he needs me. I know it.

I strip quickly, folding my hood and clothes, then tucking them beneath a hollow log. The night air raises goose bumps along my bare skin. I've got just enough stupidity left in me for one more reckless act.

I close my eyes, surrendering to the change that always lurks beneath my skin, waiting. The shift crashes through me like lightning striking a tree. Bones crack and re-form, muscles stretch and reshape, and skin prickles as fur erupts across my body. The pain burns and lasts only seconds.

When I open my eyes again, the world has transformed. Colors are sharp, and scents explode into vivid detail. The mineral tang of river water, the sweet decay of fallen leaves, the lingering musk of a deer—all of it painting a picture more detailed than sight ever could.

My wolf form is smaller than most, lithe and quick rather than powerful. Fur, the color of the silvery moonlight with subtle blue undertones, covers my body.

Then I run, staying low to the ground, paws barely making a sound on the carpet of fallen needles. I know the way to Theron's village. He showed me once, though we never ventured close enough to risk detection. It's a long journey, at least five miles through treacherous territory, but my wolf form eats the distance hungrily.

The forest grows darker the deeper I penetrate into Tenebris territory. The trees press closer, their twisted trunks forming grotesque shapes in the dim light. Strange sounds echo through the darkness—the scrape of claws on bark, the rustle of wings too large to belong to any normal bird, the occasional distant howl that makes my fur stand on end.

My heart thunders in my rib cage.

In these woods dwell creatures that my pack speaks of only in whispers—shadow beasts, spirits bound to ancient trees. But I don't fear them tonight. Something worse consumes me—the gnawing certainty that Theron is hurt, and I'm too late.

A twig snaps somewhere to my right, and I freeze, ears swiveling toward the sound.

I sniff the air, not picking up new scents.

Nothing emerges from the shadows. After a tense moment, I continue, moving faster now. The need to see him, to know he's safe, has become an obsession that drowns out my better judgment.

After an hour of running, I catch the first scent of woodsmoke, roasted meat, and the mingled smells of many wolves living in close proximity. I slow my pace, careful now to stay downwind as I approach the outskirts of the village.

Their village is nothing like our scattered stone dwellings. The Umbra wolves build upward—multilevel structures of dark wood and stone that rise from the forest floor. Torches line the main paths, casting flickering shadows against walls decorated with trophies and symbols of the pack's victories. Skulls hang from posts at regular intervals. A warning to enemies. A warning to me.

The Umbra pack's idea of home looks like my pack's idea of a nightmare.

I creep closer, staying within the tree line, my silver fur a liability in this darkness. Wolves gathered in clusters, the sound of laughter and conversation carrying to where I hide.

And then I see him.

Theron stands near the largest structure, his father's home. He's dressed formally in black leather armor accented with silver, his hair tied back to reveal the sharp angles of his face. Even from a distance, he steals my breath. The moonlight illuminates the strong curve of his jaw, the powerful breadth of his shoulders, and the scar on his collarbone.

My heart lurches painfully in my chest. He's alive. He's unharmed. He's... not alone.

A woman stands beside him, tall and sleek, with hair the color of midnight that falls in a glossy curtain to her waist. Her dress, blood-red and clinging to every perfect curve, marks her as high-ranking. One delicate hand rests on Theron's arm. When she laughs at something he says, her entire face transforms, revealing stunning beauty.

My insides knot into a sickening twist. I want to look

away, but I can't. It's like watching my own heart being carved from my chest.

The Pack Alpha of the Umbra Wolves, Theron's father, Magnus Shadowmane, is an imposing figure and impossible to mistake. Even from here, I spot the crimson gleam of his gaze as he watches his son with the woman. He says something that makes the woman smile wider, her hand tightening possessively on Theron's arm.

And Theron—my Theron, who whispered promises against my skin and swore that nothing would keep us apart—doesn't pull away. His expression remains neutral, unreadable at this distance, but he makes no move to reject her touch or her closeness.

The ground lurches beneath me. I've been a fool. A complete, utter fool.

As I watch, frozen in place, the woman leans closer, pressing her lips to Theron's cheek. She lingers there, whispering something in his ear that makes his jaw tighten. Magnus places a heavy hand on his son's shoulder, his smile a predatory slash across his face.

A betrothal. It has to be. The formal clothes, his father's presence, the public display—Theron is to be mated to this woman. Has it already happened? Has he already made her his while I waited by the river like a lovesick idiot?

Everything inside me shatters. Not just cracks but implodes, leaving a jagged hole where my heart should be. I can almost hear the pieces hitting the ground.

This is why he didn't come. This is why he broke his promise. He's being mated to another.

Bile rises in my throat, bitter and burning.

I was never going to be enough. An Elios wolf, daughter of his father's enemy—what future could we have had? But oh, how I believed him when he whispered that we could change things, that together we could heal the rift between our packs.

What a fucking joke.

A soft whimper escapes me before I can stop it. Too quiet for the celebrating wolves to hear but enough to release the first crack in the dam of my control. The pain is right behind my ribs, taking my breath and blurring my vision.

I loved him. Goddess help me, I still love him, even as I watch him with her.

A gust of wind shifts direction, carrying my scent to the village. Theron stiffens suddenly, his head turning toward the trees where I hide. For one terrible moment, our gazes meet across the distance, his widening with recognition and shock.

I don't wait to see more. I turn and run, pushing my body harder than I ever have before. Branches whip against my face and stones cut into my paws, but I barely feel the pain. It's nothing compared to the agony tearing through my chest, the knowledge that every sweet word, every tender touch, every promise was a lie.

Or worse—that they were true, and still not enough to make him choose me.

Behind me, I hear a commotion. Shouts. The crashing of someone large moving through the underbrush. I push harder, fear mixing with my heartbreak that sets my blood on fire.

I dart between trees, changing direction frequently, using every trick I learned growing up in forests just like these. Glancing back, I spot a shadow rushing amid the woods like a demon, coming after me.

Heart thumping against my rib cage, I sprint faster.

The river appears ahead, its silver surface now a barrier I desperately need to cross. Just a few more yards...

Something heavy crashes into me from behind, sending me tumbling across the forest floor. Pain explodes in my side as I slam into a tree trunk, the impact forcing a yelp past my lips.

My attacker looms over me—a huge black wolf. Not Theron, but one of his pack. A guard, by the look of him, his muzzle scarred from numerous fights.

I try to scramble away, but he pins me with a paw, claws digging into my shoulder. Blood wells, hot and sticky, matting my fur. I snap at him, teeth catching only air as he jerks back.

His jaws open wide, revealing teeth designed to rend flesh from bone. At that moment, I know I'm going to die. Here, in enemy territory, with no one knowing where I am or why I came. They'll find my body in the river, if they find it at all, and never know that I died for love. Then a war between the packs will ensue.

A blur of black crashes into my attacker, tearing him

away from me with force. The guard yelps in surprise as he's thrown against a tree, his body crumpling to the ground.

Theron stands between us, his wolf form even more impressive than I remember. He's all sleek muscle and deadly grace, his midnight fur shimmering with subtle silver highlights in the moonlight.

In seconds, he transforms, standing tall, nude, and he's frowning, fury burning in his eyes.

"What the fuck do you think you're doing, Varus?" he snarls at the guard still in wolf form.

Varus struggles to his feet, blood trickling from a cut above his eye.

"I'll handle this enemy." Theron moves closer, teeth bared in a snarl that raises the hair on the back of my neck. "You'll say it was nothing but a deer, or I'll finish you. Understood?"

Enemy. The word cuts deeper than any physical wound. That's all I am to him now. Perhaps all I ever was.

Varus glances between us, then gives a nod.

"Go back to the village. That's an order."

For a moment, I think Varus will refuse. His muscles bunch as if preparing to attack. Then, with a final glare in my direction, he turns and limps away, disappearing into the darkness of the forest.

The moment he's gone, Theron turns to me, his expression shifting from rage to something more complex. "Lyra, what the hell were you thinking? You could have been killed."

I scramble onto all four paws, ignoring the pain that lances through my shoulder. Blood drips from the wounds, but they're not deep enough to be life-threatening. Physical pain is the least of my concerns right now.

Without responding, I dash toward the river, where my clothes still lie hidden beneath the hollow log. I need to shift back, needing to get home, and fast, and not leave my clothes behind as evidence. I grit my teeth against the agony as bones reshape and fur recedes. My hands shake as I drag my clothes and robe on, pulling them on with desperate, jerky movements.

Behind me, the sounds of Theron's footsteps approach. I don't turn around. I can't bear to see him, to look into the face that's haunted my dreams for months.

"Lyra," he says softly. "Look at me. Please."

"Why?" I ask, the word scraping my throat raw. "So you can lie to my face?"

I turn slowly, the movement sending fresh pain through my injured shoulder. Blood seeps through the fabric of my robe. Theron stands a few feet away, shadows concealing most of him, except his face... and those hypnotic, pale gray eyes, almost silver.

"Why did you cross the river?" he asks, sounding strained. "Do you have any idea how dangerous that was?"

A bitter laugh escapes me. "We were supposed to meet here. Did you forget?" My voice cracks on the last word. "But you never came."

"I couldn't—"

"I saw you," I cut him off, the words like acid on my tongue. "With her. With your father. Some kind of betrothal celebration, wasn't it?"

His face pales, the scar on his collarbone standing out stark against his skin. "You shouldn't have seen that."

"You think?" I spit, tears burning behind my eyes. "Because I'm your enemy, right? You just said it yourself."

He reaches out for me, but I step back.

"Lyra, it's not what you think. I'm not—"

"Fuck you." The tears spill over now, hot tracks down my cold cheeks. I hate that he sees them, hate that I can't stop them. "What am I to you, Theron? Just some fun on the side? A novelty? The forbidden Elios bitch you could play with until it was time to settle down with a proper Umbra wolf?"

He flinches as if struck. "It was never like that. You know it wasn't."

"I don't know anything anymore." My response breaks, betraying the depth of my pain. "Except that I was stupid enough to believe you when you said you loved me."

"I do love you." Theron steps forward, one hand reaching for mine again. "Everything I said was true."

"Don't." I jerk away from his touch as if it burns, my back hitting a tree. "If you loved me, you wouldn't be with her."

"It's complicated, Lyra. My father—"

"I don't care!" Angry tears pass my lips in a near scream. "I don't care about your father or your pack politics or whatever excuses you've crafted. You made a choice, Theron... and it wasn't me."

I'm trembling now, my entire body shaking with the force of my emotions. My chest feels like it's caving in, tight and suffocating, as if my ribs might crack beneath the pressure. My breath comes in shallow gasps, each one sharp and ragged as though I'm fighting to keep myself from falling apart completely.

It's not all right. None of this is all right.

A hot tear slips down my cheek, and I swipe it away roughly as if denying it will somehow keep the rest from falling. My throat tightens, a painful knot forming as I try to choke back the sob threatening to break free. My breath stutters, a sharp, shaky inhale that catches in my chest.

I sniff hard, forcing it down. *Don't cry. Not now. Not in front of him.*

But the tears keep coming, blurring my vision until I can barely make out his face. My fingers curl into fists, nails biting into my palms, but it does nothing to stop the ache clawing inside me—this unbearable hollow feeling that won't leave. My heart twists, hammering so hard it feels like it might tear itself apart.

I can't take this.

"I wish I'd never crossed paths with you," I whisper, voice breaking on a sob I can't swallow down this time. "Never believed a single word you said."

The words barely scratch the surface of the storm inside me. Because the truth is, I had believed him—every promise, every look, every touch—and now those memories feel like knives carving through me.

Another sob slips out, and I press my hand to my mouth, trying to smother the sound. My shoulders shake, and I wrap my arms around myself as if holding my own pieces together might stop me from shattering completely.

"Lyra, please." Theron's face contorts with anguish, his eyes glistening in the moonlight. "Let me explain. There are things happening that you don't understand. She means nothing. It's only an agreement I have no say in."

"I understand enough." I push away from the tree, swaying as dizziness washes over me. "This is over. Whatever was between us... it's done. We never should have thought we could be anything."

He moves toward me again as I stumble.

"You're hurt. Let me help you."

"Don't touch me!" I snap and take a shuddering breath, trying to steady myself. "Just... don't. There was nothing real between us, was there? It was all just pretty lies that meant nothing in the light of day."

"That's not true," he insists. "What we had—what we have—it's the only real thing in my life."

For a moment, just a heartbeat, I almost believe him. The pain on his face mirrors my own, his hands trembling at his sides as if he's physically restraining himself from reaching for me again.

Then I remember the woman in red, her hand on his

arm, her lips against his cheek. I remember his father's approving smile. I remember the years of stories about Umbra wolves and their cruelty, their manipulation, their lies.

"Go back to your mate," I say, the words like ashes in my mouth. "Return to your father and your pack and your perfect Umbra life. Forget about the Elios wolf who was foolish enough to love you."

I turn away, unable to look at him any longer. Each step toward the river feels like walking through quicksand.

"Lyra," he calls after me, desperation edging his tone. "This isn't over. I'll find a way—"

"It *is* over," I interrupt, not turning back.

I move across the river over the stones. Behind me, there's nothing but silence. When I reach the middle of the current and finally look back, the bank is empty. Theron is gone, melted back into the shadows of Tenebris like he was never there at all.

Something inside me calcifies then, my heart turning from broken glass to stone. A sob tears in my chest. Another follows, and another, until I can barely stay upright against the current and the crushing weight of my grief.

Somehow, I make it across. Somehow, I drag myself back through the forest to my village. My legs ache, my body is sluggish and cold, but I keep moving—one foot in front of the other—barely aware of the tears still streaking down my face. The wind stings my damp cheeks, but I don't bother wiping the tears away. I just need to get home.

The village's outer torches flicker through the trees, and relief rushes through me, but before I can step into the clearing, a shadow moves.

"Lyra?"

The voice is familiar—one of my father's guards, Kian. He steps out from behind a tree, his hand already resting on the hilt of his blade. His face hardens when he sees me stumbling forward.

"What are you doing out here?" His tone is sharp, but then his eyes narrow, and he steps closer. His gaze drops to my blood-smeared clothes, the scrapes on my hands, the way my breath keeps hitching.

"Shit... are you hurt? What happened?"

I shake my head, but my throat's too tight to answer.

"I'll get you home," he says quickly. He shrugs off his cloak and drapes it over my shoulders before guiding me forward. His pace is steady but firm, as though he knows I might collapse if he lets go.

"You know your father's gonna have questions," he mutters, half to himself. "Questions and a hell of a temper."

I barely hear him. My head hangs low, tears still falling silently as I stumble beside him. Each step feels heavier, the weight of everything pressing down until I'm not sure I'll be able to breathe when I walk.

Kian doesn't say anything else. He just keeps his hand

on my arm, steady and sure, walking me home through the dark.

I stay silent, knowing no wolves in my pack will ever understand what I've done or why.

When I finally reach my room, I bar the door and collapse onto my bed. The pain in my shoulder has dulled to a persistent throb, already beginning to heal with my wolf metabolism. The wounds in my heart will take longer—perhaps a lifetime.

But I make a promise to myself. No more tears. No more dreams of a future that can never exist.

The next time I see Theron Shadowmane, it won't be as a lover.

It will be as an enemy.

And I will make him regret the day he ever spoke my name.

CHAPTER
ONE

THERON

One Year Later

Blood splatters across my face as I slam my opponent into the dirt. The metallic scent mingles with his fear, sour and acrid, as I press my forearm against his throat. He's an Elios wolf, smaller than me, but he puts up a damn good fight, and his eyes widen as I increase the pressure. The roar of the crowd pulses around us, but I focus only on the rapid thud of his heartbeat beneath my grip.

"Yield," I growl, low enough that only he can hear me.

He bares his teeth, a futile display of defiance, before survival instinct kicks in. His neck goes limp beneath my arm.

"I yield," he chokes out.

I release him immediately, stepping back as he gasps for air. The crowd of Umbra wolves behind me erupts in savage cheers, their howls piercing the night sky. I don't acknowledge them. This display—this ritual combat—means nothing. It's merely the prelude to the real battle that awaits.

Wolves from both packs clash nearby, each displaying their skills in a fierce bid to be chosen as the final champions for the ritual that takes place once every ten years. The Harvest Ritual.

A primal scream rips through the clearing, silencing the cheers. I whip around, muscles tensing as I spot the source—Drakon, an Umbra wolf known for his volatile temper. His body twists as he surrenders to the shift. Bones crack audibly as his human form gives way to the beast within.

"Shit," I mutter, already moving toward him. He's losing control.

The spectators scramble backward, creating a wide circle around Drakon as his transformation completes. He stands nearly four feet tall at the shoulder, his midnight fur bristling along his spine. Foam drips from large jaws filled with teeth designed to rend flesh from bone.

Drakon lunges, jaws clamping onto an Elios wolf's shoulder. Blood sprays as the man screams, the sound more animal than human.

I don't think. I move.

The ground disappears beneath my feet as I launch myself at Drakon. My shoulder crashes into his ribs, dislodging him from his victim. We tumble across the dirt, a tangle of limbs and fury. His claws rake across my chest, tearing through my already bloodstained shirt and leaving fire in their wake.

"Theron!" Kieran, my closest friend, shouts from somewhere beyond the fray. "Don't kill him!"

As if I need the reminder. Killing during the selection ceremony is grounds for immediate disqualification. But so is losing control of your wolf form, which Drakon has already done. There's no salvaging his chances.

I manage to get my arm around Drakon's throat, locking my elbow as I apply pressure to his carotid. His massive body thrashes beneath me, pure instinct fighting for survival. The scent of his fear—sharper now, more primal—fills my nostrils as I tighten my grip.

"Sleep," I command through gritted teeth, ignoring the burning in my chest where his claws found purchase. "Sleep, you fool."

His movements grow weaker, more erratic. After what feels like an eternity, he goes limp beneath me. I hold for another few seconds to ensure he's truly unconscious before releasing him.

The beast melts away, leaving only the man behind—naked and vulnerable on the blood-soaked ground. Covenant guards rush forward, dragging his unconscious form away. He's eliminated from the competition, his weakness exposed for all to see.

I rise to my feet, stretching my back. The claw marks across my chest sting, but they're shallow. They'll heal soon enough. My muscles ache from the exertion, but the pain feels good—a reminder that I'm alive.

Kieran reaches me first, his eyes wide as he takes in the claw marks across my chest. "Show-off," he says, the tension in his face belying his casual tone. "Always have to be the hero, don't you?"

I snort, wincing as the movement pulls at my wounds. "Someone had to step in."

"There are a dozen covenant guards who could have handled it." Kieran glances at the crowd, which has resumed its previous activity as though nothing happened. Another pair of male contestants circle each other in combat nearby. "But no, the great Theron Shadowmane had to prove his dominance."

"It wasn't about dominance," I argue, though part of me wonders if that's true. "It was about protection."

Kieran's gaze softens slightly. "I know. That's what worries me about you." He looks past me, his expression shifting. "Your father's coming. Try to look suitably brutal."

I turn, squaring my shoulders despite the pain. Father strides toward us, his huge frame parting the crowd effortlessly. His black hair, streaked with white and woven with bone beads that click together when he moves, frames a face carved from granite.

"You intervened," he says without preamble, his voice deep and resonant.

I incline my head. "Drakon lost control. He would have killed the Elios."

"And that would have been regrettable," Father says, though his tone suggests he finds nothing terrible about dead Elios wolves. And my thoughts spiral for a split second to Lyra, but I shake that away just as fast. "Still, you showed initiative. Strength." His gaze drops to the claw marks on my chest. "And a certain disregard for your own safety."

"The wounds are superficial."

Father's lips curve in what might pass for a smile on another man. On him, it looks like a predator baring its teeth. "Good, he's out. The weak have no place in the Harvest Ritual." He clasps my shoulder, his grip crushing. "Continue to make your pack proud."

He strides away, moving to speak with others.

"He's in a good mood," Kieran observes dryly, rubbing at a bruise forming on his jaw. "Must be all the violence in the air. Gets his blood pumping."

I grunt in response, watching as Father speaks with Tarek Nightsinger, a leader of the Onyx Covenant and a puppet to my father's ambitions. Melian, the second who rules alongside Tarek, remains inside the building. By law, only males are permitted to attend the selection.

Both of them are the ruling covenant over the packs, ensuring we don't murder each other, though considering the pair are wolves from our pack, they tend to take favor with my father on small matters.

But no Alpha dares challenge the Onyx Covenant outright—not unless they crave annihilation. The stone they're named after isn't just symbolic; it's a vessel of ancient fae magic, a force that once bled through this land when both moons aligned. If anyone, including an Alpha, dares to break the law by slaughtering their rivals and seizing their territory, the stone awakens.

And when it does, it releases the Onyx Warriors.

Twisted figures clad in shadow and iron, they rise from the onyx building itself, forged from the magic that once seeped into these lands. Bound to no pack and loyal only to vengeance, they hunt without rest, carving through entire bloodlines until balance is restored. Some say they are the spirits of fallen Alphas who once defied the Covenant—warriors trapped in endless torment, driven by a thirst that can never be quenched.

It's said that those who witness the Onyx Warriors never forget the screams that follow.

"You know," Kieran continues, pulling me out of my thoughts, "we could both just run. Find a nice, quiet corner of the world where Alpha politics don't exist."

"And miss all this fun?" I gesture to the fighting, the egos, the cheering for more brutality around us. "Besides, you know as well as I do there's nowhere we could hide that he wouldn't find us."

Kieran sighs dramatically. "True. Your father's not exactly the forgiving type." He tears a strip from his already shredded shirt, offering it to me. "Here, at least try to look less like you just fought a rabid wolf."

I take the cloth, wiping away the worst of the blood from my face and chest. Around us, the selection battles continue. These aren't fights to the death. They're demonstrations of skill and power meant to intimidate opponents and impress the Onyx Covenant officials who will select the champions. Every unmated male in both packs has the right to participate, though most know better than to challenge wolves like me or Kieran.

"How many do you think will make it to the final selection?" I ask, watching as two Elios wolves grapple nearby.

"Fuck knows." Kieran shrugs, his lean muscles shifting beneath skin marked with battle scars from years of training together. "Last Harvest Ritual, they selected eight from each pack."

"Doesn't it bother you?" I ask quietly, making sure no one else can hear as we linger at the edge of the battle starting to slow down, knowing Father will already get us both into the final ritual. "Being a piece in his game?"

"Every damn day." Kieran's jaw tightens. "But what choice do we have?" He gestures to the huge obsidian tower that looms behind us—the Onyx Covenant head-quarters, the neutral territory between the Eclipsia and Tenebris sectors of land. "Win the Harvest Ritual, and maybe we can change things. Maybe we can find the truth."

Truth. The word hangs heavy. The truth about my sister's death, about my mother's disappearance.

A bone-deep gong reverberates through the battles and cheers, halting the remaining fights. The sound emanates from the Onyx Covenant building, signaling the end of the selection battles.

"And so, the posturing ends," Kieran mutters, straightening beside me. He runs a hand through his sweat-soaked hair, the dark reddish strands standing up at odd angles. "Think I have time to make myself pretty for the ceremony?"

I snort. "Not enough time in the world for that, Stormwolf."

"It's Stormfang now, you ass," he corrects, punching my shoulder lightly. "Changed it last moon. Stormwolf was my father's name, and that drunk bastard doesn't deserve the honor."

"Stormfang," I repeat, tasting the name. "Suits you better anyway."

"Damn right it does." Kieran grins, flashing elongated canines that give credence to his new surname.

The crowd parts as Tarek, leader of the Onyx Covenant, emerges from the shadow of the building in his black, hooded robe. Both Umbra and Elios moons are full tonight, hanging in perfect balance in the night sky. One dark as pitch, one pale as winter frost.

Tarek stops after descending three wide steps, raising his hands for silence that has already fallen.

I watch him, my pulse thrumming beneath my skin. That will be me standing there one day—the only reason I'm even playing along with my father's twisted plan. He thinks I'll be his pawn if I win the Harvest Ritual and take Tarek's place, but I know better. This is about more than loyalty to my father. It's about ensuring no one from the enemy pack, Elios, wins. If they do, they'll control both territories for the next ten years, and that's a future he refuses to let happen.

I have other plans.

"Wolves of Umbra and Elios," he begins, his voice carrying across the clearing without effort. "Tonight, we gather as our ancestors did to choose those who will participate in the sacred Harvest Ritual."

I study the faces around me, the mingled looks of reverence and bloodlust. Both packs may hate each other, but they respect the ancient traditions that bind us.

"For six centuries, the Harvest Ritual has determined who will lead our divided nation," Tarek continues. "For fifty years, the Umbra pack has held this honor."

A roar goes up from the Umbra wolves behind me. I remain silent, my attention fixed on Father, who stands with a triumphant smile carved into his face.

"Tonight, we have decided to select five champions from each pack. Five strong Alphas who will compete for control of the Onyx Covenant, for the right to guide Wolfhaven for the next decade." Tarek's gaze sweeps the crowd. "The rules remain unchanged. When your manacle glows, you will have ten minutes to claim an unmated Omega from your pack. Together, you will face the trials set forth by our ancestors. Winners will take our place in the Onyx Covenant."

A low murmur ripples through the gathering.

"From the Elios pack," Tarek calls, unfurling a silver scroll. "I call forth the following champions: Orion Blaze, Cassius Claw, Nyx Ember, Tavian Windborn, and Zephyr Talonblade."

Half the crowd cheers heavily as the Elios wolves

move forward, climbing the steps to stand beside Tarek. I study them carefully, noting their builds and the way they move, searching for weaknesses I can exploit later. Orion Blaze stands tallest among them, his platinum blond hair nearly white in the moonlight. I've heard stories of his speed and his uncanny ability to anticipate an opponent's moves.

"From the Umbra pack," Tarek continues. "I call forth Erebus Shade, Kieran Stormfang, Maddox Daruk, Theron Shadowmane, and Nero Lup."

My name jolts through me, though I knew it was coming. Father has been grooming me for this since I was old enough to shift. Still, hearing it spoken aloud makes my blood run cold.

We move forward together to stand opposite the Elios champions.

Tarek moves between us, carrying an ornate wooden box. From it, he removes ten identical manacles—bands of polished onyx shot through with veins of silver. Ancient power radiates from them, the old fae magic that our ancestors harnessed centuries ago.

"These bindings are sacred," Tarek intones as he secures one around my wrist. The metal is cold at first, then warms rapidly against my skin. "They will connect you to the Omega you choose, ensuring that neither can abandon the other. Stray more than fifty feet apart for longer than five minutes, and the manacles will inject venom into your veins, killing you both. And if your partner meets an unfortunate death on their own, you must continue alone. If you are the unfortunate one, your Omega must continue on her own."

Fuck!

The manacle seems to thump against my pulse point as though learning the rhythm of my blood. I resist the urge to try to remove it.

"When these glow," Tarek continues, "the time will have come to select your partner and return here at midnight. It may be tomorrow. It may be a month from now. You must be ready at all times."

He steps back, surveying us with a solemn stare. "Not all of you will survive the trials ahead. Some will fall to the challenges themselves. Others..." His gaze drifts meaningfully between the Umbra and Elios champions. "Well, interference is not permitted by the ancient laws."

What he doesn't say—what everyone knows—is that interference often happens. The Harvest Ritual isn't just a test of skill and strength. It's a brutal contest designed to thin the ranks. And sometimes, death is only one way out.

Surviving isn't enough. Winning is everything.

"The Onyx Covenant thanks you for your service," Tarek concludes. "May the worthy rise... and the fallen be forgotten."

As we descend the steps, Father calls me over. We stand in the shadows, his powerful hand clamping down on my shoulder. His grip is punishing, fingers digging into muscle with unnecessary force.

"You will not disappoint me," he growls. His crimson

gaze bores into mine. "Five decades of Umbra rule, and you will make it six."

"Yes, Father," I respond, keeping my voice neutral even as my stomach twists with revulsion, with the knowledge that I have my own intentions for this game, something that will turn him against me.

He leans closer, his breath hot against my ear. "The Elios grow bolder. They think they can challenge us after all this time. You will show them their place."

I nod. Over his shoulder, I notice the Alpha of the Elios pack watching us, his expression unreadable in the moonlight.

Father follows my gaze, his lips curling in a sneer. "Remember what they did to your mother," he murmurs. "Remember why we fight."

The lie tastes bitter in the air between us. I know the truth—or enough of it to recognize his deception. Mother didn't die at Elios hands as he claims. She disappeared while investigating ancient pack histories, searching for the truth that Father has worked so hard to bury. That's all I've been able to determine so far in my findings, but it's enough to know I must seek my own truth.

Before I can respond, he releases me and strides toward the Elios Alpha. The two pack leaders meet at the base of the steps, exchanging formal bows that do nothing to mask the hatred between them.

"That went well," Kieran drawls, appearing at my side. His own manacle gleams dully against his wrist.

"Nothing says 'loving father' like threats disguised as encouragement."

I flex my hand, feeling the weight of the binding. "He's worried. The Elios haven't fielded champions this strong in decades."

Kieran studies the Elios wolves, who have gathered in a tight circle at the far side of the clearing. "They want this badly. Fifty years is a long time to be the subordinate pack."

"Can you blame them?" I ask quietly. "How many of their kind have disappeared during Father's rule? How many have died for crossing invisible lines drawn by the Onyx Covenant?"

"Careful," Kieran warns, his voice dropping. "Even here, the walls have ears."

The two pack Alphas stand so close they could kill each other in an instant, maintained only by the ancient laws that protect the Covenant land between both sectors.

Kieran follows my gaze to the Onyx Covenant building. He knows what I seek—the ancient records kept within. If I win the Harvest Ritual, I'll have access to those archives. I'll finally know why my sister was executed for helping Elios refugees and why my mother disappeared while investigating our shared past.

"Just be careful," Kieran warns. "Your father—"

"Is a monster," I finish for him. "I've never forgotten that."

The ceremony complete, servants emerge from the

Onyx Covenant building carrying platters of roasted meat. The scent of charred flesh and woodsmoke fills the air, making my mouth water despite the tension. My wolf stirs within me, hungry after the battles and the ceremony.

"Now we feast!" Tarek announces, gesturing to the food. "Tomorrow, you return to your territories to prepare. May the moons guide your path."

"Come on." Kieran nudges me toward the food. "If I have to spend our near future bound to one of our Omegas while fighting for our lives, I'm at least going to do it on a full stomach."

I follow him, and we heap our plates with slabs of roasted boar, still sizzling from the spit. I tear into the meat, savoring the rich, gamey flavor as blood runs down my chin. Around us, other wolves do the same, their manners abandoned in favor of satisfying primal hunger.

"You know," Kieran says between bites. "I've been thinking about which Omega I'll choose."

I raise an eyebrow. "You have someone in mind already?"

He grins, sharp canines flashing in the firelight. "Several someones, but I'm leaning toward Cleris. She has healing magic, which could come in handy when you inevitably get us into trouble."

"When *I* get us into trouble?" I laugh, the sound rusty from disuse. "Need I remind you who started the border incident last spring?"

"Details, details." Kieran waves a dismissive hand. "Besides, that Elios patrol had it coming."

"They were three miles inside their own territory."

"Like I said, they had it coming." Kieran tears off another chunk of meat. "What about you? Any Omega caught your fancy?"

I shrug, uncomfortable with the direction of the conversation. The truth is, I've avoided thinking about it. The idea of binding an Omega to this dangerous quest—to me—sits uneasily in my gut. My past with females is messy at best.

And then there's Lyra.

Her face flashes in my mind—the fire in her eyes when she was furious at me, heartbroken, the tears that shattered me. For a second, I let myself imagine her here, close enough for me to reach out and touch. To make her understand. And to not lose her.

But then Jess's face flickers in my mind, too. The woman my father forced on me a year ago, the one Lyra had seen me with. His grand plan to secure alliances had backfired spectacularly. Jess's family hadn't been quiet about their disappointment when things imploded—tempers flared, loyalties strained, and my father's reputation took a hit. It was chaos, but part of me had been relieved. Getting out of that mess was a blessing... but it cost me Lyra. The look on her face that night still haunts me.

I grunt under my breath and push the thoughts down hard, locking them away before they can take root. Lyra isn't mine to want. Not with the risks ahead. Not when my choices made sure of that.

"I haven't decided," I say finally. "There's time."

Kieran studies me, his usual joking demeanor slipping away. "You know, if you really wanted to piss off your father, you could choose Vale Dawn."

I nearly choke on my food. Vale?

She's the only surviving daughter of the wolves who tried to assassinate my father during an uprising. Her entire family was executed for treason, but she was just a child when it happened. The only reason she's still alive is because too many believed killing a pup would make my father no better than the ones who betrayed him.

Kieran's expression gleams with attitude. "Imagine the look on his face."

"I'd rather keep breathing," I mutter, though the idea holds a certain rebellious appeal. "Besides, Vale deserves more than to be used as a pawn in my fight with him."

Kieran shrugs, but his expression turns thoughtful. "Maybe that's the problem with all of this. We're treating these Omegas like tools instead of partners."

"Yeah, well," I mutter, stabbing a piece of meat with my fork. "That's the game we're playing, isn't it?"

Kieran's smile fades. "Funny thing about pawns... sometimes they take the king."

TWO

LYRA

One Week Later

Dawn unfurls lazy fingers across the Eclipsia forest, painting the sky in shades of pink and gold, which would be beautiful if I gave a damn about sunrises anymore. I've been up for hours, slipping out of my home while the rest of the pack still slept, my muscles sore and my mind restless. Sleep hasn't come easy in the year since that night by the river. Since *him*.

The Forest Sanctuary lies three miles from our settlement, a natural clearing surrounded by boulders that rise from the ground like the spines of ancient beasts. It's our place, mine and Aria's, where we can be ourselves away from judging eyes and traditional expectations.

I stretch, feeling the pleasant burn in my arms and legs from an hour of warm-ups. The morning air carries the scent of pine and damp earth, clean and crisp in my lungs. This is the only time I feel anything close to peace anymore—when my body is in motion, and my mind is too occupied with survival to dwell on anything else.

"You're distracted today," Aria calls from atop the largest boulder, her lithe form silhouetted against the rising sun. Wind whips her light chestnut hair across her face, strands sticking to the sheen of sweat along her brow. She pulls at the fitted leather gear that clings to her like a second skin, scuffed and dirt-streaked from their earlier sparring. A wicked grin curves her lips as she balances effortlessly, poised. "I could have taken your head off twice already."

"In your dreams." I snort, tightening the straps around my wrists. My loose pants and shirt make it easy to tuck the leather bands into my pockets, hidden from my parents' prying eyes.

Aria leaps down, landing with the grace our kind is known for. Unlike me, she doesn't hide her combat training. She's a Nightblade—one of the elite scouts who patrol our borders and gather intelligence on Umbra movements. Her father is my father's second-in-command, making her practically royalty in our pack hierarchy, second only to me.

Not that rank matters out here. Between these ancient stones, we're just two Elios pack members learning to survive in a world designed to break us.

"Ready for round two?" she asks, cracking her knuckles with a grin that shows too many teeth. "Or do you need a moment to compose elegies to your mysterious lost love?"

"Fuck off," I growl, but there's no heat in it. Aria is the only one who knows about that night, though even she doesn't know who broke my heart. Just that someone did, and that I crossed the river to find him. Some secrets are too dangerous to share, even with your best friend.

She tosses me a fighting staff—smooth ash wood, weighted at both ends. I catch it automatically, twirling it once to feel its balance. We've been training with weapons for months now, ever since I convinced her that priestess prayers wouldn't be enough if I ever faced a real threat.

"Come on, Moon Dancer," she taunts, using the childhood nickname I've grown to hate. "Show me what those delicate priestess hands can do."

I lunge without warning, staff whistling through the air toward her midsection. She blocks, the crack of wood against wood echoing across the clearing. The impact vibrates up my arms, but I don't hesitate, pivoting to strike at her legs.

Aria leaps over the swing, laughing. "Better! But still too predictable."

We fall into a familiar twirl, trading blows and blocks, feet moving across the moss-covered ground in patterns we've practiced a thousand times. Aria is stronger than me—all corded muscle and natural power—but I'm faster, more precise. What I lack in brute force, I make up for in technique.

"Heard anything about Orion lately?" I ask casually, ducking under a swing that would have connected with my shoulder.

Aria's rhythm falters for just a heartbeat, enough for me to tap my staff against her ribs.

"Point," I announce, grinning at her scowl.

"Low blow," she mutters, stepping back to reset our positions.

"All's fair in combat," I remind her, echoing the words she's said to me countless times. "Besides, you're the one who can't stop talking about him."

Orion Blaze—my father's most promising young warrior and Aria's not-so-secret obsession for the past year. He's handsome enough, I suppose, if you like the brooding, serious type. All sharp angles and intense stares, with a reputation for being utterly dedicated to pack protection.

Aria attacks again, her movements more aggressive now.

"I saw him swimming in the northern lake yesterday," she admits between strikes. "Alone."

I raise an eyebrow, blocking her assault. "Spying on him now? That's not creepy at all."

"It was reconnaissance," she insists, feinting left before striking right. I predict the move and counter, but she's ready, hooking my staff with hers and nearly wrenching it from my grip. "Besides, someone has to appreciate the view."

"And?" I prompt, dancing backward to create space. "Was the view worth your stalker tendencies?"

A flush creeps up her neck, visible even against her sun-kissed skin. "Let's just say the Goddess blessed him generously."

We both burst into laughter, the kind that makes your stomach hurt and your guard drop. Which is exactly when Aria sweeps my legs out from under me. I hit the ground hard, air rushing from my lungs, the tip of her staff at my throat before I can blink.

"Point," she says sweetly. "Never let your guard down, priestess."

I knock her staff aside with the back of my hand. "Cheater."

"Survivor," she corrects, offering me a hand up. I take it, then use her momentum to flip her over my shoulder. She lands with a thud and a curse that would make even the most hardened warrior blush.

"Survivor," I echo, standing over her with my own staff now pointed at her chest.

Aria stares up at me for a moment, then breaks into a wide grin. "You're learning. Good."

I help her up, and we move to sit on one of the smaller boulders that edge the clearing. The sun has fully risen now, bathing the forest in golden light that dapples through the canopy above. Sweat cools on my skin as I take a long drink from my waterskin.

"What about you?" Aria asks after a comfortable

silence. "It's been a year since you met that gorgeous, mysterious guy you barely told me anything about. How come you haven't seen him again?"

I shrug. "I guess life happened. He went his own way. I went mine."

"Life happened?" Aria arches a brow. "That's it? No lingering glances or wistful letters penned by candlelight?"

I laugh, though it comes out flat. "Please. He wasn't exactly the write-me-poetry type."

"Still..." Aria leans in, a teasing grin spreading across her face. "You liked him."

"Maybe." I pause, my smile fading. "But liking someone doesn't mean they'll stick around." The memory is bitter, but I've had plenty of practice telling myself to move on. "Besides, you know my father. He'd go ballistic if I showed interest in anyone he hasn't personally vetted and found worthy of his precious daughter."

Aria makes a sympathetic noise, but her facial expression is too knowing for comfort. She sees more than I want her to—always has.

The truth is, I still wake from dreams of silvery eyes and promises whispered against my skin. Still feel phantom touches on nights when the moon is high and my defenses are low. Still hate myself for it.

"Your mother's been dropping hints," Aria says, twisting a lock of brown hair around her finger. "About you needing to choose soon."

I roll my eyes, though anxiety curls in my stomach. "I'm aware. Apparently, at nineteen, I'm practically ancient. On the verge of spinsterhood."

"You're the Alpha's daughter. His only heir. They want to secure the bloodline."

"I know what they want," I snap, then take a breath. "Sorry. It's just... I'm more than a broodmare for the continuation of some pure bloodline."

Aria bumps her shoulder against mine. "Hey, I get it. That's why we're out here, right?"

I nod, gazing up at the sky where the Elios moon still hangs faintly visible despite the morning light—strong and unwavering, just like the stories say. Around it, a few other moons linger lower on the horizon, their pale forms barely visible, distant and quiet. None shine like Elios or cast the heavy shadow of Umbra, but they're there, the silent watchers of our planet, Lunaterra. There are thirteen moons in all.

"I respect what my mother does, bless her," I say quietly. "The moon priestesses have kept our traditions alive for generations. They say Elios is the protector, the moon that never falters, always guiding the strongest warriors. That's why the priestesses focus on this moon in our district, which comes so close to our land. The light keeps the shadows at bay."

I pause, watching the faintest flicker of another moon disappear behind a stretch of clouds.

"My parents always believed I'd follow that path. Said

it was fitting since they'd named me Lyra after the Daughter Sun herself." I smile faintly. "I used to believe that, too." My gaze drifts back to Elios. "My faith's still strong," I add, almost defensively. "But lately... I don't know. The passion just isn't there anymore, not like it used to be."

Aria snorts softly. "Yeah, well... endless lessons on healing magic and cryptic prophecies would kill anyone's excitement."

"I want to be able to defend myself, not rely on others for protection." I pick up a small stone and turn it over in my hands, feeling its rough edges. "I want choices."

Aria's face tilts toward the sun. "And you're good at fighting, Lyra. Really good. You could join the Nightblades."

The thought makes me laugh out loud. "Can you imagine my father's face if I told him that? His head would explode."

"It might be worth it just to see—"

A howl cuts through the morning air—deep and resonant, the Alpha's call demanding attention. It's the signal for all wolves to return to the main settlement immediately.

Aria and I exchange glances. "Shit," she mutters, already gathering her things. "What now?"

"Could be anything. Community hunt. Pack meeting." I shrug, but unease prickles along my spine. The call came early, even by my father's standards.

We make quick work of hiding my training weapons in a hollow beneath the largest boulder. Can't have evidence of my unladylike activities floating around. The priestesses would have a collective fit if they knew their prized pupil was learning to fight instead of perfecting her healing prayers.

"Race you back?" Aria suggests, eyes glinting with challenge.

I grin, already dropping into a runner's stance. "Loser takes the winner's temple duties for a week."

"Deal. On three. One—"

I'm already running, her shout following me into the trees. Fighting dirty isn't just for physical combat.

The forest blurs around me. I could navigate these woods blindfolded, each root and fallen log mapped in my memory. The wind whips my hair behind me, and for a few precious moments, I feel free, unbound by expectations and heartbreak and duty.

Aria catches up halfway back, her longer legs giving her an advantage once she gets going. We're neck and neck as our village comes into view, its stone structures gleaming in the morning light.

She pulls ahead in the final stretch.

"I'll win next time," I pant.

"Keep telling yourself that, priestess," she calls back, slowing as we approach the settlement's edge.

We compose ourselves before entering, smoothing our hair and adjusting our clothes to look like we've been doing anything but fighting. Aria's path takes her toward the Nightblades' quarters, while I need to rush back into my family's home unnoticed.

"See you at whatever this gathering is," she says, giving me a quick hug. "And, Lyra? Maybe give your father a chance. He might be more reasonable than you think."

I snort. "You give him too much credit. See you soon."

The central plaza is already filling with wolves answering the summons as I make my way along the back paths toward my home. I'm nearly there when a voice stops me cold.

"Lyra Mooncrest."

I turn slowly, my heart sinking. My mother is in the doorway, arms crossed over her blue ceremonial robes, her expression one of disappointment. Behind her, our house stands taller than others in the village, the heavy stone archway carved with old runes that mark my family's status as the Alpha's bloodline.

"Morning," I say, aiming for innocence.

"Where have you been at this hour?" she asks, though the question is clearly rhetorical. She knows I wasn't in my bed, as she would have checked. Before I can fabricate an excuse, my father appears behind her, his imposing figure filling the doorway.

Alpha of the Elios pack, he's not a man who tolerates disobedience, especially from his only child. His white hair is pulled back in the traditional warrior's braid. His pale blue eyes—so unlike my lavender ones, which I inherited from my mother—narrow as they take in my appearance.

"Inside," he snaps, the single word carrying all the authority of his position.

I catch a glimpse of Aria slipping away through the gathering crowd, offering me a sympathetic grimace before disappearing. Traitor.

The door closes behind me with finality. Our home is larger than most in Wolfhaven—a sprawling stone structure with multiple rooms and ancient magic humming in its walls. The main room, where we now stand, features a currently cold central hearth, as the summer heat makes fires unnecessary.

"You were told to be ready," Father says without preamble. "We discussed this last moon. The Royal Wedding is at the capital of Solmane tomorrow. And today, they are holding the United Houses Luncheon."

Oh. Shit.

Memory rushes back—a conversation I'd deliberately buried because I had no intention of complying. The United Houses Luncheon... a matchmaking circus disguised as diplomacy.

"I thought I made it clear I wasn't going," I say, lifting my chin in defiance.

"We're not going there to marry you off, dear," Mother cuts in, her voice smooth but laced with warning. "We're going to pay our respects and meet the other families. That's all."

I snort. "Right. Because dragging me to a room full of preening nobles and their desperate heirs just happens to be about respect."

"We can't just skip it," she counters, her smile tight. "Especially with the Beast Prince finding a bride, and tomorrow is his Royal Wedding. The Hunter's Eclipse is set to only pass over Solmane country during the ceremony. That's a rare blessing, one we can't afford to ignore."

The Hunter's Eclipse... the last time Lunaterra passed between Avarix and Lyra, blocking the Daughter Sun's light, its shadow had stretched across Solmane alone then, too. Yet the First Moon's shadow had been felt across the entire planet.

"We're expected to be there," Father adds. "The pack can't appear weak. This is about more than just you."

"More than me?" I bark out a laugh. "You mean you're hoping I can snare some pompous heir to strengthen us against Umbra's pack. Admit it. I'm the prize."

Father's face darkens, but Mother's silence has me regretting my outburst.

"You should change," she says instead. "We're leaving within the hour."

Father's jaw tightens. "That's not a request, Lyra. It was an order. As Alpha, I am required to attend, and as my heir, so are you."

Mother steps forward, her expression softening. "Lyra, please. This is important."

A sigh rolls past my lips.

"Get dressed. Pack for three days," Father states. "The portal from the capital awaits. I'm going to announce it to the village."

He strides from the room, leaving Mother and me in uncomfortable silence.

"I know you don't want to go," she says after a moment. "But our family presence matters." She gives me a small rub on my arm, and I don't miss the tightness around her mouth. These social gatherings are painful, and I hate them.

When she's gone, I rush to my room and sink onto my bed, pressing the heels of my hands against my eyes until spots dance behind my eyelids.

I don't want to go for one main reason...

Theron will be there.

I'm going to be sick.

Probably his betrothed, the beautiful woman in red alongside him, attending the wedding.

I thought I was over him. Thought I'd excised him from my heart like poison from a wound. But the mere possibility of seeing him again has my pulse racing and my stomach aching.

"Pathetic," I whisper to the empty room. "Still not over him after a year."

Eventually, I rise, moving to where my ceremonial robes lie spread across a wooden chest.

Perfect for the role I need to play—Lyra Mooncrest, daughter of the Alpha, priestess in training, unclaimed Omega, perfect Elios princess. Not Lyra, who crosses rivers for forbidden kisses. Not Lyra, who trains in secret to fight her own battles. Not Lyra, who still dreams of silver eyes and broken promises.

I will see Theron Shadowmane again soon. And when I do, I'll show him exactly what he lost, what he threw away for his father's approval and an Umbra bride.

I'll show him a wolf who doesn't need him. A wolf who has forgotten him. A wolf who could destroy him without a second thought.

Even if every word of it is a lie.

THREE

LYRA

I hate portals. The ancient magic pulls at my insides, stretching and compressing me until I'm not sure where my body ends and the void begins. For three nauseating seconds, I exist everywhere and nowhere, my consciousness scattered across dimensions.

Then reality slams back into place, and I stumble forward onto gleaming marble floors, my stomach lurching violently. Father and Mother step through behind me with irritating grace, as though traveling through portals is no more disorienting than a casual stroll. The two guards carrying our bags follow, looking only slightly green around the face.

"Welcome to Solmane," a crisp male voice announces.

I straighten, blinking away the disorientation as my eyes adjust to the light flooding through stained-glass windows. We've arrived in the Portal Pavilion, a grand circular chamber with arched doorways leading to different parts of the sprawling capital city.

Solmane. The capital jewel of the kingdoms and host to today's United Houses Luncheon.

The last time I was here, I was sixteen. We never even made it to the actual event. Some diplomatic crisis had Father rushing home, leaving Mother and me to spend precisely four hours shopping in the merchant district before being whisked back through the portal.

In those four hours, I'd seen enough to know that Solmane represented everything I didn't want—artifice, political games, and marriages arranged for power rather than love.

Not that love had worked out any better for me. My chest tightened at the thought.

"Alpha Mooncrest," the voice continues, belonging to a tall, slender man in elaborate gray robes. "Lady Elara. Lady Lyra. The Covenant welcomes you to Solmane for the United Houses Luncheon and the Royal Wedding."

Father inclines his head, every inch the dignified pack leader. "Thank you, Master Calloway. It's been too long."

"Indeed it has." Calloway's gaze flicks briefly to me, assessing in a way that makes my skin crawl. "If you'll follow me, your accommodations have been prepared in the Rise Tower."

We step out of the pavilion into blinding sunlight, and Solmane unfolds before us in all its ostentatious glory.

Holy fuck.

The city is more beautiful than I remember—and

more alien to a wolf raised in the forests of Eclipsia. Glass spires twist toward the sky like frozen waterfalls, catching the sun and reflecting it in prisms that paint the streets in rainbow hues. Bridges of pale wood and shimmering metal connect buildings at various levels, creating a three-dimensional maze of architecture that defies gravity.

Unlike our stone dwellings that grow organically from the forest floor, everything here seems designed to impress, to announce its own importance. Vines with purple and blue blossoms cascade down the sides of buildings, perfectly cultivated to appear wild while actually being meticulously maintained.

The streets below teem with life—not just wolves, but beings from across the planet. Humans with their quick, nervous movements. Fae with their iridescent wings.

Banners in deep crimson and gold hang everywhere, displaying the crest of the Hunter's Moon.

"The city has changed since your last visit," Calloway observes, noting my wide-eyed stare. "The Crystal Quarter has been expanded, and the new Lunar Gardens were completed just last month."

"It's very... shiny," I manage, earning a warning glance from Mother.

Calloway's lips twitch. "Some find it overwhelming at first, but I assure you, Rise Tower offers a more... rustic aesthetic that may be more to your liking."

Rustic. His polite way of saying it's been designed to

make forest-dwelling wolves feel less out of place. *How considerate.*

We're led to a sleek carriage pulled by creatures that resemble horses but aren't quite—their coats shimmer with a metallic gleam, and their eyes hold an intelligence no normal horse possesses.

"Kelpies," Mother whispers to me as we climb inside. "Fae-bred."

The carriage moves with unnatural smoothness through streets that part for us like water. I sink into plush velvet seats, watching the spectacle of Solmane slide past the windows.

Vendors line the avenues, hawking everything from moonstone trinkets to pastries shaped like crescent moons to ribbons in every imaginable color.

It's beautiful. It's impressive.

I hate it.

Every gleaming surface, every perfectly arranged flower, every carefully designed vista screams artifice. There's nothing real here, nothing authentic. Back home, our stone houses bear the marks of centuries of wolf habitation—claw marks, scent markings, and the occasional bloodstain from territorial disputes. Our forest paths wind naturally through the trees, shaped by generations of paws rather than some architect's grand vision.

This place is a costume, a mask. Just like the one I'm wearing now—dutiful daughter, perfect priestess, future mate to some worthy Alpha. But not today.

"We're here," Father announces unnecessarily as the

carriage stops before a tower that, true to its name, appears to be carved from some pale stone that captures the pearlescent quality of moonlight.

Rise Tower goes to at least twenty stories, its facade decorated with carvings of wolves and moons in various phases. Unlike the glass spires of the city center, this building has a solidity to it, a permanence that speaks to wolf sensibilities.

Calloway leads us through doors carved from a single piece of silver-white wood into a lobby that manages to be both elegant and primal. Chandeliers crafted from antlers hang from the vaulted ceiling, casting warm light over stone floors inlaid with lunar phases in blue and silver tile.

"Your suite occupies the entire fifteenth floor," he informs us, guiding us to an elevator operated by actual magic rather than mechanics. "The United Houses Luncheon begins in four hours, which should give you ample time to rest and prepare."

The doors slide open directly into our accommodations, revealing a space that would comfortably house my entire pack's covenant. Floor-to-ceiling windows offer panoramic views of Solmane, the city stretching out below us like a jeweled carpet.

"This is... adequate," Father says, which, in his lexicon, is high praise indeed.

Calloway bows slightly. "If you require anything, simply speak your needs to the moonstone by the door. A servant will attend you promptly." With that, he disappears back into the elevator, leaving us to explore our temporary home.

"Well," Mother says after a moment of silence. "Shall we settle in?"

The next few hours pass in a blur—unpacking, staring out at the beautiful city, checking out our quarters. The air smells faintly of cedar and something sweeter. Then, it's time to prepare for the luncheon.

I pause at the mirror, expecting to see a familiar reflection. Instead, I find myself staring at a stranger.

The woman who looks back at me bears little resemblance to the wolf who was training with staffs at dawn. My white-blonde hair, usually worn in practical braids, has been arranged by Mother in an elaborate updo with moonstone pins that catch the light when I move. My ceremonial facial markings, the delicate silver lines that identify me as a priestess in training, have been enhanced with some shimmering powder that makes them appear to glow from within.

The dress is something else entirely.

Unlike the formal robes I expected to wear, Mother provided a gown that is daringly modern. The bodice hugs my torso in pale silver silk, embroidered with phases of the moon in white thread so fine that it's barely visible. From the waist, the skirt flows in layers of gossamer fabric the color of twilight, darkening from silver to the deep blue of midnight at the hem. The back dips low, exposing more skin than I'm comfortable with, while the front offers a modest neckline that keeps me just on the respectable side of pack tradition.

"You look beautiful," Mother says, appearing behind me in the mirror. She's dressed in similar colors but a more conservative style, as befits her status as Luna of the pack.

"I look like someone else," I mutter, tugging at the bodice.

"Sometimes that's what's required of us," she replies, her hands gentle as she adjusts one of my hairpins. "To be who our pack needs, rather than who we wish to be."

The words hit too close to home, stirring the restlessness that's lived in my chest since childhood. "And if who I am isn't who the pack needs?"

Something soft flickers in Mother's eyes. "Then you find ways to be both, in different moments." She touches the spiral birthmark on my wrist, visible despite my attempts to cover it with bracelets. "The moon has many phases, Lyra. So do we."

Before I can respond, Father's voice booms from the main room. "It's time."

Mother squeezes my hand once, then releases it. "Remember who you are today. Whose daughter."

"I don't plan to find a mate today, just so we're clear," I whisper so Father doesn't hear and set off on a rant. "I'm here, forced to attend the Royal Wedding."

She smiles too sweetly and pats my hand like this has been some clever trick they used to get me here. Then, without another word, she turns and strides toward the door.

I grind my teeth and follow, steeling myself for a gathering of political niceties and thinly veiled matchmaking attempts.

The ballroom where the United Houses Luncheon is held occupies the entirety of the central building, a massive structure of white stone and gold. We approach along a grand hallway lined with portraits of past leaders, their stern faces watching our progress with painted eyes that seem to follow our movements.

Father and Mother pause every few steps to greet acquaintances, their social obligations slowing our progress to a crawl. I hover awkwardly behind them, searching the crowd with a growing sense of dread.

He won't be here, I tell myself. Why would he be? The Royal Wedding isn't until tomorrow.

But even as I think it, I know I'm lying to myself. Of course he'll be here. His father is Alpha of the Umbra pack —he wouldn't miss a chance to show his face, to remind everyone that his family has dominated the Onyx Covenant for fifty years. Even if he's not here for matchmaking, this is still the perfect stage to flaunt his power.

The hallway opens into an antechamber where guests gather before entering the main ballroom. Crystal chandeliers cast rainbow light over a sea of formal attire.

Then I see him.

Theron Shadowmane stands alone near a window, a glass of something amber held loosely in one hand. He's dressed in formal black, the severity of the color broken only by silver accents at his collar and cuffs. His hair, longer than I recall, is pulled back, revealing the sharp angles of his face and the intensity of his gray eyes as they scan the room.

I stumble, my heel catching on the hem of my gown. Goddess, he's even more beautiful than I remember. More dangerous.

My attention darts around, searching for the woman in red, his betrothed. I don't see her, but I do spot his father holding court in a corner, surrounded by others hanging on his every word. Theron's father radiates menace, even in this formal setting.

Heat floods my body. I should look away from Theron. Should pretend I haven't seen him.

Instead, I stare like a rabbit hypnotized by a predator, my heart hammering.

"Lyra," Mother murmurs, touching my elbow. "Are you all right? You look flushed."

I blink, breaking the spell. "Fine," I manage. "Just... warm in here."

She follows my gaze, hers landing on Theron. Something shifts in her expression. It's not a surprise, exactly, but a sharpening of interest that makes me uneasy.

"Come," she says, her voice gentle. "Your father wants to introduce you to some families."

She guides me away, deeper into the antechamber where Father stands with a cluster of important-looking individuals. I go through the motions of greeting them, smiling and nodding at appropriate intervals while my mind remains fixated on the wolf by the window.

Why isn't his betrothed with him? Did something happen to her? Did he change his mind?

Hope flares, unwelcome and deadly, before I ruthlessly extinguish it. It doesn't matter. Whatever happened or didn't happen between Theron and the woman in red has nothing to do with me. He made his choice a year ago.

Finally, we're ushered into the main ballroom, a space so vast and opulent that it momentarily distracts me from my emotional turmoil. The ceiling soars at least four stories above, painted with a mural of the night sky so realistic it seems to move. Actual stars—or magical approximations of them—twinkle, casting a soft glow over the guests.

The floor is a masterpiece of wood and stone.

My parents immediately drift toward a group of officials, leaving me momentarily unattended. I seize the opportunity to move over to the nearest wall, seeking some semblance of cover in a room designed to put everyone on display.

I can't breathe properly. Can't think. My eyes keep finding him, no matter how determinedly I try to look elsewhere. He's moved into the ballroom now, still alone, still studying the crowd as though searching for someone.

For me? The thought sends a jolt of electricity down my spine.

No. Not for me. Never again for me.

I need to escape, to find a moment to collect myself.

The bathrooms must be nearby, where I can splash cold water on my face and remember all the reasons I hate Theron Shadowmane.

I push away from the wall, intent on escape.

"Excuse me, but are you Lyra Mooncrest?" a male voice asks.

I turn to find a young man watching me with open admiration. He's handsome enough—tall, with deep brown hair and friendly matching eyes. A human, by the looks of him, or perhaps a wolf with unusually subtle features.

"I am," I confirm. "And you are?"

"Damien Croft," he says with a slight bow. "House of the Midnight Star. I've heard so much about you from mutual acquaintances."

I doubt that very much, considering I have approximately two friends, neither of whom would run in his circles. I smile politely, falling back on years of training in proper pack etiquette.

"All good things, I hope."

"Only the best." When he smiles, he seems genuine. "They said you were beautiful, but they failed to mention you'd be the most striking woman in the room."

Under normal circumstances, such an obvious line would make me sigh. Tonight, desperate for any distraction, I find myself almost appreciating his compliment.

"That's very kind," I respond. "Though I think there are many who would dispute your assessment."

"Not from where I'm standing." He gestures to a

passing server, collecting two glasses of sparkling wine. "Would you care for a drink? I promise it's not an attempt to lower your inhibitions—merely to help you endure what promises to be a tedious evening of political maneuvering disguised as social niceties."

A surprised laugh escapes me. "You're not a fan of these gatherings, either?"

"I find them exhausting," he confesses, handing me a glass. "My mother insists I attend to make connections, but I'd rather be in my workshop."

This piques my genuine interest. "Workshop?"

"I design mechanical contraptions," he explains, a hint of embarrassment coloring his voice. "Mostly useless things that amuse me, occasionally something practical. My latest is a device that automatically waters plants based on soil moisture."

"That actually sounds useful."

"For someone who consistently kills houseplants, perhaps." His smile widens. "So, what would you rather be doing than standing here making small talk with a stranger?"

Training with Aria, I think immediately. Running through the forest in wolf form. Anywhere but here, where Theron's presence presses against my awareness like a physical weight.

"Reading," I say instead, the lie coming easily. "I'm studying ancient healing techniques."

"Ah, yes, you're training as a priestess, aren't you?" So someone has been talking about me... my parents instantly come to mind. "I've read that your healers can mend bones with just a touch and the right incantation."

"It's a bit more complicated than that." I take a sip of the wine, welcoming its coolness. "The moon grants us access to—"

I stop mid-sentence, my spine stiffening as awareness prickles across my skin. He's watching me. I can feel it.

My eyes flick up involuntarily, meeting Theron's gaze across the room. He stands less than thirty feet away, his expression unreadable as he stares at me and my companion. Something dark flashes in his eyes—something that looks dangerously like possession—before he turns away, drawn into conversation by someone I can't see.

"Is that your partner?" Damien asks, following my gaze.

I nearly choke on my wine. "God, no. Never."

"Well, he's looking at you as if he'd like to either kill me or drag you away. Possibly both."

"He's what?" I can't help but glance back, and sure enough, Theron is watching us again, his jaw clenched tight enough to crack stone.

"Ah, complicated history," Damien surmises. "Say no more. I've had a few of those myself."

I turn back to him, conscious of Theron's stare burning into my back. My heart beats so loudly I'm certain Damien can hear it, but a sudden reckless thought takes hold. Why shouldn't Theron see me enjoying someone else's company? Why shouldn't he get a taste of what I've felt this past year?

"You know what?" I say, finding my voice. "He's nobody important. Just someone who once made promises he couldn't keep."

"Ah." Damien's eyes sparkle with understanding. "The plot thickens." He leans in slightly, voice dropping conspiratorially. "If you'd like to make him jealous, I'm happy to play along. I'm excellent at pretending to be utterly captivated."

The petty, wounded part of me—the part that has cried itself to sleep more nights than I care to admit—rises to the surface.

"You know what? I'd like that very much."

"Wonderful." Damien grins, offering his arm. "Shall we give him a show to remember, then?"

I take his arm, my smile feeling almost natural for the first time today. "Lead the way."

We stroll along the edge of the ballroom, Damien keeping up a stream of witty commentary about the other guests that has me genuinely laughing. I'm acutely aware of Theron's gaze following our progress, and I can practically feel the tension radiating from him, even across the crowded room. And it's wonderful.

"He's moving closer," Damien murmurs. "And if looks could kill, I'd be six feet under."

"Let him be jealous," I say, though my heart hammers against my ribs. I lean in as though Damien has just said something delightfully scandalous, letting my hand linger on his bicep.

"Brave woman." He chuckles. "I think he might actually be growling."

"Good," I say, loud enough to be heard by anyone nearby. Then I laugh, high and musical, tossing my head back in a practiced gesture I've seen other women use to display their throats in subtle invitation.

Damien plays along beautifully, his hand coming to rest lightly on the small of my back as he leads me toward a less crowded area. I catch a glimpse of my parents across the room, my father deep in conversation with some dignitary, while my mother watches me with a mixture of curiosity and concern.

"I should be careful," I murmur. "My parents are watching."

"Mine, too," Damien admits. "Though they're probably thrilled to see me talking to someone from a proper pack family instead of hiding among the potted plants." He tilts his head, studying me. "You know, you have the most fascinating eyes. Like twilight captured in—"

"Mooncrest."

The deep voice comes from directly behind me, dark and dangerous and achingly familiar. Damien's expression shifts from playful to wary as his eyes lift to meet those of the man standing over my shoulder.

"Shadowmane," Damien acknowledges, his arm tensing beneath my fingers. "I was just—"

"Leaving," Theron finishes for him, stepping to my side. He towers over both of us, radiating the kind of lethal grace that reminds everyone he's not just a man in formal attire but a predator in a thin veneer of civilization. "Alone."

The command in his tone makes Damien hesitate, clearly torn between gentlemanly obligation to stay with me and self-preservation. I decide to spare him.

"It's all right, Damien," I say, squeezing his arm once before releasing it. "An old friend who's forgotten his manners, nothing more."

Theron's jaw tightens exactly as I'd hoped it would.

"If you're certain," Damien says, skepticism clear in his tone.

"She's certain," Theron growls, his hand closing around my upper arm. Not painfully, but with enough pressure to make his intentions clear.

Damien gives me one last questioning look, which I answer with a nod.

"A pleasure meeting you, Lady Mooncrest," he says, backing away with a formality that feels like armor. "Perhaps we'll continue our conversation... later."

The subtle emphasis makes Theron's fingers tighten infinitesimally on my arm. Damien turns and disappears into the crowd, leaving me alone with the wolf who broke my heart.

"Get your hand off me," I hiss, quiet enough that only he can hear.

"We need to talk," he responds, equally quiet but with an undercurrent of barely contained fury. "Now."

I glance around, aware of curious eyes watching our interaction. Making a scene would only draw more attention, something neither of us can afford.

"Fine," I concede, yanking my arm from his grasp. "But not here."

Without waiting for his response, I turn and stride toward the nearest exit, a set of glass doors leading to a balcony. My skin burns where he touched me, anger and something far more dangerous coursing through my veins.

I burst through the doors onto the balcony, gulping the cool air. Solmane sprawls below, but I barely register the view. I twist around toward Theron as he steps through the doors behind me, shutting them.

"How dare you?" I spit. "You have no right to dictate who I speak with."

Theron's eyes gleam dangerously. "Are you trying to make me jealous?"

"Why would you be jealous?" I counter, standing my ground despite the urge to retreat from his overwhelming presence. "You don't care about me, remember? I'm the *enemy*."

"Is that what you think?" His tone drops. "That I don't care?"

I don't wait for his response, turning and pushing along the long balcony that circles the building, needing distance from him. We're alone out here, and for a moment, I pause, my knuckles on the railing white with the effort of holding myself together.

"Lyra."

Of course he followed me. Of course he couldn't let me escape.

"Go away, Theron," I say without turning. "We have nothing to say to each other."

"I disagree." His response is closer now, just behind me. "We have a year's worth of things to say."

I spin to face him, anger easier to embrace than the alternative.

"Like what? Like how you were betrothed to another woman while stringing me along? Like how you never bothered to tell me the truth? Or maybe you'd like to explain why you're here without her. Did she finally see through you, too?"

Pain lashes across his face, quickly masked. "Is that what you think happened?"

"I know what I saw."

"You saw what my father wanted everyone to see." He takes a step closer, and it takes everything in me not to retreat. "If you had stayed, if you had let me explain—"

"Don't." I hold up a hand, unable to bear whatever justification he's crafted. "I don't care anymore. You made your choice, Theron. Live with it."

I take a step away.

"If you didn't care, you wouldn't be running from me right now. You wouldn't be looking at me the way you are," he continues.

"And how exactly is that?" The words come out harsh, edged with the pain I can't quite hide.

"Like you still love me." His voice drops to a whisper. "Like you hate that you do."

My heart stutters painfully in my chest. "You're delusional."

"Am I?" He reaches out, his fingers hovering just shy of touching my cheek. "Tell me you've forgotten everything between us, and I'll leave you alone. Tell me you don't feel this, and I'll walk away."

I open my mouth to say exactly that, to cut the last thread binding us together, but the lie sticks in my throat.

"Where's your mate?" I ask instead the question that's been burning inside me since I first saw him alone.

His hand drops. "I don't have one."

A bitter laugh escapes me. "What happened? Did you kill her off already?"

"If you must know," he says, "she rejected me after my father arranged it. Apparently, the honor of being Magnus Shadowmane's daughter-in-law wasn't worth risking her life. She said she'd heard stories about my father and feared I was exactly like him."

This revelation catches me off guard. Of all the reasons I'd imagined for his broken betrothal, this wasn't one of them.

"She was afraid of you?"

"Of becoming another of my father's victims by proxy." His expression softens slightly. "Not that it matters. I never intended to go through with it, Lyra."

"And now you know the feeling of rejection," I say,

unable to process his claim that he never meant to mate with her. It's too much, too late.

"I knew how it felt the night you walked away from me." The raw honesty in his tone threatens to unravel my defenses. "I've known it every day since."

We stand frozen in a moment that feels balanced on a knife-edge. The city hums below us, and between us stretches a year of silence and pain.

Suddenly, Theron flinches, his eyes widening as he glances down at his wrist. I follow his gaze, confused, then gasp when I see what's captured his attention.

Around his wrist, a band of polished onyx shot through with veins of silver pulses with an inner light that grows stronger by the second.

A manacle—the binding used in the Harvest Ritual to connect champions to their chosen Omegas.

"What's happening?" I whisper, staring at the glowing manacle with horrific realization dawning. "Your manacle... it's activated. Here? Now? In the middle of the United Houses Luncheon?"

Before I can process what's happening, Theron lunges forward, his movements predatory and precise. His hand clamps around my left wrist, grip like iron—not painful, but a clear statement that I won't be escaping. His skin burns against mine, fever-hot with magic and intent.

I try to wrench away, but the gleam in his storm-gray eyes tells me it's exactly what he expected. Something cold and heavy materializes against my skin—a perfect twin to the manacle on his wrist, binding us together with ancient, ruthless magic.

"What have you done?" I snarl, watching in horror as my manacle begins to pulse with sickly light, matching the rhythm of his. White-hot pain shoots up my arm like a lightning strike, tearing a scream from my throat.

Theron doesn't flinch. There's no shock on his face, only dark satisfaction as he watches the manacles connect.

"Why would you do this?" I demand, pacing now, yanking at the cruel metal as if I could tear it from my flesh. "How could you?"

Theron steps closer. "You know why."

"This shouldn't even be working," I hiss, still pulling against the bond. The pain has receded, replaced by a pulsing warmth that terrifies me more. "We're from opposite packs. No one has ever matched from Elios and Umbra in the Harvest Ritual. These manacles only bind champions to Omegas from their own pack, so one pack takes the Onyx Covenant positions."

A cruel smile plays at the corners of his mouth. "And yet, here we are."

"Take it off," I demand.

"I can't," he adds, and for a moment, I think I hear regret beneath the steel in his words, but then his eyes darken, almost black now. "Maybe this is simply the Shadowed Moon's will, bringing darkness to light."

"Don't you dare," I spit. "Don't invoke your cursed

moon when you've trapped me in this. The Veiled Moon would never sanction such a betrayal."

"Isn't it more of a betrayal to disappear for a year?" he asks, following as I try to put distance between us on the balcony. The manacles pull taut, forcing me to stop. "I went to our meeting place every week, Lyra. You never showed."

"You made your decision," I bark, the memory of seeing him with her flashing before my eyes.

"And now I'm undoing it," he growls, stepping closer until I'm backed against the railing. His scent—pine needles and winter frost with smoky amber—surrounds me, achingly familiar. "This challenge gives me the right to claim what should have been mine all along."

"By adding me to this dangerous fucking ritual without my consent?"

"I'll keep you protected," he promises, and he lowers his lips to my ear. "No harm will come to what's mine."

"You're insane," I whisper, hating how my body betrays me, leaning toward him even as my mind screams to run. "The Alphas will kill us both for this."

His laugh is dark velvet. "Let them try. We're guarded by the Onyx Covenant rules."

The manacle pulses again, and beneath the anger and fear, a dangerous thrill courses through me, the wolf in me responding to the irrevocable claiming, my traitorous heart remembering what it was like to be his. The moon priestess in me knows this bond is forbidden, but the woman I am wonders if it's true that fate has drawn us together.

Theron's fingers brush against the ceremonial markings on my face, a touch that's almost tender despite everything.

"You can hate me for this, Lyra," he murmurs. "But I won't lose you, and you cannot deny what flows between us."

Gods help me, I can't.

The doors to the balcony burst open behind us, and we spring apart. Theron's father, Magnus, stands framed in the doorway, his crimson eyes taking in the scene with frightening calculation. Behind him, my parents appear, my father's face a mask of confusion that rapidly turns to horror as his gaze locks on our wrists. They all pour out onto the balcony.

"Theron?" Magnus snarls. His tone is directed at his son, but his murderous glare is fixed on me.

"Father," Theron begins, stepping slightly in front of me in a protective gesture that doesn't go unnoticed by anyone.

"Lyra, are you all right?" My mother's voice breaks through the tension, her eyes wide with disbelief. "How is this possible?"

My father pushes past Magnus, reaching for my arm to examine the manacle. "This is outrageous," he growls, looking up at Theron with pure hatred. "An Umbra champion cannot claim an Elios Omega! It violates the most sacred rules of the Harvest!"

"Yet the magic has accepted the claiming," my mother observes quietly, her fingers hovering over the glowing band. "Look... the patterns match perfectly."

She's right. The silver veins running through both our manacles have arranged themselves into identical patterns, pulsing with the same rhythm. According to everything I've ever been taught about the Harvest Ritual, this shouldn't be possible. The Alpha and Omega team must be from the same pack, ensuring the winner comes from only one pack to take over the Onyx Covenant.

"I will have this undone," Magnus declares. "The Onyx Covenant will hear of this perversion."

"They can't undo it," Theron replies, standing his ground despite the threat emanating from his father. "Once the manacles have accepted the pairing—"

"You dare to lecture me on ancient law?" Magnus cuts him off, taking a menacing step forward. "This is a deliberate insult to our pack. To claim an Elios wolf, and not just any Elios—the daughter of their Alpha?"

My father turns to Magnus, his anger momentarily redirected. "If anyone should be outraged, it's me. Your son has trapped my daughter in a ritual that could get her killed!"

The full weight of the situation settles on me. I'm bound to Theron Shadowmane. We will face the trials together, our lives literally dependent on each other's survival. After a year of heartbreak and hatred, fate has forced us back together in the cruelest possible way.

"This changes nothing," Magnus blurts out. "You still

need to present yourself with your... chosen Omega at the Onyx Covenant by midnight to begin the Harvest Ritual." He spits the words *chosen Omega* like they're poison. "As for this... abomination..." His gaze shifts between Theron and me, contempt evident in every line of his face. "The Onyx Covenant will decide what to do about it."

With that, he turns and stalks back into the ballroom.

My parents remain, my father looking as though he might physically tear Theron limb from limb, my mother's face unreadable as she studies our bound wrists.

"I need to speak with my daughter," my father says finally, the tightly controlled rage behind his words making me flinch. "Alone."

"We can speak in the adjacent room," my mother suggests, gesturing to a small antechamber back inside the building. "The binding allows for up to fifty feet of separation."

The thought of being able to put even that small distance between us brings momentary relief until I remember that this invisible tether will remain for the duration of the Harvest Ritual.

"I'll wait here," Theron states. "But don't go farther than the next room. The pain starts gradually, but it becomes... intense."

My father's jaw tightens dangerously, but he nods once, sharply, and nudges me toward the antechamber. The moment we cross the threshold, I feel it—a slight tugging sensation at my wrist, not quite painful but definitely present. A constant reminder that I'm no longer completely free.

"What has he done to you?" my father demands the moment the door closes. "How is this even possible?"

"I don't know," I admit, my own shock still making it difficult to think clearly. "The manacle activated, he grabbed my wrist, and…" I gesture helplessly at the glowing band.

"And the magic accepted it," my mother finishes, her eyes fixed on the manacle with unsettling intensity. "This is unprecedented. In all the history of the Harvest that I'm aware of, there has never been a cross-pack claiming. And there's a reason for that—to ensure the team who wins will be the one pack that takes control of the Onyx Covenant for the next ten years."

"It's forbidden!" my father explodes. "He's trapped our daughter. The trials are designed to be lethal. How many participants don't return each decade? And now she's bound to the son of our greatest enemy!"

"I'm right here," I remind them, frustration cutting through my shock. "And I can handle myself. I'm not some helpless Omega who needs protection."

Both my parents turn to look at me incredulously.

"Lyra," my mother says carefully. "You don't understand what this means. The Harvest Ritual isn't just a physical challenge. It tests the bond between Alpha and Omega, forces them to work together in ways that—"

"That require trust," I finish for her. "I know the stories."

What I don't say—what I can't say—is that Theron and I once had that trust. Before he shattered it. Before I spent a year trying to hate him.

"We need to get back to Wolfhaven immediately," my father decides. "The Onyx Covenant might be able to dissolve this binding. If a partner requests removal on grounds of inability or unfairness, it's not too late. And Theron can still continue the games on his own."

I don't say anything, as I'm still in shock myself.

My father curses, a rare display of raw emotion from the usually composed Alpha.

Mother turns to me, her expression softening slightly. "Lyra, is there something you're not telling us about you and the Alpha's son?"

My heart stops for a beat, then races to catch up. Does she know? Has she somehow figured out what happened between us?

"What do you mean?" I manage, trying to keep my voice steady.

"The ancient magic wouldn't have accepted such an unprecedented pairing without... something binding you already. Some connection." Her eyes are too knowing, too perceptive.

"There's nothing," I lie quickly, even as the manacle seems to warm against my skin as if contradicting me. "He's the enemy. Always has been."

My mother doesn't look convinced, but before she can press further, the door to the balcony opens. Theron stands in the doorway, his tall frame filling the space.

"We should go," he says. "My father has already left for the portal back to Wolfhaven."

My father steps between us, a growl building low in his throat. "You're not taking my daughter anywhere."

"With all due respect, Alpha Mooncrest," Theron responds, his tone careful, "neither of us has a choice now. If we don't present ourselves to the Onyx Covenant by midnight, we'll be disqualified, and the binding will remain until the Harvest Ritual concludes anyway. Our best chance is to go through with this."

My mother places a restraining hand on my father's arm. "He's right. Let's go back and talk to the Covenant."

For a moment, I think my father might attack Theron, consequences be damned. Then his shoulders slump fractionally, defeat and fury warring in his eyes.

"If anything happens to her, if she comes to any harm because of you or your pack, there won't be a place in any of the kingdoms where you can hide from me."

Theron meets his gaze unflinchingly. "Understood."

My mother steps forward, taking my hands in hers.

One thought cuts through all others—tonight, the man who broke my heart has bound our fates together irrevocably. What scares me most isn't the deadly trials ahead of us; it's the treacherous hope buried deep in my chest that refuses to die.

FOUR

LYRA

Night crawls across the sky as I stand at the edge of the Onyx Covenant grounds, the moons already high and casting their dual glow—Elios veiled in silver mist, Umbra cloaked in shadow. The air feels electric, charged with the approaching chaos.

The enormous clearing surrounding the Covenant building stretches before us, an expanse of ancient cobblestones worn smooth by centuries of rituals and ceremonies. Tall pine trees encircle the area like silent guardians. Torches line the perimeter, their flames dancing wildly as if sensing the tension that hangs in the air.

My parents have just arrived, their faces grim in the flickering light. We remain within the shelter of the trees, not yet exposed to the dozens of wolves I know await us in the clearing. Father pauses, glancing around to ensure we have relative privacy, though I'm aware of Theron standing about thirty feet away, providing us space while still remaining within the required distance. I appreciate his discretion.

"Lyra," Father says. "I need you to understand the gravity of what's happening."

I glance down at the manacle encircling my wrist. The black metal seems to absorb the moonlight rather than reflect it, save for the thin veins of silver. I've seen these artifacts in ceremonies my entire life but never imagined wearing one, especially not one that connects me to an Umbra wolf.

"I understand," I reply, running my finger along the smooth edge of the manacle. "But the binding is already complete."

"The Onyx Covenant must reverse this." Father shakes his head, concern etching deep lines around his mouth. "They will. You aren't trained for the trials that lie ahead, Lyra. The Harvest Ritual claims lives every year—seasoned warriors who've prepared their entire lives."

"I'm not as helpless as you think," I say, the words sounding small even to my own ears.

He frowns, placing a gentle hand on my shoulder. "This isn't about being helpless. You are a priestess in training, a calling highly revered above even our Nightblades. Your path serves our pack in different ways."

"But I'm nineteen," I argue, straightening my spine. "Old enough to make my own decisions."

"No." Father's voice firms, though his eyes remain

kind. "Not while you're under pack rule. Like everyone else, you follow our laws—laws that have kept us safe for generations."

Mother steps closer, her hand finding mine. "He only wants to protect you, Lyra. We both do."

I want to argue further, but the words die in my throat. They can't understand what this means to me, this unexpected chance to prove myself, to be more than just the Alpha's sheltered daughter. And they certainly can't understand the storm of emotions Theron's actions have unleashed inside me.

Betrayal. Anger. Confusion.

"We should join the others," Mother says softly. "The Covenant is waiting."

As we emerge from the tree line, the full force of the gathering hits me. The clearing is packed with wolves from both packs, carefully maintaining distance from each other, the invisible boundary between Elios and Umbra territory evident even here on neutral ground. Conversation dies as we pass, curious gazes following our progress across the cobblestones.

I hold my head high, refusing to shrink under their scrutiny. Let them stare. Let them whisper. I may not have asked for this, but I won't cower from it, either.

My parents stride toward the imposing obsidian structure of the Covenant building, where the members wait on the steps, their black robes blending into the night. I follow several paces behind, and my attention is drawn to the other participants gathered near the entrance.

The champions stand around chatting. Theron joins his friends. He's taller than the others, his broad shoulders and lean frame accentuated by the fitted black shirt and tight-fighting pants he wears. A curved blade hangs at his belt, and his wild black hair flutters in the breeze.

"Lyra!" Aria's voice rings out, and I turn to her jogging toward me, her face bright with excitement. Unlike the formal ceremonial attire most have chosen for this gathering, she's dressed practically in fitted leathers, ready for action at a moment's notice. Unlike me, still in my simple blue dress with silver embroidery along the hem. I'd insisted on stopping at home before coming to the Covenant grounds to change my clothes, making him wait outside while I traded a constricting dress for something I could at least move in. A simple knee-length dress with a black belt cinched at my waist that holds a small dagger—barely ceremonial, but better than nothing.

"There you are," she says, embracing me quickly. "I thought you might not come."

"Did I have a choice?" I hold up my wrist, displaying the manacle that binds me to Theron. "The moment he bound me, I couldn't leave the grounds even if I wanted to. Not unless I want to be injected with poison from the manacle. You've heard the stories of what happens when Harvest Ritual couples stay apart for too long."

Aria's eyes widen, too busy focusing on my wristband

than my words. "Holy shit, it's real. I heard the rumors, but... by the Veiled Moon, Lyra, how did this happen?"

I shrug, unable to explain what I don't understand myself. "He grabbed my arm, and the manacle just... appeared."

"That's not how it's supposed to work. The manacles only bind compatible champions and Omegas from the same pack." Her gaze narrows suspiciously. "Unless..."

"Unless what?"

"Unless there's more between you two than you're letting on." She studies my face closely, and I'm reminded of Mother's suspiciousness. "He's the one, isn't he? The reason you've been moping around for the past year?"

I hesitate, then nod once, the admission feeling like surrender.

"I knew it!" Aria exclaims. "It all makes sense now. But Theron Shadowmane? Seriously? You couldn't have fallen for someone less... I don't know, lethal?"

"It wasn't exactly planned," I mutter, unable to stop myself from glancing in his direction again. He's watching me. A shiver runs down my arms.

"Can't blame you, though," Aria continues, following my gaze. "Look at him, all broody and mysterious with those shoulders and chest. And the way he moves... No wonder half the females in both packs are drooling over him." She nudges me playfully. "How'd you two even meet? Secret rendezvous in the forbidden zone?"

Despite everything, I feel my lips curving into a small smile. "He almost shot me with an arrow."

"What?"

"I was gathering moonberries near the border. He was hunting, didn't see me until the last second, and redirected his shot. The arrow missed me by inches." I pause, remembering the moment—the shock on his face, the immediate regret, the strange tension that sprang between us like lightning. "We started talking, and something just... happened. Like I couldn't bear to be away from him."

"Instant attraction." Aria nods sagely. "The most dangerous kind."

"Not that it matters now," I state. "He showed his true colors a year ago. There's nothing between us."

"Sure doesn't seem that way," she replies, glancing meaningfully toward Theron.

I make the mistake of looking up, meeting his gaze directly. The intensity in his stare sends heat flooding through me. I glance away quickly, cursing myself for the reaction.

"It's complicated," I say finally, the understatement of the century.

Aria holds up her own manacle, changing the subject. "Well, I'm officially in, too. Orion chose me as his Omega. Can you believe it?" Her eyes sparkle with excitement. "The top warrior in Elios, and he picked me!"

I force myself to focus on her news, genuinely happy for my friend despite my own turmoil. "Of course he did. You're the best fighter. I know you'll make our pack proud." I squeeze her hand. "Just stay alive, okay?"

"Please," Aria scoffs. "You know me better than that. I'm too stubborn to die in some ancient ritual." She studies me for a moment. "The real question is, what are you going to do? Are you really going through with this?"

I stare down at the manacle. Am I? The thought of participating in the Harvest Ritual terrifies me. I've trained in secret with Aria, yes, but nothing approaching actual danger. And being bound to Theron adds layers of complication I can barely begin to untangle.

I'm torn in a way I've never felt before, caught between fear and pride, duty and desire. Between the safety of the path carved out for me... and the chaos that waits beyond it. And then there's Theron. The sting of his betrayal still claws at me, even after a year. I still see him with her, the woman his father deemed more suitable. Like I was never even a choice.

"I don't know," I admit, the weight of indecision heavy on my shoulders. "Part of me wants to run as far from this as possible. Another part wants to prove I can do this, that I'm more than just a priestess reciting prayers in a temple."

"And another part?" Aria prompts gently. "The part that still feels something for him?"

I close my eyes briefly. "That's the part I trust least of all."

A hush falls over the gathering, drawing our attention to the steps of the Onyx Covenant. Tarek and Melian Nightsinger stand side by side. Though not related by blood, their matching ceremonial black robes and synchronized movements give them an eerie, other-worldly quality. Both in their thirties, they emanate power and authority that silence even the most contentious voices.

"Champions and Omegas of Elios and Umbra," Tarek calls, his words carrying effortlessly across the clearing. "The hour of selection has arrived."

My parents stand before them, alongside Magnus Shadowmane. The contrast between the two families could not be more stark—my parents with their light coloring and concerned expressions, and Magnus, dark and imposing, radiating barely contained hostility.

"The Harvest Ritual is our most sacred tradition," Melian continues in a melodic yet powerful tone. "Through it, we honor the moons that guide us and select those who will join the Onyx Covenant to lead our packs through the next ten years."

My pulse quickens as I listen. Controlling the Onyx Covenant has always been crucial to our packs. It gives the pack controlling the Covenant final authority to decide on pack disputes and to negotiate trade agreements with neighboring countries that subtly favor their pack's interests, even while representing our entire nation. They also have the right to command joint hunting expeditions and distribute the spoils during the harsh winter months in their favor. No wonder Father's been preparing our pack warriors for this moment all year.

"We are aware of the unusual situation that has

arisen," Tarek states, his gaze scanning the crowd until they find me. "A binding has taken place between members of different packs."

Murmurs sweep through the gathering like wind through the surrounding pines. The weight of dozens of stares grows heavier on me. Beside me, Aria stands a little straighter, a silent show of support.

"Alpha Mooncrest has requested this binding be dissolved," Melian announces. "Alpha Shadowmane has demanded the same."

My father steps forward. "My daughter is a priestess, not a warrior. This binding places her in grave danger unnecessarily."

"And such a mixing of bloodlines violates our most ancient traditions," Magnus Shadowmane adds. "The ritual is meant to select the strongest pair from each pack, not create abominations that blur the lines between Elios and Umbra."

I flinch at his words, and Aria's hand finds mine, squeezing gently.

"We have consulted the sacred texts," Tarek replies calmly. "We have communed with both moons."

Melian raises her hands, silver light emanating from her palms. "The manacles are not mere metal but manifestations of the moons' will. They respond to compatibility on the deepest level—soul to soul, heart to heart. That such a pairing has occurred between Elios and Umbra is unprecedented but not impossible.

"Perhaps," she continues, "this is a sign that the

divide between our packs is not as absolute as we have believed. Perhaps the moons themselves seek to bring us together rather than keep us apart."

"This is blasphemy," Magnus growls. "The Umbra moon would never sanction such a union."

"And yet," Melian replies with quiet authority, "the manacle bearing the mark of Umbra now rests on your son's wrist, bound to a daughter of Elios. Would you claim to know the moon's will better than the moon itself, Alpha Shadowmane?"

Magnus falls silent, though the fury in his eyes speaks volumes.

My father glances over at me, then back to the Covenant members. "What of my daughter's safety? The other champions have trained their entire lives for this ritual. Lyra has not."

"The manacle would not have chosen her if she were truly incapable," Tarek responds. "Perhaps there is more to your daughter than even you have seen, Alpha Mooncrest."

My heart swells at these words, even as fear continues to gnaw at my insides.

"Our decision is made," Melian declares. "The binding stands. Lyra Mooncrest and Theron Shadowmane will participate in the Harvest Ritual as bound partners."

Magnus steps forward, his huge frame radiating menace. "And when this... experiment fails? When the ritual is corrupted by this aberration?"

"Then we will bear responsibility," Tarek says simply.

"But the will of the moons cannot be denied, Alpha Shadowmane. Not even by you."

For a moment, I think Magnus might challenge them, but he merely inclines his head in a mockery of respect and steps back, his crimson eyes finding mine across the distance. The message in them is clear: This isn't over.

I swallow hard.

"Now," Melian continues. "Let the remaining selections proceed. Champions, step forward with your Omegas."

The Covenant members take records of each couple. When that's complete, Tarek raises his hands for silence.

"The Harvest Ritual will commence at midnight tomorrow. Everything you need will be provided."

"All champions and their Omegas must remain on the Covenant grounds from this moment forward," Melian continues. "The binding magic requires proximity—no more than fifty paces between bound pairs at any time. Behind the Covenant building are lodgings where you will stay tonight, simple quarters with separate rooms for each pack, though none larger than thirty feet in any direction, offering ample space to accommodate for the binding's constraints."

"Training will commence at dawn. Families and friends must depart within the hour. Say your farewells now," Tarek adds.

With those words, the two Onyx Covenant members turn as one and disappear into the building, the obsidian doors closing behind them with a sound like distant thunder.

The crowd begins to disperse, champions and their chosen Omegas huddling together to discuss strategy, families offering last-minute advice. My father approaches, his anger now replaced with quiet resignation.

"I wish we had more time," he says. "But it seems the moons have other plans."

I nod, suddenly exhausted. "I know."

"I'll help her get ready," Aria offers.

Father hesitates, then nods. "Very well." He embraces me, his arms strong and secure around my shoulders. "Whatever happens, know that we are proud of you, Lyra. And we will be waiting when you return."

When, not if. The confidence in his voice brings tears to my eyes, which I quickly blink away. "Thank you, Father."

Mother presses a small pouch into my hand. "Moondust," she whispers. "For protection. Use it wisely." She kisses my forehead and steps back. "Trust your instincts, Lyra. They've never led you astray."

"We'll be watching from the ceremonial viewing area until you leave for your mission." Father adds, "Remember your strength."

With final embraces, they turn to leave, joining the other departing families. I watch them go, feeling suddenly adrift despite the dozens of people still milling around the clearing.

"Well," Aria says once they're out of earshot. "That was intense. Ready to become a warrior overnight?"

I glance across the clearing to where Theron stands. I hate how my breath catches. It's not just the pull between us—though there's still that, damn him—it's something deeper. As if we both know there's no going back from this moment.

All entrants start moving to the structures behind the onyx building.

"Come on." Aria tugs me in that direction, too. "We should check out our quarters and get you ready for tomorrow."

I follow her, acutely aware that Theron isn't too far behind, alone, more of the contestants, including Orion, farther behind coming this way. I see how Orion stares at Nadia, another Elios Omega. I wonder if Aria noticed?

Turning back around, I take in a shaky breath. This is *actually* happening.

And the weird thing is that beneath all the fear and anger, there's a spark of excitement I can't quite squash. Like maybe, finally, I get to show everyone who I really am.

And if Theron Shadowmane thinks I'm going to make this easy for him, he's about to learn just how wrong he is.

FIVE

THERON

Alongside her friend, Lyra strolls to the bunkers, the blonde of her hair disappearing into the darkness of the tree line. She glances back in my direction, but there's no reaction on her gorgeous face, and it fucking kills me.

My jaw clenches as I stroll after her until she reaches the stone building nestled farther behind the onyx building. Our home for tonight is a low and imposing structure —smooth gray walls gleaming under moonlight, carved with ancient runes. Two heavy ironwood doors stand side by side, sitting open, one marked with Elios's crescent moon, the other with Umbra's shadowed orb, designating the separate quarters for each pack. Narrow windows, more like arrow slits, pierce the stone.

Lyra pauses by her door, her slender fingers tracing one of the glowing runes etched into the stone. Even from this distance, I sense her hesitation and can see the tension in her shoulders before she disappears inside with a final glance in my direction. I linger close, remaining outside, desperate to drag her somewhere alone—just the two of us—to talk, to show her I'm not the asshole she thinks I am. Like old times.

Other participants from both packs file inside, chatting among themselves. No one spares me a glance, even though I know they've all been talking about Lyra and me.

Fuck. This all went to shit, didn't it?

The binding wasn't supposed to happen like this, but when I saw her standing there on the balcony in the capital, something primal and undeniable took over. The manacle activated before I could think it through.

Her face, when it happened, one of shock and devastation, is burned into my memory. Like I'd betrayed her all over again.

"Enjoying the night air?" Kieran pauses at my side near the bunkers, his voice low enough that only I can hear.

"Shut up." I don't take my eyes off the door she entered.

"Just saying, you could've given some warning before deciding to upend pack law and tradition."

"It wasn't exactly planned."

"No shit." He follows my gaze toward the tree line. "She looked ready to gut you where you stood."

"She'll learn to accept it."

Kieran raises an eyebrow but doesn't press. He's one

of the few who know pieces of what happened between Lyra and me—not everything, but enough to understand the weight of what I've done tonight.

"Don't look now," Kieran mutters. "But Daddy Dearest is coming, and he doesn't look happy."

"When does he ever?"

Kieran quickly heads inside.

My father's hand clamps down on my shoulder like a steel trap, fingers digging into muscle hard enough to leave bruises. Without a word, he steers me to the edge of the bunker, where there are no windows. I could resist— part of me wants to—but causing a scene would only make things worse.

"You've created a real fucking mess!" His voice is a low growl, and his crimson eyes are gleaming.

"The binding is done," I say, keeping my voice level, not wanting anyone to hear us. "The Covenant accepted it."

"The Covenant," he spits the word like poison, "is composed of idealistic fools who believe in peace and unity." He steps closer, the bone beads in his braids clicking together like death rattles. "I raised you better than this. Trained you to be a leader, not some Elios-loving weakling who binds himself to the enemy."

"The packs weren't always enemies," I say, the words slipping out before I can stop them.

His eyes narrow dangerously. "What did you say to me?"

"Nothing." Too late to take it back, but too dangerous

to elaborate. The journals hidden beneath my floorboards contain truths my mother discovered that would get me killed if he knew I'd discovered them.

"Nothing," he repeats, mockery dripping from the word. "Just like your pathetic excuses for why you bound yourself to that Elios bitch."

My hands curl into fists at my sides, nails digging into my palms to keep from striking him. "Don't call her that."

A cruel smile spreads across his face. "Ah, there it is. The real reason. You actually care for her." He laughs, the sound devoid of any warmth. "Just like your mother— weak for anything with a pretty face and Elios blood."

The mention of my mother sends ice through my veins. "Leave her out of this."

"Why? She left herself out years ago, didn't she? Escaped into the night without a trace, only for me to discover she was seeing a fucking Elios man behind my back. Then she disappeared... that same pack she adored would have killed her for breaking the law." He leans closer, his breath hot against my face.

I don't look away. I let him see the fury in my eyes when he brings up my mother. He does it to provoke me. He always fucking does. The bastard knows exactly where to cut. How can I blame her for running when she was shackled to my father in a marriage she never chose? But he does—he blames her for leaving, for disappearing, for breaking the image of the perfect little family. Claims she was murdered, as though that's easier to believe than the truth. But they never found a body. Just silence. And it screams louder than any lie he tells.

"Here's what's going to happen," he whispers, his voice low and venomous, glancing over his shoulder like the walls might be listening. "The first night of the ritual, when the little blonde priestess is asleep and dreaming of gods who'll never save her, you're going to end her. Slit her throat. Snap her neck. Hell, push her off a fucking cliff if that's what it takes. I don't care how you do it. Just make sure she doesn't see the morning."

Rage explodes through me, hot and volatile.

"Do you understand me?" His eyes lock on mine, blazing with ruthless intent. "I will not let your bleeding heart destroy everything we've built. We didn't claw our way to the top of the food chain just to lose it all because you hesitated." He leans closer. "The only reason our pack survives the dead of winter with full bellies is because we own the Onyx Covenant. Because we take what we need without apology. And now you're gambling all of it—our future—because you can't bring yourself to kill one pretty little girl?"

My vision edges as I fight to keep my wolf contained. The audacity—to order me to murder her, to speak of her like she's nothing but an obstacle.

"You dare?" I growl, voice dropping to a dangerous timbre that causes even my father to tense. "You speak of pack power while ordering me to kill my bound partner?"

His lip curls. "Grow up. Do your fucking duty. Or I'll find someone who will."

I step closer, towering over the man who raised me to be his weapon. For the first time, I see a flicker of uncertainty in his crimson eyes. Good. Let him fear what he's created.

"I am not your attack dog, Father." The title tastes bitter on my tongue. "And Lyra is not your sacrifice. This binding happened for a reason. Maybe it's time our packs stopped circling each other like wounded predators."

His face twists with disgust. "You sound like a lovesick pup, not the Alpha heir of Umbra. She's made you weak."

"She's made me see." I match his stare, refusing to back down. "Everything you've taught me about power and control, it's all fear. Fear dressed as strength."

The shadows around us deepen as my father's anger manifests in tendrils of darkness. Let him try to intimidate me. I am done cowering.

"You will do as I command," he hisses.

The wolf inside me roars, desperate to protect what's mine, but I've learned from a lifetime under my father's rule. Showing my hand now would only endanger her further.

"Then you're not the son I raised. And I have no use for disappointments in my bloodline."

"You've made your position clear," I say, voice flat. "Is that all?"

"For now." His eyes narrow. "But remember, boy… I'm watching." He turns and marches away.

Fury and fear are warring for dominance inside me. The one thing I don't feel is regret. Whatever comes next, binding myself to Lyra was the right choice—the only choice.

"Well, that looked pleasant." Kieran emerges from the doorway farther down the building. "Still breathing, I see."

"Fuck him."

"What did the mighty Magnus want?" Kieran moves closer. "Besides your head on a spike, that is."

"He wants me to kill her."

Kieran stumbles, catching himself quickly. "Fuck. He actually said that? In those words?"

"Yep."

"That psychotic fuck!" Kieran's face hardens. "Fuck." He runs a hand through his hair, a gesture I recognize from years of friendship—something he does when strategizing. "So, what's the plan? We still continuing with ours?"

"Nothing's changed." I glance back at the Covenant building, its obsidian walls gleaming in the moonlight. "We find the proof, we expose him, we end this."

"Except now your father's actively trying to murder your ritual partner and, by extension, you." Kieran's voice drops lower as we approach the entrance. "And let's not forget that *she* probably wants to murder you."

I let out a dry chuckle. "Never had so many people lining up to take my head." With a loud exhale, I shift gears, tired of circling the topic of my death. "Anyway... you never told me who you chose as your partner?"

"Rachel." He grins. "She's solid in a fight and hot to look at." He winks.

"Better than solid," I correct, remembering the fierce Umbra female who nearly took down three opponents single-handedly in last year's combat trials. "She's lethal with those twin blades."

"Yeah, well, we can't all bind ourselves to blonde priestesses and cause pack-wide scandals." He nudges my shoulder with his. "Some of us have to settle for partners who might actually help us survive."

Movement catches my eye—a flash of platinum blonde hair and lithe, lethal grace. Selene, the female my father had all but promised would be my partner. The best fighter among Umbra females, ruthless and cunning, with a particular talent for making deaths look like accidents. She stands with her newly chosen champion, Erebus Shade, but her ice-blue eyes are fixed on me, promising retribution.

"Selene looks ready to flay you alive with her finger-nails," Kieran murmurs.

"She'd have to get in line." I touch the scar over my collarbone—a souvenir from a previous encounter with Selene's particular brand of affection. "Besides, she's dangerous but predictable. I'm more concerned about my father's next move."

"You should be concerned about all of it," Kieran says bluntly. "Especially if half our own pack wants you dead."

"And the other half is just waiting to see which side wins," I add grimly.

As Selene and Erebus approach the doorway, they give their best hard stares.

"Welcome to the Harvest Ritual," Kieran suddenly declares with exaggerated formality. "May the worthy rise and all that shit."

"Fuck you," Selene barks.

"Such eloquence," Kieran replies, clutching his chest. "Your way with words truly brings tears to my eyes, Selene."

Erebus, towering over even me, narrows his dark eyes. "Save your breath for tomorrow, jester. You'll need it when I leave you in the dust."

"Oh, please," Kieran scoffs, leaning casually against the stone wall. "The last time you tried to outrun me, you tripped over your own feet and face-planted into a thornbush. Still have the scratches, or did Selene kiss them better?"

Selene's eyes flash dangerously. "Save your pathetic trash talk."

"At least I'm loyal to my pack," Erebus fires back, glancing pointedly at me, knowing Selene desperately wanted me to pick her, but she ended up with him. And that I brought Lyra into the challenge.

"They're just intimidated by my superior skills." Kieran waves dismissively. "Something you wouldn't understand."

Despite everything, I feel my lips twitch into the ghost of a smile. The animosity between them is as amusing as it is predictable—pack mates who'd die for each other in a heartbeat but would also happily trip each other during a race.

"Coming inside, traitor?" Erebus directs at me, ignoring Kieran entirely. "Or are you camping outside to be closer to your... pathetic choice of partner?"

"Don't worry about his choices," Kieran interjects before I can respond. "Worry about yours. Like that haircut—who convinced you that was a good idea? A blind squirrel?"

Erebus growls low in his throat, but Selene tugs him through the doorway before he can escalate further.

Kieran claps a hand on my shoulder. "Let's get some rest. We'll need it."

I nod, following him through the heavy wooden door marked with Umbra's symbol. The narrow hallway is dimly lit with torches that cast long, dancing shadows across the rough stone walls. The air smells of pine resin and perspiration, a combination that makes my wolf stir restlessly beneath my skin.

We emerge into the main chamber, where the rest of our pack is already claiming beds. Ten simple pallet beds line the walls—five for Alphas, five for their Omegas. Except in our case, there's one bed that will remain empty tonight.

My gaze falls on it, and the reality of my situation lingers in my thoughts. While every other champion will sleep with their Omega nearby, mine is in the next room with her pack.

I move to the bed farthest from the door but closest to the wall.

Kieran gives me a knowing look as he claims the bed beside mine. "Try not to brood all night," he murmurs. "Your face might get stuck that way."

I ignore him, stretching out on the thin mattress and staring at the ceiling. The stone is etched with ancient patterns that seem to swirl and dance in the torchlight—moon cycles, wolf packs running through endless forests, the eternal dance of Elios and Umbra across the night sky.

My father's words echo in my mind... *Slit her throat. Snap her neck. Hell, push her off a fucking cliff if that's what it takes. I don't care how you do it. Just make sure she doesn't see the morning.*

I close my eyes, feeling the weight of what lies ahead.

When the Harvest Ritual begins tomorrow, nothing will be the same again. Not for me, not for Lyra, and not for the two packs who have spent generations keeping us apart.

Let them all come for me. Let them try.

SIX

LYRA

Sleep escapes me in the stone bunker, despite my exhaustion. I shift uncomfortably on Aria's borrowed blanket, the hard floor beneath digging into my hip. Around me, the soft breathing and occasional snores of the Elios candidates fill the darkness. Ten of them, all with proper beds. And then there's me—the unwanted addition, the priestess who doesn't belong.

"Fuck this," I mutter, staring at the ceiling, tracing the cracks in the ancient stone.

How did I end up here? Yesterday morning, I was preparing for a routine moon-blessing ceremony. Now I'm bound to Theron Shadowmane, forced to participate in a ritual that claims lives every year. My father's disappointed face flashes in my mind, along with the whispers that followed me tonight. The Alpha's daughter, bound to an Umbra wolf. A betrayal, they called it, as if I'd chosen this.

Then I finally drift off...

Branches tear at my skin as I run, heart pounding, lungs burning. The forest stretches endlessly in every direction, thick with shadows that move when I blink. Behind me, thunderous footsteps and low growls vibrate through the trees. I don't look back. I know what I'll see. I've seen it before. The gleam of his eyes—Theron's eyes—glowing in the dark, twisted with something feral. Wrong.

I trip. Cold earth slams into me. Before I can scramble up, he's there, on me, crushing the breath from my lungs. Claws bite into my shoulders, and I scream as his jaws part above my throat, hot breath washing over my skin.

I wake with a gasp, choking on it. My heart's racing, hair stuck to my forehead. The scream never left my lips, but it still rings in my head.

Godsdammit. I wipe my face with shaking hands. The darkness presses in, the weight of stone above me suddenly suffocating. I need air. Space. Anything to escape the tightness in my chest.

Rising silently, I navigate between the sleeping forms of my pack mates to reach the rear door in the room. None of them offered to push the super-narrow beds together with Aria's so that I didn't sleep on the floor, not even those who've smiled at me during temple ceremonies. The message couldn't be clearer—I've crossed a line by being connected to an Umbra wolf. I'm no longer fully one of them.

The Covenant buildings have running water, a rare

luxury that the elders engineered generations ago, combining advanced plumbing with old magic. Something only reserved for those of importance... Not Elios wolves.

I fill a wooden cup from the sink and gulp it down, the cool liquid doing little to calm the storm inside me. A bowl of fruit sits nearby, and I grab a handful of grapes, popping them into my mouth one by one, barely tasting them.

What the fuck am I doing here? I'm not a warrior, despite my training sessions with Aria. The other candidates have been preparing for this their entire lives. They know how to fight, how to survive the trials that await us.

The right decision would be to get myself eliminated somehow, to leave... I thought earlier that maybe I deserved a chance to prove myself. Now that I'm in the thick of it, I'm not so sure.

And Theron... that arrogant bastard. After a year of silence, why bind himself to me now? What does he gain?

The memory of his face when the onyx bracelet materialized on my wrist burns in my mind—that look of satisfaction, of getting exactly what he wanted. Does he think he can just force his way back into my life?

First love, first heartbreak, and now he's dragged me into a fucking death trap. Great track record.

I reach for more water, trying to focus on tomorrow's training, but the thought that I choose to stay lingers like a shadow in my mind.

My grip tightens around the cup. With everything he's done, I stayed and I know why.

It's him.

Even after his betrayal, after watching him with her, I couldn't bring myself to break the bond. Some stubborn, bleeding part of me still aches for what we were... or maybe what I thought we could be. And that's the part that's killing me.

Because no matter how much I try to deny it, I'm still not ready to let him go.

A sound comes so faintly I almost miss it, a whisper of fabric against stone, a breath held too long. I freeze, cup halfway to my lips. I'm not alone.

Before I can turn, something rough and heavy slams down over my head—a bag of thick, scratchy fabric scrapes my face, sealing me in suffocating darkness. I open my mouth to scream, but a fist drives into my stomach like a hammer. The air is punched from my lungs, and the scream dies in my throat, the cup tumbling from my grasp. I lean over, gasping, hugging my gut. Panic floods me.

"Don't you fucking scream," a voice hisses near my ear. The tone is forced—low, distorted—but there's a sharp edge to it. Female. Trying not to sound it. "One noise and we'll cut your throat."

Hands clamp around my arms like iron. Another slams into my back, shoving me forward. I stumble, nearly fall, head pounding, the bag clinging to my face like a second skin. My breaths come shallow and fast. I can't get enough air. I can't see. I can't think.

Instinct takes over. I twist hard, yank free just enough, and throw out a wild kick, one Aria drilled into me over and over. It connects with something solid—a grunt of pain from one of them.

A sudden crack against my neck and I whimper. Another blow to my ribs, brutal and fast. White-hot pain erupts in my side, stars bursting behind my eyes, even in the pitch black.

I collapse to my knees with a strangled cry, agony lancing through my body. Every breath feels like knives. My heart hammers, screaming to run, but my limbs are heavy, slow.

"Bitch fights like a rabid wolf," one of them mutters. "Didn't expect that from a temple flower."

"Just get her away from the building," the second voice snaps, also female, also masked in false depth. "Before someone hears."

My heart slams against my ribs as they drag me forward, the rough fabric of the bag scratching my face, choking me with every panicked breath. The ground shifts beneath my feet from stone to dirt, each step disorienting. I can already feel the manacle on my wrist buzzing slightly. We're not past the edge of the fifty-foot radius, but perhaps I'm getting close.

Five minutes to get back, or Theron and I are dead.

"Just let me go and I won't tell anyone," I press, all

while rage rises hotter than the fear, curling through my veins like fire.

They laugh at me. "We're not idiots."

Fuck them.

"I beg to differ."

Who the hell do these girls think they are, threatening me like I'm nothing? Like I'm prey? Just another passive priestess too soft to fight back?

My parents, the temple, every smug face that ever looked at me like I was breakable. I'm not just some girl in robes whispering prayers in the dark. I can fight. I will fight. And I'll make damn sure they regret ever thinking I wouldn't.

So I plant my feet, jerking back hard enough to make the one holding my arm stumble. "Let me go!" My voice echoes in the night, ragged and desperate, so I scream.

Crack.

Pain explodes across my face. A sharp, brutal punch through the bag.

I stagger, my legs giving out for a split second as the world tilts.

Focus. Don't go down.

My pulse pounds like war drums, but my body feels sluggish, my senses dulled from the hit.

They drag me forward by an arm, shove me at the back, my feet scraping against the ground.

My jaw throbs, my head spins, but the fire inside me refuses to go out.

They wanted a docile priestess?

They're about to get a fucking storm.

"Move faster," one of them snaps. "The gorge is just ahead."

The *gorge*. They're going to throw me over the edge. My brain catches up with their plan instantly.

My hand inches toward my side, remembering I have a small blade tucked into my belt, seeing as we all slept in our clothes.

"This is far enough," one of them rasps, jerking me to a stop. The roar of water fills my ears—the gorge.

"Any last words, priestess?" a voice sneers as the bag tightens around my neck. My lungs seize. I can't breathe, can't think. Panic claws up my throat like a wild thing.

"Fuck you!"

"Feisty!" another taunts. "So no pleading to spare your pathetic life?"

My fingers curl around the hilt of my blade. And I swing at them with the weapon.

A cry rings out, sharp and shocked, followed by the sudden thud of footsteps. One of them shoves me hard from behind. My boots skid across loose earth. I stagger, and the ground turns to loose rubble beneath my foot, descending in front of me. I flail wildly, my heart exploding in my chest.

"You don't deserve to be here!" one of them hisses as I scramble back to catch my footing. "You're nothing. Go die like the weak little wolf you are."

Then they shove me in the back harder.

I fall.

Air tears past me, the roar of the gorge rising like a scream. My arms fling out, desperate, and catch a thick branch that lashes across my stomach. I grab it with both hands, fingers locking around bark and splinters, body swinging hard against the cliffside.

Pain explodes through my shoulders, but I hold on. I fucking grip that branch with my life depending on it.

With a cry, I claw my way back up, every inch a war. Dirt crumbles beneath my boots. My heart is a drumbeat of survival and fury. I rip the damn bag off my head just in time to see two shadowy figures vanish into the building. To the side of the building, the glow of a torch—a man approaches, shouting.

"Who's out there? Show yourselves!"

But I'm already running back to the sleeping quarters.

Barely breathing, legs screaming, I sprint across the field. I won't stop. My lungs burn.

I'm not leaving. I'm not crawling away like a coward in the dark. I'm going to survive this. And when I do... I'm going to find those bitches. I'm going to look them in the eyes, and I'm going to make them regret ever touching me.

I slam into the side of the building just as the pain eases, the manacle no longer buzzing, and I breathe easily.

The guard is suddenly there, a fiery torch blazing across my face, and I squint against the bright light.

"What happened to you? No one should be out of the sleeping quarters at this hour."

"Needed some air," I manage, wiping blood from my split lip. Then I shove past him, chest heaving, blade tucked in the back of my belt.

I made it back.

Inside, I stumble to the washroom next to the kitchen. I splash cold water on my face, gasping as it stings my split lip. My side aches and will most likely be bruised.

The mirror above the basin shows what I already know from the pain—a bruise darkening beneath my right eye, another on my jawline, blood smeared across my chin. I look like I've already been through the first trial.

My hands shake as the adrenaline begins to ebb, leaving in its wake a bone-deep exhaustion and the full awareness of how close I came to dying tonight. Not from beasts or Onyx Covenant challenges, but from my fellow wolves.

Who were they? The obvious suspects are the Umbra females, but for all I know, it's two of my pack. Their voices were hard to determine, their scents masked. And right now, I don't pick up on that unique smell in our quarters, telling me Umbra wolves must be responsible.

I clean away the blood as best I can, wishing I had some of Mother's healing salve. The bruises will be impossible to hide in the morning.

As I make my way back to my makeshift bed on the floor, I cast a wary gaze over the rear doorway.

I clasp the blade firmly in my hand beneath the blanket. I close my eyes anyway, forcing my breathing to regulate despite the throbbing pain in my face and side.

This is just the beginning, I realize. The ritual hasn't even officially started, and already, someone wants me dead or at least removed from the competition. And if these are the lengths they'll go to now, what will happen once we're in the wilderness? Once there are no guards to intervene?

I grip my blade tighter, a promise to myself in the darkness. I won't be caught off guard again. I won't be the weak link, the easy target.

Now, more than ever, I want to win this damn ritual to prove them all wrong.

Morning comes too quickly, harsh sunlight streaming through the high windows of the stone bunker. I rise stiffly, every movement sending fresh stabs of pain through my ribs. The night's attack has left its mark, not just in the visible bruises but in the way my body protests even the simplest movements.

Around me, the other Elios candidates are already up, gathering their things and preparing for the day ahead. Some cast curious glances my way, but none approach.

None ask if I'm okay. Their silence speaks volumes. Aria's not in her bed, so I assume she's in the kitchen or bathroom.

A female guard enters, arms full of identical, folded clothing, the color of the deepest blue night sky. "Leave everything behind except your chosen weapon," she announces, her voice echoing off the stone walls. "These are your ritual garments. Each is named for your size."

She distributes the clothing—tight-fitting pants, stretchy tops, jackets with buttons down the front, and sturdy boots. Military in style but made from fabric that moves with the body.

Aria's there, in yesterday's clothes, but her cheeks rosy and hair wet from a shower. She collects her bundle from the woman, then returns to my side.

"Holy fucking shit, what happened to your face?" Her gaze is wide with shock.

"Keep your voice down," I mutter.

"Yeah, sure, but everyone's gonna see that." She gestures to the bruise under my eye, the split lip. "You look like you got trampled by a shadow beast. Who did this?"

I grab her arm, pulling her closer. "Two girls tried to throw me into the gorge last night."

"What?" Her hand instinctively moves to the dagger at her hip. "Names. Now. I'll gut them before breakfast."

Quickly, I relay what happened, the attack, the female masked voices and scents.

"Those fucking bitches," Aria seethes, her face

flushing with rage. "I swear by both moons, I'll find out who did this and feed them their own entrails."

"I don't know who it was," I remind her, wincing as I bend to lace up my boots.

"Moonshadow root," Aria nods grimly. "Mixed with black pine tar. Nightblades use it during stealth missions. Burns the nostrils of anyone who catches the scent but completely masks wolf traces." She studies my face. "You should report this. The Covenant takes—"

"No," I cut her off. "I'm not giving anyone the satisfaction of knowing they got to me."

"This isn't about satisfaction, Lyra. This is about survival. If they tried once..."

"They'll try again," I finish for her. "I know. And I'll be ready next time." I check my blade, securing it at my hip, where it's hidden by the jacket but easily accessible.

"Fuck them. You're twice as smart as most of the warriors here, and after last night, I'd say you've got more guts, too."

"Thanks." Her faith in me creates a warm spot in the cold dread that's settled in my chest since the attack. "But I think it's time our pack kicked those Umbra assholes aside and took the reins. An Elios victor is a win for all of us."

Aria studies me for a moment, then nods. "All right, but we're still figuring out who they were. No one gets away with that shit."

I hesitate, then lower my voice. "I cut one of them last night."

Her stare sharpens. "Excellent!"

"I got her with my knife as I tried to break free." I glance around to make sure no one's listening, then add, "I had the blade smeared with kevrin powder before I left home. My mom taught me how to mix it—it slows healing, even for wolves. Makes it ten times harder for the body to mend."

Aria grins wickedly. "Smart. That'll leave a mark. If they're here... they'll be nursing that wound for days."

"Maybe longer," I mutter. "It burns like fire, too."

Aria's expression hardens. "Good. That'll make them easier to spot." She glances at the bathroom door, and an Elios girl emerges. Aria drags me by the arm. "Come on, it's your turn to take a quick wash before breakfast. Training starts after."

I hurry into the bathroom with my new clothes. Once I'm dressed and clean, Aria is ready, too, and we file out, making our way to a large tent set up near our sleeping quarters building. Despite the situation, I can't help noticing how the ritual clothing suits her athletic frame, highlighting the muscles she's built through years of Nightblade training.

Inside the mess hall, long tables are arranged with food laid out—plates filled with bread, fruit, and meats, enough to fuel warriors for the trials ahead.

The Umbra candidates are already seated at one end, their black clothing a sharp contrast to our deep blue garments despite the identical style. I keep my head down as we enter, but I sense stares on me immediately—on the bruises I can't hide.

Stay calm.

I scan the Umbra females, looking for any reaction to my appearance. A flicker of guilt. Satisfaction. Fear. But none meet my gaze directly.

I glance at their arms, their hands, anywhere a fresh wound might show. Nothing.

Aria murmurs beside me, her voice low. "See anything?"

"Not yet." I grab a plate and follow her down the line, but my mind is still on them. They wouldn't leave the wound exposed... but they'll show it when they move.

Aria and I take seats with our plates of food at the far end of the Elios section. "Eat," she commands. "You'll need your strength."

I force myself to take bites of bread and meat, knowing she's right. Whatever the day brings, facing it hungry won't help. But my appetite vanishes when I feel a particular gaze burning into me from across the tent.

Theron strolls over to join his Umbra wolves, his presence commanding the space with every step. The ritual clothing clings to him, dark leather stretched taut over his broad shoulders and powerful chest. The fitted long sleeves do little to hide the muscular lines of his arms, the fabric pulled snug across biceps that flex with restrained power.

His hair, wild and tousled, looks like the wind had its way with it—longer at the top, falling in messy strands across his brow, while the sides and back are shorter, highlighting the sharp angles of his jaw. And then there are his eyes, piercing, molten silver that gleam with unreadable intent. Even now, even after everything, my pulse betrays me, pounding harder.

His gaze is currently fixed on my bruised face with an expression of concern.

I drop my attention back to my plate, but I'm acutely aware of him watching me throughout the meal.

"He looks ready to murder someone," Aria murmurs, staring at Theron. "Think he knows about last night? Well, actually, we haven't heard of anyone being killed yet, so I guess he doesn't know."

I laugh softly as I stab a piece of meat with unnecessary force.

When breakfast ends, an older woman in black Covenant robes enters the tent.

"Training will begin shortly. You will be working with your bound partners today to prepare for tomorrow's first trial and learn the meaning of trust."

A ripple of murmurs passes through the group.

As we rise to follow her out, a hand closes around my upper arm, pulling me toward the back of the tent. I know who it is before I even turn from the captivating scent alone.

"Get your hand off me," I hiss, yanking my arm away.

Theron doesn't release me, instead drawing me behind a stack of supply crates where we're hidden from view. His stare rakes over my face, darkening as it takes in the bruises and the split lip.

"Who did that to you?" he demands, tone low and deadly.

"None of your business," I snap, lifting my chin defiantly despite the pain. "And I don't need your concern."

"It is when we're a team, and I plan to win this." His hand rises, fingers hovering near my bruised cheek before the tips trace lightly under the worst of the damage. His touch is featherlight, and for one treacherous moment, I find myself leaning into it, my gaze settling on his full lips. Memories flood back of that mouth against mine, against my neck, whispering promises in the darkness. Heat rushes through me, overwhelming and unwanted.

I jerk away, batting his hand from my face. "Don't."

"I won't have anyone mess with what's mine," he says, his voice a dangerous rumble.

"Yours?" I repeat, incredulous anger flaring in my chest. "I am not yours, Theron. I stopped being yours a year ago."

A muscle in his jaw ticks, something feral flashing behind his eyes. "Whether you want to accept it or not, Lyra, it's you and me against the world in this ritual. Most aren't happy about this pairing."

I try to move past him, but he blocks my path, his massive frame an immovable obstacle. Up close, he's even more devastatingly handsome—the ritual clothing defining every hard plane of muscle, the scent of him filling my senses with unwanted memories of stolen moments in the forest. Moments I shouldn't be thinking about.

Focus, Lyra.

But it's not just the heat rolling off him or the way his presence stirs something dangerous inside me. It's the weight of what happens if we win. Umbra wins. And that means... Theron takes the title. Alpha. I become his Omega. Bound to Umbra, to the very people who tried to break me.

I can't let that happen.

My throat tightens as the realization sinks deeper. If Elios wins, my pack thrives. We gain advantage on supplies shared by the country. But if Theron and I win... we lose everything.

So... do I sabotage him? Throw the ritual so Elios takes the victory to win the Harvest Ritual?

The thought twists in my gut, leaving a bitter taste. Sabotage means betraying myself if I want to win for me, to prove to everyone else I'm not weak. I need to prove that I'm a strong Omega.

But at what cost?

My fingers curl into fists at my sides. If I win, I lose. But if I lose, I still lose.

Theron's gaze is locked on me, steady and unreadable, but I feel the tension thrumming between us. He doesn't know what's going through my mind, doesn't see the war raging beneath the surface.

Do I fight for myself? Or do I fight for what's best for my pack?

"I don't need you to protect me," I murmur, but the words taste hollow. I don't even know what I'm protecting anymore.

Theron's expression darkens, as if he senses the turmoil I'm barely holding together. "We're in this together, Lyra."

But for how much longer?

"Whatever is happening, whoever hurt you... tell me," he implores, an edge of command to it that sends a shiver down my arms. "Because if this ritual goes the way I plan, it was always going to be us standing together at the end. Us against them, right? Just like it would have been, anyway."

He smiles then, a dimple appearing in his cheek, and I hate how my insides liquefy at the sight. Just as quickly, he schools his features.

"Stop it," I hiss. "The smiles, the flirting. I'm immune to your trickery now."

He laughs, the sound rich and knowing, and I clench my thighs together against the wave of heat it sends through me. Damn him.

I push past him, but his hand catches my arm, grip firm but not painful.

"Listen to me, Lyra. No one out there is on your side once we begin, but I am." His voice drops to a whisper that ghosts across my ear. "Remember who is enemy and who is friend."

"Friend?" I scoff, stepping back just enough to meet his gaze. "They didn't just attack me, Theron."

His expression hardens instantly, the teasing wiped clean.

"They tried to shove me over the gorge." My tone is steady, but the memory makes my blood run cold. "They wanted me dead."

Theron's jaw clenches, his body going still. "Fuck!"

"And not just me," I continue, stepping closer. "They clearly wanted you gone, too. Seeing me falling would break our fifty-feet rule, then we'd both be poisoned by our manacles."

Theron's nostrils flare, but his gaze burns with something lethal. "Umbra you think?" His tone is ice.

"I don't know for sure," I admit, though the suspicion claws at me. "But it seemed like it..." I let the implication hang heavy between us.

Theron's eyes darken, his silence more dangerous than any words.

"They don't care about your title." I step closer, the space between us crackling with tension. "They'd rather see us both fall than let you win."

"Then we make damn sure that doesn't happen." His voice is calm, but I feel the storm beneath it.

I fall silent, my own decisions warring inside of me.

His gaze holds mine, steady, intense.

"Looks like we're the only ones we can trust." His words are quiet, but they settle like a promise. "So we need to stop pretending we're enemies."

I can't bring myself to respond. My throat tightens

when someone calls out for us to join the group. Then we're on the move.

Two enemies.

Two broken hearts.

Two fates hanging by a thread.

The most dangerous part of this ritual isn't the challenges ahead or even the rivals waiting to strike. Because if I let my guard down, even for a second, Theron won't just cost me the ritual for my pack.

He'll cost me everything.

CHAPTER
SEVEN
THERON

I march toward the training grounds with everyone else already there, fury burning in my veins with every step. The purple bruises on Lyra's face bloom against her golden skin. Someone thought it was acceptable to hurt her because I selected her as my Omega in the Harvest Ritual.

Someone believed they could touch what's mine and walk away unscathed.

My gaze sweeps over the gathered members of my Umbra pack, studying their faces as I approach. The way they glare at both me and Lyra tells me everything I need to know. They're making her pay for my decision, punishing her for my sins. And I'm not fooled to know my father would have a hand in this.

I *know* I have to bide my time. The Harvest Ritual demands focus, requires control, but seeing Lyra again after a year apart has unleashed something animalistic in me. I'd forgotten how her presence affects me. For twelve long months, I've ached for her—for her touch, the sound of her laughter, her voice—and now she's here, forced to stand at my side once more.

I will make her mine again, even if she pushes me away now, even if she claims to hate me. Some bonds can't be broken, not completely. And ours... ours was forged in fate and shadows.

The training field stretches at the side of the Onyx Covenant building, an expanse of emerald grass. Beyond it, ancient pines stand, their shadows barely touching the field's edge. Twenty contestants—ten pairs.

Kieran falls into step beside me, his perpetual smirk firmly in place. "You look ready to commit murder," he states, nudging my shoulder. "Not the best strategy for winning friends and influence."

"I don't need new friends," I growl. "I need answers."

"About your priestess's face?" When I shoot him a dangerous look, he raises his hands in mock surrender. "Relax. Wasn't me. Though several of our pack mates are discussing it like a trophy."

My fingers curl into fists. "Names, Kieran."

"I already grilled the bastards who were running their mouths," Kieran says, his voice dropping lower. "Said they had no clue." He spits the last word like it tastes foul. "Let it go for now, or you'll get disqualified for starting a fight before the event even begins. Once the ritual starts?" He shrugs. "Have at them. No rules against *accidents* during trials."

The darkness that's been growing inside me since discovering my mother's notebooks in the house rises to the surface, a tide I can barely contain. It would be so easy to let it consume me.

"I'll find them," I hiss. "And they'll beg for death before I'm done."

Kieran studies my face, his usual humor gone. "You're starting to sound like him, you know."

I don't need to ask who he means. The comparison to my father sits like acid in my stomach.

"Besides," he adds, nodding toward the center of the field. "Our esteemed teacher has arrived."

Melian glides across the grass, dressed in flowing black robes that billow around her tall, lithe frame. Despite being in her mid-thirties, she carries herself with the manner of someone far older. Her dark hair is pulled back in intricate plaits interwoven with metal rings that catch the morning light. Her face is striking rather than just pretty—high cheekbones, lips set in a serious line, and eyes so dark they appear almost black in certain light. The Covenant member's presence silences the murmurs instantly.

"I hope you all slept well," she announces, her voice carrying effortlessly across the field. "You have a long day ahead. One day of training, of learning the basics. Afterward, you begin in earnest." Her gaze sweeps over everyone. "These rituals aren't just about winning for your pack but also discovering if you've made the right choice in your partner to serve alongside you in the Onyx

Covenant for the next decade... someone to trust implicitly."

Beside me, Kieran snorts. "Trust. Right. Because nothing says trust like throwing people into deadly trials."

I turn my attention to Lyra, who stands apart from the others.

She shouldn't stand out. Not here. Not in the middle of all this chaos.

But she does.

Fuck, does she.

The leather armor clings to her curves, molded to her body like a damn invitation. My gaze drags lower—her full breasts, the dip of her waist, the flare of her hips, the way the tight straps highlight the curve of her ass. I shouldn't be looking. Not now. Not when I know what it cost her to be here.

But my body doesn't give a shit about that.

Her still-damp hair falls halfway down her back. I remember how it felt tangled in my fists. How it spilled across my chest, her pale lavender eyes locked on mine when she stared down at me.

My chest tightens. *Don't go there.*

It's too fucking late.

The bruises on her skin appear darker in the morning light. It twists something savage inside me. But even bruised and battered, Lyra doesn't shrink. She holds herself like a warrior—head high, eyes sharp.

That's what gets me.

Not just her beauty. Not just the curves that still haunt my fucking dreams.

It's the fire inside her. The strength. The way she refuses to break, no matter how much this world tries to crush her.

And fuck me... I crave her.

Even when she's pushing me away.

"Today's lesson," Melian continues, drawing me out of my fantasy, "is all about trust. Later, we'll conduct a ritual that will reveal more about the truth you hold for your partner."

I have no idea what that means, but it sounds ominous. Whispers ripple through the gathered contestants.

"What truth?" Kieran mutters. "I'd trust a snake not to bite before I'd trust that whatever trials we have coming up won't kill us." He grins smugly as a few around us chuckle.

"Kieran of Umbra," Melian calls out. "You seem to have a lot to say. Come, let's do a practice run."

He grins, stepping forward with that cocky swagger that's gotten him into trouble more times than I can count. "Always happy to volunteer, Covenant-sister."

"Excellent." Melian's smile is razor-sharp. "Stand here." She positions him before us, then walks ten paces away, her back to him. "Attack me."

Kieran glances around, confused. "You want me to... attack you? From behind?"

"If you can," she says simply.

Kieran shrugs, then charges, silent and quick—I'll give him that. Before he's taken three steps, Melian whirls, drops to one knee, and sweeps her leg in a wide arc. Kieran goes down hard, the breath knocked from his lungs as his back hits the grass.

Laughter erupts from the onlookers.

"The first lesson of trust," Melian says, offering Kieran a hand up, "is to recognize when you can't trust your own assumptions. I told you to attack me. I never said I wouldn't be ready."

"Lesson learned." Kieran accepts her help, his grin unwavering despite his wounded pride. "Though I maintain its poor form to humiliate your students so early in the morning."

More laughter, and even Melian's lips twitch. "Pairs, find an empty spot near the edge of the woods that surround us."

Kieran brushes grass from his clothes as he rejoins me. "Go find your priestess. And try not to look so murderous. You're scaring the children."

I bark a laugh and leave him, making my way toward Lyra, who's already waiting for me. We head toward the perimeter of the woods.

"So," she says. "What are we meant to do? Fight each other?" A ghost of a smile touches her lips. "That could be entertaining."

"I wouldn't fight you," I say as we pause by a lofty pine. "That's unfair."

She raises an eyebrow. "Because I'm a priestess and—"

"You should stop talking," I interrupt. "Before you embarrass yourself more."

Her shoulders shoot back. "Excuse me?"

"I wouldn't fight you because you'd lose," I clarify, enjoying the flash of indignation in her eyes. "And I take no pleasure in easy victories."

"Is that what you tell yourself about us?" she counters. "That I'm an easy victory?"

"You know I don't." I step closer, unable to stop my gaze from trailing over every perfect inch of her body. The leather bodice cinches her small waist. Even bruised and angry, she's the most beautiful thing I've ever seen.

"Up here, big boy," she calls me out, snapping her fingers in front of my face.

I laugh, deep and genuine, just as Melian approaches us.

"Theron. Lyra." The Covenant member glances between us. "Your task today is simple in concept, difficult in execution."

"Isn't everything?" I mutter.

Melian produces two black silk scarves from her robes. "You will be blindfolded."

Lyra tenses beside me. "Both of us?"

"Yes," Melian says. "You'll be connected by this." She holds up a thin rope the length of my arm. "Wrist to wrist. You must traverse the forest and return with the token hanging from the heart tree."

"While blindfolded and chained together," I clarify. "Anything else? Maybe set the forest on fire for ambience?"

"The forest has its own challenges," Melian says cryptically. "You'll need to communicate. To trust each other's instincts. And most importantly"—her gaze locks with mine—"protect each other. Not all dangers will be physical."

With that, she binds the rope to my left wrist, then to Lyra's right, leaving about a hand's length of rope between us.

"Each pair must find their own path. You'll know when you've found yours."

"That's helpfully vague," Lyra mutters.

Melian's lips curve. "The ritual doesn't reward those who need everything explained. Last year, three pairs never returned."

"What happened to them?" I ask, though I suspect I know the answer.

"They weren't worthy of the Covenant." She ties the blindfold around my eyes, plunging me into darkness, then presumably does the same for Lyra. "May the moons guide you."

She takes our bound hands and guides us several steps, then turns us.

"You're now facing the woods. Go north and stay true on that path until you scent the mountain moss. Follow it to the heart tree, which will offer you a token. Find yourself on a pebbly stone floor, and you have veered in the wrong direction. Coming back, you must remain blind-folded. And remember, trust is also in being honest in the test without cheating… you will be watched." She releases us, and her receding footsteps soften.

I breathe in the scent of damp earth and pine trees.

"Well," Lyra says after a moment. "This should be interesting."

I feel her shift, the rope pulling slightly against my wrist.

"North," I say, and I tilt my head back, orienting myself by the warmth of the sun on my face and the sounds of the forest.

"Slightly to your right," Lyra says just as the words are about to leave my lips. Clever girl.

I take a step, then pause when she doesn't move with me. "You need to—"

"I know how to walk, Theron," she says tartly. "Contrary to what you might think, I didn't spend the last year sitting around weeping over you."

I laugh it off. "Good to know the claws are still sharp."

She's finally moving forward with me.

We take the first steps together, awkwardly at first, then find a tentative rhythm. I take hold of her hand, and the sudden contact with her skin sends electricity up my arm.

"What are you doing?" she demands.

"Making it easier to walk," I say innocently. "Worried you might like being so close to me?"

"In your dreams."

"Every night," I admit, the truth slipping out.

Her breath catches, and we both fall silent.

Then the air changes—cooler, damper. We've reached the deep forest's edge.

"Woods will be denser, bigger, more broken branches on the ground and shrubbery," Lyra says, her shoulder brushing mine, sending another current of awareness through me.

"So now we trust each other," I say, surprising myself with how easily the words come.

We move forward when my foot hits a root jutting across the path. I stumble, regaining my balance before I fall over.

"Step up," I warn, reaching back with my free hand to guide her. "Root across the path."

Her fingers brush against my arm as she navigates the obstacle. "Yep, got that from you lurching."

We continue, my arm stretching outward as my navigation to ensure I don't walk into anything. I assume she's doing the same, as I feel her swaying as if reaching around her. Her scent fills my nostrils—night-blooming jasmine and fresh rain—stronger than I remember, more intoxicating. My inner wolf stirs, restless and hungry in a way that has nothing to do with food.

"You still smell the same," I murmur.

"And you're still inappropriate," she snaps, but her quickening pulse betrays her. "Focus on the task."

"I am focused," I state. "Just not on what you think."

She makes a sound, half frustration, half something else entirely. "You're impossible."

"Yet you're bound to me anyway."

"Not by choice," she reminds me.

"Are you sure about that?" I can't resist pushing. "You could have refused the pairing."

She doesn't answer immediately. When she does, her voice is quiet. "So could you."

The ground becomes uneven, sloping upward. I sense Lyra tense beside me as small rocks shift beneath our feet.

"Careful," she murmurs, her grip tightening. "Ground's unstable here."

Suddenly, Lyra stops.

"Wait. Do you hear that?"

I go still, focusing beyond the forest sounds. There—a low growl, coming from our left.

"Something's watching us," I whisper.

The growl intensifies, and I catch its scent on the breeze—predator, territorial, agitated.

"Mountain lion," Lyra breathes, her pulse quickening. I can practically taste her fear in the air.

"Don't move," I say, positioning myself slightly in front of her.

The growl comes closer from our right. Without thinking, I drop into a crouch, pulling Lyra down with me. My own growl rises from deep in my chest, louder and more terrifying than any natural predator. I feel the change ripple through me—not a full shift, but enough that my senses sharpen to painful clarity, my canines lengthening in my mouth. My growl becomes a roar that echoes through the trees, primal and possessive.

Silence follows, then the sound of retreating paws.

"That was..."

"Necessary," I finish for her, straightening. My partial shift recedes, leaving me slightly breathless.

"I was going to say terrifying," she admits, and I can smell the adrenaline coursing through her. "Sometimes I forget how scary you can be in your wolf form. Anyway, we should keep moving."

We press on, the forest growing denser, both of us going slower, bumping into trees. Suddenly, something whips across my face—a low-hanging branch. I duck too late, feeling it scrape across my forehead.

"Damn it," I mutter.

"What?" Lyra asks, concern breaking through her controlled tone.

"Branch. Watch your—"

She makes a small sound of pain as the branch must have caught her, too. She stumbles into me. I catch her instinctively, my arm wrapping around her middle as she collides with my chest. My back hits a tree, bracing us both.

For a moment, we're frozen, her body pressed against mine, our faces inches apart. Her breath dances on my lips. She's softer than I remember, yet stronger, too—the curve of her waist, the firmness of muscle beneath, the cushion of her breasts against my chest.

"Your heart is racing," I whisper, unable to resist. I

inhale deeply, drawing in her scent. "Gods, I've missed how you smell. Like midnight and magic and everything I've ever wanted."

Her pulse jumps. "Let go of me," she says but makes no move to pull away.

"Why?" I ask, my lips almost brushing her ear. "You're fighting so hard to resist me. Why bother when we both know how this ends?"

"I still hate you, if you've forgotten," she whispers.

I laugh softly. "No, you don't. You wish you did. It would be easier, wouldn't it? But hate doesn't make your body react like this." I run a hand lightly up her spine, feeling her shiver. "Hate doesn't dilate your pupils or quicken your breath."

"You can't see my eyes," she points out, a hint of her usual sharpness returning.

"I don't need to see to know," I murmur. "I remember every detail of you, Lyra. Every. Single. One."

She pushes against my chest with one flat palm, and I release her, though our bound hands remain locked together.

"For someone who wants to win this competition, you're not taking it very seriously."

"It's just training," I say, grinning, though she can't see it. "We have time for more."

"More what?"

"Truths," I suggest, my voice dropping. "More confessions. More of whatever this is between us that refuses to die."

"You're delusional," she murmurs.

"Am I? Then why can I still sense your desire from here? Why can I—"

"There's something blocking the path," she interrupts, clearly desperate to change the subject. "Feels like fallen trees. Two of them crossed over each other."

I reach out, my fingers finding rough bark—massive and immovable. "Too high to climb over while blindfolded and bound."

"We need to find another way around," she says.

"Wait," I say, inhaling deeply. The scent hits me like a memory, damp, earthy, ancient. "Wintermoss." I recognize what Melian described. "That mossy ground she mentioned—our destination."

"I smell it, too," Lyra breathes, her voice dropping to something almost intimate. I hear her inhaling deeply, sniffing the air. "To the right. It's stronger there."

I run my hand along the fallen trunk, fingers catching on rough bark. "We follow it, then, as it's fallen in that direction."

With each step, the wintermoss scent grows more potent, pulling us closer. Then—

The ground vanishes beneath my foot.

My stomach lurches as I pitch forward into nothingness. "Fuck, it's a cliff!" tears from my throat.

In an instant, Lyra snatches the back of my shirt with surprising strength. She yanks me backward, hard. I stumble, losing balance in the opposite direction. We both tumble to the ground, my back hitting the earth with Lyra half sprawled across me, both of us breathing hard.

"That," she gasps, "was too close."

My heart hammers against my ribs, adrenaline coursing through me.

"Well," I manage once I catch my breath. "I think we found an edge. Guessing the moss is down there. They do tend to grow in valleys, so it makes sense."

We sit there for a pause. Her hand rests on my chest, probably unintentionally, but I cover it with mine before she can pull away.

"I knew you still cared about me," I state, unable to resist.

"I'm not a monster, Theron," she says with an exasperated sigh. "I don't want you dead."

I chuckle at how badly she lies, her pulse quickening beneath my fingers. "Just maimed, then? Or merely suffering?"

"Don't tempt me," she warns.

She gets up abruptly, the rope tugging on my wrist. "Let's move." She nudges me with her foot. "We've got a tree to find."

I rise to my feet, staying close to her. "What's your plan?"

"Let's test the edge slowly," she suggests, already moving carefully toward where the ground dropped away. "See if it's just a small valley or a cliff. Though there shouldn't be any big cliffs on this part of the mountains."

"You sound very sure of that for someone who can't see a damn thing right now."

"I've studied these forests," she says, and I can hear the priestess in her voice—confident, knowledgeable. "Part of my training. Now, get on your ass."

"Excuse me?"

"We're going to slide down gradually until we're sure we're not free-falling off a cliff," she explains, already lowering herself to the ground. "Unless you've got a better idea?"

"Always so commanding," I tease but follow her lead, sitting at the edge. "I'd forgotten how bossy you get when you're nervous."

"I'm not nervous," she insists. "I'm cautious. There's a difference."

I grin to myself as we ease forward, testing the slope with our feet. It's steep but not a sheer drop, maybe a forty-five-degree angle of loose soil and rocks.

"It's not too bad," I say, already sliding down on my backside. "Steeper than I'd like, but manageable."

We descend slowly, testing each section with our foot before committing our weight. Eventually, the ground levels out enough that we can stand, still moving carefully.

"Stop for a bit. I need a rock," Lyra says.

We both lean forward cautiously. I hear the soft scrape of Lyra's movements, her fingers rustling against dirt and stone as she searches the ground near us.

"Got one," she murmurs. I feel her knuckles accidentally brush against my thigh as she shifts position. The rope tugs at my wrist, forcing me to move with her as she repositions herself.

A light clicking sound reaches my ears as she must be rolling the rock between her palms. "This should work."

I sense her arm tensing beside me, the subtle change in air pressure as she moves. Her shoulder presses briefly against mine before I feel her motion—the pull on our bound wrists as she throws the stone.

The silence stretches for a heartbeat—two—then a soft thud echoes back to us. Not far. Not deep.

"See?" she breathes, relief evident in her voice. "Not a cliff."

"Never doubted you," I lie smoothly.

"Sure you didn't." Her voice is dry, but I can hear the smile in it. "Now, let's find that tree."

We head forward, our fingers intertwined, and just being close to her leaves me grinning like an idiot. The wintermoss's damp, mushroom-like scent grows stronger with each step.

"Tell me, Theron," she asks out of the blue, her voice casual. "Why did you really select me as your partner in the Harvest Ritual? Was it to torment me further?"

The question hangs between us, heavy with all the things we've never said.

"Selfishness," I admit truthfully. "To get you to finally talk to me, listen to me, not pretend I don't exist." I take a breath, the darkness of the blindfold somehow making it easier to be honest. "You've haunted me, Lyra. Every night. Every damn dream. I wake up reaching for you. I can't..." My voice catches. "I can't get you out of my head. Out of my blood."

Her fingers tense in mine.

"I also didn't want anyone from my pack," I continue, the words spilling out now. "Not for this mission. Not for anything that matters."

"Against your father's wishes?" The surprise in her voice is genuine. "He was pissed... maybe more than mine."

"My father is a fucking bastard," I growl, the words dark with loathing. I don't elaborate. "This Harvest Ritual is my way to make a difference, to stop his brutality my way."

She's quiet for several steps before responding.

"Like the mountain hunt last month? The one where our packs joined forces to go into the high peaks? There were those huge wild wolves, but also great game." Her voice turns pointed. "Did you know that our pack only got a quarter of the catch, even though we had more hunters than your team?"

The question takes me by surprise. "I didn't." The news settles like a stone in my gut. "But it sounds exactly like something he would do."

"If your goal is to knock your father aside, then I'm with you," she says, her words fierce. "As long as you don't plan to follow in his steps."

Something in me breaks that she could think so little

of me. "You don't know me if you say that," I say, my voice rough with hurt.

"I thought I knew you, Theron." The simple statement carries years of pain.

I stop walking, tugging her to a halt beside me. Even in darkness, I turn to face her, my free hand finding her shoulder.

"Then use this time to get to know me again," I say, pouring everything I feel into the words. "We start fresh. No assumptions. No past. Just you and me, as we are now."

She goes quiet, and when we start walking again, the silence stretches between us like a living thing. Her fingers remain laced with mine, neither pulling closer nor pushing away, and she never responds. But she doesn't have to—I pick up the way her pulse beats faster and stronger.

It's not forgiveness. Not yet. But it's a beginning.

The ground begins to soften, and we're both crouching low, hands tentatively exploring our surroundings.

"Moss," I confirm, fingers tracing over the soft, cushiony surface. It's moist to the touch and springy under pressure. "We've reached the mossy ground Melian mentioned."

"So the heart tree must be here," Lyra says.

I stand slowly, careful not to pull on her as I do. The air here is different, still and heavy with the scent of vanilla flowers that seems to come from all directions. I turn in a slow circle, taking her with me, trying to catch any hint of the massive tree.

I run a hand through my hair. "This feels like an open field. The tree could be anywhere."

"We keep going until we find it."

So that's what we do, moving cautiously across the mossy ground, hands outstretched like sleepwalkers. After several minutes of finding nothing but more moss, Lyra sighs.

"This is insane. How are we supposed to find one tree in what feels like acres of open space?" It doesn't stop us from walking around aimlessly.

"Maybe we should—" My words cut off as my boot catches on something hard and gnarled, sending me stumbling. "Shit!"

"What is it?" Lyra asks, steadying herself as I regain my balance.

I crouch down, my hands exploring what tripped me. "Tree root. A big one." I trace my fingers along its length, feeling the woody texture. "Really big, actually."

"The heart tree," Lyra breathes. "It has to be. Follow it!"

We both laugh at the sudden breakthrough. We use our feet to trace the root, shuffling ahead carefully.

"This way," I say, following the root as it grows thicker.

We travel in tandem, one foot sliding forward to find the root, then the other foot joining it. It's awkward but effective. The root widens beneath our steps, rising higher from the ground.

"It's close," Lyra whispers, excitement making her voice tremble slightly. "I can feel it."

More careful steps and my outstretched hand collides with something solid. Rough bark meets my fingertips, warm and alive in a way that ordinary trees aren't.

"Found it," I say, my palm flattening against the huge trunk. It pulses faintly beneath my touch, like a sleeping giant's heartbeat. "This must be the heart tree."

"Oh, she feels huge. Now we need to find the token."

We circle the tree, hands exploring its surface. The trunk is enormous. It would take four people with outstretched arms to encircle it.

"I hear something," Lyra says suddenly. "Like parchment fluttering in the breeze. Up high."

I cock my head to the side and listen. She's right. There's a faint rustling above us. I raise my free hand, stretching for the fluttering object, but I can't reach it. And by the direction of the sound, it should be right above us.

"Our token. I'll lift you," I suggest. "You could stand on my shoulders."

"Blindfolded? That's insane."

"You have a better idea?"

She hesitates. "No," she admits reluctantly. "But if you drop me, I swear I'll end you."

"Never," I say too seriously. "I'd never let you fall. Come on, then. I'll crouch, and you put your feet on my thighs, then I'll stand, and you can step onto my shoulders."

"This is such a terrible idea," she mutters, but her free hand finds my shoulder.

"Ready?" I ask.

"No... but do it anyway."

I crouch lower, bracing myself against the tree. She hesitates, then places one tentative foot on my thigh, gripping my shoulder for balance.

"I'm going to fall and break both our necks," she warns, wobbling slightly.

"You won't. Trust me." I can't help the grin spreading across my face.

"Stop enjoying this so much. I can hear you smirking."

"I'm not—"

"You absolutely are." She places her other foot on my opposite thigh, her body swaying dangerously. "Oh Gods, oh Gods."

I steady her with my hand at her waist. "You're doing great."

"Shut up," she hisses.

As she attempts to maneuver higher, she loses her balance, pitching forward. Her breasts bump against my face, and we both freeze.

"I... sorry," she stammers.

I clear my throat. "No problem. Though I can't say I mind the... unexpected perks of this position."

"If you make one more joke, I swear I'll—"

"Just keep going," I say, my voice strained. "Before I drop you."

She shifts upward, her hand finding my head for support. When I breathe in, I catch the faint scent of her perfume, something delicious and light. It's intoxicating and absolutely not what I should be focusing on right now.

"Can you... just a little higher..." she says, her fingers tangled in my hair.

"Working on it," I grunt, slowly beginning to stand. Every muscle in my body strains with the effort.

She steps higher, one foot finding my shoulder.

"Focus on not falling, would you?"

Her second foot lands on my other shoulder. I'm steadying her with my hands on her thighs, her bound arm pulling against the rope and giving her one arm to stretch up. She's light, but the position is awkward. My back presses against the rough bark of the heart tree, giving me the stability I need to hold her. The muscles in my shoulders and arms burn with the effort, but it's a good pain—purposeful, necessary.

Standing slowly, I widen my stance and plant my feet more firmly on the moss-covered ground. She shifts her weight, leaning more heavily on my right shoulder as she extends herself further.

"Almost there," I encourage, voice strained from the effort. "Can you reach it?"

"Nearly," she breathes. I feel every subtle shift as she balances herself. "I can feel it brushing my fingertips."

"Hurry," I urge, feeling a tremor start in my legs. No matter how light she is, holding anyone above your head while blindfolded is no small feat. "Not to rush you, but I'd rather not drop you."

"Just… a… little…" Her body tenses, extending that final crucial inch.

"I can feel it," she says, excitement breaking through her reserve. "It's a piece of parchment that must be tied to a branch. Just a little higher…"

I groan for her to hurry up.

"Got it!" she exclaims. "Let me down."

I steady myself as I prepare to help her descend.

Her foot searches blindly for purchase as she begins to move down.

Her body slides against mine, and my hands instinctively find her waist.

"Gods, this is so awkward," she mutters as she slips a little, her body pressing firmly against my chest.

"Really?" I can't keep the smile from my voice. "I'm in heaven right now."

"Gods," she says, but there's a laugh hiding beneath her words.

My hands grip her waist more firmly as she continues her descent, the heat of her body radiating through her clothes. Without sight, everything feels magnified—the slight catch in her breath when my fingers accidentally graze the skin where her shirt has ridden up and the softness of her hair brushing against my chin.

"Your heart is racing," she whispers, and I realize her palm is splayed against my sternum.

"Can't imagine why," I reply, my voice rougher than I intended.

When her feet finally touch the ground, neither of us moves.

"You can let go now," she says quietly.

My hand remains at her waist, thumbs tracing small circles against the fabric of her shirt.

"Do you *really* want me to let you down?"

She's quiet, and her breath flutters, quick and uneven, against my face. We're too close. Dangerously close.

"Theron," she says, her voice lower than before, almost a warning. "Don't make this harder for us."

"Harder?" I can't help the suggestive tone that creeps into my voice. My fingers tighten slightly at her waist. "I think we're well past that point, my little moon."

The paper rustles between her fingers as she shifts in my grip. "Let's not do this."

"Why? Because you still care for me," I say, not a question but a statement. "Because you still want me. Do you dream of me, Lyra? The way I dream of you?"

"How is that conducive to not making things harder for us?" There's an edge to her voice.

"Just answer the question," I persist, unwilling to let this moment slip away. Her body is warm against mine, her scent surrounding me, clouding my judgment.

She sighs, the sound filled with frustration. "Yes. You happy now?"

I can't stop the grin that spreads across my face, thankful for the blindfold that hides how much that simple admission affects me.

"It's all I need to know."

"Whatever." The parchment crinkles again as she fidgets with it. "Anyway, what do you think the note says?"

I shrug, mostly to myself, as I finally lower her, our bodies sliding against each other in a way that feels both deliberate and accidental. "Guess we'll find out soon enough."

She's already moving, pulling me by our bound rope. "Come on. We need to retrace our steps."

There's no hiding the truth—whatever broke between us a year ago isn't completely shattered. The pieces remain, jagged and dangerous, waiting to be reassembled into something new.

Returning seemed to take us less time.

"Congratulations!" Melian's voice comes from nearby. Her hands are there, untying my blindfold, then the rope binding me to Lyra. "You're the first to return successfully."

Light floods my vision, momentarily blinding me. When my sight clears, I glance at Lyra blinking beside me, a small scratch on her brow from the branch. She's never looked more beautiful—wild and fierce and alive in a way that makes my chest ache.

Melian holds out her hand, and Lyra places the folded parchment in it. Instead of taking it, Melian smiles. "This is yours to keep—a message from the heart tree. When you're ready, make your way to the side of the training yard. We'll be practicing defense moves next."

As Melian walks away, I glance down at Lyra, something vulnerable flickering across her face.

"What does it say?" I ask, glancing at the parchment in her grasp.

She raises and unfolds it.

"Two paths diverged in ancient woods,

Yet shared one destination.

Trust not the common solitude,

But the uncommon alliance."

She stares at the words. "What do you think it means?"

"Maybe that some battles aren't meant to be fought alone," I say, holding her gaze. "Whatever lies ahead, we're stronger together than apart."

"Poetic," she states, but there's no mockery in her tone.

"I have my moments."

"Come on," she says, tucking the parchment into her pocket. "Let's show them what an *uncommon alliance* can do."

"Is that what we are now?" I ask, unable to keep the hope from my voice. "Allies?"

Her gaze meets mine. "It's a start."

Those eyes still hypnotize me. There's dirt on her cheek and that scratch on her brow, but they only make her look more alive. More real. More mine.

She's changed this past year—leaner, harder. The soft priestess edges worn away to reveal something dangerous beneath. Something that matches the wolf inside her.

I want to run my thumb across that scratch, taste the salt on her skin, and press her against the nearest tree until those lavender eyes go dark with wanting. Until she admits what we both know.

As we walk toward the training field, I can't help but smile. She can pretend all she wants that the wall between us is still intact, but I felt it crumbling in that forest, touch by touch. And now that I've found a crack in her defenses, I won't stop until I've torn them down completely.

She may not be mine yet. But she will be. It's only a matter of time.

EIGHT

LYRA

The Hall of Champions steals my breath away the moment we enter. Towering obsidian pillars stretch toward a vaulted ceiling where thousands of crystals dangle like frozen stars, scattering the light from massive iron chandeliers dripping with thick white candles. Their flames dance and flicker, casting long shadows that seem to move with a life of their own across the midnight-blue walls inlaid with silver runes that pulse with ancient fae magic.

A table stretches the length of the hall—ancient ironwood polished to a gleam, the surface so dark it reflects our faces like a still lake at midnight. Silver platters overflow with steaming food, goblets gleam in the candlelight, and the air is heavy with the scent of roasted meats, spiced wine, and freshly baked bread.

I salivate at the smells.

I adjust the sleeve of the new training clothes we were

given for dinner—soft leather pants and a fitted tunic in Elios deep blue. Over the top of that is a fitted jacket I carry in my hands for now.

"Stop fidgeting," Theron murmurs as he pulls out my chair, his breath warm against my ear. "You look like you're planning an escape."

"Maybe I am," I shoot back, sliding into the seat as he takes my jacket and sets it on the back of my chair, which is carved with moon phases.

Theron drops into the chair beside me, his thigh pressing against mine beneath the table. His dark hair falls loose across his brow, framing sharp cheekbones and those storm-silver eyes that always stare at me. Like the rest of us, he's dressed in the ceremonial training gear, though his is Umbra black, the fabric stretching across broad shoulders that seem to take up too much space beside me.

"That would be ill-advised," he says, his lips quirking upward. "I'd have to come after you, and we both know I'd catch you."

I half laugh. "You sound awfully confident for someone who needed my help to win today's challenge."

"Is that what happened?" He leans closer, and I catch the scent of pine and winter frost that clings to his skin. "I remember things differently."

"You would." I try to ignore the heat that spreads through me at his proximity, focusing instead on the feast laid before us.

Aria slides into the seat beside me, her movements

fluid. She's cleaned up for dinner, but her cheekbone still bears a scratch from training, angry red against her honey-toned skin. Her chestnut hair falls in waves past her shoulders, and her amber eyes sparkle with her grin.

"Holy mother of moons," she whispers, eyeing the spread of food. "If I die tomorrow, at least my last meal was spectacular. I don't remember ever seeing so much food."

"Don't even joke about dying," I hiss, glancing around to make sure no one heard.

"Please." She rolls her eyes. "Everyone's thinking it." She reaches for a platter piled high with roasted pheasant, the skin crisp and glistening with a honey glaze. "Besides, if we're going to die, we might as well do it with full bellies and smiles on our faces."

On her other side, Orion sits with his back ramrod straight, looking out of place in his formal training clothes. His emerald eyes remain fixed on the others at the head of the table.

"You could at least try to look like you're enjoying yourself," Aria tells him, nudging his arm with her elbow.

He doesn't even glance at her. "This isn't a celebration. It's another test."

"Does everything have to be so serious with you? I'm sure this is just them spoiling us before the big event." She piles food onto his plate regardless of his dour mood.

Orion's lips twitch, the closest thing to a smile I've seen from him. "Pure stubbornness might keep us alive tomorrow."

She grins triumphantly when he finally picks up his fork.

I turn away, giving them privacy, only to find Theron watching me with an intensity that has my cheeks burning up. He's already filled his plate, but he hasn't touched the food.

"What?" I demand, reaching for a small loaf of bread still steaming from the ovens, along with the butter.

His eyes follow my movements with that predatory focus I'm starting to recognize.

"Just wondering if you've accepted your fate yet... being stuck with me."

I narrow my eyes. "You mean being forced into this nightmare because you broke every rule selecting an Omega from the enemy pack? No, I haven't *accepted* anything."

His smile is sharp, dangerous. "Though you can't deny we work well together. Or have you forgotten how I lifted you up that heart tree to collect the token? The way you *climbed me* to reach those higher branches." He's grinning like a fool.

I laugh at him as I spread butter on my bread, watching it melt into the warm crust. "I told you yesterday and the day before—selecting me was a mistake."

"We'll see about that." He leans closer.

My body buzzes all over at his whispered words.

Before I can respond, Kieran slams his goblet down on the table, sitting next to Theron, drawing everyone's attention. Dark hair wild around his strong face, a faint shade of growth on his jawline, his smirk bright in the candlelight.

"To all of us making it through today's trust mission!" he announces, raising his goblet high. "Though some of us"—he winks at Theron and me—"did it with a bit more style by coming in first. May tomorrow's trials be just as successful!"

Cheers erupt from half of the wolves, though a few others can't help but smile at Kieran's infectious enthusiasm. He has that effect on people—making you like him even when you know you shouldn't.

Rachel, his Omega partner, yanks him back into his seat by the hem of his jacket. "Do you ever shut up?" she asks with a teasing smile.

"Never," he replies with a wink. "It's part of my charm."

"Sure it is," Theron mutters, but his lips twitch with his own grin.

Kieran leans across Theron, his eyes finding mine. "How's our little priestess holding up? Not too over-whelmed by my friend's sunny disposition, I hope?"

"I've survived worse," I reply dryly.

"Have you now?" He waggles his eyebrows suggestively. "Care to share details? For research purposes, of course."

Theron elbows him. "Mind your own business, Stormfang."

"When has that ever been fun?" Kieran laughs,

rubbing his side. "Besides, someone has to make conversation. You two look like you're plotting murders instead of enjoying a feast."

"Who says we can't do both?" I reach for my goblet, and both men laugh. Aria, next to me, watches, smirking. There's something comforting about having her here with me, as though I'm not alone in this chaotic mess.

Across the table, Selene's ice-blue gaze narrows to slits. She's an Umbra wolf and hasn't touched her food, her pale fingers circling the rim of her goblet as she watches us... watches me.

"Something amusing?" she asks, her voice dripping with false sweetness. "Or have you simply forgotten which side you're on?"

The table falls quiet, all attention shifting between us.

"I know exactly which side I'm on," I say, meeting her gaze steadily. "My own."

"How convenient." She tosses her deep brown hair over one shoulder, the movement deliberately sensual.

"At least she faces her opponents directly," Theron interjects, his voice deceptively soft. "Instead of hiding behind others and pecking at weaknesses from safety. Like an unintelligent coward."

Selene's face flushes an ugly red. "What the fuck is that supposed to mean?"

"If you don't understand, you're proving his point," Kieran butts in.

She turns to Erebus, her hulking partner with shoulders like small mountains and a perpetual scowl. "Are you going to let them talk to me like that?"

Before Erebus can respond, Kieran lets out a dramatic sigh. "Calm your damn heels, everyone. We're trying to eat here!" He pats his stomach. "Some of us have important digestive business to attend to."

"Is that what you call stuffing your face?" Rachel asks.

"I call it preparing for survival." He grins, tearing into a turkey leg with exaggerated enthusiasm. "Can't fight on an empty stomach!"

"Or a full one, either," she points out.

"Watch me."

Servers start coming into the room, bringing more platters—steaming vegetables sprinkled with herbs, sweet pastries drizzled with honey, and pitchers of fruit juice and water. I notice there's no alcohol, which makes sense. The Covenant wants us sharp for tomorrow.

"Is your friend always this... much?" I ask Theron quietly, nodding toward Kieran, who's now performing an elaborate tale for those around him, complete with sound effects.

Theron's lips twitch. "Always." He laughs out loud.

"And yet you keep him around."

"He grows on you." He takes a sip from his goblet, eyes never leaving mine over the rim. "Like a fungus you can't quite get rid of."

"I heard that!" Kieran calls out. "And I prefer to think of myself as a rare and valuable truffle."

"Rare, definitely," Theron replies, chuckling.

As the men continue their banter, I fill my plate with roasted venison and herb-crusted potatoes, my stomach growling despite the tension, and then eat.

Aria leans in close beside me. "See the ice queen across the table?" Her voice drops to a whisper as she tilts her head subtly toward Selene.

I follow her gaze, noting how Selene's attention remains fixed on Theron, nibbling on her food as she studies him laughing with Kieran. "What about her?"

"Found out something interesting today." Aria spears a glazed carrot, pretending to be casual. "That's who Theron was supposed to select as his partner for the Harvest Ritual. Everyone expected it... including her."

I nearly choke on my food. "All right, that explains the animosity."

"Mm-hmm. Her father and Theron's had some kind of arrangement." She takes a sip from her goblet. "Until Theron went rogue and chose you instead."

"She might be responsible for my attack, then," I whisper in her ear.

"Jealousy's an ugly thing." Aria shrugs, but her expression is serious. "Watch your back with that one. Wounded pride makes people dangerous."

That's when Selene leans forward, practically draping herself across the table.

"I was surprised to see you paired with the priestess, Theron. Especially after what happened between us in the western forest last moon."

My hand freezes halfway to my mouth, curious as much as everyone else at the table now listening.

Theron's jaw tightens, but Selene answers before he can.

"Oh, he didn't tell you?" Her voice drops to a stage whisper. "We were hunting, just the two of us. One thing led to another, and…" She trails off with a suggestive smile. "Let's just say his mouth is good for more than just giving orders."

Heat floods my face, but it's not from embarrassment. It's from fury. I don't have any claim on Theron, yet the thought of him with Selene makes me want to leap across the table and claw her eyes out.

"Is your memory really that bad, or do you just enjoy rewriting history?" Theron asks mildly. "What actually happened was you tripped over your own feet and took us both down a ravine. The only thing my mouth did that day was curse when I hit every rock on the way down."

Kieran bursts out laughing. "That was the time you came back looking like you'd wrestled with a pig in the mud!" He slaps the table. "And you"—he points at Selene—"you claimed a twisted ankle and had three warriors carry you back to camp on a stretcher!"

Even some of the Elios join in the laughter, and Selene's face contorts with rage.

"Laugh all you want," she hisses. "We'll see who's laughing when the trials are over."

"Probably still Kieran," I say, and more laughter erupts.

She huffs, folding her arms over her chest.

Erebus fills his plate with more food, glancing over at her. "You started it, so I can't help you out. Maybe just enjoy the meal," he says simply before returning to his plate.

Selene's mouth drops open in shock, and even I'm surprised. The massive Umbra warrior has barely spoken two words all evening.

"Trouble in paradise?" Kieran stage-whispers, earning a death glare from Selene.

I glance around the table, taking stock of everyone. Most of the Elios are clustered together, speaking in hushed tones while shooting suspicious glances at their Umbra opponents. Some seem to be getting along, heads bent close in conversation, while others look like they're planning how to murder each other in their sleep.

"They're all staring at us," I murmur to Theron.

He follows my gaze around the table. "Let them wonder."

"You don't care what they think?"

"Do you?"

The question catches me off guard. Do I care? The Elios have never fully accepted me anyway—too scholarly, the Alpha's daughter—and the Umbra see me as an outsider, a potential threat. Maybe that's why being paired with Theron doesn't feel as wrong as it should.

"I care about surviving," I finally admit.

His hand finds my knee under the table, and I nearly

jump out of my skin at the contact. "Then we're on the same page."

I should push his hand away. Instead, I find myself hyperaware of the heat of his palm through the thin fabric of my pants and the slight pressure of his fingers.

"Your friend is mooning over Orion again," Theron says, nodding toward Aria, who keeps stealing glances at Orion.

"She could do worse."

"She could do better."

I raise an eyebrow. "Such as?"

His gaze flicks toward Kieran, who's engaged in animated conversation with his selected Omega, Rachel, and another male from the Umbra pack. "Just an observation."

I'm not sure what to make of his suggestion. Did Kieran mention being interested in my friend?

Aria turns to me, her cheeks flushed. "Is it hot in here, or is it just me?"

"Definitely you," I tease. "Especially when you keep staring at Orion like he's the last piece of chocolate cake."

She groans, dropping her head into her hands. "Am I that obvious?"

"Only to everyone with eyes."

"Great. Do you think he's noticed?" she whispers.

I glance at Orion, who's engaged in what appears to be a serious conversation with Cassius. "I think he's too busy plotting battle strategies to notice much of anything."

"Maybe I should throw myself at him. Make it impossible to ignore."

"Or maybe you should focus on surviving the trials first, then worry about your love life."

She sighs dramatically. "You're no fun. What's the point of possibly facing danger tomorrow if I can't at least try to kiss the man of my dreams tonight?"

"The point is staying alive," I say dryly.

"Oh, please." She reaches for her goblet. "Even you're not immune to a little pre-battle romance. I've seen how you look at Theron when you think no one's watching."

Heat creeps up my neck. "I have no idea what you're talking about. I hate the guy."

"Sure you do." She takes a long drink, then makes a face. "This juice tastes strange. Almost... spicy?"

I take a sip from my own goblet, only tasting the slight bitterness beneath the sweetness of berries. "Tastes the same to me."

Aria shrugs and returns to her food.

Voices grow louder, laughter more raucous as everyone enjoys the feast and seems to be getting along more. At the far end of the table, Maddox from the Umbra pack suddenly stands, swaying slightly before staggering toward the door, hand pressed to his mouth. Others are arguing loudly.

Theron's hand slides higher on my thigh, and I nearly knock over my goblet in surprise.

"What are you doing?" I hiss, trying to push his hand away.

He catches my fingers, intertwining them with his own beneath the table. "What I've wanted to do since they shackled us together."

Something in his voice makes me look up, and I'm startled by what I see. The carefully controlled mask he always wears has slipped, revealing an intensity that steals my breath. His pupils are dilated, nearly swallowing the gray of his irises.

"You're acting weird," I tell him.

"I'm acting honest." His thumb traces circles on my palm, sending shivers up my arm. "There's a difference."

"Honesty doesn't usually involve groping under the table."

A slow smile spreads across his face, transforming his features. Without the perpetual scowl, he's devastatingly handsome.

"You have no idea what honesty between us would look like, Lyra."

The way he says my name—like he's tasting it—makes my stomach flip.

"Why don't you enlighten me?"

It's a challenge, one I immediately regret when he leans in, his lips brushing the shell of my ear.

"Honesty would be me telling you that I dream about tasting every inch of your skin," he murmurs, his voice so low that only I can hear. "That I want to bend you over this table, tear those pants down your legs, and fuck you until you forget there was ever a time you hated me."

I jerk back, my face on fire, my pulse hammering in my throat. "Theron!"

His eyes are dark, predatory. "Honesty would be admitting that I've wanted you since the first time I saw you in the woods."

"Stop it," I whisper, but there's no conviction in my voice. My body is betraying me, responding to his words with a rush of heat and want.

"I can just imagine how wet you are right now for me," he whispers in my ear, and my thighs clench involuntarily. "How much you want me to make good on every filthy promise."

"You're insane." But am I any better? All I can think about is climbing into his lap right here, with everyone watching.

"I'm not the one with my pulse racing and my scent screaming that I want to be fucked."

Gods, what is wrong with me? This is Theron Shadowmane—the enemy. Yet I can't deny that the pull between us grows stronger now more than ever before.

"I need a minute," I mutter, pushing away from the table. I need distance, need to clear my head.

Theron's gaze follows me as I retreat, dark with promise. "Don't go too far, priestess. The manacle won't allow it."

In the corridor outside, I lean against the cool stone wall, trying to calm my racing heart. What's happening to me? To Theron?

Movement down the hallway catches my attention. In

an alcove partially hidden by heavy curtains, two figures are locked in a passionate embrace. I'm about to look away when I recognize Orion's distinctive strawberry-blond hair. He has Nadia from our pack pressed against the wall, his mouth devouring hers as her legs wrap around his waist.

My stomach drops. Poor Aria. The crush she's been nursing is clearly not going to end well.

I duck into the bathroom, splashing cold water on my face and staring at my reflection. My eyes look strange—too bright, pupils too wide. I need to calm down and not lose my head.

When I return to the hall, the chaos has escalated. Someone has overturned a platter of food, and Nero is dancing on the table, howling at the ceiling while others cheer him on. Two wolves in partial shift chase each other around the far end of the hall, knocking over a side table with a tremendous crash.

I spot Aria at the far end of the room near the curtains, deep in conversation with Kieran. Their heads are bent close together, and his hand rests lightly on her waist in a gesture that's definitely not casual.

I weave through the madness, approaching them. "Hey there." I try for casual but sound strained.

Aria jumps slightly, but her smile is unrepentant. "You think only you can have fun with the enemy?" She wiggles her eyebrows, and I notice her pupils are as dilated as mine were when I checked in the bathroom mirror.

"You know I have no issues with that," I say, glancing between them. "But be careful. Something weird is going on."

"Weird how?" Kieran asks, his hand still on Aria's waist, tugging her closer to him in a protective manner.

I gesture around at the deteriorating scene. "Look at everyone. It's like they've lost their minds."

"Or found them," he suggests with a lazy grin. "Maybe we're all finally being honest about what we want."

"Since when is honesty such a disaster?" I ask, watching as Tavian and Zephyr's argument devolves into a fistfight, silver goblets and plates crashing to the floor around them.

"Honesty has always been dangerous," Aria says, surprisingly serious despite her flushed cheeks. "It's why we hide behind pack loyalties and ancient feuds instead of admitting what we really feel."

Kieran's eyes linger on her face. "And what do you really feel, my Aria warrior?"

Something in his tone makes me feel like an intruder. "I should get back," I state, though neither seems to notice as I slip away.

I turn toward our table and freeze. Selene has taken my vacant seat, her body pressed against Theron's side, one hand on his chest as she whispers in his ear. Something primal and possessive roars to life inside me, drowning out all rational thought.

I'm already striding across the room, fingers tracing

the hilt of my blade. The only coherent thought in my head is... *Mine. He is mine.*

Just as I reach the table, a deafening horn blast cuts through the chaos. Many freeze, though others continue their revelry, too far gone to care. At the entrance, two figures in midnight-black robes stand silhouetted against the doorway.

Tarek and Melian.

"Return to your seats!" Tarek commands, his voice echoing with power. When only half the room complies, he slams his staff against the stone floor. The sound resonates like thunder, and a pulse of energy sweeps through the hall, forcing even the most wild-eyed among us to momentarily still.

I shove Selene out of my seat, reclaiming my place beside Theron.

"Touch him again, and you'll lose that hand," I whisper as she retreats, too quiet for anyone else to hear.

Her eyes widen in surprise. "My, my. The priestess isn't a kitten after all."

Theron watches the exchange, his hand on my thigh again, possessive and warm.

"I like seeing you jealous."

"Sit down, all of you!" Tarek's voice booms again. Most comply, though Nero must be physically hauled from the tabletop by Erebus, and Zephyr continues cursing at Tavian from across the room.

Tarek paces before us. The lines of his face seem

carved from stone. Melian stands eerily still beside him, her ageless face revealing nothing.

"Tonight was your final truth test," Tarek announces, his voice cutting through the strained silence. "And you have all failed spectacularly."

"I knew this was a test!" Orion bellows a bit too loudly. He's returned to the table, though his hair is mussed and his lips swollen.

"The feast was laced with veritroot," Melian explains. "A substance that strips away pretense and reveals one's true desires and nature."

Veritroot. The name crashes through my foggy mind. A rare herb that grows only in the deepest caves of the mountain. Priest-healers use it in sacred ceremonies to induce visions and union with the divine. But in larger doses...

"You drugged us?" Aria's voice rises in outrage. "Without our consent?"

"You consented when you accepted your place in the Harvest Ritual," Tarek replies coldly.

"This is bullshit!" someone calls out. "You can't just—"

"We can, and we did," Melian interrupts. "Your actions tonight reveal how you truly feel toward your partners and your competitors. Consider carefully what your behavior says about you."

My cheeks burn as I recall Theron's whispered words, my own possessive rage. Even now, I feel it deep in my veins, pulsing, escalating.

"Some of you gravitated toward your assigned partners, strengthening bonds that will serve you well in the trials to come," Tarek continues. "Others showed fractures that will need to be addressed. And still others"—his gaze lands on Orion—"demonstrated a complete lack of commitment to your team."

Orion looks away, jaw tight.

Tarek steps forward, his gaze sweeping over the wolves. "You've feasted. You've been tested. And now, the Harvest Ritual trials will commence."

Everyone starts talking at once, groaning, and protesting.

I freeze. Beside me, Theron's hand tightens on my thigh. When I glance at him, his brow furrows.

"Tonight?" Zephyr shouts, still bleeding from his fight with Tavian. "You can't be serious!"

"Not in this state," Nero protests. "You've drugged us!"

Aria grabs my wrist. "This isn't happening," she whispers. "We're not ready."

"Exactly in this state," Tarek iterates. "While your inhibitions are lowered, sort out the differences with your partner fast because you will need each other. Otherwise, consider yourself already failed."

Theron leans close. "Stay calm. We can do this." The steadiness in his voice surprises me.

"This is crazy," Nero mutters, loud enough for me to hear.

"Preparedness is a luxury you will rarely have in battle

or leadership," Tarek replies. "The strongest wolves adapt."

"Pair up with your Omegas," Melian instructs. "You will travel as a team to the Darkbone Peaks."

Murmurs ripple through the room. The Darkbone Peaks. Jagged mountains beyond both territories said to be haunted by the spirits of wolves who died in the ancient wars. Parts of the forests are also occupied by territorial trolls. Few who venture there return.

Aria's face drains of color. "Shit!" she whispers, hand squeezing mine so tightly it hurts. "All those horrid stories we've heard about the place."

I swallow hard, fear crystallizing in my gut. Theron's gaze meets mine. We're in this together now, whether I like it or not.

"Getting to the Darkbone Peaks is a transition to your trial," Tarek explains. "You will face the elements, wild beasts... and perhaps even each other."

His gaze sweeps across the room meaningfully.

"Some of you already contemplate how you might eliminate your competition," Melian explains. "That is your right. The Harvest Ritual has always been as much about survival as leadership. But remember, your actions here will echo through your reign—should you survive to claim it."

"But know this," Tarek adds. "Once you reach the Bloodmoon Field at the heart of the Darkbone Peaks, the main Harvest commences. Then, the first pair to complete it will rule the Onyx Covenant for the next decade."

I shift uncomfortably, my thoughts spiraling into dangerous territory. If Theron and I win, his pack will claim victory, but with my presence on his team, the influence of the Elios wolves won't be ignored. But it will still be weak, as I doubt Theron's father will not be involved. He wants me nowhere near the Onyx Covenant if the Umbra wolves win again.

My throat tightens as the weight of it all presses down on me. How am I even thinking about winning when I'm the weakest link on his team? I'm not a warrior like the others, and staying alive feels like a victory in itself. Yet... I can't ignore what's right in front of me. I have a dangerous, impossible chance to shift the outcome. If I hold back, if I let Theron stumble, Aria and Orion could take the lead. They could secure the win and ensure that the Elios pack controls the Onyx Covenant's positions.

I swallow hard, my heart pounding as the weight of that decision coils tighter around me.

"One final warning," Melian's voice drops. "Your partner is the only one you can truly trust. They will have your back when no one else will. Remember this when the shadows grow long and the path seems uncertain."

With those ominous words, they turn to leave, but Cassius stands.

"Wait! Just like that? No equipment, no weapons?"

Tarek pauses in the doorway. "You have the clothes on your back, the wolf in your blood, and whatever weapons you managed to conceal." His smile is knowing.

He's not wrong. My dagger is strapped to my waist

beneath my tunic, and I'd bet my life every person in this room is similarly armed.

"May the moons guide your path. Meet us outside to commence," Melian intones. Then they're gone, leaving us in stunned silence that lasts approximately three heartbeats before the room erupts into chaos.

"This is a death sentence!" someone shouts.

"It's a test of our resourcefulness," another argues.

"It's fucking lunacy," someone else declares, but he's already moving to gather what little he can from the table —a knife, a cloth napkin, anything useful.

Beside me, Theron is completely still. Then he turns to me, more focused.

"We need to move outside and start," he says. "Now, while everyone's still arguing."

"What's the rush?"

"First to leave, first to arrive." He stands, and I quickly follow him. "Besides, do you really want to be here when the alliances start forming? When they remember how much they hate each other—and us?"

He has a point.

I turn to Aria beside me, leaning in to whisper, "We're leaving now. You coming?"

Aria nods without hesitation and nudges Orion. Theron does the same with Kieran.

The six of us edge toward the side exit fast, trying not to draw attention. I catch movement from the corner of my eye—Selene watching us. Her ice-blue eyes narrow dangerously as she tugs on Erebus's arm, whispering urgently.

"Move faster," I mutter, nudging Theron. I take one last look at the chaos behind us. Half the room is still arguing, while others frantically gather supplies.

Theron's hand finds the small of my back, warm and reassuring against the sudden chill that sweeps through me.

The Harvest Ritual has begun.

Fear and excitement war in my belly. I don't know if I'm being stupid for trusting Theron, don't know if we'll survive what's coming...

But as we plunge outside together, one thought burns brighter than the rest—whatever happens in the Dark-bone Peaks, I'm no longer just the priestess in training, watching from the sidelines. For the first time in my life, I've stepped into the heart of the conflict, and there's no turning back.

For better or worse, I've chosen my path. And may the twin moons watch over us through the darkness that lies ahead.

NINE

THERON

Fire burns under my skin, my blood running hot with need. Every breath brings Lyra's scent, making my wolf scratch and claw inside me. Fuck, I need to focus, but all I can think about is bending Lyra over and fucking her.

I bite down hard on the inside of my cheek, tasting blood. Better. The pain cuts through the fog, if only for a second.

The Onyx Covenant's grand dinner was a joke—poisoning us to show our true natures, how we really felt about our partners. As if we didn't already know that. Animals dressed in human skin, pretending at civilization.

Now, the six of us stand at the edge of the Whispering Woods, waiting for Tarek and Melian to stop their ceremonial bullshit and send us on our way. Tall torches flank the ancient path that disappears into darkness, their flames casting dancing shadows across our faces.

"Stop fidgeting," I tell Kieran, who's been shifting his weight from foot to foot for the past five minutes, Rachel by his side. Her dark hair is pulled back in a tight braid, her black Umbra uniform making her nearly invisible in the night.

"I'm ready to get going before the rest of the mob follows." He smirks. "Hate to kill fellow pack members when they inevitably piss me off."

Lyra makes a choking, laughing sound.

"I mean the Elios twins, Cassius and Nyx," Kieran clarifies. "Heard they've been practicing synchronized throat-slitting."

"Their technique is sloppy at best," Orion scoffs, his rigid posture making his dark blue Elios uniform look even more formal. "I wouldn't waste your energy worrying about them."

"You've been watching them train?" Aria asks, her loose hair blowing in the night breeze. Unlike Lyra, whose blonde locks practically glow in the moonlight, Aria blends into shadows almost as well as my Umbra pack does.

"Know your enemy, even those in your own pack," Orion says simply.

Lyra steps closer to me, and the heat from her body pulses over to me. "They're not our immediate enemies," she says. "Our priority is completing our objective in one piece."

I glance down at her, taking in her seriousness and how adorable she looks. Dressed for battle, she's fucking hot and fierce. The monster in me wants to grab her by that hair and—

"They're ready for us," Aria murmurs, nodding toward the path where Tarek and Melian have finally taken their positions.

"About fucking time," I growl, stalking forward with the other five following close behind.

Tarek stands tall. Beside him, Melian's obsidian robes absorb the light, making her seem like a hole cut from reality itself.

"The initial champions have arrived," Tarek announces, his voice carrying across the clearing.

Melian steps forward, her features expressionless. "You stand at the threshold of your destiny. The Harvest Ritual begins now."

Tarek gestures toward the bundle of backpacks on the ground behind them. "Basic supplies. Blanket, firerod, rope."

"Back in the hall, you said there would be no advantages given," Rachel points out, her tone challenging.

"We said we wouldn't arm you with weapons," Melian corrects coldly. "Now stop wasting time and get going."

I snatch up a pack, feeling its weight. Light. Too light for comfort, but better than nothing. "Which way to the Darkbone Peaks?"

"The path will guide you," Tarek says cryptically. "Stay on it, and you will reach your destination."

Kieran mutters under his breath, "Nothing in these woods is that simple."

"The Darkbone Peaks are just visible on the horizon," Orion says, squinting into the dark distance. "The valley between them is our goal."

"Not exactly," Tarek mutters, his gaze narrowing as he points toward them. "That's no ordinary valley. It's higher up, wedged between the mountains like a scar carved into the stone. The path is steep. Getting there won't be easy. Surviving it... even harder."

"May the moons guide your journey," Melian states, stepping aside to clear our path. "Their light shines brightest on those worthy of their gifts."

"Let's move," I snap, stepping onto the path first, my wolf already alert to the dangers lurking beyond the torchlight.

The others fall into step behind me, the crunch of boots on dirt and the occasional rustle of clothing the only sounds. The forest looms ahead, ancient trees reaching skyward like clawed hands grasping for the moons.

"Any particular plan besides walking until something tries to kill us?" Kieran asks, coming up alongside me.

"Stay together, move fast, reach the valley before the others," I reply. "Simple."

The path narrows as we enter the true forest. I take point, keeping a steady pace that the others can maintain.

The canopy closes overhead, blocking out most of the moonlight and plunging us into almost complete darkness. For normal humans, it would be impenetrable black, but our wolf eyes adjust quickly.

Lyra's footsteps are nearly silent behind me, where I want her. An hour passes. The forest whispers around us, alive with sounds—rustling leaves, snapping twigs, the distant calls of animals and birds.

"This is taking too fucking long," Kieran finally says, his voice low. "At this rate, we'll still be walking when the next ritual comes around."

"We need to move faster," Rachel agrees.

I come to a stop, the others halting behind me. "We switch to four legs."

"What about our supplies?" Orion asks, already shrugging off his pack.

Lyra steps forward, her movements confident as she sets her pack down. "We wear them before we shift. Our wolf forms will adapt around them."

"Best way to travel," Aria adds.

"Great plan. Let's do it." I start unbuttoning my jacket, watching as the others do the same. There's no awkwardness—we're shifters, and nudity is part of our lives—but I still find myself drawn to Lyra as she slips off her blue uniform.

She catches me looking and doesn't glance away. Instead, there's a challenge in her eyes, a heat that mirrors my own. The serum might be making things worse, but this attraction has always been there, buried under politics and pack rivalries.

I turn and strip off my shirt, revealing the ancient runes tattooed down my spine. When I glance back, Lyra's eyes are tracing the marks.

"Like what you see?" I ask, my voice low enough that only she can hear.

"I've seen better," she replies, but the flush on her cheeks tells a different story.

"Highly doubt it." I grin, taking my time with my belt, making sure she gets a good look. Her eyes narrow, but she doesn't look away as I strip completely.

Around us, the others are doing the same. Kieran and Rachel are already naked, stuffing their clothes into their packs. Orion keeps his back turned as he undresses. Aria is quick and businesslike, her movements economical.

Lyra is the first to finish, her clothes neatly packed away, the dark and the shadows concealing everything I want to see. She slips the straps of her backpack over her shoulders, securing it firmly.

"Ready?" she asks me, her blonde hair spilling down her bare back.

"Always," I reply, shouldering my own pack.

She closes her eyes, and the change takes her. It's fucking beautiful to watch—blonde hair becoming fur as her body flows seamlessly from woman to wolf. When it's complete, she stands before me as a sleek silver wolf with subtle blue undertones, her pack still on her back as she predicted.

"Clever trick," I tell the others, nodding toward Lyra.

"Looks like the Elios wolves are smarter than us after all," Kieran states with a laugh, already securing his bag. Rachel follows suit, while Orion and Aria have already figured it out, their packs in place and bodies in wolf form, both light-colored gray wolves.

I finish securing my own, then call to my wolf. The change rips through me—bones snapping and re-forming, muscles tearing and rebuilding, skin giving way to fur. There's pain, but it's clean, familiar, almost welcome after the insidious burn of the serum.

When it's done, I stand as a black wolf with silver streaking my flanks. I shake out my fur, feeling the weight of the pack settle between my shoulders.

Lyra's scent hits me stronger now, and my wolf's sense of smell picks up nuances my human nose missed —the subtle musk of her own arousal that she's been trying to hide. The poison isn't just affecting me. Good to know.

I meet each wolf's eyes, establishing the hierarchy through gaze alone. Then I turn and lead the way along the path, our six-wolf pack moving through the midnight forest.

We cover ground rapidly now, our pace a steady trot that eats up miles without exhausting us. The forest opens to us.

Lyra keeps pace at my right flank, her fur flowing like moonlight. Kieran takes my left, his russet fur nearly black in the darkness. Rachel stays in the middle, while

Orion and Aria bring up the rear, watching for threats from behind.

Must be a couple of hours that pass this way, the exertion burning away some of the poison's effects. My head clears, though my awareness of Lyra's presence never diminishes. Her scent, her movements, the occasional brush of her fur against mine when the path narrows—all of it feeds the hunger inside me.

When we reach a gurgling creek cutting across our path, I slow to a stop. The water is clear and cold, rushing down from the peaks ahead. I lower my head to drink, the cool water soothing my parched throat.

The others spread out along the bank, drinking deeply after our long run. Lyra laps at the water near me. Kieran and Rachel drink side by side, their shoulders touching casually. Orion keeps watch while Aria drinks.

An owl calls from a high branch while some small critters rustle in the underbrush, the wind sighing through ancient trees.

I've just lifted my head from the creek when I hear it —a howl rising from somewhere to our east. Not one of the entrants. The pitch is wrong, the cadence different. This is a wild wolf, one of the vicious packs that call the deepest woods home.

Another howl answers, then another. My ears swivel, tracking the sounds. Lyra tenses beside me, her body pressed against my side. Kieran moves closer, head low, hackles rising.

These aren't ordinary wolves. The ones that survive in

the Whispering Woods are larger and fiercer than their cousins elsewhere. Some say they're touched by old magic. Whatever the truth, they're dangerous—and territorial.

I let out a low growl, bringing my pack together.

More howls join the chorus—at least ten distinct voices, maybe more. Too many to fight, especially when we're carrying no weapons but teeth and claws.

I can almost count the seconds before I catch the first flicker of movement between the trees, a shadow detaching from shadow, low to the ground, moving with predatory purpose. Then another. And another.

We're being hunted.

I snarl and leap across the creek, the others following without hesitation. The water might dilute our scent trail, but it won't buy us much time. We need distance, and we need it now.

We run—not the measured trot of before, but a full sprint, each of us pushing to our limits. I lead them through the trees, trying to find the path again while avoiding the worst of the underbrush. Lyra stays close to my side. Kieran occasionally drops back to snap at shadows that venture too close, his teeth flashing in the darkness.

Through breaks in the canopy, I catch sight of the Darkbone Peaks looming closer under the moonlight, twin spires of rock reaching for the night sky. But the howls behind us are gaining, coming from both sides now as well as behind.

They're herding us.

A fallen log appears in our path. I clear it in a single bound, hearing the others jump after me. But a sharp yelp tells me someone has fallen. I skid to a stop, turning to find Aria struggling to her feet, blood darkening the fur of her left hind leg. Lyra is at her side in seconds.

Orion stands over her protectively, his teeth bared at the darkness. Rachel circles back to help, too, while Kieran takes up position beside me, facing the approaching threats.

A gray wolf slides from the shadows, lips peeled back to reveal yellowed fangs. He's big, almost as large as Orion, with battle scars crisscrossing his muzzle. The pack Alpha, no doubt. Behind him, more pairs of eyes gleam in the darkness—fifteen, twenty, more.

I could take him one-on-one. Shifters are stronger than their wild cousins, and I've been trained to kill since childhood. But this isn't one wolf. It's an entire pack, and they are closing in.

I grunt, jerking my head to the right, away from the main concentration of wild wolves. Orion understands immediately, taking the lead position while I drop back with Kieran to guard our flanks and rear. Rachel helps Aria up, and we're on the move again.

Protect the pack. *Protect Lyra.* The thoughts pulse frantically with each heartbeat as we sprint through unfamiliar territory, the howls at our heels driving us forward without time to choose our path.

The trees thin, and the ground beneath our paws

changes from soft earth to hard stone. For a moment, the howls seem to fade, and I think we might have outrun them.

Then Orion slides to a sudden halt ahead of us, the rest of us nearly crashing into him. We've run straight to the edge of a cliff, a sheer drop with the river churning far below. The roar of a waterfall fills the air, and I can barely make out the white water waiting to claim us.

The wild pack's howls sound near once more. Orion stares at me, then at the water below. A choice passes between us without words. He turns to Aria and Rachel, who presses her muzzle briefly against his in understanding.

Then he leaps, his powerful form arcing out over the abyss before disappearing into the darkness below. Rachel follows without hesitation, her gray form vanishing into the mist. I hear the splash of their bodies hitting water, but in the chaos, there's no telling if they've survived the fall.

A snarl from behind jerks my attention back to the immediate danger. Three wild wolves have broken through the tree line, the gray Alpha the largest in the lead. I don't wait for them to attack. I charge, using my larger size and shifter strength to slam into him.

My teeth find his throat, ripping through fur and flesh until I taste blood. He thrashes wildly, claws scoring my sides, but I hold firm. Kieran is beside me in an instant, taking down a second wolf that tries to flank me. His fighting style is all controlled fury—quick, vicious, and efficient.

I throw the Alpha aside, his body limp and broken. But more are coming. Many more, their eyes reflecting moonlight as they close in.

"Go!" I try to shout, but it comes out as a commanding bark. I lock eyes with Aria, then jerk my head toward the cliff edge. She understands, limping quickly to the edge before gathering herself and leaping into the void.

Kieran snarls beside me, refusing to leave. Loyal to the end, the stubborn fool. I growl at him, baring my teeth until he backs away. Then he turns and makes his own jump, his russet form briefly silhouetted against the mist before he's gone.

I turn to find Lyra still standing there, her silver form trembling but her stance defiant. Why the fuck hasn't she jumped? The wild wolves are regrouping, at least a dozen of them edging closer, emboldened now that only two shifters remain.

I rush to her side, nudging her roughly toward the cliff edge. She resists, her lavender eyes wide with fear. Not of the wolves, I realize, but of the fall. The wild wolves charge, and there's no more time for coaxing.

I grab her by the scruff of her neck, my teeth gentle but firm in her silver fur. She struggles for a second, then goes still, trusting me. I'm already moving, carrying her with me as I make a powerful leap from the cliff edge.

For a moment, we're suspended in air, the twin

moons our only witnesses as we fall together into darkness. I loosen my grip, not wanting to injure her when we hit the water.

The impact is brutal, the cold shocking even through thick fur. The waterfall breaks the water, making the fall not as deadly as it could have been.

The current drags Lyra farther from me. I fight to the surface, lungs burning, head twisting to catch any glimpse of silver among the churning black water.

But with the current pulling me, I slam hard into a rock, pain exploding through my skull. The world spins, water filling my lungs as I struggle to stay conscious. The last thing I see before darkness claims me is a flash of silver fur in the moonlight, then nothing.

Lyra...

TEN

LYRA

Cold. So fucking cold it burns. The impact slams into me like a thousand blades, stealing my breath and shocking my system. The current tears me away from Theron instantly.

Something primal kicks in, and I surrender to the shift, letting my wolf form melt away. The transformation is swift, bones and muscles re-forming as my human body emerges. In water, I've always been stronger as a human—my mother made sure of that, forcing me to swim in icy rivers since before I could walk.

My head breaks the surface, and I gasp, lungs burning as they fill with precious air. The roar of the waterfall crashes behind me as the current drags me downstream. My bag clings to my back somehow, the weight pulling at my shoulders.

"Lyra!" Aria's voice carries over the rushing water. Thank the moon she's all right.

"Here!" I shout back, catching glimpses of bodies farther downstream—Kieran's dark, reddish hair, Orion's broad shoulders, Rachel struggling against the current.

The river is carrying them away, but I can't follow. Something's wrong. Something's missing.

"Theron?" I call out, spinning in the water, scanning the dark surface.

Nothing.

Then I see him—face down, unmoving, his human body bobbing lifelessly in the current a dozen yards away. His black hair spreads across the water like spilled ink, blood mixing with it in sickening swirls.

My veins turn to ice.

"No!" The word tears from my throat as panic floods my system.

I dive forward, arms cutting through the freezing water with desperate strength. The current fights me, trying to drag me along the same path as the others, but I battle harder. Every swimming lesson, every hour spent in frigid waters with my mother's stern voice pushing me to be stronger—it was all for this moment.

"Don't you dare," I gasp between strokes. "Don't you fucking dare."

Above us, shapes line the cliff edge—the shadow wolves watching, waiting to see if we'll survive the fall only to drown in the river. They most likely won't follow us down, not with the cliff so steep, but they'll wait. They're patient hunters.

I reach Theron and grab his shoulder, flipping him

onto his back. His face is deathly pale in the moonlight, blood smeared across his forehead. His chest doesn't move. He's not breathing.

"No, no, no." I loop my arm across his chest, kicking furiously to keep us both afloat. "Wake up, damn you!"

His head lolls against my shoulder, unresponsive. I spot a rocky bank about fifteen yards downstream and adjust my course, pushing against the current with everything I have. My muscles scream in protest, but I refuse to let go.

"You don't get to die on me," I hiss into his ear. "Not like this."

The shore seems impossibly far away, but I shove forward inch by excruciating inch. The river doesn't want to give him up, pulling at him like it has a personal vendetta. Maybe it does. The waters of Wolfhaven have always had their own will, their own hunger.

When my feet finally touch stone, relief surges through me so strongly that I almost collapse. But I can't. Not yet. I drag Theron's limp body onto the rocky shore, his dead weight nearly impossible to move.

"By the moons, you're heavy," I grunt, hooking my arms under his and heaving with the last of my strength. Then I drag his backpack off him so he's lying flat on the river's grassy bank. "All that brooding must weigh a ton."

Once he's fully out of the water, I collapse beside him, my lungs burning, my arms trembling with fatigue. But there's no time to rest. He's still not breathing.

I press my ear to his chest, searching for a heartbeat. There's nothing there.

"Don't you fucking leave me," I whisper, positioning my hands over his chest. "You hear me, Theron? You're not going to die."

I push down hard, again and again, the way I was taught in priestess training. Healing is supposed to be our domain, though most of our methods involve herbs and prayers, not this desperate physical struggle against death itself.

"Breathe," I command, pumping his chest rhythmically. Water trickles from the corner of his mouth, but he doesn't respond. "Breathe, damn you!"

In the distance, I can hear the others calling to each other, their voices growing fainter as the river carries them away. I should be worried about them, but all I can focus on is the man beneath my hands.

After everything—after he broke my heart, after seeing him with that Umbra bitch he was supposed to mate with, after a year of forcing myself not to think of him—here I am, fighting to keep him alive with a desperation that terrifies me.

"You don't get to choose me for this ritual and then leave me alone in it." My voice breaks as tears mix with the river water on my face. "You don't get to look at me like you did back there, like I'm yours, and then just... just..."

The tears come harder now, blurring my vision as I

continue compressions. I'm so focused I almost miss the slight tremble of his chest, the first tentative rise and fall of breath.

But nothing happens after that. His chest remains still, his face pale and lifeless.

"Gods," I sob, a new wave of panic washing over me. "Please, no."

Then I remember—the moondust. My mother pressed the small sachet into my hand before I left for the ritual, her eyes grave as she warned me to use it only in the direst need.

It can bring someone back from the threshold of death, she'd once said. *But it must be mixed with the blood of one who cares for them truly.*

I scramble for my backpack, yanking it open with shaking hands. Water streams from everything inside, but I find the small leather pouch tucked into the pocket of my pants where I'd put it when we changed clothes before dinner. Something I planned to carry with me, along with the blade. When I open it, my heart sinks. The white powder is soaked through, clumping at the bottom of the bag.

"Fuck, no," I whisper, digging my fingers in to scrape out what I can. There's powder there, wet and paste-like but present. It will have to do.

I find my small blade. With a quick motion, I slice my thumb, barely feeling the sting as blood wells up.

"Blood calls to blood," I murmur, the priestess's

words coming automatically as I squeeze my thumb over the moondust, watching as crimson drops mix with white. "Life calls to life."

I add a splash of river water from my soaked shirt, stirring the mixture with my bleeding thumb until it forms a thin paste. The moondust begins to glow faintly —a good sign. Even wet, its power remains.

Kneeling beside Theron again, I cradle his head with one hand, lifting the small pouch to his lips with the other.

"Drink this," I plead, tipping the mixture into his mouth. "Please, Theron. I don't know if it will work, but you have to try."

When the paste disappears between his lips, I work my fingers on his throat, encouraging him to swallow. Then I resume compressions, putting all my remaining strength into each push.

"Come back," I whisper. "Please."

For several agonizing heartbeats, nothing happens. The night seems to hold its breath around us, the river's angry cry the only sound besides my ragged breathing.

Then Theron convulses suddenly, his body jerking beneath my hands. He coughs violently, and I quickly roll him onto his side as water pours from his mouth. His eyes fly open, wide and disoriented, as he gasps desperately for air.

After a small moment, he quiets down.

"Thank the moons," I whisper. "Welcome back from the dead." Relief leaves me lightheaded.

He blinks rapidly, coughing up more water, struggling to focus on my face. "What...?"

"You died," I tell him, unable to keep the tremor from my voice. "Fuck, I would have been so pissed if you died."

A surprised laugh escapes him, followed by more coughing. He reaches up to touch the wound on his head, wincing when his fingers come away bloody.

"*You* would have been pissed?" he asks, voice raspy.

"Don't you dare ever die on me, understand?" I snap, the fear I felt still too raw, too close.

His gaze softens as he focuses on my face. "See? I knew you loved me."

I look away, unwilling to let him see how true his words might be. "You're delirious from nearly drowning."

Theron tries to sit up, grimacing with the effort. "Something feels gritty in my throat." He makes a smacking sound with his mouth, running his tongue over his teeth. "Tastes like... what the hell did you give me?"

"Moondust," I admit. "Mixed with my blood."

His eyes widen. "What the...?"

"Hey, it worked, didn't it?" I shoot back defensively.

"You gave me blood magic?" There's no disgust in his voice.

"It's not blood magic," I correct him. "It's an ancient healing remedy. Moondust is made from rare plants that grow only in the Valley of Mists, combined with powdered moonstone and... yes, fine, some animal bone dust. My mother gave it to me before the ritual."

His expression softens, and he reaches for my hand. "Where are the others?"

"The river took them downstream. I saw them briefly, but they were already far ahead when I got you out." I squeeze his hand, then release it, suddenly aware of our naked state. "We need to rest and patch up that head wound. You got hit hard."

Only then does Theron's gaze drift over my nakedness, a familiar heat igniting in them despite his weakened state.

"Even on your deathbed?" I state, arching an eyebrow.

"Well, deathbank, I suppose." His mouth quirks in that half smile that always made my heart skip. "Not the most dignified place to die and come back."

I roll my eyes but can't stop my own smile. "Can you stand? We need to find shelter."

With considerable effort, I help Theron to his feet. He sways dangerously, and I slip under his arm, taking his weight. We move slowly along the river's edge, searching for better shelter than the exposed bank.

The wolves are visible on the cliff above, their stares gleaming in the darkness as they pace restlessly. I want to get out of their sight as quickly as possible in case they are waiting to see where we settle before they attack.

"Shadow beasts," Theron mutters, following my gaze upward. "That's what my father calls them. Says they're not true wolves, that they're tainted by old magic from before the packs formed."

"The priestesses call them moonshades," I reply.

"They say they refused to choose between Umbra and Elios, so both moons cursed them to never shift, to remain forever in one form."

"Poetic," he says with a weak chuckle. "But right now, I'm just glad they can't climb down that cliff."

"Not for lack of wanting to," I observe as one particularly large beast snaps its jaws in frustration.

After I grab his backpack, we start a long walk of slow progress. I spot a dark opening in the rock face near a wall of stone close to the water's edge.

"There," I say, adjusting my grip on Theron. "That might be a cave."

We make our way toward it. The entrance is narrow but tall enough to enter without stooping. I pause at the entrance, sniffing carefully.

"No recent scents," I announce after a moment. "Nothing's been living here."

Theron nods, leaning heavily against the stone wall. "Good. We can rest and regroup. My head's spinning."

The cave opens into a small chamber, dry and protected from the wind. Moonlight filters in through the entrance, casting everything in silver and shadow. I guide Theron to a relatively flat spot inside the cave and ease him to sit against the stone floor.

"Let me check what we have left." I open my bag, searching its contents beneath my wet clothes. The firerod survived, protected in its waxed case. The thin emergency blanket is protected in a waterproof case as well. There's a small waterskin and some other survival items.

"We should count ourselves lucky," I say, holding up the firerod. "At least we can have warmth. And we have two blankets," I note. "Let me spread yours out on the ground. You need to lie down before you fall over."

"I can help," he insists, stumbling to his feet.

"You can barely stand," I counter, rushing to steady him as he sways.

Once I lay both blankets next to each other, easily offering a double-sized bed in seating, I help Theron get off his feet. He's heavier than he looks. By the time he's settled, I'm already thinking about what else needs to be done.

"We need water," I murmur, grabbing both waterskins and heading back outside. The cool night air brushes against my skin, carrying the distant scent of damp earth and pine.

The mountains loom closer than I expected, their twin peaks silhouetted against the night sky. The Darkbone Valley lies directly between them, our intended destination. From here, I can see why it has its name. The peaks look like massive dark bones jutting from the earth, sharp and unyielding. I frown, tilting my head as a chill creeps down my spine. Did we take a shortcut? The mountains feel too close.

Shaking the unease from my mind, I glance up at Elios's moon, her veiled face just visible through a thin layer of mist.

"Guide us safely through the darkness," I whisper, the prayer coming automatically. "Light our path with your hidden wisdom."

Then I make my way toward the stream, kneeling at the edge and dipping the waterskins into the cool, crystal-clear water. As I wait for the skins to fill, something catches my eye—a cluster of bright green leaves with deep purple buds just on the shore.

My brows lift in surprise. Sweetclover. Small delicate herbs that help with dizziness. Their sweetness lingers, making them a favorite for keeping breath fresh, too, and Theron said he tasted the powder I gave him to drink.

I pluck a handful, cradling them gently in my palm as I head back to the cave with the water.

When I return, he's sitting up, looking marginally more alert but still dangerously pale. He's completely naked, with his bag on the stone floor in front of him as he paws through it, his jaw tight with frustration.

"No food in the bags," he mutters. His head tilts back against the stone wall. "I'd kill for some jerky right now."

"I brought you something else," I say softly, stepping inside and holding out the handful of sweetclover leaves.

He lifts a brow, his expression flat and unimpressed.

"Grass?" he deadpans, lips curling slightly. "You brought me grass?"

I kneel beside him. "They're sweetclover," I correct, nudging his hand until he takes them. "They'll help with the dizziness... and take that dusty taste out of your mouth." A small smile tugs at the corner of my lips. "They're used to freshen breath, too, did you know?"

He stares at me for a moment, then lets out a low grunt. "Huh."

But he doesn't argue. Instead, he pops a few leaves into his mouth, chewing slowly. After a beat, his expression softens just a fraction as the sweetness kicks in.

"Not bad," he murmurs.

I hand him one of the full waterskins, watching as he takes a long, grateful drink. Some color returns to his cheeks, but the exhaustion on his face remains.

"I'll be right back," I say, standing and brushing the dirt from my hands. "I need to gather some sticks and dry leaves for the fire."

He doesn't respond, too focused on chewing through the rest of the sweetclover.

When I return, arms full of kindling, I stop short, eyeing the empty palm of his hand.

"You ate them all?" I ask, a touch of amusement in my voice.

Theron lifts a shoulder in a lazy shrug, his lips quirking at the corners. "What? You said they were good for me."

I laugh at him, arranging the kindling in a small circle of stones I'd gathered from around the cave, then use the firerod to strike sparks. It takes several attempts before the dried twigs catch, a tiny flame fluttering to life. I blow on it, nurturing it carefully, adding more wood gradually until we have a small but steady fire.

The cave fills with warm light, pushing back the shadows and taking the edge off the cold. I rummage through my backpack again, finding the sticky bandages and salve. Using a strip of fabric torn from my soaked shirt, I shuffle over to Theron's side.

"Hold still," I instruct, kneeling beside him. "This might sting."

"I think I can handle it after apparently dying," he says dryly.

I reach over and pat the wound carefully, wiping away blood to reveal a deep gash across his forehead. "You did die. Trust me, I was about to lose my mind."

He winces as I apply pressure. "I like that you worried about me."

I shrug and try to be gentler, acutely aware of his gaze on me as I work. Our naked state suddenly feels more significant with the firelight playing across our skin. I notice his gaze lowering down my body.

"So, you just died, and you're checking me out," I say, trying to lighten the mood and distract myself from the fire within me, sparking alight for him.

"Hard not to when you're in front of me nursing me while naked," he replies. "No man could resist this."

I apply the salve to his wound, leaning closer to make sure I cover it completely. His breath warms my skin, his gaze never leaving me.

"You're still staring," I murmur.

"You're beautiful," he answers simply.

I reach for a semi-wet bandage with edges that are

sticky for adhering, determined to finish my task without giving in to the fire burning between us.

"Hold this in place," I instruct, positioning the bandage over his wound.

As he raises his hand to hold the bandage, his fingers brush mine, and the contact sends jolts of desire through my body. Our gazes lock.

Without warning, Theron's hand moves to the back of my neck, drawing me toward him until our lips meet. The kiss is unexpected, urgent, a claiming rather than a request. And Goddess help me, I respond instantly, as if my body has been waiting for this since the day I walked away.

The familiar sensation of the poison from dinner rises through my blood again, a liquid fire that shouldn't still be there but undeniably is. Or maybe it's just Theron—the taste of him, the scent of him, the feel of his skin against mine—that's the real intoxicant.

His lips are soft despite the urgency behind them, his tongue tracing the seam of my mouth in a plea for entry. I grant it without hesitation, a small sound escaping my throat as the kiss deepens. I've dreamed about it more often than I care to admit.

"Lyra," he exhales the word against my mouth, his hand sliding into my damp hair. The tenderness in the gesture nearly undoes me.

I shouldn't want this. Shouldn't want him, not after everything—the heartbreak, the betrayal, the year of forcing myself to hate him—but my body remembers his.

My skin recalls the exact pressure of his fingers, the precise heat of his mouth. Muscle memory takes over as I press closer, my hands finding their way to his shoulders, feeling the coiled strength there.

Theron draws back just enough to look into my eyes, his pupils dilated with desire. "I need to feel you against me," he murmurs, his voice a rough caress. "Need your skin on mine."

"Not sure we should do this," I manage to say.

His lips find the sensitive spot just below my ear that he somehow still remembers. "Why?"

I open my mouth to list them all—our packs, our families, his father, who would kill me without hesitation—but his lips drag across my neck, and every rational thought disintegrates.

"Can't think of any, can you?" he murmurs, a smile in his voice as his hands slide down my sides.

I gasp as his mouth moves to my collarbone.

"You're irresistible." He draws me fully against him so I'm kneeling between his spread legs, our chests pressed close.

The contact is electrifying, overwhelming. I forget where we are, forget the danger that drove us here, forget everything but the feel of him beneath me. I trace my fingers up his powerful biceps to his shoulders, then skate them up his neck and into his wet hair.

His mouth finds mine again, more demanding this time, one of possession and hunger. His hands cup my face, holding me steady as he devours my mouth as if he could consume the very essence of me. And I let him, opening to him, matching his desire with my own.

I've missed him desperately. For all our differences, for all the reasons we shouldn't be together, there's always been this undeniable pull between us. Like gravity. Like fate.

"I've thought about this every day," Theron admits against my lips, his voice rough with emotion. "Every fucking day since I lost you."

The confession strikes deep. "I'm still struggling with that pain, still angry, still broken that you chose your pack over me," I admit, unable to keep the hurt from my words.

Something shatters in Theron's expression. He's usually so guarded, but now it reveals everything—the agony, the regret, the raw longing that's been eating him alive. His hands tremble slightly as they cup my face.

"I would apologize for every star in the sky, and all the ones we can't even see, if it would earn your forgiveness," he whispers. "Seeing you that night, watching you witness that charade with her, gutted me."

His warm breath flutters on my lips.

"I made the choice to protect you, not because I didn't want you. Never that. I knew what my father was capable of, knew I needed to stay in his good graces to ensure I got into the Harvest Ritual. To finally find a way to end his torment."

He pulls back just enough to stare at me, his thumbs brushing away tears trickling from my eyes.

"And it came at the devastating cost of losing you.

Something I've never forgiven myself for. I'm so sorry, Lyra."

"Fate had other plans," I whisper.

"Fate," he agrees, a bitter smile playing on his lips. "Or my stubborn refusal to live without you any longer." His hands slide into my hair, cradling my head. "I think it was fate that chose you for this ritual with me. To have you by my side, to be saved by you from death."

His attention drops to my lips.

"To finally claim what's mine."

The possessiveness in his tone should anger me, but instead, it sends heat spiraling through my body. We're like the twin moons—forever circling each other, forever pulled apart, but always drawn back together.

"Our families will never accept this," I whisper, even as I lean closer to him.

"Then we'll change the fucking world," he growls before capturing my mouth with his.

The kiss is desperate, savage with need and the knowledge of how easily we could lose each other again. His hands grip me like he's afraid I'll disappear, and I match his brutal love, pouring months of longing, hurt, and hope into every touch.

The cool blanket beneath my knees does little to ease the heat building inside me. Theron's stare is locked on me—stormy silver and filled with a hunger that takes the air from my lungs. The firelight pulses over his bare skin. His chest rises and falls, each breath heavier than the last.

"You're shaking," he murmurs, his voice low and

edged with something dark and dangerous. His fingers trail lightly over my arms, leaving a path of heat in their wake. "Are you afraid, Lyra?"

I swallow hard, my body betraying me with the way I instinctively lean into his touch. "No," I whisper, my voice barely above a breath.

"Good. Because I don't want you afraid." His head dips, lips brushing against my collarbone. "I want you desperate... aching for me." His tongue slips out and licks along the top of my breasts. I gasp. "Just like in the hall." His tone is pure sin, a dark promise that has a buzz traveling across the apex between my thighs. "When I whispered in your ear... I felt how close you were. You almost came... didn't you, Lyra?"

I can't speak, my throat tight as my body remembers the heat of that moment. My fingers dig into his arms as I nod, my breath coming faster.

"Say it," he commands softly, his teeth grazing my earlobe before he sucks it gently into his mouth. The sensation sends a bolt of pleasure right to my core.

"Yes," I breathe, barely holding back a moan. "Fuck, it was so good."

A dark chuckle rumbles in his chest, and his fingers thread through my hair at the back of my head, drawing me closer until our lips are a whisper apart.

"Good girl," he murmurs, his breath hot against my skin. Then his expression shifts, something darker, more dangerous flashing in his eyes. His grip tightens.

Before I can react, Theron shifts beneath me. His

hands leave my waist long enough to guide me back slightly as he shuffles to no longer have his back to the cave wall and slides down to lie on the blanket, staring up at me.

"Come here," he rasps, his stare filled with sinful intent. His fingers curl slightly, beckoning me forward as he lies sprawled out.

"Sit on me, Lyra," he murmurs, and his words send a pulse of molten heat straight through me.

My cheeks flush, heat blooming under my skin as my gaze tumbles to his bare chest. The firelight casts dancing shadows over the carved muscles and runes etched into his skin. I lower my attention to where he's so erect, so big. I swallow hard as he takes my hand and guides it to wrap around his cock. I pump him several times, just like the few times we'd done in the past. He hisses, grinning at me. Then I straddle his lap, my knees pressing into the blanket on either side of his hips. The hard length of his cock presses against me, and my body reacts instinctively, heat coiling inside me.

His hands settle firmly on my waist, grounding me. When I glance up, I see the wicked gleam on his face—like he's amused by something I don't yet understand.

"I..." I swallow. "Theron... I've never been..." My voice trails off, the words catching in my throat as I try to summon the courage to say out loud what I've never told him before.

A slow, wicked grin spreads across his face. "I know. I'm going to be your first, my little moon." His thumb brushes softly against my breast, circling and plucking an erect nipple that draws a moan from my lips, my body arching into his touch.

I gasp. "You do?"

"I remember the first time you let me touch you..." His words are a velvet caress against my senses, sending a shiver down my back. "When my fingers slid inside you... you were so damn tight, so beautiful, coming apart in my hand."

Heat pools between my thighs at the way he watches me—as though he's reliving every moment.

"But I remember something else," he murmurs, his thumb teasing my nipple again, making me gasp. "The spots of blood on my fingertips after..." His voice softens, almost reverent. "Do you know how much I adored you in that moment?"

My heart pounds as his words sink into me, wrapping around my soul like a possessive embrace.

"I didn't realize you noticed."

"You gave yourself to me," he murmurs. "Letting me be your first... trusting me completely." His other hand slides up to cradle my face, thumb brushing gently over my lips.

I'm captivated, every inch of me buzzing, and I'm dripping; already, I feel how wet I am.

"And now..." His lips curl into a dangerous smile. "I'm going to finish what I started."

I'm trembling at his words, heat swirling through me as his thumb drags lazily down my jaw.

Then his hands slide lower, gripping my hips firmly, possessively.

His fingers flex against my skin. "I asked you to sit on me."

He lifts me slightly, guiding me upward along his body. The hard heat of him brushes against me as I shift, and I bite my lip, my pulse pounding.

"I was..." I whisper, my voice trailing off, flustered by his words.

Theron's low, wicked laugh vibrates against my skin, sending a fresh wave of heat straight between my thighs.

"On my face, beautiful one." His grin is pure sin as he tilts his head back slightly, his tongue brushing across his bottom lip as if he's already tasting me. "That's what I meant."

My stomach flips. "Oh..." The single sound escapes on a breath, my cheeks burning as realization sinks in.

I can't look away from him, the hunger in his stare, the raw need carved into every sharp line of his face. My body tightens with anticipation, my pulse hammering in my ears as I hover above him, desperate for the aching desire that refuses to be ignored.

"Lyra," he murmurs, his voice softer now but no less commanding.

Despite the heat scorching my skin, I feel a spark of nervous hesitation, but the way he studies me—as if I'm his whole damn world—strips away the doubt.

My heart pounds as I shuffle forward, my knees finally

pausing on either side of his head. Every moment feels like a leap off a cliff.

"That's it," Theron murmurs, his voice a low growl vibrating against my skin. His hands settle on my thighs, strong and steady, while I'm hovering just above his mouth.

A wave of uncertainty crashes over me. What am I doing?

"I..." My voice is barely a whisper as I hesitate. "Theron..."

"Shh..." His thumbs brush soothing circles along my bikini line, but his eyes remain locked on mine—dark, hungry. His lips curve into a wicked smile. "I've got you."

Then he pulls me down.

The moment his mouth meets me, everything changes.

A gasp rips from my throat, my head falling back as his tongue slides against me, soft at first, a gentle tease. An inferno floods through me, and I instinctively try to draw away, but his grasp tightens on my thighs, holding me exactly where he wants me.

"Stay," he growls softly. "Let me devour you, little moon."

My body obeys before my mind catches up, surrendering to the sensation as his tongue moves with slow, devastating wickedness. Soft strokes, then firm, teasing circles that leave me breathless.

"Oh... Gods," I breathe as my hips rock against him. The wet heat of his mouth, the way he sucks my lips, leaves me with unrelenting focus—it's too much and not enough, all at once.

"Theron..." I gasp, my tone a breathless plea. I can't believe I'm doing this—straddling his face—but I'm powerless to stop.

I don't want to stop.

"Fuck, you taste so sweet," he growls against me, the words muffled but sending a shiver through me. He's never gone down on me before, and now I wonder why I didn't ask him to do it earlier.

His tongue dips deeper, pushing into me, and I'm shaking all over, moaning louder, rocking my hips.

My thighs clench around his head, a strangled grunt escaping me as fire coils tighter and tighter in my core. His tongue flicks the sensitive spot that leaves me arching.

"Don't stop doing that. Oh my Gods..." I whimper, my hips moving with a mind of their own. "I... I can't..."

"Yes, you can." His voice is rough, vibrating through me as he devours me with renewed intensity. "Let go, Lyra. Give it to me. Come all over my face, beautiful. I fucking need this!"

The command shatters whatever control I had left.

I break.

My body bows, a strangled cry tearing from my lips as my release crashes over me like a tidal wave. Desire pulses through me violently, my legs quaking as Theron holds me steady, his tongue licking me so fast I scream.

I can't breathe. I can't think. All I can do is feel.

My fingers tighten in his hair, my body trembling as the last aftershocks ripple through me. I'm boneless, weightless, completely undone.

And yet... he doesn't stop.

"So fucking beautiful," he murmurs, his voice dripping with praise and raw hunger as he presses one last kiss against my spread lips, making me cry for more. "But I'm not done with you yet, little moon."

I'm gasping for air as he gently guides me down, and I kneel on the blanket beside him. My limbs feel like jelly, my mind spinning, and I'm buzzing all over, every nerve alight with the aftermath of what he just did to me.

"That was..." I trail off as a soft purr escapes my lips. "Incredible."

Theron's hands never leave me, one trailing lazily down my side, the other brushing along my thigh, possessive and steady. His smile is devious, his lips, nose, and chin glistening.

"Oh, Lyra..." His voice is a low, dangerous drawl that makes my core clench all over again. Before I can ask what he's thinking, his body shifts as he pulls himself up. He sits back against the cool stone wall, his broad chest rising and falling rapidly.

Then his strong hand wraps around mine, tugging me effortlessly toward him.

"You're too far away," he growls softly, dragging me onto his lap, my legs instinctively straddling his hips as he sits with his legs outstretched. His cock presses against me, where I'm slick from my orgasm.

"I'm ready," I whisper, my hands finding purchase on his shoulders, but his grip on my waist tightens, pulling me flush against him. Heat burns off his skin.

"Fuck, Lyra... do you have any idea how good you taste?"

I smile like a fool, yet the dark savageness in his expression has me pressing myself against him, needing to feel him skin to skin.

"So, so sweet," he murmurs, kissing me along my jaw. "And sinful at the same time." His mouth trails down my neck, making me quiver. "When you came on my tongue... You drenched me, little moon. And I fucking loved being covered in you."

I gasp, my body buzzing as the ache between my thighs reignites.

"I could've stayed between your thighs all night," he growls, his hands on my rear. "Tasting you. Feeling you. Owning you."

A blush creeps down my neck. "I like it when you talk dirty." My words are barely above a whisper, but it's enough. "It... turns me on."

"Good. Because I fucking adore saying it to you."

His touch slides to my waist, bringing me closer until I'm grinding against his erection.

"Now... I want to feel all of you."

My body tenses as I realize what he's asking. The hard press of him against me leaves no doubt.

I moan, my heart pounding. "I... I don't know..."

"Shh..." His lips brush against my jaw, his tone softer

now, full of gentle reassurance. "I'll help you, Lyra. Let me. Will you let me do that?"

I blink, drawing in a sharp breath. "Yes, I think I'm ready."

His hands slide down to my hips, positioning me perfectly over him, the tip of him pressing just barely inside my entrance. I tense, instinctively trying to pull back, but his grip holds me steady, his touch gentle but firm.

"Slow, little moon." His words are full of raw control, his thumb stroking lazy circles against my hip. "Take your time."

I bite my lip as I gradually lower myself onto him, inch by inch. The stretch is intense—an ache that makes me pause, my breath hitching. My nails dig into his shoulders, and my forehead rests against his as I try to focus on breathing.

"Relax," he murmurs. "You're doing so well."

I shift slightly, feeling him push deeper, and the burn eases just enough for the pleasure to start edging in. The ache is there.

"Almost there, little moon." His voice is strained, his jaw clenched as if he's holding himself back. His eyes, so dark, so full of want, are locked on mine. "You feel so fucking perfect."

When I finally take him fully, a strangled moan escapes me as I adjust to the overwhelming sensation. I feel stretched, filled, fucking amazing.

"Oh, it's..."

"That's it," he growls softly, his hands flexing on my hips. "You're taking me so well."

I try to move, but he holds me still, giving me a moment to shift around. His lips find mine, a kiss grounding me in the moment.

"Move for me, Lyra," he murmurs against my lips. "Ride me."

Drawing in fast breaths, I slowly start to move, my hips rolling instinctively. The initial discomfort fades, replaced by a deep, aching pleasure that coils tight in my core.

"Fuck..." Theron's guttural groan tears from his throat as I take him deeper. "Just like that, little moon."

The friction is intoxicating, and soon, I'm moving with more confidence. His lips find my breast, sucking my nipple into his mouth, and I cry out, my body arching as pleasure spikes through me.

"Theron..." I moan as he lavishes attention on me, teeth on my nipples, making it hurt just enough to make me shiver.

I'm moving faster now, grinding down on him with desperate urgency.

"I... I'm..." My voice hitches as the pleasure crashes through me again, my body convulsing as I come undone, coming so hard my world turns to stars. But Theron doesn't stop.

"Good girl... but I'm not done." He holds my hips harder, guiding me through the aftershocks. I'm overly sensitive, my body shaking, but the hunger on his face tells me he's far from satisfied.

"I'm not sure I can..." I gasp, but he doesn't let up, his pace relentless as he drives me higher all over again.

"Yes, you can," he growls, his grip unwavering. "I'm going to make you come again, little moon. I'm going to fucking ruin you."

I can't stop. My body responds to his every touch, and just as another climax starts to build, I hear his strained voice, rough and raw with need.

"I want to fill you, Lyra..." His jaw clenches, his control fraying as his hips drive up into me. "I want to mark you as mine."

His words push me closer, but a sliver of uncertainty pierces the haze.

"Theron, wait." My words are shaky, my mind struggling to think clearly through the fog of pleasure. "No..." I press a hand against his chest, my breath ragged as I shake my head. "Not yet..."

His growl vibrates through me, full of frustration and barely restrained control, but he listens. His grip tightens as he pulls out, his cock slick and throbbing, and before I can think, I slide off his lap, my body moving on instinct.

"Lyra, fuck, don't do this," he growls, but when I meet his gaze, I see the arousal there.

"I want to taste *you*," I whisper, surprising myself with the boldness in my tone.

"Fuck, Lyra..."

I kneel between his legs, lowering myself until I'm eye

level with his hard, throbbing cock. I wrap my fingers around him, and he's wet from me. My touch is tentative at first, but when I hear his sharp intake of breath, confidence surges through me.

I press my lips over his tip, inhaling his muskiness as well as mine. He tastes salty and sweet, and I moan softly at the sensation. His hand slides into my hair, not pushing, just guiding. I take him deeper, hollowing my cheeks as I move slowly, savoring the power of making him come undone. There's something so rewarding about making a strong man like Theron fall under your spell.

"Fuck..." His head falls back against the wall. "You're so fucking perfect... taking me so well, little moon."

I move faster, my tongue swirling around him, my lips tightening, never stopping, not even when his tip hits the back of my throat and my eyes tear up. His hand cups the back of my head. I don't want to disappoint. I want him to never forget this moment... me.

His groans turn into ragged curses.

"I wish I hadn't hit my head," he groans. "Or I'd pin you to the ground and fuck you until you screamed." His voice is low and dangerous.

I hum softly around him, and that's all it takes. His body stiffens, a guttural growl tearing from his throat as he comes, filling my mouth with his hot seed. The taste of him floods me, and I rapidly swallow. It feels messy and chaotic, but I love the feeling of him losing control because of me. It's intoxicating.

When I finally pull back and sit on my heels, my lips

swollen and my insides thrumming, he stares, filled with awe, desire, and love.

"My little moon." He reaches over and cradles my jaw.

"You're mine forever, little moon."

He means every word. I can feel it in my bones. Gods, I've longed to hear them, but this isn't just about us. Loving him risks everything—my pack, our future, all the lives tied to mine. And still, I hate how much of me already belongs to him.

ELEVEN

THERON

Fuck, my head aches.

I blink against the faint early-morning light filtering through the cave entrance. Every muscle in my body feels like I've been thrown off a cliff. Oh, wait, I was.

Lyra's naked body is draped over my chest, her breathing deep and steady against my skin. She's warm and soft, and I can't help but slide my hand down the curve of her spine, appreciating the feel of her pressed against me. Last night comes rushing back—her mouth on mine, her body moving on me, the way she said my name when she came undone.

A moment I will never forget.

But we need to move. The ritual is happening, and we're wasting daylight.

I move, and pain lances through my skull. I touch my forehead and remove the bandage, but there's nothing but smooth skin. My wolf's healing has done its work, though the spot is still tender as hell.

Carefully, I untangle myself from Lyra, smirking as she makes a small noise of protest in her sleep. The fire has nearly died, just embers glowing softly in the dim cave. Our clothes are spread nearby, mostly dry now. Smart woman, thinking ahead while I was busy nearly dying. I add wood to the dying embers, coaxing the fire back to life.

I grab my pants, grimacing at the lingering dampness as I pull them on. My shirt and jacket follow, still damp in spots but good enough. Then my socks and boots. We don't have time for perfect.

Kieran. Rachel. Orion. Aria. Where the fuck did they end up? They're strong, capable fighters, but that river was brutal.

And Lyra saved me. I actually fucking died, and she brought me back. I'm still dealing with the reality of that.

Stepping outside, the cool morning air hits my skin. The river flows below, calmer now as the sun starts to rise over the horizon. The Darkbone Peaks loom closer than I expected—the cliff and river cut a significant chunk off our journey. At least something's working in our favor.

My stomach growls, reminding me that neither of us has eaten since the shitshow dinner. I can fix that.

Moving silently through the underbrush takes focus, but hunting has been drilled into me since childhood. It doesn't take long to spot a fat rabbit, oblivious to the predator tracking it. One quick chase, and it's over—neck snapped cleanly.

I skin and clean it outside the cave. No need to make a mess inside.

When I return to the cave, Lyra's still sleeping, her blonde hair splayed across the blanket, one arm stretched to where I'd been lying. Something tightens in my chest at the sight, a feeling I've spent the last year trying to bury.

I spear a branch through the rabbit and hold it over the flames, then sit down near my Omega. The cave fills with the scent of roasting meat. My mouth waters, reminding me how long it's been since I've eaten.

Soon, Lyra stirs, her nose twitching slightly. Her eyes open, immediately alert and focused on me.

"Hey, beautiful," I say with a grin.

She stretches, unconcerned with her nakedness, then sits up.

"You're looking better than the last time I saw you conscious."

"Hard not to, considering I died and was bleeding out."

She scans my body, lingering on my forehead. "Your wound's gone. Fast healing."

"Still sore as hell, though. Feels like I got kicked by a fucking horse."

She wraps the blanket loosely around herself as she moves closer to inspect my head. "The moondust you drank probably helped accelerate the healing."

"Whatever it was, it worked." I turn the rabbit over the flames. "Hungry?"

"Starving," she admits, tucking her legs beneath her. "I didn't realize how much energy it takes to drag your heavy ass out of a river."

I snort. "Could've left me there."

"And miss the opportunity to lord it over you for the rest of your life? Not a chance."

I tilt my head, smirking. "Pretty sure the real reason you're drained is from riding my face like you were chasing God... and the way we fucked afterward." I glance at her flushed cheeks. "Dragging me out of the river was just the start."

She snorts. "Keep talking, and I'll shove you back in the river."

"You didn't deny it."

"Too tired to argue. Next time, you get to drown."

There's the sass I remember, the sharp wit that caught my attention when we first met. I watch as she tucks a strand of hair behind her ear. Even half wrapped in a blanket, she's the most beautiful thing I've ever seen.

"The rabbit's going to take longer, but we don't have time," I say, tearing my gaze away. "But it's edible. Then we need to get going."

"Any idea where the others might be?" she asks, her tone shifting to something more concerned.

"River probably carried them downstream. Hopefully, they made it to shore." I check the rabbit again, the skin crisping over the flames at least. "Kieran's been through worse. That damn wolf has more lives than a shadow cat."

"What about Aria and Orion?" Lyra's brow furrows. "Aria's a strong swimmer, but if she was injured from the fall..."

"Rachel would look after her," I say, trying to sound reassuring. "And Orion strikes me as the responsible type."

Lyra sighs, her fingers fidgeting with the edge of the blanket. "Aria's like a sister to me. She's an orphan, you know. No one knows who her parents are."

"That's fucking awful." I turn the rabbit, letting her continue a bit longer.

"No one would claim her," Lyra continues, her voice softer now. "A family volunteered to raise her; both parents are in Nightshade, our warrior division. So she's determined to be like them, to prove herself. She's the most incredible fighter I know, but sometimes I think she pushes too hard, as if she's trying to earn her place."

"Must be hard, not knowing where you come from," I say, pulling the rabbit from the fire.

Lyra nods, her expression troubled. "Sometimes, I wonder if her parents are still in the pack, just not telling anyone she's theirs. It would kill her if she found out."

"Political reasons?" I ask, breaking the rabbit in half and offering her the larger portion.

"Or fear," she suggests, accepting the meat with a nod of thanks. "Not everyone believed in the old ways of dealing with mixed-pack relationships. Some might have hidden children to protect them."

The possibility that Aria might be half Umbra could make her parents fearful of revealing the truth when people under my father's reign have died for less.

"She's going to be fine," I say. "She has you."

Lyra takes a bite of the rabbit, her eyes closing briefly in appreciation. "This is good," she murmurs.

"Don't sound so surprised," I retort, tearing into my own portion. "I do know how to feed myself."

"I just never pegged the great Theron for a cook," she teases, a small smile playing on her lips. "Thought you'd have servants doing that for you."

"My *father* has servants," I correct, the mention of him souring my mood. "I prefer to handle things myself."

"Speaking of your father," Lyra begins. "He clearly wants you to win the ritual. How will you deal with that if you do win? I'm pretty sure he will die of a heart attack if I don't die and win alongside you."

The question catches me off guard.

"It's not that simple," I say, tossing a bone into the fire. "For him, this is about winning, holding on to power. It's personal for me."

Her eyes study my face, searching for something.

"Because of your sister? I remember you once told me briefly about her."

I nod, the familiar rage building at the memory of Rina. "He executed her when I was twelve. Blamed her for helping Elios refugees escape a culling." My jaw clenches tight enough to hurt. "Public execution. Made me watch."

Ice fills me, my hatred for my father so deep I lose all sense of emotions. No empathy, no understanding for him.

"Theron..." Lyra's voice softens, her hand reaching out to touch my arm.

"That's just the start," I continue, the words bitter in my mouth. "After that, my mother changed. Started asking dangerous questions about pack history, about the Onyx Covenant. Then one day, she was just... gone." I stare into the fire, seeing my father's cold eyes as he announced her disappearance. "He told everyone she'd run off with an Elios male, that they'd both been killed by rogue wolves in the borderlands."

"But you don't believe that," Lyra says softly.

"Fuck no. I found her journal notebooks hidden under the floorboards in our home. She wrote that my father had been lying, manipulating both packs, and betraying the Onyx Covenant itself. Said there was proof hidden somewhere in the Covenant chambers."

Lyra blinks at me, her face paling. "Oh, fuck! That's why you want to win the ritual. To get access to the Covenant building."

"I think my father has been silencing people while erasing our history." The fire pops, sending sparks dancing into the air. "The last pair of Elios who won the ritual mysteriously died after a few months in their reign, and he forced the packs to run the Harvest Ritual again for new candidates. Before them, Umbra was in charge for three consecutive terms.”

“You think he killed them,” Lyra says, her voice barely above a whisper.

“I’m certain he did,” I reply. “Just like I know he killed my mother when she got too close to the truth. I need to find proof, expose him, change the fucking way things are run by him.” I squeeze her hand, needing her to understand. “He wants Elios exterminated, Lyra. Completely wiped out. And I won’t let him do it, even if it means him against me.”

Silence falls between us, heavy with the weight of my confession. I’ve never told anyone this much—not even Kieran knows the full extent of my suspicions. But Lyra needs to know what we’re really fighting for, what’s truly at stake.

Without warning, she moves forward, abandoning her food and the blanket to wrap her arms around my neck. The sudden embrace comes as a surprise, her naked body pressed against mine, her face buried in my neck.

“I’m so sorry about your mother and sister,” she whispers against my skin. “Makes me fucking loathe your father even more than I already did.”

I encircle my arms around her, pulling her closer, letting myself take comfort in her warmth. For so long, I’ve carried this alone—the suspicion, the rage, the grief. Having her understand, having her believe me without question, feels like putting down a weight I didn’t realize was crushing me.

"That's why I need to win this," I murmur into her hair. "For them, for everyone my father has hurt or plans to destroy. I need to end his reign before he ruins both packs."

She hugs me more, then pulls back, still touching, and she wears the pain, too.

"But I worry that I'm more like him than I want to admit," I counter. "The rage, the violence, the ability to do whatever it takes—that's his blood in me."

"You're nothing like him," she says fiercely. "Nothing."

Her faith in me is staggering, unearned. It reminds me of why I was drawn to her from the beginning—not just her beauty or her fire, but the way she saw me. Really saw me, beyond the Umbra markings and the Shadowmane name, beyond the reputation and the rumors. She saw the man I was trying to be, not the monster my father was grooming.

"When I met you at the border," I say slowly. "It was the first time in years I felt like myself. Not my father's son, not the future Alpha, just... me."

She smiles, a genuine one that lights up her whole face. "I remember thinking you were the most arrogant ass I'd ever met."

I laugh, caught off guard by her candor. "And yet you kept meeting me."

"What can I say? I have terrible taste in men."

"The worst," I agree, pulling her closer again, savoring the feel of her against me. "We need to win, Lyra. For your pack, for mine. For us."

She hesitates at first, then says, "For us."

We finish our meal quickly, aware of time slipping away. Lyra returns to her clothes, dressing fast, and I can't help but watch. She catches me staring as she pulls her shirt over her head.

"You didn't get enough last night?" she teases.

"Never," I reply honestly.

A light blush colors her cheeks, but she doesn't look away.

"Save it for after we win."

"Is that a promise?"

"Might be." She laces up her boots, then gathers her pack. "Ready?"

I put out the flames, kicking dirt on the spot, then shoulder my bag and nod. "Let's find the others and head up into the mountains."

We step outside into the full morning light. The river gleams below, reflecting the clear sky. The Darkbone Peaks dominate the horizon. From here, I can make out the dark gap between them—the valley that's our destination.

"We made better progress than I thought," Lyra observes, shielding her eyes as she studies the peaks. "The fall and river cut miles off our journey."

"Small mercies," I grunt, scanning the terrain ahead. Rocky ground gradually rises toward the mountains, scattered trees thinning as the elevation increases. "We should shift. Cover more ground that way."

"Agreed." She turns to me, her expression serious. "Do

you really think we can do this? Find proof against your father, change things between our packs?"

The doubt in her voice is reasonable; what we're attempting seems impossible. Two wolves against generations of hatred, against an Alpha who's ruled through fear and manipulation for decades.

"I don't know," I admit. "But I know we have to try. I'm tired of living in his shadow, tired of watching people suffer for his ambition."

"If we fail—"

"We won't," I cut her off, not willing to consider the alternative. "We can't."

She studies me for a long moment, then nods once, decision made.

"Then we'd better win this ritual."

We secure our packs more tightly, preparing to shift. Lyra rolls her shoulders, loosening muscles still sore from yesterday's ordeal.

"Stay close to me out there," I tell her. "I don't trust the quiet."

"I'm not the one who needs protection," she tells me. "I wasn't the one who died last night."

"Don't remind me," I grimace, touching the spot where my wound had been. "Still can't believe you fed me your blood."

"Saved your ass, didn't it?"

"That it did." I glance at her, suddenly serious. "Thank you. For that, for listening, for... everything."

She holds my gaze, a slow smile spreading across her face. "You're welcome. Now, let's go win a ritual."

TWELVE

LYRA

Rain slices through the air like daggers, pelting my fur until it hangs heavy against my skin. The storm came out of nowhere. Now, each step is a battle against the weather's fury and the treacherous mountain path beneath our paws. The ground has turned to slick mud, threatening to send us sliding back down with every careful movement.

Theron presses forward ahead of me, his black form barely visible in the sheets of rain.

We've been trekking since dawn, exhausted and drenched, with no sign of our friends. The raging river tore us apart last night, and I've been scanning for any trace of them since we started going uphill, but the downpour has washed away any scent trails that might have guided us.

In that frozen moment, I smell the metallic scent of blood. Dread curls in my chest.

As thunder cracks overhead, splitting the sky with a blinding flash that illuminates the forest for a heartbeat, I catch sight of something that doesn't belong—a splash of unnatural color against the browns and greens of the forest floor.

I halt, my instincts screaming caution even as curiosity drives me forward. Theron senses my change in direction and circles back, a low, questioning rumble vibrating in his chest.

The rain parts for just a moment, and I see it clearly.

A body.

Not just any body. The blue uniform of Elios clings to the lifeless form, now sodden and dark with rain and something else—blood, so much blood. I step closer, my heart hammering against my rib cage, praying to both moons that it isn't Aria.

It's not, but the recognition hits me hard.

Zephyr Talonblade.

One of our pack's warriors, renowned for his speed and precision. Now, he lies broken on the forest floor, his skull caved in on one side, congealed blood matting his light brown hair. His eyes stare unseeing at the storm-darkened sky, his mouth frozen in what might have been a final scream.

I shift into my human form without conscious thought, the change rippling through me in a painful wave. Dropping to my knees beside Zephyr, a keening sound escapes my throat.

"No, no, no..." I reach out with trembling fingers,

touching his face, already knowing it's too late. His skin is cold, the spark of life long fled.

Zephyr's Omega, Kay, is nowhere in sight. I pray she got away, that she's still running. Because if she didn't... I force down the panic clawing at my throat. The ritual doesn't pause for grief. But with him gone, if she survived, it's up to her to finish the Harvest Ritual. Alone.

Theron shifts beside me, his human form materializing. He doesn't speak, just places a steadying hand on my shoulder as I struggle to process what I'm seeing.

The wound on Zephyr's temple is grotesque—not a clean cut from a blade or a puncture from claws, but a massive crushing injury. Whatever hit him did so with tremendous force, shattering bone and pulping the flesh beneath.

"I think I'm going to be sick," I whisper, bile rising in my throat.

Theron kneels beside me, his eyes scanning our surroundings. "We need to keep moving, Lyra," he says, his voice low and urgent. "I think we're in troll territory."

"We can't just leave him here," I protest, even as the rational part of my mind acknowledges the truth in Theron's words. "He deserves a proper burial, a prayer to guide his spirit to the moons—"

My words die as I turn and spot another crumpled form about twenty yards away, half hidden by undergrowth. I gasp. This one wears the black uniform of Umbra.

Theron follows my gaze, his body tensing beside me.

He moves swiftly to the second body, and I follow on unsteady legs, dreading what we'll find.

It's Maddox Daruk, one of the Umbra tributes selected for the ritual. His death mirrors Zephyr's—the same crushing head wound, the same frozen expression of terror. Theron growls low in his throat, a sound so feral and pained that it raises the hair on my arms.

His Omega isn't anywhere either, and just like Zephyr's, Maddox's manacle is dead—no silver threads, no light. The moment its host dies, the magic in it snuffs out, too, like it senses the soul slipping free.

"They died fighting," he says after a moment, gesturing to Maddox's bloodied knuckles and the defensive wounds on his forearms. "They didn't go easily."

I look around more carefully now, noticing what I missed in my initial shock. Signs of a violent struggle are everywhere—broken branches, trampled underbrush, splashes of blood washed pale by the rain. This wasn't a quick ambush; it was a battle.

"Trolls. Do you think they're responsible?" I ask, glancing around frantically.

Thunder cracks directly overhead, making me flinch. The storm is intensifying, the sky darkening to a premature twilight, though it can't be past midday. But in this gloom, the forest's predators might grow bold earlier than usual.

"Could be," Theron replies grimly, scanning the tree line. "And that's exactly why we need to move... and fast.

Trolls are territorial. If they've killed once today, they won't hesitate to do it again."

I glance back at Zephyr, my heart clenching at the ache of his parents finding out.

Theron's gaze meets mine, grim determination in their gray depths. "Let's go. Now." He nods toward our packs, which we left at the edge of the small clearing when we shifted.

"I can't just—"

"You can and you will," he cuts me off, his voice firm but not unkind. "Zephyr and Maddox are beyond our help. We're not."

The rational part of me knows he's right, but something in me rebels at the thought of abandoning our pack mates to the mercy of scavengers and the elements.

"We'll come back for them," Theron promises, reading my hesitation. "Once we've won, once we're safe, we'll return with others and give them the rites they deserve. But right now, we focus on staying alive."

A flash of lightning illuminates the clearing again, and in that stark, blue-white light, I see something that sends ice through my veins. Massive, misshapen footprints pressed into the mud—too large for any wolf or bear, with splayed toes that end in blunt, almost rectangular depressions under the trees where the rain hasn't washed them away yet.

"Theron," I whisper, pointing to the tracks. "Look."

He follows my gesture, his expression hardening as he recognizes the threat.

"Fucking hell," he mutters.

I don't hesitate. The change tears through me, bones cracking and re-forming as my body contorts into the powerful frame of my wolf. The pain is sharp but brief, and then I'm on four paws, senses heightened despite the storm's interference. Theron is in his wolf form just as quickly, and we're off.

The wind howls amid the trees, bending trunks and sending branches crashing down around us.

We're forced to a slow, cautious pace as we continue upward, hyperaware of every sound, every shadow. As we advance farther, more signs become clear—trees torn out by their roots rather than fallen naturally, strange circular clearings where nothing grows.

Definitely trolls.

Suddenly, a deep rumbling sound carries through the storm—not thunder, but something moving. The ground under our feet trembles with heavy footfalls.

A hulking silhouette appears between the trees ahead, at least eight feet tall and broad as a bear. The figure moves with surprising speed for its size, navigating the slick terrain.

We freeze in the shadows of the trees.

I hold my breath, willing my racing heart to quiet. The troll pauses, its huge head swinging from side to side as it scents the air. Now that it's closer, I can make out more details—grayish-green skin like weathered stone, knotted muscles bulging, arms so long the monstrous hands nearly brush the ground. A jutting brow ridge shadowing small, deep-set eyes, a flat, almost nonexistent nose with flared nostrils, and a mouth full of blunt, rock-like teeth.

The evidence of Zephyr's and Maddox's shattered skulls tells me those stories were, if anything, understated.

The troll takes another step forward, and a twig snaps under its large foot. Its head swivels in our direction, those small eyes narrowing as they lock on to us. At that moment, the wind blows in our direction, bringing its repulsive scent of rot and swamp water. I gag just as the troll's roar deafens me, vibrating in my ears and chest.

Fear drives us forward, weaving between trees frantically. The mud squelches beneath my paws, sometimes firm enough for traction, sometimes slick enough to send me sliding. Rain pelts my fur, soaking through to my skin despite the protective undercoat. Each breath pulls in the metallic tang of the storm, the mossy decay of the forest floor, and the stone-and-rot smell of troll.

Heavy footfalls behind us send tremors in the ground that I feel through the pads of my paws.

A boulder flies past, missing me by inches and crashing into a tree with enough force to splinter it. I wince and swerve away from it. Theron veers left, and I follow instinctively.

My lungs burn, and my muscles scream.

The troll gains ground, its massive fist slamming into a tree trunk just beside me. Splinters of wood sting my flank, spurring me to greater speed.

A yelp slips past my throat, panic driving me forward faster.

Theron gives a short, sharp bark, urging me on. I don't need to be told twice. He changes direction again, heading toward what appears to be a wall of dense vegetation. As we get closer, I realize it's not a wall at all but the edge of something—a ravine or gorge, its far side obscured by the rain and mist. A primitive rope bridge spans the gap, swaying precariously in the wind.

Fuck!

I skid to a halt at the edge, hackles rising, a growl of disbelief rumbling in my chest. Theron stops, too, looking back at me with intense eyes. He nudges me toward the bridge with his muzzle, then steps onto it himself, testing it with his weight.

The structure creaks ominously but holds. He looks back at me, ears forward, tail straight—a clear command to follow.

He takes more steps and starts moving forward, glancing back at me, grunting to follow him.

The troll's roar behind us makes the decision for me. I step onto the first plank, feeling the entire bridge sway alarmingly under my weight. Through gaps in the wooden slats, I glimpse a mist-filled chasm, the roar of rushing water suggesting a river far below. My sensitive ears pick up the creaking of rope fibers.

Theron moves ahead. I match his pace, focusing on him. Behind us, the troll reaches the edge of the ravine. Its frustrated growl is followed by the ominous splintering of wood as it sets foot on the bridge.

The bridge sways dangerously.

I freeze, my heart about to give out.

A warning snarl rises from Theron's throat. His pace quickens, and I follow suit, pulse hammering in my veins.

A rotted plank gives way beneath my paw, and I scream, plunging through, back legs scrabbling at empty air. A yelp of terror escapes me as I cling desperately to the remaining planks with my front paws.

Theron spins around, ears flat against his skull, eyes wide with alarm. The bridge tilts crazily as the troll advances, its weight causing the entire structure to sag dangerously. The ropes stretch and groan, ancient fibers beginning to snap one by one.

With a desperate surge of strength, I pull myself up, muscles trembling with the effort. Theron seizes the scruff of my neck in his jaws, helping haul me back onto what remains of the walkway. The bite is painful but steadying.

We scramble forward as a tremendous crack echoes across the gorge. The main support rope has snapped under the troll's weight. The entire bridge lurches sideways, and we're reduced to scrambling, claws scrabbling for purchase on the remaining planks as the structure begins to collapse around us.

Theron reaches the far side first, leaping to solid ground before turning back. His bark is sharp and urgent, commanding me to jump as the final planks begin to fall away beneath me.

I'm still several feet away, clinging to what's left of the rope railings as the bridge continues to fall apart. It's too far, but staying put means certain death. With a desperate lunge, I launch myself toward the edge, front paws extended, muscles straining.

For one heart-stopping moment, I'm suspended in the open air, nothing but mist and death below me.

Then my front paws catch the edge of the ravine, claws digging into mud and rock. I scrabble wildly, back legs kicking at nothing as I fight to pull myself up. Theron's jaws close around my scruff again, and with a grunt of effort, he drags me the rest of the way. We collapse onto solid ground as the last of the bridge plummets into the gorge.

A furious roar echoes across the chasm. The troll is clinging to the opposite cliff face, its body too heavy for the bridge but strong enough to save itself from the fall.

I struggle to my feet, sides heaving with each desperate breath. Theron rises beside me, nudging me with his muzzle—a wordless command to keep moving. His growl is low and urgent. He turns and bolts into the forest, and I follow, rain beating against us.

We run for what feels like hours. Only when we've put miles between us and the ravine do we finally slow, both of us heaving with exertion. We've climbed higher, following a narrow game trail that winds through increasingly rocky terrain. The trees are thinning, and through gaps in the foliage, I catch glimpses of our destination—the twin spires of the Darkbone Peaks, with the valley nestled between them.

Theron stops in a small clearing, shaking his black fur to dislodge some of the water. I follow suit, though it does little good in the continuing downpour. He tilts his head, eyes questioning, and I understand without words. We're relatively safe now, at least from the trolls. We can rest, if briefly.

I sink onto my haunches, grateful for the break. My entire body aches, muscles pushed beyond their limits, the pain in my shoulder from the bridge rescue a persistent throb. But beneath the physical discomfort lies a deeper wound—the image of Zephyr's broken body, the knowledge that the ritual has already claimed lives.

How many more will die before this is over?

Theron moves closer, his big black form settling beside me, offering warmth and silent comfort. I allow myself to lean against him, drawing strength from his solid presence.

After a few minutes, he nudges me gently with his muzzle, indicating we should continue. I rise reluctantly, knowing he's right. We're close.

Ahead, the valley comes into clearer view with each step. From this vantage point, I can see that it's enclosed by a lofty wall of dense greenery—some kind of natural barrier. In the center, barely visible at this distance, stands a pair of towering metal gates.

And gathered before those gates are figures—other

participants who have survived the journey. My heart leaps at the sight. Aria has to be among them. Orion? Have our friends made it after all?

We shift back to human form beneath the last stand of trees, our packs still on our backs.

"Well," Theron says, dragging his wet clothes out and getting dressed. "At least we're somewhat decent."

I quickly do the same. Glancing down at myself, I have to suppress a hysterical laugh. My clothes are clinging to me.

"Very decent," I agree dryly, crossing my arms over my chest. "I'm sure the Covenant will be impressed with our formal attire."

Theron's gaze lingers on my chest for a moment.

Heat rises to my cheeks, but I resist the urge to squirm under his attention.

"See something interesting?" I ask with forced casual-ness, arching an eyebrow at him.

His gaze meets mine, unashamed and intense. "Some-thing beautiful," he admits. "Even soaking wet and nearly eaten by trolls, you're the most captivating thing I've ever seen."

That was too close. "I've never seen trolls before," I breathe, still trying to catch up to what just happened.

He steps in close, sliding a hand beneath my chin and gently tipping my face toward his.

"Are you hurt?" His voice is low, rough with emotion. "The troll... the bodies... it's fucking gut-wrenching to lose people. I've seen too much of it." His thumb brushes over my jaw, slower than it needs to be. "But I couldn't take it if I lost you."

The world around us is chaos, but for a breath, all I can feel is him—steady, grounding, protective.

Then a shout comes from the group across the open field, and the moment shatters. We have to move. But his touch lingers like a promise.

I shoulder my pack. Theron does the same, and we begin the long trek toward the gates.

"The trolls usually stay higher in the mountains," Theron replies, running a hand through his wet hair. "The storm might have driven them down."

Then we walk mostly in silence, the rain slowing, thankfully.

As we draw closer, I scan the figures waiting at the gates as more emerge from the tent set up near the wall.

Wait...

"I can't see Aria," I whisper, my voice hitching. My pulse quickens, the momentary relief crumbling into fresh fear.

Theron squints, his jaw tightening as he surveys the small group. "I can't see Kieran either," he murmurs, concern evident in his tone. "Maybe they're in that tent near the wall."

My stomach twists into a knot, hoping he's right. After everything we've endured—the storm, the trolls, the treacherous bridge—this new uncertainty is almost too much to bear.

"We need to hurry," I say, already quickening my pace,

mud splashing beneath my boots as I half run, half slide down the remaining slope.

Theron matches my stride. The gates remain firmly closed, offering no answers, no welcome. Just cold metal standing between us and safety—or whatever lies beyond.

My mind threatens to spiral with each step closer. The image of two opponents' shattered skulls flashes unbidden in my thoughts, and I have to bite my lip to keep from crying out.

The surviving participants turn to watch our approach, but right now, all I can think about is Aria.

THIRTEEN

LYRA

We burst into the clearing of the gate, where others stare at us, looking just as startled. The valley stretches before us, cradled between the towering Darkbone Peaks that loom overhead. Their jagged silhouettes pierce the storm clouds, dark against darker, watching our approach with stony indifference.

"Aria!" I call out, scanning the gathered entrants. "Aria, where are you?"

The rain continues to fall, gentler now but persistent, but I can't see her and hurry toward the tent.

Tavian steps forward, his expression grave. The relief of seeing him alive is immediately overshadowed by the absence at his side.

"Where's Aria?" I demand, my voice breaking. "Has she returned?"

His jaw clenches. "She, Orion, Kieran, and Rachel haven't returned."

Panic rises, sharp and acidic in my throat.

He shakes his head and moves back into the tent, out of the rain.

Theron steps up beside me, his presence solid and reassuring. All I can think about are the trolls in these mountains. Aria could be injured, trapped—or worse.

I wrap my arms around myself, shivering.

Nearby, several elaborate attached tents have been erected. They're constructed of a gray and faintly luminescent material, as if woven from moonlight itself. Small glowing orbs hover above each entrance, casting cool blue light across the muddy ground.

"We need to go look for them," I say, already turning back toward the mountainous path we just descended.

Theron catches my arm. "Lyra, wait."

"No, we can't just—"

"Priestess Mooncrest." A stern voice cuts through my protest. I turn to see Tarek and Melian approaching from within the tent.

Unlike the rest of us—battered, soaked, and filthy from our journey—the two Covenant representatives look immaculate. Their ceremonial robes are perfectly dry, without a speck of mud or a single wrinkle. Their hair and skin are clean, as if they'd just stepped out of a bath rather than traveled the same treacherous mountain we did.

"We need to find my friend," I say, facing Melian

directly. "There are four of them still out there somewhere."

Melian's expression remains impassive. "The Harvest Ritual continues regardless of individual circumstances. Those who have arrived may proceed. Those who have not must find their own way and will be eliminated if they don't arrive."

"Are you serious?" I step closer, disbelief making me reckless. "There are trolls out there. We found Zephyr and Maddox dead already. And you're just going to... what? Leave them to die?"

"We do not interfere," Tarek states firmly. "Each participant is responsible for themselves and their partner. This is the way it has always been."

Theron continues at my side, hand at my back, urging me to move away from the Covenant members. He leans in close, saying, "Kieran has survived worse than this. If anyone can find a safe path through this mess, it's him. Let's not panic yet."

I want to believe him. I need to believe him. But the image of Zephyr's crushed skull flashes before my eyes, and my throat tightens.

"You leave, you nullify your continuation in the ritual," Melian says, her voice as cold as mountain stone. "Everyone is responsible for themselves. This is why your team member is most important."

"We wait," Tarek states with finality. "They have until midnight. If they don't arrive by then, they forfeit their positions in the final trial."

The declaration falls like a stone. Midnight. Hours away still, but with the storm and the mountain's dangers...

"Come," Melian gestures toward the tents. "There is food and dry clothing. You'll need your strength for what's to come."

I want to refuse on principle, to stand in the rain until Aria appears, but Theron's hand on the small of my back guides me into the tent.

"We're no use to them exhausted and hypothermic," he murmurs close to my ear. "Besides, Aria would kick your ass if she knew you were standing in the rain like an idiot instead of getting dry."

Despite everything, a small smile tugs at my lips. He's right. Aria would absolutely give me hell for being dramatic.

"Fine," I concede.

Inside, the space is larger than it appeared from outside—impossibly so, as if the canvas walls contain more space than they should. Soft rugs cover the ground, intricately patterned in blues and silvers that remind me of Elios ceremonies. Plush cushions are arranged around low tables laden with food, and several braziers provide warmth without smoke.

The other survivors are scattered throughout, some already changed into dry clothes provided in neat stacks at the tent's edges.

He leads me to a stack of dry clothes that appear to be

my size. "Get changed," he says softly. "Then we'll grab some food."

The clothes are similar to what we're wearing but dry. I change quickly behind a discreet screen, the fabric heavenly against my skin after so long in wet clothes.

When I emerge, Theron is waiting for me with a smile. "Feel better?" He's changed as well into black pants, a charcoal tunic, and a dark jacket.

I nod, and we go to collect some food before settling on the cushions. The meal is simple but satisfying—slices of hard cheese and cured meat, rough-crusted bread still warm from the hearth, and small bowls of dried fruit and quince preserves.

As I finish eating, I gather our plates and cross the tent to place them on a stack near the entrance. A jug of water rests beside them, and I pour myself a cup, letting the warmth of the food settle in my belly.

Near the back of the tent, I spot Kay, Zephyr's Omega, next to Maddox's Omega, grief etched into their faces. They don't speak, just pick at the food on their plates. My heart aches for them—for whatever horror they survived to make it back without their partner.

Across the space, I catch a glimpse of Theron speaking quietly with Erebus, their heads bent close, their voices too low to hear.

That's when I feel it. A stare.

I turn slightly and find Selene watching me from her spot near the far wall. Her blue eyes are sharp as blades, her face is scratched, and her dark hair is tangled in a way that suggests more than just the storm is to blame.

I try to ignore her, sipping my water.

She rises and stalks toward me, her steps sure and stiff with anger.

"I almost died today because of you," she groans with no subtlety, just venom.

I blink, caught off guard by the accusation. "Excuse me?"

"I bet you were safe with Theron at your side," she continues, poison dripping from every word. "While we were attacked by fucking Bloodmoths."

Ah. That explains the scratches, the tangled hair, and the storm of rage she's barely holding back.

I raise a brow, tilting my head just slightly. "You were afraid of moths?"

Her eyes flare, the fury in them igniting like dry kindling. "They feed on your skin, you idiot... ripped through clothes like it was paper."

"Sure," I drawl, not even bothering to hide the edge in my voice. "If there's a massive swarm. Was it?"

She opens her mouth, then hesitates, just for a second, but it's enough.

I see the truth flash across her face before she can hide it.

It wasn't.

She glares harder, jaw tightening like she wants to lunge at me, and grinds her teeth.

"I was supposed to be with Theron, not you, bitch!"

She practically spits the last word, her hands curling into claws at her sides.

I step closer, keeping my voice low but razor-sharp. "Listen, Selene, I don't care what little fantasy you had planned. I just found two of our kind with their skulls crushed, nearly died on a collapsing bridge, and my best friend is still out there somewhere. Your hurt feelings are the least of anyone's concerns right now."

Selene's beautiful face contorts with rage, her body tensing as if preparing to spring. "You think this is about hurt feelings?" Her voice is a venomous whisper, barely audible to the others resting nearby. "This is about tradition. About bloodlines. About maintaining the purity of what we've built for generations."

"Spare me the purity speech," I hiss back. "We both know this is about your wounded pride."

Her eyes gleam with cold fury. "You have no idea what you've stepped into, Elios trash. You're nothing but a temporary distraction for him. When this is over—if you even survive—he'll come to his senses."

"The only thing coming to an end is your delusion," I counter, feeling my own anger rising to match hers. "Theron made his choice. Deal with it."

Something shifts in her expression then—calculation replacing blind rage. She leans in closer, her words meant for my ears alone. "You know, I should have made sure you died in the gorge that first night. My mistake."

The admission hits me like ice water. She'd tried to murder me before the trials even properly began.

"It was you," I breathe, realization turning quickly to white-hot fury. "You pushed me."

Her smile is all venom and pride. "And next time, I won't fail."

Something snaps inside me. With a snarl, I lunge forward, my fist connecting with her jaw before she can react. "You fucking bitch!" The words tear from my throat as she staggers backward.

Selene recovers quickly, her hand dropping to the blade at her waist. The metal gleams as she draws it halfway from its sheath.

Suddenly Theron is between us, his broad back to me as he faces Selene. One hand is raised toward her, the other extended behind him to hold me back.

"That's enough," he states sternly, his voice carrying quiet authority.

"She attacked me!" Selene hisses, though her hand stills on the blade.

"After you admitted to attempted murder," I spit, trying to move around Theron. He shifts slightly, keeping himself as a barrier between us.

"She doesn't deserve to be here," Selene continues, her gaze locked on me over Theron's shoulder. "An Elios priestess? She'll be useless in the final trial. You've doomed yourself by choosing her."

"Selene." Theron's tone drops even lower, a warning rumble like distant thunder. "Your father's influence got you into this ritual, but it won't keep you alive through it. The mountain just taught everyone a valuable lesson about who can be relied on. Take the hint and focus on survival instead of petty rivalries."

His words do nothing to dampen the hatred in her eyes. "This isn't over," she mouths to me, her fingers still wrapped around her blade's hilt.

"You're right about that," I murmur, just loud enough for both of them to hear.

Selene's eyes narrow to slits of pure hatred. For a moment, I think she might attack anyway, consequences be damned. Instead, she turns on her heel and stalks out of the tent, her rigid posture screaming of humiliation.

As soon as she's gone, Theron turns to me. "What happened? What did she say to you?"

I consider telling him. But something stops me. This is my fight, not his.

"Nothing worth repeating," I say instead, forcing my breathing to steady. "Just her usual poison."

His eyes search mine, clearly not believing me. "Lyra—"

"Not here," I cut him off, nodding toward the others pretending not to watch our exchange. "Trust me. This is something I need to handle."

He hesitates, then gives a slight nod. He takes my hand, guiding me to a quieter corner of the tent, where a small table holds bread, cheese, and what smells like mulled wine. "You should eat more. The final trial won't be easy."

We sit close together, the shared warmth a stark contrast to the chill of worry that's settled in my chest. I pick at the food, my appetite diminished by worry for Aria.

"Tell me," I say after a while. "Why are you so confident Kieran will keep Aria safe?"

Theron's expression softens slightly. "We've been friends since we were pups. His mother helped raise me after mine disappeared." He tears off a piece of bread, rolling it between his fingers absently. "He comes across as a smart-ass, but he's the most loyal wolf I know. And the most resourceful. When we were fifteen, we got lost in the northern territories during a hunting trip. Blizzard came out of nowhere and separated us from the rest of the party. Kieran not only found shelter, but he also managed to catch food, start a fire with practically nothing, and track our way back once the storm cleared."

We lapse into a comfortable silence, the worry still present but somehow more bearable shared between us. Outside, the rain slows, pattering against the tent. Occasionally, thunder rumbles overhead while I keep picking at the food, and Theron and I exchange stories of the silliest things Kieran and Aria have done.

The waiting is torture. As night stretches over the land, bringing with it a deeper chill, my hope begins to falter. What if they don't make it by midnight? What if they don't make it at all?

"They're coming," someone says from outside the tent.

I sprint out of the tent, hope tight in my gut, Theron at my side.

Voices call out, feet splash through mud, and my heart leaps into my throat. Four of them are pushing themselves toward us, and I let out a relieved sound to see them alive.

They finally reach us, drenched, breathing hard, flushed with exertion but gloriously, wonderfully alive.

"Aria!" I launch myself at her, nearly knocking her over with the force of my embrace. She staggers but stays upright, her arms closing around me with equal fervor.

"I thought you were dead," I sob into her neck, not caring who sees my moment of weakness. "When you didn't come back, I thought—"

"Takes more than a river to kill me," she replies, her voice rough but strong. "Though it wasn't for lack of trying."

I pull back to examine her face, the bags under her eyes. Exhaustion is evident in the slope of her shoulders, but she's here, solid and real beneath my hands.

Beside us also stand Orion and Rachel, appearing just as worn. Theron and Kieran engage in a rougher version of the same reunion—a fierce hug followed by Theron shoving Kieran's shoulder hard enough to make him stumble.

"Cutting it a bit close, aren't you?" Theron growls, though the relief in his voice is obvious.

Kieran grins. "Had to make a dramatic entrance, didn't we? Besides, your Omega's friend here insisted on taking the scenic route."

Aria rolls her eyes at him, but I notice something odd

in her expression—a softness when she looks at Kieran that wasn't there before.

"What happened?" Cassius asks.

"The river carried us around to the eastern side of the mountain," Kieran explains, running a hand through his soaking red hair. "By the time we managed to get out, we were halfway to the fucking Hallowlands."

"The current was too strong to swim against," Aria adds. "We had to hike back, and then we ran into damn wolves."

"But you got away," I say, still holding her arm as if afraid she might disappear again.

"Obviously," Kieran smirks. "Aria here is quite the fighter. Took down the Alpha with nothing but sheer stubbornness."

Rachel clears her throat loudly nearby. "We were there, too, you know. It wasn't just The Aria Show."

Kieran shoots Rachel a crooked grin, but it's the way Aria's lips twitch—just barely—and the faint color lingering on her cheeks that really catch my attention.

Aria never blushes.

There's something going on between those two.

Orion is also soaked and scowling. "Glad you're all enjoying the drama. Next time I get dragged into a river and chased by monsters, I'm sending a fucking raven ahead."

That earns another round of laughter, and the tension finally starts to ease.

"You four should get dry," Tarek, who has been sitting

back quietly, finally says, nodding toward the tent. "There's food as well."

"Thank the fucking moons," Kieran groans. "I'm starving."

As they move indoors and I follow, I pull Aria aside, leading her to a relatively private corner of the tent.

"Are you really okay? What actually happened out there?"

Aria wipes her face with one of the towels provided, then grabs a cup of water and drinks deeply.

"It was just as Kieran said. The river split us up from you and Theron and carried us miles east. We had to spend a full day hiking back."

"And the rogue wolves?" I press, watching her face carefully.

"Came at us just as we were nearing the valley. But we handled it." She sounds casual, but there's something in her voice—a slight catch, an undercurrent of tension.

As she reaches for more water, I notice a pinkish mark on her neck, partially hidden by her collar. Then another, lower down, disappearing beneath her shirt.

I lean in, eyes widening. "What is that?"

Aria blushes furiously, quickly adjusting her collar to cover the marks. Her eyes dart reflexively toward Kieran, who's enthusiastically recounting their adventures to a group of entranced listeners.

"Oh, Aria," I breathe, realization dawning. "Did you and he..."

"Shh! Gods, do you want to scream it for the whole

world?" She glances around nervously, but no one is paying attention to us.

"What happened? Why?" I lower my voice to an urgent whisper. "What about Orion? You were crushing on him for months!"

"I don't know." She shrugs, unable to meet my eyes. "Kieran is... he's not what I expected. He's actually amazing, and he flirts so well, and then we had to spend the night in the woods to rest. We caught fish and he found these mushrooms to make tea with, and maybe the mushrooms were a bit special, or the serum from that dinner was still in our system, but..." She glances around once more, then leans in close. "We fucked in the woods while the others slept!"

I gasp, though I'd already guessed as much. Aria looks simultaneously embarrassed and pleased with herself, her eyes bright with a new energy despite her exhaustion.

"He's your enemy, you know that," I remind her, though I can hardly throw stones, given my own situation. "In this game, at least."

"So is Theron," she counters, one eyebrow raised in challenge.

"Yeah, but at least he's my partner for the ritual."

"Well, we talked about it, and we're going to help you and Theron win," she says, surprising me.

"You talked about it?" I stare at her, not quite comprehending. "And what do your actual ritual partners think about this plan? Or the fact that you're okay with Umbra wolves winning? As the Alpha, Theron will win, and we Elios will be second again..."

Her expression grows serious. "So, what's your plan? To make Theron lose?"

The question pauses me. I frown, suddenly unsure.

"I don't know. I'm torn. I don't want Elios wolves to always come up second best, disadvantaged... but Theron..." I glance over at him, remembering the things he told me in the cave last night. His sister's execution. His mother's disappearance. His father's murderous ambitions.

"But it's a risk," I continue slowly. "If he wins, he might be able to remove his father from leadership and find evidence of his crimes. But in the meantime, am I gambling with the lives of Elios, who struggle more each year? The lack of help from the Covenant, the unfairness, the attacks on our people that we can't hold his father responsible for because the Covenant never takes our side..."

I feel almost sick, the weight of the choice crushing down on me.

"What if... what if I help you win instead?" The words taste like a betrayal on my tongue. I'd be betraying Theron... after everything we've shared.

Aria studies me for a long moment, her lips pressed into a thin line. Then she sighs. "For a priestess, you have remarkably little faith in the moons."

"What?"

"You're always trying to control everything, plan for

every outcome," she explains, her voice gentler now. "Maybe it's time to trust that the moons have a path laid out, even if you can't see it yet."

I start to open my mouth to respond—

"Attention!" Melian stands at the center, her black robes making her seem like a piece of the night sky given form. "The Harvest Ritual trial is beginning. Everyone outside, please. Leave your belongings behind and only take what you're wearing. Pair up with your partners."

A ripple of tension passes through the gathered wolves as we file out of the tent into the cool evening air. The rain has slowed to a gentle drizzle, more mist than proper precipitation now. Above, the clouds have thinned enough to reveal glimpses of the twin moons—Umbra dark and full, Elios veiled in partial shadow.

We gather before the enormous gates that mark the entrance to the trial grounds. I hadn't paid them proper attention before, too consumed with worry for Aria. Now, I stare in awe at the intricate construct—towering gates of intertwined thorns, branches as thick as my arm woven together in complex patterns that seem simultaneously natural and deliberately crafted. The thorns themselves are enormous, wickedly sharp, and faintly luminescent in the gathering darkness.

My skin ripples with goose bumps. There's old magic here, powerful and wild, neither Umbra nor Elios but something more primal than both.

Tarek and Melian take positions before the gates, their

ceremonial robes now adorned with elaborate head-dresses that echo the lunar cycles.

"Before we begin," Tarek announces, his voice carrying easily across the field. "Let us acknowledge those who did not complete the journey."

A moment of silence falls as he names Zephyr and Maddox, offering a traditional prayer for their spirits. I lower my head, grief for my pack mate a dull ache beneath my breastbone.

"The journey to this point has tested your strength, your courage, your resourcefulness," Melian continues once the prayer concludes. "The final trial will test something else entirely—your understanding of what truly matters."

She gestures toward the entrance, which remains firmly closed.

"Behind these gates lies the true Bloodmoon Field—a labyrinth of choices and consequences. Each team will enter through a different path, but all paths may eventually converge. Your goal is to locate any of the five Moon Shrines hidden within and use the clues they provide to find the Onyx Moonstone."

"The first team to retrieve the stone and return it to the Sacred Circle at the labyrinth's center will win the leadership of the Onyx Covenant for the next ten years," Tarek adds. "Their pack will guide both Umbra and Elios until the next Harvest Ritual."

"Sounds easy enough," Kieran calls out, earning a few nervous chuckles from the gathered attendees.

"Indeed, it is a race," Melian acknowledges with a thin smile. "But not as simple as you might think. There are dangers beyond this wall that you won't expect, so be cautious of everything you encounter."

"There is no time limit," Tarek explains. "But be warned—those who become lost may wander the labyrinth for months or years before finding their way out again. Some never do."

A shiver runs through me at his words. Beside me, Theron stands tall, his expression determined rather than fearful.

"One rule above all must be observed," Melian states firmly. "Once found, the Onyx Moonstone must be freely given to the Sacred Circle. It cannot be forced or coerced into position. Only a worthy team, acting in true harmony, will be able to complete this final task."

Tarek steps forward, raising his arms to the thinning clouds above.

"May the twin moons guide your paths and illuminate your true purpose. May your hearts be light and your spirits strong. The Harvest Ritual's final trial begins... now."

With a grinding creak that vibrates through the ground beneath our feet, the massive gates begin to swing inward. Heat and shadow roll out from the opening, but it's not total darkness—flaming torches cast a flickering glow that makes everything feel far too alive.

We're ushered forward in pairs, each team directed to different entrances that are arched gaps carved into a towering wall of living thorns, pulsing faintly as though it breathes.

Theron is shoulder to shoulder with me, both of us staring incredulously at where our path leads. The ground dips suddenly in front of me—and my breath catches.

A vast maze sprawls below, winding paths twisting and looping so far across the valley that they disappear into shadow. The torchlight doesn't reach the far end, leaving the edges to bleed into pitch blackness. From where I stand, it looks endless.

"Gods," I murmur. "We're going to get lost and die in there."

From a few entrances down, Kieran's voice pipes up. "Speak for yourself. I have an excellent sense of direction —just not when I'm hungry, tired, or mildly inconvenienced."

Laughter breaks some of the tension, but only for a moment.

Beside me, Theron exhales slowly, his gaze locked on the maze as if he's already memorizing every twist and turn.

"Stay close. The maze is alive. It will try to separate us."

A chill creeps down my spine.

The walls tower at least fifteen feet high, constructed entirely of thorns and tangled, dried branches so dense that no light penetrates through them. The only illumination comes from small round orbs spaced along the walls at irregular intervals—like fireflies trapped in circular glass, giving off a faint, bluish glow that barely pushes back the darkness.

"Holy shit," I whisper, stopping at the threshold. "How are we supposed to find our way through there?"

Theron takes my hand, his grip warm and steady. "Together," he says simply. "We'll find our way together."

I look up at him, searching his face for any sign of doubt or fear. There is none—only determination and something else, something that makes my heart flutter despite the terror of what lies ahead.

"Are you ready?" Melian asks, standing beside our entrance.

I'm not. I'm absolutely not ready for whatever nightmare labyrinth they've constructed for us, but I square my shoulders and nod.

"Good luck to you both," she states, and it almost sounds sincere. "Remember, not everything in the labyrinth is as it appears. Trust your instincts... and each other."

With that cryptic warning, she gestures us forward. Theron steps through first, holding my hand, and I follow close behind.

The moment we cross the threshold, the world changes. The air grows thick and oddly sweet smelling while sounds become muffled as if we're underwater. Behind us, the entrance disappears, replaced by more thorn walls, sealing us in the labyrinth completely.

"No going back now," Theron murmurs, his voice sounding strangely distant despite his proximity.

I swallow hard, fighting down the surge of panic that threatens to overwhelm me. "Forward it is, then."

"Stay close." He squeezes my hand, a silent reassurance that somehow penetrates my fear. "Whatever happens in here, we face it together."

Together. One word, so simple yet so complex given everything between us—our packs, our histories, the night in the cave, and now this final challenge that will determine the future for our pack wolves.

The path ahead splits almost immediately, offering our first choice—left or right, without any indication of which might lead to success.

Theron looks down at me, waiting. Not commanding, not deciding for us both, but genuinely waiting for my input.

"Left," I say, trusting the instinct that whispers through me. "We go left."

He nods, and together, we step into the unknown.

The thorns seem to shift slightly as we pass.

This is no ordinary maze. This is something ancient, something powerful, something that knows exactly who we are and what we carry within us—our hopes, our fears, our secrets.

The real trial has only just begun.

FOURTEEN

LYRA

The first thing that strikes me about the maze is how it breathes. Not metaphorically—it literally inhales and exhales, the massive thorny walls expanding and contracting in a slow, deliberate way. With each breath, tiny motes of silver-blue light drift from the black vines, hovering momentarily before dissolving into the darkness.

"Did you see that?" I whisper to Theron, pointing to where the wall just rippled.

He nods, eyes narrowed. "This place is alive."

We've been walking for what feels like hours, though time seems distorted in this labyrinth. The narrow path beneath our feet has transformed from mud to something more unsettling—a mosaic of flat, dark stones inlaid with what looks disturbingly like fragments of bone. Small symbols are etched into each piece, ancient glyphs that seem to shift and change when viewed from different angles.

The rain has finally stopped, but the air remains heavy with moisture. It reminds me of the ceremonial incense used in moon priestess rituals, but darker, more primal.

"We should have found something by now," Theron mutters, pausing at yet another junction. "A shrine, a clue —anything."

The maze seems to mock our frustration, offering three identical paths forward. Each corridor stretches into shadow, walls glistening with moisture that catches the faint blue light from the hovering orbs. Unlike normal torchlight, these spectral globes cast no warmth, only an eerie illumination that makes shadows dance and colors fade to muted shades of blue and gray.

I close my eyes, reaching for my priestess intuition, though I've never fully trusted it. "This way," I say finally, pointing to the leftmost path. "I can't explain it, but it feels... less wrong."

Theron doesn't question me, just nods and marks our path with another scrap of fabric he tears from his shirt and ties to a protruding thorn.

The passage narrows as we proceed, forcing us to walk single file. Theron takes the lead, his broad shoulders nearly brushing the walls on either side. I follow close behind, trying not to think about the thorns that seem to flex and reach toward us as we pass.

"Wait," Theron whispers suddenly, stopping so abruptly I nearly collide with his back. "Listen."

I hold my breath, straining to hear past the subtle whispers of the maze itself. Then it comes—a distant, haunting melody floating on the damp air. Someone is singing, the voice ethereal and oddly familiar, though I can't place it.

"What is that?" I breathe, my skin prickling with goose bumps.

"A trap," Theron says grimly. "Has to be."

But even as he says it, I feel drawn toward the sound. The melody reminds me of something from childhood—a lullaby my mother used to sing, something about moon blossoms and silver dreams. Without conscious decision, I slip tightly past Theron, moving toward the sound.

"Lyra, wait." His hand catches my arm, his grip firm but gentle. "Let's think about this."

The music grows slightly louder, more enticing. I shake my head, trying to clear the fog that's suddenly settled over my thoughts. "You're right," I admit. "But we need to find the shrines, and this is the first real sign we've encountered."

"Could be leading us straight to danger," he points out.

"Everything in this maze is dangerous," I counter. "At least this is something different."

He can't argue with that logic. With a resigned sigh, he releases my arm. "I'll go first," he insists, moving ahead of me once more.

We follow the haunting melody around several bends, the passage gradually widening until it opens into a circular chamber, unlike anything we've seen so far. The walls here aren't made of thorns but of smooth, dark stone that gleams like polished obsidian. The floor is covered in a carpet of luminescent moss that pulses with soft blue-green light in rhythm with the music.

At the chamber's center stands a fountain—not of water, but of what appears to be liquid moonlight that's slightly translucent, cascading over a series of black tiers into a basin below. The singing emanates from this impossible fountain, rising and falling with the flow of the water.

"Is this a shrine?" Theron asks, his voice hushed with wonder despite his earlier suspicion.

I approach cautiously, drawn by the beauty of the spectacle. "I think so, but where's the clue?"

As if in response to my question, the liquid in the fountain ripples, its surface clearing to reveal an image—not a reflection, but a vision of another part of the maze. I lean closer, mesmerized by what I see—a huge clearing dominated by a stone circle, at its center a pedestal upon which rests a black stone that pulses with inner light.

"The Onyx Moonstone," I breathe, recognizing it from descriptions in ancient texts.

Theron moves beside me, equally entranced by the vision. The image shifts, rippling outward from the center to show the path leading to this important location—a series of turns and landmarks that I try desperately to memorize. Left at the weeping willow, right at the stone archway, straight past the pool of shadows...

"We need to remember this," I say urgently, still watching the vision unfold.

"No need," Theron responds, his voice oddly flat. "I know exactly where that is."

I turn to him, surprised. "How could you possibly—"

The words die in my throat as I see his face. His eyes have gone completely black, reflecting the obsidian walls around us. His expression is slack, vacant, as if something else is looking out through his features.

"Theron?" I whisper, fear clutching at my heart. "What's wrong?"

He doesn't respond, just continues staring at the fountain with those unnervingly black eyes.

I reach for him, grabbing his shoulder. "Theron! Snap out of it!"

The moment my hand makes contact, a jolt of energy surges between us, not painful but powerful enough to make us both gasp. Theron staggers backward, blinking rapidly, his eyes returning to their normal gray.

"What the fuck just happened?" he growls, shaking his head as if to clear it.

"You were... gone," I explain, still gripping his shoulder. "Your eyes went black. You said you knew where the moonstone was."

He frowns, confusion evident in his expression. "I don't remember that. Last thing I recall is looking into the fountain and seeing the stone circle."

My unease deepens. "The fountain was showing us

the path to the moonstone, but something happened to you when you watched it."

We both turn back to the fountain, but the vision is gone. The moonlight water continues to flow, but it shows nothing now except its own luminescent ripples.

"I don't like this," Theron mutters. "The maze is playing games with us."

Before I can respond, a chilling scream echoes through the chamber—raw, terrified, and abruptly cut short. My blood runs cold.

Theron's head snaps up, his body instantly alert. "Which direction?"

I pivot, trying to pinpoint the source of the sound. "I think... that way." I point to a passage on the opposite side of the chamber from where we entered.

Without hesitation, we sprint across the moss-covered floor, the glowing plants leaving trails of blue light beneath our feet like spectral footprints. The new corridor is wider than the others, the walls here composed of both stone and thorns intertwined in an elaborate latticework.

We run blindly, guided only by instinct and fear for our friends. The passage twists and turns, branching occasionally, forcing quick decisions based on nothing more than gut feeling. The maze seems to respond to our urgency, the walls pulsing faster, the whispers growing louder, more insistent.

After what feels like an eternity of desperate searching, we burst into another clearing, this one vastly different from the fountain chamber. Here, the ground is covered not in moss but in pale white flowers that close at our approach, their petals folding inward like tiny fists. The air is thick with their floral perfume.

"Careful," Theron warns, placing a protective arm in front of me. "Something's not right."

In the clearing's center stands a massive willow tree, its trunk black as night, its drooping branches composed not of leaves but of thin silver chains that tinkle softly as they sway. Beneath the tree, a figure sits cross-legged on the ground, back toward us, head bowed.

I step forward despite Theron's restraining arm.

The figure doesn't respond or turn. As we approach cautiously, I realize it's large enough to be a male.

"That's—"

"Kieran," I finish for him as we circle around to see the figure's face.

Theron's friend sits motionless, eyes closed, breathing so shallowly I can barely detect it. His skin has taken on an ashen quality, and thin silver lines—like the chains hanging from the willow—trace patterns across his exposed skin.

"Kieran!" Theron drops to his knees beside his friend, shaking him roughly. "Wake up!"

Kieran doesn't respond, doesn't even flinch at the contact. It's as if he's fallen into some deep trance or enchanted sleep.

"What happened to him?" I ask, kneeling on Kieran's

other side and checking his pulse. It's there but slow and faint.

"I don't know." Theron's voice is tight with concern. "Kieran! Come on, man, snap out of it!"

A soft laugh echoes above us, sending ice through my veins. I look up to see a figure sitting among the willow's branches, partly concealed by the hanging chains, and I swear they were not there moments earlier.

"He can't hear you," the figure says, voice melodic yet unsettling. "He's walked too deep into the dream."

I stand slowly, trying to make out the speaker's features. "Who are you? What did you do to him?"

The chains part as the figure leans forward, revealing a face both beautiful and terrifying. It appears female, with skin so pale it's almost translucent, showing a network of silver veins beneath. Her eyes are completely white, without iris or pupil, and her hair flows around her like a living shadow.

"I did nothing," she says, smiling to reveal teeth as sharp as the thorns that form the maze walls. "He came willingly, searching for something lost. The tree merely granted his desire—to see what cannot be seen, to know what cannot be known."

"What the fuck does that mean?" Theron demands, rising to his feet. "Release him. Now."

The creature's smile widens. "I cannot release what does not wish to be released. Your friend chose to drink from the roots of the Whisper Willow. His mind wanders pathways of possibility now."

"The scream," I say suddenly, remembering why we came running here in the first place. "We heard someone yell out. Was it Kieran? Or Rachel? Where is she?" I glance around.

She shrugs and smiles again. "The dark female wolf? She's hiding somewhere close, terrified."

"How do we help Kieran?" Theron asks, his voice slightly less hostile now that he knows the creature didn't directly harm his friend.

The willow-woman gestures to the tree's roots, where I now notice a small pool of silver liquid similar to what flowed in the fountain. "He drank to see. You must drink to find him and lead him back."

"That's not happening," I say firmly. "We saw what that stuff did to Theron at the fountain. It's some kind of mind control."

The creature laughs again, the sound like glass breaking in slow motion. "Not control, little priestess. Revelation. The waters of the maze show truth—painful, beautiful, terrible truth. Some minds cannot bear it. Others..." Her white eyes fix on Theron. "Others are already touched by old magic and respond... differently."

I glance at Theron, who stares at Kieran with conflicted emotions playing across his face. I know what he's thinking—he won't leave his friend here, trapped in some magical coma.

"I'll do it," he says finally. "I'll drink and find him."

"No!" I grab his arm. "We don't know what that stuff will do to you. There has to be another way."

"There isn't," the creature says simply. "One dreamwalker must find another. Such are the rules of the Whisper Willow."

"Then I'll go," I decide, surprising even myself. "You had a bad reaction to the fountain. It might be worse here."

Theron shakes his head vehemently. "Absolutely not. I'm not risking you."

"And I'm not risking you," I counter. "Kieran is your friend, but you're my partner. If something happens to you, I'll never forgive myself."

The creature watches our exchange with evident amusement. "Both bound by concern for the other. How... touching." The word drips with sarcasm. "But time passes differently in the dream. While you argue, your friend walks further away."

I stare down at Kieran again, noticing that the silver lines on his skin have spread, now covering most of his visible flesh. His breathing has grown even shallower.

"I'm doing this," I say with finality, meeting Theron's eyes. "I've had priestess training. Mental discipline. If anyone has a chance of navigating this 'dream' without getting lost, it's me."

Theron holds my gaze for a long moment, his jaw clenched in frustration. Finally, he sighs. "If you're not back in five minutes, I'm coming after you both."

"How gallant," the creature mocks. "But it doesn't work that way. Once entered, the dream must reach its natural conclusion."

"And how long might that take?" I ask, suddenly wary.

The creature shrugs, an oddly human gesture from something so clearly not. "Moments. Days. Years. It depends on what your friend seeks and how desperately he clings to the illusion."

Great. I kneel beside the small pool at the tree's roots, the silver liquid reflecting my face in rippling distortions. It smells sweet, like honeysuckle and moonflowers, with something darker beneath.

"Just find him and bring him back," Theron says, his hand warm on my shoulder. "Don't get... distracted. I want you back alive."

I nod, cupping my hands and dipping them into the pool. The liquid is cool and tingles against my skin, almost vibrating with potential. Before I can reconsider, I raise my hands to my lips and drink.

The effect is immediate and overwhelming. The world dissolves around me, reality peeling away. I'm falling, floating, flying—all at once.

I see my mother as a young woman, fierce and determined, standing before the Onyx Covenant with a proposal that would unite the packs.

I see Theron as a child, watching in horror as his father slices his sister's throat in the village square... Flashes of the atrocity pop into my vision.

I see myself growing old, wrinkled hands still performing the moon rituals, surrounded by young priestesses who hang on my every word.

None of these are my memories or experiences, yet they feel undeniably real. I struggle to maintain my sense of purpose, repeating to myself... Find Kieran. Bring him back. Don't get lost.

The visions shift and swirl, gradually manifesting into a new scene. I'm standing in a sunlit clearing, the air warm and fragrant with summer flowers. Before me stands a small cottage, smoke curling from its chimney, the door standing invitingly open.

This must be where Kieran's consciousness has retreated. I approach cautiously, noting details that seem strangely specific—wind chimes made of wolf teeth hanging by the door, a garden of herbs I recognize from healing rituals.

"Kieran?" I call, stopping at the threshold. "It's Lyra. I've come to bring you back."

Laughter emanates from inside, along with the clatter of cookware and the smell of something delicious. I step through the doorway into a cozy interior, where Kieran stands at a hearth, stirring something in a pot. He turns, grinning when he sees me.

"Lyra! Perfect timing. Dinner's almost ready."

He looks... happy. Relaxed in a way I've never seen him, the perpetual tension he carries completely absent from his shoulders. But what truly stops me in my tracks is the other figure in the room, setting places at a small wooden table.

"Aria?" I whisper, shock rolling through me.

My best friend looks up, her face lighting with a smile.

She's dressed differently than I've ever seen her—a simple linen dress in place of her usual scout leathers, her hair loose around her shoulders instead of tightly braided.

"About time you got here," she says warmly. "We've been waiting ages."

I struggle to remember that this isn't real, that we're still in the maze, that this domestic scene is nothing but a dream spun from Kieran's deepest desires.

"Kieran," I say carefully. "This isn't real. We're in the maze, remember? The Harvest Ritual? You drank something from a tree called the Whisper Willow, and now you're trapped in a dream."

His smile doesn't falter. "Don't be ridiculous. The ritual ended weeks ago. We decided to stay here, away from all that pack politics nonsense." He gestures around the cottage. "This is our home now."

"Our home?" I repeat, looking between him and the dream version of Aria.

"Of course," dream-Aria says, moving to stand beside Kieran, her hand finding his. "After everything that happened, did you think we'd go back to the way things were? Living apart, pretending we're enemies because of some ancient grudge?"

My heart aches at the scene before me. I understand now what the willow-woman meant—Kieran has constructed a perfect dream where he and Aria can be together, free from the complications of pack rivalry and ritual obligations.

"It's a beautiful dream," I say gently. "But that's all it is, Kieran. A dream. The real Aria is still in the maze, possibly in danger. Theron is waiting for you. We need to complete the ritual."

His expression darkens slightly. "Why? So Theron's father can consolidate his power and continue his crusade against anyone who opposes him? To not have a choice in which Omega I want to be with? What's the point of it all?"

"The point is to change things," I insist. "Together. Remember? That's why we entered the ritual in the first place. For Theron to find evidence against the Alpha, to create a new leadership."

Dream-Aria steps forward, her expression suddenly cold. "She's trying to take you away from me," she says to Kieran, her voice hardening. "She wants everything to go back to the way it was—you with your pack, me with mine, never allowed to be together."

"That's not true," I protest. "Aria—the real Aria—feels something for you, too. I saw it when you both returned to the camp. But this illusion, this fantasy of a perfect life together? It's not helping either of you."

Kieran looks torn, glancing between dream-Aria and me. "How do I know you're telling the truth? How do I know this isn't the reality and you're the dream?"

It's a fair question, one I'm not entirely sure how to answer. Then I remember something—a detail so small but so distinctly Aria that no dream could replicate it perfectly.

"When Aria gets nervous," I say carefully, "she touches the small scar at the base of her throat—the one she got when we were kids, climbing trees near the river. She does it unconsciously, a habit she's never been able to break." I look pointedly at dream-Aria. "But your version doesn't have that scar, does she? Because it's not a detail you would know about."

Kieran's gaze snaps to dream-Aria's throat, which is indeed flawlessly smooth. Doubt creeps into his expression, and the edges of the cottage seem to waver slightly, like heat rising from summer-baked stones.

"She's lying," dream-Aria insists, but her voice sounds different now—higher, strained, less like the friend I know.

"No," Kieran says slowly, backing away from her. "She's right. The real Aria has a scar... and she would never wear a dress like that. She hates anything that restricts her movement." His eyes clear, he focuses on me with new intensity. "This isn't real, is it? None of it."

As he speaks the words, the cottage begins to dissolve around us, the walls melting away like wax, the dream-Aria fading into nothingness with a howl of rage that chills my blood.

"How do we get back?" Kieran asks, grabbing my arm as the ground beneath us starts to disintegrate.

"I don't know," I admit. "I was told to find you and bring you back, but not how to actually return."

The world continues to collapse around us, replaced by swirling silver mist that obscures everything beyond a few feet. In the distance, I hear a voice—Theron, calling my name, his tone frantic with worry.

"We need to follow that voice," I say, pulling Kieran toward the sound. "Focus on Theron. Remember who he is to you, what he means. He's your anchor in the real world."

Together, we push through the mist, which grows thicker and more resistant with each step. It's like wading through honey, every movement requiring tremendous effort. Kieran's hand clutches mine with bruising force, as if afraid we'll be separated in this formless void.

"Theron!" Kieran shouts. "We're here! We're coming back!"

The mist swirls faster, taking on a violent quality, trying to pull us in different directions. Kieran's grip slips, and I tighten my hold desperately.

"Don't let go!" I cry. "Whatever happens, don't let go!"

A tremendous force yanks us apart, and I scream as Kieran's hand is torn from mine. The mist engulfs me completely, and for a terrifying moment, I'm utterly alone in the void, panic clawing at my throat.

Then strong hands grasp my shoulders, shaking me roughly. "Lyra! Come back to me. Come back right now, damn it!"

Theron's voice is so close now. I reach blindly toward it, and suddenly...

I gasp, my eyes flying open to find myself back in the clearing under the Whisper Willow. Theron kneels before me, his face inches from mine, eyes wild with dread and relief. Behind him, Kieran is sitting up, rubbing his head and blinking rapidly.

"You did it," Theron breathes, pulling me against him in a fierce embrace. "Gods, I thought I'd lost you both. You went completely still, just like him, those silver lines appearing on your skin."

I glance down at my arms, but the lines are already fading, leaving no trace of their presence.

"What happened?" Kieran asks, his voice hoarse as if from disuse. "I was… somewhere else. Somewhere perfect."

"The willow shows what you most desire," purrs the creature, still perched in the branches above. She looks disappointed, as if she'd hoped we wouldn't return. "Few have the strength to recognize illusion and reject it. Fewer still can lead others out of the dream."

I struggle to my feet, Theron's arm supporting me as my legs tremble with exhaustion.

"We most likely heard Rachel scream. Where is she? What happened to her?"

The creature sighs, a sound like wind through dead leaves. "As I told you, she's hiding somewhere near." She tilts her head, considering. "The maze speaks in many voices, using memories, fears, and desires. What you heard may not have been real at all."

"The maze was mimicking a scared female voice?" Anger flares in my chest. "Why? To lure us here?"

"Perhaps," the creature admits with a shrug. "Or

perhaps to show him"—she gestures to Kieran—"what he truly fears to lose."

Kieran looks away, unwilling to meet my gaze. Whatever he experienced in that dream cottage with the illusion of Aria, it's affected him deeply.

"We've wasted enough time here," Theron states.

"Such confidence," the creature mocks. "As if the maze will simply yield its secrets because you demand it."

"Maybe not," I say, standing straighter as strength returns to my limbs. "But we've already passed one of its tests. The fountain showed us where to find the moonstone. And now we've faced the Whisper Willow and emerged with our minds intact."

"Two shrines found when most find none," the creature acknowledges, sounding almost impressed despite herself. "Perhaps you will survive this labyrinth after all."

"We'll survive," Theron states, his arm still protectively around my waist.

The creature smiles her terribly sharp-toothed smile. "We shall see, wolf of shadow. We shall see."

As we turn to leave, Kieran still unsteady on his feet but determined to continue, the creature calls after us.

"Follow the chains that shimmer silver, like tears of the veiled moon. They will lead to what you seek."

I glance back, but the willow-woman is already melting into the branches of her tree, becoming indistinguishable from the hanging chains.

"Can we trust anything she says?" Kieran mutters.

I look at the fading form of the willow-woman, her

essence returning to the tree. "I'm not sure we have much choice."

The silver chains hang motionless now, no longer swaying. In the eerie glow of the dark moon overhead, they cast thin, spidery shadows across the ground.

"Rachel," Theron calls out, glancing around at the several entrances into the clearing we're in with the tree. "It's safe to come out again." Theron snorts. "If she's hiding, how is she meant to battle?"

I take in the several shadowed exits that branch off from our current position. The maze stretches in multiple directions, each opening a black maw of thorns and uncertainty.

"We should split up," Theron suggests, his eyes scanning the various exits. "Cover more ground."

"Great idea," Kieran drawls, leaning heavily against a section of wall where the thorns are less dense. "Let's all wander alone in the murder maze. What could possibly go wrong? And you two can't split up for long, remember?" He points at his own manacle.

Despite the situation, I almost smile at his sarcasm.

"Just to check the entrances," Theron clarifies, giving Kieran a hard look. "Yell if you find anything."

We each take a different opening, peering into the darkness beyond. The entrance I choose seems to curve sharply to the left after only a few feet, making it impossible to see further without actually entering. The air from within feels colder, carrying a faint metallic scent that reminds me of old blood.

I'm about to turn back when I catch a glimpse of movement deep in the shadows—a hunched figure pressed against the far wall where the path bends.

"Rachel?" I call softly, stepping just inside the passage. "Is that you?"

The figure stiffens but doesn't respond.

I take another cautious step. "Rachel, it's Lyra. You're safe now. Kieran is safe."

As my eyes adjust to the deeper darkness, I can make her out more clearly now—knees pulled up to her chest, arms wrapped tightly around them, head bowed. She looks small, vulnerable. Nothing like the confident Umbra girl who sneered at me during training.

"Rachel, are you hurt?" I move closer, moonlight from behind me spilling just far enough to illuminate her face as she looks up.

Her face is flushed, but a small smile tugs at the corner of her mouth. She struggles to stand, and I notice her flinch as she straightens.

As she rises, her shirt rides up slightly on one side, revealing a strip of pale skin across her waist. There, livid against her flesh, is a fresh wound—a clean slice that's still an angry red.

I freeze on the spot, unable to stop staring at the wound, a familiarity rising through me.

Rachel notices me staring and quickly yanks her shirt down, covering the injury. Her eyes flick past me toward the main chamber.

I glance back, but from this angle, I can't see Theron or Kieran. We're alone.

"When did you cut yourself?" I ask, my voice barely above a whisper.

I turn just in time to see Rachel's face shift—vulnerability vanishing, replaced by cold hatred.

She lunges.

A dagger flashes in her hand, the blade slicing through the air—straight for my face.

FIFTEEN

LYRA

Rachel's blade flies at me.

Panic thumps in my chest.

I jerk my head to the side, feeling the blade whistle past my ear. My foot catches on something—a root or stone—and I stumble backward, hitting the ground hard. The impact knocks the breath from my lungs, but adrenaline propels me into a clumsy roll as Rachel comes at me again, her blade slicing through the air where I'd been only a second before.

"What the fuck are you doing?" I shout, scrambling to my feet and backing away.

Rachel's face is contorted with rage, her eyes burning with hatred.

"You should have withdrawn from the ritual, Elios filth!" She slashes again, this time grazing my arm. A line of fire blooms across my skin. "Your kind doesn't belong here!"

I twist just in time, bringing my forearm up to catch her strike. The impact rattles through me, sharp and jarring, and the cut she gave me earlier flares with pain—but I shove it down, refusing to give her an inch.

"You're insane! We're supposed to be competing, not killing each other!"

"This was never about the competition," Rachel snarls, feinting left, then striking right.

I catch her wrist, twisting hard. She counters with a brutal sweep to my legs, and we hit the packed dirt with bone-grating force, tangled in a flurry of limbs and snarled breaths.

Her elbow drives toward my ribs, but I shift, using my knee to lever her weight just enough to slip free. My hands scrape against the dirt as I lurch upright, unsteady but fast.

She's still half risen when I drive a kick into her side. The impact lands with a dull thud, forcing a grunt from her throat.

Snarling, she slashes upward with her knife. I jerk back—just in time—the blade missing my stomach by a whisper. Rachel scrambles to her feet, eyes wild, lips peeled back in a snarl.

She lunges, but I twist and catch her, using her momentum to drive her backward. Her shoulders slam into the wall of thorns, and there's a wet hiss as they pierce through her tunic and dig into her skin.

She claws at me, wild and furious, but I grab her wrist —the one holding the dagger—and slam it hard against the thorny wall. Her fingers loosen just enough so I can wrench the blade free.

Before she can recover, I pivot, driving my forearm across her chest and pinning her to the wall. Thorns dig deeper into her back. She snarls, trying to twist free.

I raise the stolen dagger and press it to her throat, the point steady against her pulse. Her breath catches. I lean in, close enough to feel her heartbeat stuttering beneath the blade.

Panting for breath, I think about the cut on her side and how it looked fresh and unhealed. How I always use kevrin powder on my blade to slow down the healing of any cuts.

"You're trying to kill me? And it was you, wasn't it? You attacked me in the sleeping quarters behind the Covenant building. You and some other loser."

"For the Alpha of Umbra." Rachel's eyes burn with undiminished hatred. "For him. For our pack's survival."

"What the fuck is happening?" Kieran demands from farther behind me.

I don't take my eyes off Rachel.

Her lip curls into a sneer. "You're a bitch who doesn't deserve to draw breath." Her gaze shifts to Theron and Kieran. "And you two... traitors to your own kind. Betraying your pack for Elios scum." Her eyes lock on Theron. "What would your father say, seeing his son and heir protecting her instead of slitting her throat when she fights me? You're a disgrace to the Shadowmane name."

She turns to Kieran, blood trickling from her split lip.

"And you, Stormfang. Your father sacrificed every-thing for the pack. He'd vomit at the sight of you now." Her voice grows wilder, more frantic. "Kill her! Kill her now and show the pack you're strong, not weak! Show your father you're worthy of the Umbra name, Theron!"

Kieran steps to my side and suddenly drives his blade straight into Rachel's throat.

The sound is sickening—flesh splitting, cartilage giving way with a wet crunch. Her eyes snap wide, not with fear but with disbelief. Blood pours over Kieran's hand, thick and fast, bubbling from her lips as she jerks once, then begins to crumple. I feel something splash on my face.

The silver lines on her manacle pulse—then fade into nothing.

She hits the ground hard.

I don't move.

"Fuck!" My breath catches somewhere between my ribs, my limbs frozen as the heat of what just happened rushes past me like a wave I didn't see coming. The dirt smells of iron and sweat.

Kieran doesn't even look at her, just wipes the blade against his sleeve and turns away like it's nothing.

But it isn't.

Not to me.

"What the hell did you just do?" I ask, stumbling back, frantically wiping my face with the sleeve of my jacket.

"That was on me to finish," Kieran says grimly, his voice hollow. "I asked the fucker to be my partner, and she betrayed us all. Fuck!" He rakes a hand through his matted hair, smearing mud and blood across his forehead.

I stare at Rachel's body, watching her blood seep into the dirt. My hand trembles as I lower my blade.

Theron finally steps forward, silent until now. He glances at Kieran, jaw tight, then shifts his gaze to me. His eyes soften.

"She would've killed you," he says evenly, as though he needs to say it out loud for all of us. "You did what had to be done."

Even as he says it, he moves toward me, not Kieran.

His arms go around me, strong and steady, pulling me into his chest. I don't even realize I'm shaking until I feel the heat of him, the weight of his hand cradling the back of my head.

"She made her choice," he murmurs. "And we made sure it ended with us."

"I'm sorry," I whisper, unable to take my eyes off her now-lifeless form.

"You have nothing to be sorry about," Theron says, staring down at me. His body is warm. "She was going to kill you for my father. That bastard won't stop until he's destroyed everything good in our territory."

"You killed her," I say to Kieran, the words coming out flat and disbelieving. "She's dead."

"She lost her privilege to live," he grunts.

"He's right," Theron says. "In the wilds, the law is clear—attempt to take a life, forfeit your own."

I break away from Theron, suddenly needing space. "This is supposed to be a sacred ritual, not a bloodbath!"

"It became a bloodbath the moment my father decided to try to murder you," Theron states firmly. "Rachel was just a pawn... expendable, like we all are to him."

Kieran crouches beside Rachel's body, searching her pockets. He pulls out a small leather pouch.

"I didn't want this." I stare at Rachel's body, at the crimson seeping into the mud. "Any of this."

Theron cups my face, turning me away from the corpse to look at him. His eyes are dark with emotion, almost black in the dim light. "This isn't your burden to carry. Everyone will need to know what happened here, but first, we need to finish what we started."

"We keep moving," Kieran agrees, standing up. "If Rachel was working for your father, then perhaps so are the rest of the Umbra wolves."

Something shifts at the edge of my vision.

I blink, my gaze snapping back to Rachel's body. The dirt around her is... moving. Subtle at first, like a breath rising from the ground itself. Then I see them—pale, slender roots emerging from the ground like tendrils, twitching and curling as they slither toward her limbs. One coils around her wrist, another wraps her ankle, and then more, writhing like they're alive.

They pull her slowly downward to where the ground cracks open. Inch by inch, she's claimed.

Blood-smudged dirt sinks beneath her weight as the roots weave over her chest and throat, sliding under her clothes and through her hair. Her fingers vanish next, then her boots, until only her face with wide-open eyes remains, staring straight through me.

And just like that, she's gone. Swallowed whole.

I take a step back, my breath caught somewhere between a gasp and a curse.

"All right," Kieran mutters beside me, his voice a little too loud in the silence. "That's new. Nature's got a real flair for drama."

He's trying to play it off, but I catch the way his hand tightens around his blade.

Theron's gaze stays fixed on the spot where Rachel vanished, the dirt now smooth and undisturbed as if she were never there at all. He finally exhales, a sound low and grim.

"The maze doesn't leave reminders."

We stand there in silence at first, then Theron turns to the wall of thorns.

"The tree woman said, 'Follow the chains that shimmer silver, like tears of the veiled moon. They will lead to what you seek.'"

I quickly tuck Rachel's blade into the back of my pants as we return to the chamber with the hanging chains, which seem to glow more brightly now. One chain in particular shines brighter than the others, swaying slightly despite the still air, pointing to an entrance door across from ours.

"That one," I say. "It wants us to follow its direction."

As we walk away, I can't help looking back at the passage where Rachel's body was. My stomach twists painfully. I've seen too much death today.

Theron takes my hand, entwining our fingers. "We stick together," he murmurs, glancing at me and Kieran. "We find the moonstone, we win this damn thing, and then we deal with my father. One step at a time."

The dark moon continues to shine overhead, casting long shadows that seem to point the way forward, deeper into the heart of the maze.

Kieran walks ahead, one hand always on his blade.

"You okay?" I ask quietly, catching up to him while Theron investigates a side passage.

"Fucking fantastic," he mutters, then sighs. "Sorry. My head's still... not right. Like there's a fog I can't shake." He rubs his temples. "And I just killed someone, so there's that."

The blunt admission startles me. "I'm sorry."

His amber eyes meet mine, hard and unflinching, then he shrugs. "I've made my peace with it."

"Just like that?"

"Just like that." He looks away.

Before I can respond, Theron rejoins us. "Nothing that way but more thorns," he says. "The chain is still leading us forward."

We continue on, the maze growing denser and disorienting. The walls seem to shift when we're not looking directly at them, changing configuration subtly. More than once, I glance back to find that our path has disappeared, replaced by a solid wall of thorns, but the silvery chain woven into the wall remains ahead of us.

"The maze doesn't want us going backward," I observe after the third time this happens.

"Or someone doesn't," Theron replies grimly.

The chain suddenly brightens, pulsing with an urgent light. It leads to a narrow opening barely wide enough for one person to squeeze through.

"I don't like this," Kieran says, peering into the gap. "Perfect spot for an ambush."

"The willow-woman said to follow the chains," I remind him.

"And we're just trusting a creepy tree spirit now?" Kieran arches an eyebrow.

"You have a better idea?" Theron challenges.

"Fine." Kieran sighs dramatically. "But if I die horribly, I'm haunting both of you." He turns to me with a twisted smile. "Especially you, Mooncrest. I'll be the ghost in your bedroom, watching you undress every night."

"Fuck off, Kieran," Theron growls, shoving him lightly.

"Just trying to lighten the mood," Kieran mutters with a wink at me. "Someone's gotta keep things interesting." But I notice how his hand trembles slightly as he reaches for his blade, how sweat beads on his forehead despite the cool air.

"I'll go first," I say, moving toward the opening.

Theron catches my arm. "Lyra—"

"I'm the smallest," I point out. "And I can recoil back faster if needed."

Theron hesitates, then nods reluctantly. "Be careful."

I edge through the narrow opening sideways, thorns catching at my clothes and hair. The passage is barely shoulder width and completely dark except for the faint glow of the chain ahead. After about ten feet, it widens suddenly, opening into a small circular chamber.

In the center stands a pedestal of rough-hewn stone, and upon it rests a gleaming object that glints from the moonlight filtering down from above and is hard to see at first. The chain we've been following dangles directly over it, its tip nearly touching it. It's so bright my eyes hurt.

"I think I found something!" I call back. "There's space in here!"

Theron squeezes through next, shuffling sideways, his steps careful as he takes in the chamber.

Behind him comes a loud grunt from Kieran. "If I lose a nipple to these thorns, I'm blaming both of you." A rustling pause. "Seriously, who designs a maze with bramble-covered birth canals?" Another sharp snag on his trousers. "Ow! Great. That's it. These pants are officially enemies." He finally stumbles through, looking like he wrestled a wild bush—and lost.

"What is this place?" Theron asks, eyes scanning the circular chamber.

The walls here are different—less thorny vines and more ancient stone—covered in faded carvings. I run my fingers lightly over a massive wolf, its head raised toward a full moon carved in gleaming silver. Around it, smaller wolves knelt or bared their teeth in challenge—it's hard to tell which. Another panel shows hooded figures encircling a bound shape beneath a bleeding crescent, the lines worn but unmistakably deliberate.

A story, half erased by time.

"These are old," I murmur. "Older than the Onyx Covenant, perhaps. They look like..."

"The original pack markings," Theron finishes, examining another section of the wall. "Before the split. When Elios and Umbra were one."

"What's that on the pedestal?" Kieran asks, stepping toward the center of the room.

"Careful," I warn, but he's already reaching for the object.

As his fingers touch it, the entire chamber floods with brilliant silver light. Kieran jerks back. When the light fades, we can see the object clearly—a key, ornately crafted from what appears to be moonstone, its handle carved in the shape of a wolf's head.

"The Bloodstone Key," I breathe, recognizing it from the ancient texts in the temple. "It's real."

"What does it open?" Kieran asks, rubbing his eyes.

"According to legend, the door to reconciliation,"

Theron says, his voice hushed with awe. "The way back to unity between our packs."

"Great," Kieran mutters. "A metaphorical key. Very helpful."

"I don't think it's metaphorical," I say, reaching out tentatively and wrapping my fingers around the key. It pulses faintly in my palm, warm to the touch, almost like it's alive. For a second, I brace for another flash of light, another trap, but nothing happens. Just a soft hum against my skin.

We fan out, searching the chamber. I hold the key tightly, scanning the pedestal, the floor, and even the carved walls for any sign of a matching keyhole.

"Could be hidden under something," Theron mutters, running his fingers along the base of the pedestal. Then he turns to the stone walls, squinting at the faded carvings. "These symbols... some kind of sequence. Could be a locking mechanism."

"Could also just be very old art," Kieran calls from the opposite wall. "Or the world's worst interior decorator."

I catch the edge of a laugh, then freeze.

A sound. Faint but distinct. A soft rustling from the narrow passage behind us.

I glance at Theron. He's already gone still.

Kieran hears it next. "What the hell was that?"

I don't answer. My fingers close around the key, and I shove it deep into my pocket.

Then the ground trembles.

A dull, distant thud, followed by another. Louder. Closer.

"We need to move," Kieran says sharply, his sarcasm gone in an instant. "Now."

"There!" Theron points to a break in the stone wall, half obscured by hanging moss and shadows.

We don't hesitate. I sprint for it with Theron in front of me and Kieran bringing up the rear, his blade already drawn. Behind us, a bone-splitting screech tears through the chamber.

Kieran swears and shoves me forward. "Go! Go!"

The corridor beyond the arch is narrow and crooked, its walls more stone than thorn. We rush through it blindly, the path twisting as it slopes upward. The screeching behind us grows louder, angrier, joined now by the sound of heavy, deliberate footsteps—each one a thunderous quake through the floor.

My breaths are racing, dread thumping through me.

"Don't look back!" Theron shouts.

So I don't.

Until I do.

I risk a glance and catch only a glimpse—just long enough to make my blood run cold.

It's tall. Hulking. Broad shoulders hunched beneath twisted, bark-like armor. Its skin is dark and glistening, streaked with something slick. Its face is a ruin of bone and exposed muscle, two molten eyes glowing in its skull. And the sound it makes—it's not a roar.

It wants to hunt.

"Go!" I scream, and this time, I run faster.

Theron leads us deeper, the stone passage a blur of gray and shadow. I lose track of time, of distance. There's only breath, burning legs, and the pounding in my ears. The beast doesn't follow us directly, but the echoes haunt every turn.

Eventually, the sound fades.

The ground begins to level out. The walls widen. And then, suddenly—grass.

Blades beneath my boots, soft underfoot. We stumble into a narrow clearing, barely more than a pocket of space carved into the maze, the thorn walls high on every side.

Kieran collapses first, landing on his back with a groan. "Good news... not dead. Bad news... probably still gonna die."

Theron presses a hand to the wall, chest heaving. "It didn't follow us."

"Or it's circling around for a dramatic entrance," Kieran mutters. "Real flair for theatrics, that one."

I wipe sweat from my brow. My limbs are shaking. My hair is a nest of leaves and blood and who knows what else.

I let out a long yawn, sudden and dragging.

Kieran raises a brow. "You're kidding. You're actually tired right now?"

I rub my eyes. "We've hit a dead end. If that thing didn't come this way, it's not likely to. We can retrace our steps after some rest."

Theron gives the wall another once-over. "One entrance. Defensible."

We all exchange a look, then wordlessly sink to the grass.

"We'll take turns watching. I'll go first," Theron says.

"I'll take second," Kieran grumbles, already half horizontal.

"And me third."

SIXTEEN

THERON

"Do you think Aria's okay?" Lyra asks, her voice cutting through the heavy silence.

"She's with Orion," I explain. "She'll be fine. He won't let anything happen to her."

If I were with Aria instead of Orion, I'd tear apart anything that threatened her—not because I feel anything for Kieran's little obsession, but because she matters to Lyra. And anything that matters to Lyra is under my protection, whether she wants it or not.

Kieran sprawls on his back a few feet away, one boot half off like the lazy fuck couldn't be bothered to finish the job. Despite everything, affection tugs at me. There's no one I'd rather have at my back in a fight, even if he drives me insane the rest of the time.

"She's feisty," he says, eyes fixed on the stars above us. "Takes no shit. Great with a blade. Kind of terrifying, actually."

I catch the slight softening in his voice when he mentions Aria. For all his swagger and endless parade of conquests, Kieran's showing a vulnerability toward the girl.

Lyra smirks. "Yeah, you would know."

Kieran's head twists toward her. "Ah. She told you, hey?"

Lyra hums in response, the sound making Kieran narrow his eyes suspiciously.

"Girls share things," she says, a teasing lilt to her voice that makes my skin heat. "Everything. Every detail, you know."

I fight back a grin as Kieran props himself up on one elbow. For all his bragging, the idea of being discussed by the women makes him squirm. Hilarious.

"Yeah? Like that?" he counters. "Then I need to know exactly how she painted me—just to ensure fairness. Can't have you walking around thinking I'm anything less than fucking legendary."

A harsh laugh escapes me. "Pretty sure it's not an issue. Lyra only cares about me."

The words come out as a claim, staking territory that part of me knows isn't mine to claim anymore.

Lyra's laugh is tender, but I don't miss the darkening of her lavender eyes as they meet mine. She still wants me. The knowledge burns through me like fire.

Kieran looks between us, and a slow, wolfish grin stretches across his face.

"Oh. I see. You two as well, huh? Did the dirty deed in the woods? Rolled in the ferns? Howled at the full moon?"

Memories flood my mind unbidden—Lyra riding me, her legs wrapped around my waist, firelight painting her skin. Her nails dug into my skin as she came apart in my arms. The taste of her, like night-blooming jasmine, is addictive.

"Fuck off," I growl at Kieran playfully. My lips curl into a smile that's all teeth. "Jealous?"

"Always," he fires back instantly. "Just wondering if our Alpha-in-training here actually knows what to do with a woman like Lyra or if he just stands around brooding dramatically while she does all the work."

"Trust me," I say, eyes locked on Lyra's as a flush spreads across her cheeks and down her neck. "I know exactly what to do with her."

I remember every inch of her body—the sensitive spot at the nape of her neck that makes her gasp when kissed, the way she arches when I trail my fingers along her spine, the small sounds she makes when she's close to breaking. *Mine.*

Kieran flings an arm over his mouth and nose dramatically. "For fuck's sake, control your pheromones. Some of us are trying not to get eaten by the murder maze, remember?"

Lyra covers her face with her hands, but not before I catch the quickening of her breath. "Oh Gods," she groans.

My body responds instantly to her reaction, my cock

hardening painfully against my pants. I shift my position, grateful for the single orb of light hanging off the walls and the shadows that hide my erection. Not the time. Not the place. But fuck if I don't want to cross the clearing and remind her exactly what she means to me.

Kieran lies back down with a theatrical sigh, drawing me from dangerous memories. "You know, it's moments like these I realize I'm the real romantic soul of this group. All heart. All class."

Despite the blood and dirt covering him, despite the fact that he killed a woman tonight without hesitation, there's something undeniably charming about Kieran's bullshit. It's why he's my right hand, my brother in everything but blood.

"And definitely all modesty," Lyra replies dryly.

"Exactly," he says without missing a beat. "Someone's gotta keep the tone high while the rest of you fuck like animals. Some of us have standards, you know."

"Like pinning Aria against a tree while others sleep?" Lyra's chuckling.

It's a low blow, but Kieran's laughing.

"That was... tactical," he says, an unusual defensiveness creeping into his voice.

"Tactical?" Lyra asks, curiosity getting the better of her.

"Absolutely." Kieran nods with mock solemnity. "Confined space. Strategic positioning. Excellent use of available surfaces."

"Shut the fuck up with your tactical crap," I say. For all

his faults, Kieran is the only person besides Lyra who sees me as more than just the heir to Umbra, the next in line to carry on my father's bloody legacy.

Lyra's smiling, and the sight of it loosens something tight in my chest. There's been too little laughter tonight, too much blood, betrayal, and death. I'd kill a hundred Rachels just to keep that smile on her face.

I watch her, memorizing every detail—the way her hair spills across the grass like liquid moonlight, the gentle curve of her hips, the delicate lines of her moon priestess markings that shimmer faintly in the darkness on her brow. If we die in this maze, I want her image burned into my mind as the last thing I see.

Kieran's eyes are beginning to close despite his efforts to stay alert. One hand still rests on his dagger, ready even in exhaustion.

"Rest," I order, the command flowing naturally from years of training warriors. "Both of you. I'll keep watch."

The twisted branches surrounding our clearing shift slightly, though no wind stirs them. I don't trust this momentary peace.

"You need sleep, too," Lyra argues, her voice already thick with exhaustion.

"I'll wake you when it's not my turn," I lie, knowing I have no intention of sleeping while we're exposed like this. Not when my father has proven he's willing to sabotage a sacred ritual to see her dead.

She wants to protest—I can see it in the stubborn set

of her jaw—but her body betrays her. Within minutes, she curls onto her side in the lush grass, blonde hair fanning out around her.

Kieran's already snoring softly, his body surrendering to exhaustion despite his best efforts. In sleep, the cynical mask falls away, revealing the boy I grew up with before my father's cruelty hardened us both.

I move closer to Lyra, positioning myself between her and the most obvious entrance to our clearing. Not touching—I don't trust myself to stop if I start—but close enough to feel the heat radiating from her body, to catch the scent of night-blooming jasmine that clings to her skin despite the blood and dirt of the maze.

"Sleep," I murmur, pitching my voice low enough that it won't disturb Kieran. "I won't let anything hurt you."

The dark moon watches from above, witness to the blood we've spilled and the blood yet to come. I know my father, know the depth of his hatred for the Elios pack.

I settle into a crouch, back to Lyra and Kieran, facing outward toward the maze. Let the thorns come. Let my father send his assassins. Let the ancient evils of this place rise against us.

They'll find me waiting, a shadow among shadows, guarding what's mine.

The night deepens. My muscles ache from maintaining the same vigilant posture, but I don't dare move. Behind me, Lyra's breathing remains deep and steady, occasionally punctuated by Kieran's soft snores.

A sound breaks the silence—faint voices carrying on the still air. I tense, hand tightening around my blade's hilt.

I strain to hear, to make out words or recognize the speakers, but the voices are too distant. They echo strangely, bouncing off the maze walls, making it impossible to pinpoint their direction.

Are they other competitors? Something else entirely?

My eyelids grow heavy as the dark moon reaches its zenith. The knife feels heavier in my hand with each passing moment. I shake my head, trying to clear the fog that's settling over my thoughts.

Just exhaustion. Just the aftermath of combat and poison and death. Nothing more.

The voices come again, louder this time, then fade to nothing.

My head nods forward.

I jerk it back up, blinking hard.

The stars blur overhead.

I dig my nails into my palm, using pain to stay alert.

The dark moon watches.

My eyes close.

Just for a second.

Just to rest them.

Just...

I jolt awake with a gasp, disorientation flooding my system.

Sunlight. Pale and watery, but definitely sunlight—not the dark moon's silver glow.

Fuck.

I passed out. After swearing to keep watch, I fucking passed out.

Panic surges through me as I take in our surroundings. We're no longer in the circular clearing where we stopped to rest. Instead, we lie in the middle of a wide path, thorny walls rising on either side—but not the same walls as before. These are shifting before my eyes, branches untangling and reweaving themselves in new configurations, opening passages that weren't there seconds ago, closing others that had seemed permanent.

The entire maze is rearranging itself in the dawn light.

Kieran still sleeps a few feet away, one arm flung over his face. Lyra lies between us, her white-blonde hair spread across the ground, her face peaceful in slumber.

I scramble to my feet, blade in hand, spinning in a slow circle. Which way did we come from? Which way were we headed? The maze's transformation has erased all familiar landmarks.

"Kieran!" I blurt out, kicking his boot. "Wake the fuck up!"

He groans, rolls over, and then his eyes snap open as consciousness returns. "What's your problem?" he mumbles, then pauses mid-stretch as he notices our changed surroundings. "What the fuck?"

"We moved," I say tersely, continuing to scan for threats. "Or the maze moved us while we slept."

Kieran sits up, rubbing his eyes, then freezes as he takes in the shifting walls. "Shit. Are those...?"

"Moving? Yes." I watch as a thick branch untangles itself from the wall to our right, snaking across to join the opposite side, forming a new archway where a solid barrier had been moments before.

Kieran gets to his feet. The rising sun casts long shadows across his face, highlighting the exhaustion and dried blood still caked along his hairline.

"You fucking fell asleep, didn't you?" he accuses, scrubbing a hand over his face. His eyes widen as he takes in the shifting walls.

I don't deny falling asleep. Can't deny what's obvious. I shrug.

"Well, shit on my grandfather's grave," Kieran says with a low whistle, watching as another section of wall unravels and reknits itself farther down the path. "Gotta hand it to the Onyx Covenant—they really know how to throw a party. Nothing says *sacred ritual* like a maze that decides to redecorate while you're sleeping." He runs a hand through his matted hair, grimacing when his fingers catch on dried blood.

"Some say this maze and its life force have been here way before the Onyx Covenant was established, and now they simply bow to its power."

"That's not terrifying at all. So what's the plan?"

I crouch beside Lyra. "Lyra," I say, gently shaking her shoulder. "Wake up. We need to move."

She doesn't respond, her body limp beneath my touch.

"Lyra?" I shake her harder, alarm building in my chest. "Lyra!"

Nothing. Not even a flicker of her eyelids.

"Fuck, she's not waking up," I growl, pressing my fingers to her throat. Her pulse beats strong and steady, and her breathing is normal. She looks like she's in a deep, peaceful sleep—too peaceful for our circumstances.

"What's wrong with her?" Kieran asks, crouching on her other side.

"I don't know." I check her body for new wounds or new signs of poison but find nothing. "She was fine when we fell asleep."

"Uh, Theron?" Kieran's voice has an odd note to it.

"What?"

"Her fist is fucking glowing like a moonlit beacon."

I look down at her other side, and he's right... Lyra's right hand is clenched into a tight fist. Sure enough, faint light pulses between her fingers, leaking out in thin rays.

"The key," I growl, remembering the Bloodstone Key

she'd found in the heart of the maze. "Looks like she's holding it."

The delicate silver lines of her moon priestess markings on her brow begin to illuminate, pulsing in perfect synchronization with the light in her fist. The spiral birthmark on her wrist glows brightest of all, its light so intense I can see it through the thin fabric of her sleeve.

"What the actual fuck is happening to her?" Kieran hisses, backing away slightly. "Is this normal Elios priestess bullshit, or should we be running for our lives right now? Because I vote for running."

I remain at Lyra's side, torn between fascination and terror. The silver light spreads, following the network of barely visible priestess markings that cover her body—lines I've traced with my fingers and lips in darkness now revealed in brilliant luminescence. They form a complex pattern across her skin—not random decorative markings, as I'd always assumed, but a map. A fucking map.

"It's old magic," I say, recognizing the signs from ancient texts in my mother's hidden journals. "Veiled moon magic. The strongest fucking kind."

"Great," Kieran drawls, edging closer despite his obvious unease. "Because what this nightmare needed was ancient magic. Is it hurting her? Because if she dies, I'm blaming you, and I'm not explaining it to her terrifying friend with the knives."

"I don't think so." I shake my head, though I'm far from certain.

Lyra's body suddenly rises several inches off the

ground, suspended by nothing but the silver light pulsing through her. Her hair floats around her face as if underwater, her clothing rippling with unseen energy.

"Fucking shit," Kieran breathes, taking another step back. "This is some ancestral spirit nonsense right here. Next thing you know, she'll be channeling every dead Alpha since the First Pack."

The walls of the maze react to her transformation, their movement accelerating. Branches twist and unravel faster, thorns retracting and extending, new passages forming and old ones disappearing in the span of heartbeats.

"It's responding to her," I realize aloud. "The maze... it's changing for her."

"Or because of her," Kieran counters, his usual sarcasm replaced by genuine awe. "Either way, this is seriously scary, even for this ritual."

Lyra's suspended body begins to rotate slowly, her head tipping back as if she's listening to something beyond our perception. The light from her markings intensifies until it's almost painful to look at her directly.

"We need to do something," I say, reaching toward her, then hesitating. What if touching her makes it worse? What if this is part of the ritual—a test we weren't told about?

"Like what? In case you haven't noticed, we've got a floating, glowing girl and a maze that's rearranging itself by the second. I don't think the Onyx Covenant manual covered this scenario."

I reach for her hand, finding it cooler to the touch.

"Theron," Kieran says quietly. "I don't think we can stop this."

I grip Lyra's hand tighter, watching helplessly as her eyelids flutter, revealing just the whites of her eyes.

"I can't lose her," I say, my voice breaking. "Not like this."

SEVENTEEN

LYRA

I stand in a vast, empty space filled with silver mist. There's no ground beneath my feet, no sky above, just an endless swirling fog that glows with the gentle radiance of moonlight. I don't remember how I got here or where here even is. The last thing I recall is falling asleep in the maze clearing with Theron keeping watch.

The mist before me begins to gather and condense, forming a figure of pure light. Its shape is never constant, flowing and shifting. The glow it emanates matches exactly the intense silver-blue light that adorns the sacred walls in the inner sanctum of the moon priestess temple. The light pulses like a heartbeat, sending waves of energy rippling through the mist around me.

This can only be one being—the Elios Moon God, the ancient deity our pack has worshipped since the First Pack split. I've seen the carved images in the sacred chambers where *only high priestesses are allowed, chambers I snuck into as a child, hungry for knowledge forbidden to me.*

"You have to give in to him," a voice resonates, not through my ears but directly into my mind. "Help Theron win."

My shoulders pull back instinctively, rejection immediate. "What? But then our pack—my pack—the Elios will lose again." The words taste like ash on my tongue. "Is that what you want? For Umbra to dominate us once more?" I'm starting to wonder if this is some trickery by the Umbra moon.

The light shifts, patterns changing, almost like expressions crossing a face. "Your distrust, your indecision, is what is blocking you and will continue to do so. You will be stuck in this maze for eternity until you choose."

"Choose what?" I demand, feeling a surge of anger. "To betray my people? To submit to Umbra rule?"

"Trust him. Help him win." The figure's light dims slightly, then flares brighter. "The path forward requires blood and trust. Old divisions must fall for new growth to emerge."

I shake my head, feeling the weight of generations of conflict pressing down on me.

"You don't understand. It's not that simple. If Umbra wins—"

"If Theron wins," the figure corrects, and somehow, I know the distinction is crucial.

The luminous being pulses. "Your path lies not in the outcomes you fear but in the unity you have forgotten. Five rights. That is your path."

"Five rights?" I repeat, confusion momentarily displacing my internal turmoil. "What does that mean?"

The being doesn't answer.

"Why should I trust him?" I challenge, thinking of how Theron broke my heart, how he chose his pack over me once before. So, he could do it again, right? Yet the thought alone aches deep under my rib cage. "He's Umbra. His father wants me dead."

"He is not his father," the light pulses more intensely. "And you are more than your pack designation."

I feel myself beginning to spiral into deeper confusion. "But my people—"

"Will suffer if the division continues," the being interrupts. "As will his. As will all."

The images shift again, showing me glimpses of a future I don't want to see—bodies strewn across contested territories, children crying, blood soaking into soil that yields no harvest.

"This is what awaits if the old hatreds persist." The voice grows somber. "This is what your indecision feeds."

"That's not fair," I protest, feeling tears burn behind my eyes. "This isn't my responsibility alone."

"No," the being agrees. "But your choice now will determine if change becomes possible. Your destiny is within your grasp, Lyra Mooncrest. Not as an Elios victory or an Umbra defeat, but as something new entirely."

I close my eyes, trying to center myself amid the chaos of emotions. My loyalty to my pack wars with my feelings for Theron, with my own ambitions, and with the weight of expectations I've carried my entire life.

"I don't know if I can do this," I admit, voice cracking. "I don't know if I'm strong enough."

The light pulses gently now, almost comforting. "You need to let go."

"Let go of what?" I whisper.

"Of who you believe you should be. Of the boundaries that limit what you could become."

As the being speaks, I feel something within me shifting, like a key turning in a lock I didn't know existed. The silver light grows brighter, enveloping me completely, and I feel myself falling, spinning—

I gasp awake, the sensation of falling jerking me back to consciousness. Instead of hitting the ground, I feel strong arms catch and cradle me against a solid chest. Theron. His scent fills my senses as my eyes flutter open.

"I've got you," he murmurs, his silvery gaze smiling at the corners. "You're back. Thought I'd lost you."

"What... what happened?" My voice comes out raspy, my throat dry.

"You don't remember?" Theron asks, helping me stand, though his hands linger on my arms as if worried I might collapse again.

Kieran hovers nearby, his usual cocky expression replaced by something close to awe. "You went full moon priestess on us. Floating, glowing, the whole ancestral spirit package." He gestures vaguely at my face. "Your brow is still doing the glow thing, by the way."

I reach up, feeling warmth under my fingertips, where

the most intricate of my priestess markings trace a delicate pattern across my forehead.

"You were possessed or something," Kieran continues, keeping a careful distance. "That's some serious priestess shit, even for an Elios." Despite his flippant words, I can see he's genuinely unsettled. "I was expecting you to start prophesying the end of the world or demanding virgin sacrifices."

"Shut up, Kieran," Theron growls.

I take a steadying breath, images from my vision still vivid in my mind. "I think I just spoke with the Elios Moon God."

"The what now?" Kieran blinks.

"The deity of my pack," I clarify. "At least, I think that's who it was. A being of light, ancient, powerful."

Theron's expression grows serious. "What did it want?"

I look at him, really look at him, at the man who once held my heart and perhaps never truly relinquished his claim on it. The vision's message echoes in my mind.

"I need to be honest," I say, the words feeling like stones in my throat. "I've been struggling with something..." I pause, gathering courage. "I've been battling with the idea of you winning, with my pack coming second again, with whether I should ensure Aria and Orion win instead."

Theron's expression doesn't change, but something in his eyes darkens. He says nothing, just watches me, his jaw tight.

"Don't ask me how I could do it, but I've been torn," I continue, needing to get this out. "Part of me has been holding back, wondering if I should sabotage our chances."

A muscle twitches in Theron's jaw as he glances down, then back up at me. The silence stretches between us, heavy with unspoken emotions.

"I think it's been holding me back, us back," I admit. "Working against everything we've accomplished together. It goes against everything I want for myself, but..." I take a deep breath. "The vision showed me that I need to help you win. That it's what the Elios Moon God wants. This must be a vision for a reason, right?"

Theron is quiet for a long moment, his expression unreadable.

"I can't say it doesn't hurt to hear that, Lyra, but I can't blame you." He runs a hand through his dark hair. "The division between our packs has brought up so much anger and hatred when we should be one. That's my goal —to unite the packs, not suppress yours."

I blink at his sincerity. He's hinted at similar things before, but I wasn't sure how he would actually ever achieve that without a full-out war.

"But your father..." I start. "And the others who don't want that..."

"Will have to be dealt with," Kieran interrupts, stepping closer. His amber eyes burn with determination. "Listen, Lyra, you just had a fucking divine vision. A god spoke to you. So let's go change this shit." He grins suddenly, wild and reckless. "Fuck the old farts. We have a god on our side!"

Despite everything, I feel a laugh bubble up from somewhere deep inside me.

Theron steps closer, his eyes finding mine, unwavering.

"Then we do this together, all the way," he says, his voice low and resolute. "No more doubts between us. My father, the packs, all of it—we face it as one." He extends his hand to me, a gesture that carries more weight than words could express. I accept it, and he drags me into a powerful hug. I melt into it, and my next breath hiccups all the way down to my lungs.

"The vision gave me a message," I say, remembering. "*Five rights*. That's what it said is our path."

Theron's brow furrows in thought. "Could be as simple as us taking five right turns on our journey." He gestures to where the maze has created a new passage before us. "Let's try it."

We set off, following the cleared path. At the first junction, we take a right, then another, and another. The maze seems to be cooperating, offering us exactly the turns we need. After the fourth right turn, a sense of anticipation builds in my chest.

"One more," I murmur as we approach another fork.

We take the fifth right turn—and find nothing. Just another winding passage that seems to lead deeper into the maze.

"What the fuck?" Kieran mutters, looking around in confusion. "There's nothing here."

We continue forward, hoping for some sign, some indication that we're on the right path, but the passage only narrows, eventually leading to a dead end—a solid wall of thorns that blocks our way completely.

"That's it?" Kieran kicks at the ground in frustration. "Your god gave us directions to a fucking wall?"

Theron approaches the wall, examining it closely. "Maybe there's something we're missing." He turns to me. "What else did the vision say? Anything that might help us?"

I close my eyes, trying to recall every word, every image. "Something about blood. I think it needs blood."

Before either of them can stop me, I step forward and press my palm against the thorny wall. Sharp points pierce my skin, and I wince but don't pull away. Blood wells from the small wounds, bright red against my pale skin, and drips onto the plants.

"Lyra!" Theron rushes to my back but doesn't move me.

My blood seeps into the thorns, disappearing as if absorbed by the very material of the wall. For a moment, nothing happens. Then a pulse of silver light, similar to the one in my vision, spreads from where my hand touches the thorns, racing along the wall in all directions.

The deadly thorns begin to soften, to change. Green shoots emerge, unfurling into leaves, then buds, and then flowers of impossible beauty—blossoms that glow with faint silver light, that seem to sing without sound as they open to the morning sun. The transformation is breathtaking.

The wall isn't disappearing—it's transforming, becoming something alive, vibrant, and welcoming instead of a barrier.

"Holy shit," Kieran breathes, his usual sarcasm abandoned in the face of the marvel before us.

I feel a strange draining sensation, as if the wall is pulling more than just the blood from my cuts. My vision begins to blur at the edges, my knees weakening.

"It's taking too much," I gasp, suddenly unable to pull away from the wall, my head spinning. The flowers continue to spread, more and more of them erupting along the thorny surface, but my strength is fading with each new bloom.

"Lyra!" Theron's voice seems to come from far away. Strong hands grasp my shoulders, pulling me back, breaking my connection to the transformed wall.

I stumble into his arms, the world spinning around me. "I'm okay," I mumble, though I'm not sure that's true. My head feels light, my limbs heavy.

"You're not okay," Theron growls, his arms tightening around me. "What the fuck was that?"

Before I can answer, a sound like stone grinding against stone fills the air. We turn to see the flowered wall sliding aside, revealing a hidden passage beyond.

Kieran peers into the darkness. "Looks like your blood sacrifice worked."

With Theron's help, I stand straighter, fighting off the lingering weakness.

"Let's go," I suggest, determination returning. "We've come too far to stop now."

We step through the opening into a small chamber hewn from ancient stone. The walls are covered in carvings—the old language, symbols that even I, trained in the temple, barely recognize.

And there, in the center of the chamber, bathed in a shaft of sunlight, rests an object that makes my breath catch.

The Onyx Moonstone.

Not the key we found earlier, but what the key was meant to unlock. A perfect sphere of translucent crystal that seems to contain the essence of moonlight within it, swirling, alive, and calling to something deep within me.

It rests in an elaborate cradle of interwoven silver and obsidian branches. The branches form a complex cage around the stone, with narrow gaps between them just barely wide enough to glimpse the treasure within. The entire structure sits atop a circular pedestal carved with ancient symbols.

Small thorns protrude from the metallic branches, positioned in a way that makes simply reaching in impossible without being pierced from multiple angles.

"Well, that's just fucking perfect," Kieran mutters, eyeing the apparatus. "Why can't anything ever be simple?"

EIGHTEEN

LYRA

The Moonstone gleams in its prison of thorns and metallic branches, suspended in the center of the chamber like a captured fragment of night sky.

I step forward, drawn to it. The intricate cage of interwoven branches looks both beautiful and deadly. Dozens of thorns jut from the metallic arms, promising to draw blood from anyone foolish enough to reach directly for the treasure they protect.

"Gods above," I breathe, circling the structure slowly. The air feels charged, heavy with the weight of centuries.

Theron moves silently beside me, his presence solid and reassuring despite everything between us. He studies the pedestal.

"What do you make of these?" he asks, gesturing toward the markings etched into the stone base.

I kneel before the pedestal. The stone feels cool

against my knees. I study the markings. "They're celestial runes," I say. "Similar to what we use in the Elios Temple."

Kieran whistles low, crouching on the other side of the Throne. His reddish hair falls across his face as he examines the intricate cage.

"Lucky for us, we've got someone who can actually read this cryptic nonsense," he says with a grin. "I'd be trying to poke everything in sight by now."

"And you'd be full of thorns like a pincushion," Theron replies. He turns to me, his expression growing serious again. "Can you translate them?"

I trace my fingers just above the surface of the runes. They form two overlapping circles around the base of the pedestal, with intricate lines connecting various points.

"Give me a moment," I murmur, focusing intently. "They're dialect variants... older than what I'm used to seeing."

"Take your time," Theron says, leaning in closer to me. "We've come too far to rush now."

His closeness sends welcome warmth spreading through me.

"Hey," Kieran says suddenly, moving to the wall of the chamber to our left. "Anyone else hear that?"

We fall silent, listening. Faint voices echo from somewhere beyond the wall, muffled but drawing closer.

"Someone's coming," Theron confirms, straightening to his full height. The transformation is immediate—the relaxed posture vanishes, replaced by the coiled readiness of a predator.

"I count two distinct voices," he continues, head tilted slightly. "Moving parallel to us."

Kieran presses his ear against the wall. "Definitely getting closer."

The voices suddenly become clearer, as if they've turned down a corridor that brings them alongside our chamber.

"...should be around here somewhere," a female voice says, frustration evident. "The clues pointed in this direction."

"We'll find it before they do," a deeper voice replies with smug confidence.

I exchange glances with Theron. "Selene and Erebus," I mouth silently.

He nods, a muscle twitching in his jaw.

That bitch who attacked me in the sleeping quarters, trying to kill me.

"Oh, perfect," Kieran mutters.

Theron gestures for us to return to the pedestal. "They don't know we're here yet," he whispers. "Let's keep our advantage."

"Hello?" Selene's voice calls out, closer now. "Is someone there?"

We freeze, exchanging glances.

Kieran raises his eyebrows in silent question. Theron shakes his head fractionally—a command to remain quiet that Kieran accepts with a slight nod. The wordless communication between them speaks of years fighting side by side, trusting each other with their lives.

"I could've sworn I heard voices," Selene says, her words clear enough now that she must be just on the other side of the wall.

"Your imagination again," Erebus replies dismissively. "Come on, this passage loops around. I think I see a chamber entrance ahead."

The urgency crystallizes my focus. I turn back to the runes, pushing all else from my mind.

"The markings are a celestial map," I say quietly, tracing the flowing script. "It references our two moons and their alignment during what it calls... the Blood Harmony."

"The Bloodstone Moons," Theron translates, his eyes lighting with recognition. "That's what my people call them when both moons take on the reddish hue during harvest season."

Kieran runs a hand through his hair. "How does that help us get the shiny rock without becoming thorn decorations?"

I continue studying the runes, translating fragments. "There's something here about *five points* and a *crown of night*."

"The Hunter's Crown," Theron says immediately. "It's a constellation visible only during the Blood Moon alignment—five stars that form a crescent. My people use it for navigation during the hunts."

I look up at him, surprised by the connection between our packs' astronomical systems.

"We call it the Reaper's Sickle in Elios," I say. "But yes, the same formation."

"Touching cultural exchange," Kieran interjects, "but those two assholes out there might be finding the Moonstone any moment now, and I'd rather not share our prize."

He's right. The sounds of footsteps and voices have faded slightly as Selene and Erebus moved around the curve of the maze, but they'll find their way to us soon enough.

I refocus on the pedestal and notice something I missed before—five small indentations arranged in a crescent pattern among the runes, each one the size of a fingertip.

"Look," I say, pointing them out. "These match the pattern of the Hunter's Crown—the Reaper's Sickle."

Theron kneels beside me, examining them closely. "Pressure points," he suggests.

Kieran leans over from the other side. "So, we press them, and the cage opens? Seems too simple."

"No," I say, continuing to translate. "There's more here. *When crowns of night align, five points of power must awaken...*" I pause, struggling with the next symbols. "*In the order of their birth.*"

"The order of their birth?" Kieran echoes. "What does that even mean?"

Theron's eyes meet mine, and I see the same realization dawning in their gray depths. "The stars appear in sequence when the constellation rises," he says.

I nod. "The first star appears in the east, then the next, until all five form the crown—or sickle. They're born in sequence across the night sky."

"So, we press them in the same order they appear in the sky," Kieran surmises, looking between us. "East to west."

"That's my interpretation," I agree.

Kieran raises his hand to the sun and quickly says, "Northeast. The energy flow begins there."

Theron nods. "So, the sequence starts with this one." He indicates the indentation closest to the northeast corner.

"I think so," I explain, but doubt niggles at the edges of my mind. If we're wrong, who knows what might happen? The thorns could be venomous, the entire apparatus could collapse, or—worse—we could damage the Moonstone itself.

"Wait," Kieran says, frowning. "How do we know the indentations correspond exactly to the stars? What if this one—" he points to the smallest indentation, "—is actually the first star?"

It's a good question. I reexamine the runes, searching for more clues. "There's something here about size... *The smallest light first breaks the darkness.*"

"That settles it," Theron says, identifying the smallest of the five indentations. "We start with this one, then follow in increasing size."

"Hold on," I say, noticing yet another layer to the runes. "There's a warning here. *False steps wake the thorns.*"

Kieran grimaces. "Wonderful. Get it wrong, and we get skewered."

"Footsteps," Theron hisses suddenly, his head turning toward the chamber entrance. "They've found the right corridor."

My heart pounds against my ribs.

"I'll do it," I say, positioning my finger above the smallest indentation.

Theron's hand covers mine, gently but firmly moving it aside. "No," he says, his voice allowing no argument. "My responsibility."

"This isn't about protection, Theron," I snap, irritated by his assumption. "I can read the runes. I know what I'm doing."

His eyes harden, not with anger but with determination. "This isn't protection, Lyra. It's strategy. You're the only one who can read these markings. If something goes wrong, you need to be uninjured to figure out the next step."

Put that way, his logic is sound. Kieran watches our exchange with poorly concealed impatience.

"Fine," I concede. "But be careful."

Theron nods once, then presses his index finger firmly against the smallest indentation.

For a heartbeat, nothing happens. Then, a soft click resonates through the chamber, and one of the silver branches shifts slightly, rotating a few degrees clockwise.

The thorns along that branch retract into the metal with tiny mechanical whispers.

"It worked," Kieran whispers, eyes wide.

"One down," Theron says, not celebrating yet. "Which next?"

I identify the second-smallest indentation. "This one should represent the second star—it appears slightly higher in the formation."

Theron presses it. Another click, another branch shifting, more thorns retracting.

We continue through the sequence, each press followed by mechanical movement within the cage. With the fourth indentation, a narrow path opens through the structure of metal and thorns—not enough to reach the Moonstone, but close.

"Last one," I say, indicating the final, largest indentation.

Theron presses it without hesitation.

Nothing happens.

"That can't be right," I mutter, frustration building inside me. "We followed the sequence perfectly."

"Maybe there's a timing element?" Kieran suggests, shifting nervously. "The voices are getting closer."

Indeed, I can now hear Selene and Erebus clearly, their footsteps echoing just outside the chamber entrance.

"There's nothing about timing in the runes," I say, scanning them again frantically. "There must be something we missed."

That's when I notice a smaller set of symbols beneath the main inscription, partially obscured by years of dust. I brush it away carefully.

"*As above, so below,*" I translate. "*The reflection reveals the path.*"

"Reflection?" Kieran looks around wildly. "I don't see any mirrors in here."

"Not literal reflection," Theron states, his eyes fixed on the pedestal. "The stars' reflection. The Hunter's Crown is mirrored in the waters below it in the ancient sky charts."

Understanding washes over me. "It's a test of knowledge," I breathe. "The final step isn't the fifth star—it's the sequence in reverse, reflecting the original pattern!"

"So, we press them backward? Fifth to first?" Kieran asks, confusion evident.

"No," Theron says. "We completed the forward sequence, which opened the path. Now we need to complete the reflecting sequence to reach the prize."

"Starting with the fifth indentation again, then the fourth, and so on," I confirm, excitement building.

Theron positions his finger over the largest indentation once more. "Here we go."

He presses the fifth indentation again, then the fourth, third, and second in rapid succession. With each press, the path through the thorns widens slightly.

Then, just as he's about to press the first indentation again, voices echo from the chamber entrance.

"Well, well. Looks like we found the right place after all."

We turn to see Selene and Erebus standing in the arched doorway, their expressions a mixture of triumph and displeasure at finding us here first.

Selene steps forward, her dark hair gleaming in the chamber's strange light. Her eyes fix on the Moonstone, then narrow at the sight of us around the pedestal.

"The Moonstone," she breathes. "And you haven't claimed it yet."

"We're in the middle of something," Kieran says with false cheerfulness. "Mind waiting outside?"

Erebus laughs, the sound echoing harshly. "And let you take the glory? I don't think so." He steps further into the chamber, his muscular frame tense with anticipation. "The Harvest Ritual prize belongs to the worthiest competitor."

"We solved the puzzle," Theron says, his voice low and dangerous. "Back off."

"You haven't claimed it yet," Selene points out, edging closer. "The competition continues until someone holds the Moonstone."

I meet Theron's eyes, a silent message passing between us. He understands immediately, subtly repositioning to block Selene's view of the pedestal.

"You're right," he says, drawing their attention. "But we're one step ahead."

While he speaks, I quickly press the final indentation—the first in the reversed sequence. There's a louder click this time, and the remaining branches retract fully, leaving the Moonstone suspended in the air, accessible at last.

The movement draws everyone's attention. Selene lunges forward, but Kieran intercepts her, his lanky frame surprisingly solid as he blocks her path.

"Sorry," he says with a grin that's all teeth. "Finders keepers."

Erebus moves to assist his partner, but Theron steps between them, his presence alone halting the larger man in his tracks.

"Fuck off," Theron growls.

I seize the moment, reaching through the now-open cage for the Moonstone. The instant my fingers touch its surface, a jolt of energy races up my arm—a cold fire that burns through my veins, awakening something primal within me. The stone feels both freezing and vibrant, humming with power against my palm as I carefully lift it from its cradle.

"HOLY SHIT, SHE GOT IT!" Kieran explodes, his voice echoing off the chamber walls as he throws both arms into the air. "WE FUCKING DID IT!"

I barely have time to absorb his outburst before Theron's arms encircle my waist from behind, lifting me clear off the ground in a spinning embrace that makes the Moonstone's light dance across the walls.

"That's my girl," he growls into my ear, his voice thick with pride and something deeper that sends shivers down my spine.

I can't help it—a wild laugh escapes me, the sound so

foreign after weeks of tension and danger that it startles even me. I clutch the Moonstone to my chest with one hand and reach back to tangle my fingers in Theron's hair with the other.

"We won," I manage between breathless laughs as he sets me down. "We actually won."

"Did you ever doubt?" Theron's eyes blaze with intensity as he spins me to face him, his hands still possessive on my hips. Gone is the careful distance he's maintained in public—this is the Theron I know in private moments, fierce and unguarded.

Kieran is dancing across the chamber in a ridiculous victory jig that would mortify him in front of his warrior brethren. "Moon-blessed magic fingers solving ancient puzzles! They're all going to lose their minds!"

"An Elios priestess claiming the prize meant for Umbra," Selene spits from the entrance, her beautiful face contorted with anger. "You sure as fuck don't deserve it!"

Kieran spins toward her, still mid-dance. "Too late! You snooze, you lose, sweetheart!"

"Back off, Selene," Theron growls, not bothering to hide his triumph as he keeps one arm firmly around my waist. "The alliance was sanctioned by the competition rules."

"Rules," Erebus scoffs. "As if Umbra ever cared about rules."

"Rich coming from you," Kieran retorts, bouncing on his toes with excess energy. "Wasn't it your sister who got disqualified at the last Harvest Ritual for poisoning her opponent's water?"

Erebus lunges forward, but Theron intercepts him, one hand on the larger man's chest, holding him back with seemingly minimal effort.

"Enough," Theron barks, his quiet authority filling the chamber. "We've won. Accept it, or we'll make you bleed."

Before Erebus can respond, a deep rumbling fills the chamber, the stone floor vibrating beneath our feet. The pedestal begins to sink into the ground, disappearing inch by inch into the floor.

"What the hell?" Selene gasps, fear replacing anger as she backs toward the entrance.

I clutch the moonstone tighter, its energy pulsating intensely now. "What's happening?" I breathe, watching as cracks appear in the floor around us.

"The walls!" Kieran shouts, pointing wildly. "Look!"

They begin to sink, descending slowly into the ground with a grinding noise that sets my teeth on edge. Beyond them, the maze walls do the same—the entire labyrinth folding itself back into the earth.

Within moments, where there were once high walls surrounding us, there is now open space. The vast expanse of the competition grounds stretches out in all directions, revealing its true scale for the first time.

In the distance, I spot other competitors frozen in mid-motion, staring as their sections of the maze melt away around them.

"LOOK UPON US AND WEEP, LOSERS!" Kieran bellows at the top of his lungs.

His ridiculous showboating breaks the tension, and a scattered cheer rises from various parts of the field—not everyone is disappointed in our victory.

"Aria!" Kieran suddenly shouts, his theatrics forgotten as he spots a lithe figure in the distance.

My heart dances to see she's unharmed.

Kieran is suddenly running to my best friend across the exposed field, her light chestnut hair flying behind her as she does the same.

Erebus steps back, jaw tight with disappointment. He and Selene begin to withdraw.

"No need to stick around," Theron calls after them, his dismissal carrying a victorious edge. "We know how to celebrate properly."

As they slink away, Theron turns to me with a ferocity that takes my breath away. His eyes, which have haunted my dreams since we parted, are blazing with more than just the thrill of victory.

"Lyra," he murmurs my name like a prayer on his lips as he cups my face. The public mask is completely gone now, replaced by the man I fell for. "My beautiful, brilliant little moon."

Then he's kissing me. His lips are fierce and familiar against mine, his hands sliding into my hair with the confidence of someone who knows exactly how to make me melt.

I respond instantly, the moonstone clutched between us as I press against him. This is raw and real.

When we break apart, I'm breathless, my head spinning with more than just the power of the stone I hold.

Theron doesn't release me. Instead, he lifts me into his arms in one fluid motion, spinning me around as if I weigh nothing.

"This is the beginning," he says, his voice rough with emotion. "Something new, something terrifying... but it will be beautiful, Lyra." He presses his forehead to mine. "You by my side, in the Onyx Covenant, where you've always belonged."

"You're so sure?" I challenge, though my smile betrays me.

"No," he admits, setting me gently on my feet but keeping me close. "But I'm sure I'll spend every day making it worth your while as we make all the wrongs right."

I glance down at the moonstone in my hand and notice something concerning. The pulsating light within it is dimming, the swirling energy inside growing sluggish rather than intensifying as I expected.

"Wait," I say, my smile fading. "Something's wrong."

Theron follows my gaze to the stone. His brow furrows. "What is it?"

"It's not... it shouldn't be—" My words are cut off by another rumbling beneath our feet, different from before. Not the walls descending, but something else—something changing.

In the middle of the now-exposed field, the ground shifts and rises. Earth and stone rearrange themselves, forming a perfect circle approximately thirty feet in diameter. And at its center, a stone dais emerges from below, rising to waist height.

"The Sacred Circle," Theron breathes, his body tensing against mine.

Kieran, who had been halfway to Aria, stops in his tracks and looks back at us. "Wait, what's happening?" he calls, confusion clear on his face.

"We're not done," I whisper, horror dawning. "Tarek said the first team to retrieve the stone and return it to the Sacred Circle would win."

"Melian's warning," Theron says urgently. "The stone must be freely given to the Sacred Circle."

As if in response to his words, every competitor still on the field turns toward us—toward the stone in my hand. The celebration dies in an instant, replaced by a predatory stillness that makes my skin crawl.

"Oh, fuck," I breathe. "They all know."

"Lyra!" Aria shouts from across the field, pointing frantically at the Sacred Circle. "The ritual's not complete!"

Without warning, Selene and Erebus turn back toward us, their expressions transformed from defeat to renewed determination. Selene's eyes lock on the moonstone, calculating the distance between us.

"We have to get to the circle," Theron says, his voice tight. "Now."

"Run," I gasp, clutching the stone tighter. "We need to run!"

We break into a sprint toward the Sacred Circle, but we're not the only ones. The field erupts into chaos as every remaining competitor makes a desperate dash toward either us or the circle itself.

"Don't let them take it!" Theron shouts as a pair of competitors cut across our path. He barrels into them without slowing, clearing our way.

My lungs burn as I push myself faster, the moonstone clutched in my fist. From the corner of my eye, I spot Selene gaining on us, her face twisted with determination. Behind her, Erebus is plowing through anyone who gets in his way.

"They're gaining!" I yell to Theron, who glances back and curses.

Ahead of us, I see Aria purposefully place herself in the path of an opponent rushing toward us. She feigns a stumble, crashing into her legs and sending her sprawling.

"Go, Lyra!" she shouts as she scrambles to her feet.

Kieran appears at our flank, intercepting Erebus with a shoulder check that sends them both tumbling across the dirt. "Get to the circle!" he roars as he grapples with the larger man.

We're close now—twenty feet, fifteen, ten. The symbols around the Sacred Circle come into view and begin to glow.

"Almost there," Theron pants beside me.

A flash of movement to our right—Selene lunging toward us, fingers outstretched for the stone. Theron shoves me forward, placing his body between us as he collides with her.

I stumble the final few steps into the Sacred Circle alone, its perimeter tingling against my skin as I cross it. The dais at the center beckons, a small hollow carved into its top—perfectly sized for the Onyx Moonstone.

My hands shake as I place the stone on the dais, expecting it to fit seamlessly into the hollow.

Nothing happens.

"No," I gasp, pressing harder. The stone refuses to settle, rolling slightly to one side. "No, no, no!"

Theron vaults into the circle behind me, his breathing ragged. "What's wrong?"

"It won't fit!" Panic rises in my throat as I hear the sounds of others approaching. "The stone won't go in!"

Theron's hands join mine on the moonstone, both of us trying desperately to position it correctly. The stone grows warmer between our palms, the energy inside swirling faster.

"Remember what Melian said," Theron says urgently. "It must be freely given in true harmony."

Our eyes lock as understanding passes between us. Not one of us placing it, but both—together perhaps.

As Selene and some others reach the edge of the circle, Theron and I position the stone above the hollow, our fingers intertwined around its smooth surface.

"Together," I say, and we both release it at the same moment.

The moonstone drops into place with a sound like a distant bell. For a heartbeat, nothing happens. Then light erupts from the dais, shooting skyward in a brilliant column that illuminates the entire field.

The symbols around the circle flare to life, creating a barrier that ripples like water. Those rushing toward us hit it and rebound, unable to cross.

The moonstone itself transforms, its dark surface becoming translucent, revealing what looks like swirling galaxies within its depths. The ground trembles once more, but gently this time, like a contented sigh.

Tarek's voice booms across the field, magically amplified: "The Onyx Moonstone has chosen! The ritual is complete!"

Theron pulls me against him, his heart pounding against mine. "We did it," he whispers fiercely into my hair. "We actually did it."

The barrier around the Sacred Circle dissolves, allowing Kieran and Aria to join us. They crash into us in an exhausted relief.

"That," Kieran breaths, "was entirely too dramatic."

Aria punches his arm. "You loved every second of it."

Beyond the circle, Selene watches us with cold hatred, Erebus a stone-faced sentinel beside her. But they can do nothing now. The ritual has spoken.

"We did," I confirm, feeling lighter than I have in months, despite the bone-deep weariness.

"The pack Alphas will be losing their collective minds right about now," Aria says with a wicked grin. "An Elios priestess and an Umbra Alpha claiming the prize? Historical."

"Revolutionary," Theron corrects, his hand finding the small of my back. "This changes everything."

"It'd better," I say, meeting his gaze. "After what we went through to get this damn rock."

Kieran throws his arms around all three of us, creating an awkward group hug that somehow feels exactly right. "Onward to glory and free drinks!" he declares. "The tale of how we conquered the Harvest Ritual will be told for generations!"

As we break apart, laughing, I look across the now-open competition grounds toward the gates where we started the trials. Tarek and Melian await, their expressions difficult to read at this distance. The impossible task is complete, but the real challenge is just beginning.

And as Theron's fingers lace with mine, I know with absolute certainty that whatever comes next, we'll face it together.

I look down at our interlaced fingers, then up at his face—the face I once knew better than my own, the face I trained myself to hate after he broke my heart. Now, I see neither the man I loved nor the enemy I forced myself to despise, but a man standing at the same crossroads as me, facing the same impossible choice.

Together, we turn toward the entrance. Behind us, Kieran falls into step with Aria.

Around us, the last of the maze walls sink into the earth, leaving the competition grounds open and exposed. Other competitors make their way forward as well, their challenges ended with our victory.

NINETEEN

LYRA

I take a deep breath as the manacle is finally removed from my wrist, the metal clasp opening with a soft click that somehow resonates through my entire body. Freedom. The raw skin beneath is tender, marked with a faint impression that will fade but never truly disappear—a reminder of everything we survived.

"There you go, miss," says the official, nodding respectfully. "Congratulations again."

My parents rush forward. Father's face is a storm of emotions—pride battling with lingering reservations. It wasn't long ago he'd been furious about Theron choosing me, a daughter of the rival pack, calling it a political stunt or worse. But now his eyes shine as he takes my hands in his.

"My daughter," he says, voice rough with emotion. "You did it. You actually did it."

"Were you ever really worried I wouldn't?" I ask,

trying to sound light, though we both know how close we came to disaster in that ritual.

He shakes his head, a rueful smile breaking through. "I should have known better. You've always been unstoppable when you set your mind to something." His grip tightens on my hands. "I was wrong about Theron's choice. Wrong about a lot of things. And I want you to know that I'm with you now. Both of you. Whatever comes next."

The admission costs him, I can tell. Years of pack rivalry don't dissolve overnight. But he's trying, and that means everything.

"Thank you," I whisper. "That matters more than you know."

Mother pushes forward then, unable to contain herself any longer. She pulls me into a fierce embrace, and I breathe in her familiar scent—herbs and home.

"My brilliant girl," she murmurs against my hair. "Always knew you were meant for greatness."

I laugh against her shoulder, feeling suddenly like a child again. "I'm not sure surviving a deadly maze counts as greatness."

She pulls back, framing my face with her hands. "It's what comes after that will make the difference. And you'll handle that just as well."

Over her shoulder, I spot Theron across the grounds, standing with Kieran rather than beside his father. The distance between them speaks volumes. Our gazes meet briefly, and he offers a small smile that sends warmth cascading through me.

"Look at you," Mother says, following my gaze. "Already thinking like a leader."

"Is it that obvious?"

"To a mother? Always." She kisses my forehead. "We'll let you celebrate with your friends. Your father and I should mingle—make nice with people who've been sneering at us for years." Her eyes twinkle mischievously.

As my parents move away to join the growing crowd of pack members—both sides talking awkwardly on the Onyx Covenant grounds—a familiar voice rings through the murmur.

"Look who's a big deal now."

I turn to see Aria striding toward me, resplendent in a deep blue dress that reflects the flaming torchlights like rippling water. Her smile is wide and infectious.

"Aria!" I exclaim, grabbing her hands.

She loops her arm through mine, steering me toward a quieter corner of the grounds. "So how does it feel? Being the talk of every single wolf for miles around? I've heard your name so many times today I'm considering changing mine just for some variety."

The grounds around us are filling with members of both packs, old rivals now forced into an uncertain alliance. Some faces are openly hostile, others cautiously optimistic.

"Honestly? It still doesn't feel real," I admit. "Yesterday, I was fighting for my life, and today, everyone's acting like I'm suddenly important."

"Oh," Aria says, patting my arm. "You have no idea. Half the people here are absolutely seething with jealousy, and the other half are tripping over themselves to declare how they've 'always supported unity between the packs.'" Her impression of the self-important elders is so spot-on I have to stifle a laugh.

"And which half do you fall into?" I tease.

"Please. I'm in the third, much more exclusive category of people who are just here for the free food and the drama." She winks, then grows suddenly serious. "But truly, Lyra, so many people are behind this union. The younger generation especially. We're tired of the old grudges, the pointless rivalry."

I nod, feeling the weight of expectation settling on my shoulders. "I know. That's what makes it so terrifying. We can't fail."

"Speaking of failing..." Aria nods subtly toward where Theron's father stands, surrounded by his traditional supporters, his face like stone. "What's the plan for dealing with the chief opposition?"

I sigh, the worry I've been pushing down bubbling back up. "I don't know yet. Theron thinks his father will eventually come around, but—"

"But he's a stubborn old wolf who's been running things his way for decades," Aria finishes. "How long do you think it'll take Theron to wrestle control once you're officially installed at the Onyx Covenant?"

"Months, at least. Maybe longer." I run my fingers over the tender skin where the manacle had been. "Gods, Aria, can you believe it? In a week, I'll be helping run the Onyx Covenant. Me. With actual power and responsibility and—"

"And a gorgeous mate at your side," Aria cuts in with a sly grin. "Don't pretend that's not a significant perk."

I feel heat rising to my cheeks. "That's hardly the point."

"Maybe not the main point," she concedes. "But definitely a very nice bonus point." She nudges me playfully. "Look, I know your head is spinning with plans and politics and potential disasters, but maybe for tonight, just focus on one thing."

"Which is?"

Her smile turns wicked. "That you get to stand alongside the extremely hunky Theron while making history. The rest? We'll figure it out as we go. We always do."

I laugh, the tension in my chest easing slightly. "What would I do without you?"

"Bore everyone to death with your responsible leadership, probably," she quips, but her eyes are soft with affection. "You were born for this, Lyra. All of it."

The crowd around us shifts suddenly, parting like water around stone as Tarek and Melian emerge from the grand Onyx Covenant building. They stand tall on the wide marble steps, their ceremonial robes gleaming with ancient sigils that catch the torchlights.

"The victors approach," Tarek calls, his words

carrying across the grounds without effort. "Let all bear witness to what the moons have ordained."

The murmuring of the crowd grows louder as Theron approaches and takes my hand, squeezing it once before we begin walking forward. The path to the Covenant steps feels impossibly long, a gauntlet of stares—some admiring, others hostile. I can feel the unease rippling through the gathering, particularly from the Umbra side with dark expressions and clenched jaws.

"They look like they want to eat me alive," I whisper.

"Let them try," he murmurs back, straightening his spine.

As we approach the steps, a tremor runs through the ground—subtle at first, then strong enough to make several people stagger. Cracks appear in the stone steps, spreading like veins across the surface.

"What's happening?" someone shouts, panic rising in the crowd.

Tarek and Melian remain unmoved, exchanging a knowing glance. "It begins," Melian says, stepping back.

The cracks widen, and from them pour what looks like liquid shadow, pooling on the wide steps and behind them rising and taking form. A dozen figures materialize. Half-wolf, half-warrior, they tower at nearly eight feet tall with broad shoulders encased in jagged obsidian armor. Where skin should be, there's instead a shifting surface like volcanic glass that absorbs light rather than reflects it. Their faces blend canine and human features—elongated jaws filled with gleaming teeth, pointed ears that swivel toward sounds, and eyes that burn with amber fire. Ancient runes etched in silver light pulse across their midnight skin in complex patterns, briefly illuminating veins of blue energy beneath before fading and reappearing elsewhere on their bodies.

Gasps and cries of fear erupt through the crowd. Many retreat several steps, even the most hardened warriors among them.

"The Onyx Warriors," a woman behind me whispers, her voice trembling. "They haven't been summoned in generations."

The creatures arrange themselves in a semicircle behind Tarek and Melian. One steps forward, larger than the rest, its muzzle elongated into a wolf's snout. It throws back its head and unleashes a bone-chilling howl that seems to reverberate through my very soul. A shiver rushes down my arms at the Onyx Warriors everyone fears.

The crowd falls silent.

"For centuries," Tarek begins, his voice cutting through the silence. "The Onyx Covenant has preserved balance between our packs. Today, that balance shifts—not toward destruction, but toward unity."

"Many of you," Melian continues, her gaze sweeping across the crowd, "see this outcome as a threat to tradition. To the natural order." Her eyes narrow. "You are mistaken. The natural order is not static. It evolves, adapts, strengthens."

A figure pushes to the front of the crowd—Theron's

father, his face contorted with barely contained rage. "This is an abomination!" he shouts, pointing at me. "An Elios wolf in the Covenant? You forget whose pack built these very walls! What pack you both came from."

One of the Onyx Warriors shifts, a low growl emanating from its shadowy form, but Melian raises a hand to stay it.

"We forget nothing, Magnus Shadowmane," she says coolly. "Including how your leadership has brought us to the brink of civil war more times than I care to count. Perhaps what truly troubles you is not tradition but the thought of an Elios wolf having power you cannot control."

Murmurs spread through the crowd at her bold rebuke. His face darkens dangerously, but even he seems unwilling to challenge the presence of the Onyx Warriors.

"The moons have chosen," Tarek states, his voice rising. "And their will is clear. Approach, victors of the Harvest Ritual."

Theron and I climb the steps, the Warriors parting to allow us passage. Up close, they are even more terrifying —ancient beyond reckoning, with eyes that seem to hold entire galaxies within them.

"For the first time in our lifetime," Melian announces, "wolves from opposing packs have united to claim the Onyx Moonstone."

"Our ancestors," Tarek continues, producing two pendants from within his robes. "They created the

Covenant not to divide us but to remind us of our common origins."

He places the pendants around our necks—circular amulets of polished stone, half obsidian, half moonstone, with ancient symbols. The moment mine touches my skin, a warmth spreads through my chest, as if recognizing something in my blood.

"These will grant you access to the chambers within," Melian explains. "Chambers only permitted for the Onyx members."

"Let all here witness," Tarek calls to the crowd. "Theron Shadowmane and Lyra Mooncrest now stand as the Onyx Covenant. Their word is law, their judgment binding. Those who defy them defy the will of the moons themselves."

As if responding to his proclamation, the lead warrior in my father's pack steps forward, dropping to one knee before us in a sign of fealty. The others follow, their shadowy forms bowing in unison.

A cheer rises from the Elios side of the gathering, led by my father, who steps forward, arms raised high. "The Elios pack stands with the new Covenant!" he shouts. "Let this mark the beginning of true peace!"

Half the crowd joins the cheer, while the rest—primarily Umbra—remain silent, their disapproval obvious despite the Warriors' intimidating presence.

Theron turns to me, his eyes reflecting the torchlight. "There's no escaping me now, little moon," he whispers, his voice too low for others to hear. "Not that I'd ever let you run. You're bound to me by forces older than these stones—and I to you, forever."

My heart stutters at his words, heat rising to my face despite the gravity of the moment. Before I can respond, we're pulled apart as my father approaches, embracing me tightly.

"I'm so proud," he murmurs against my hair. "So very proud."

As congratulations swirl around us, we're separated by well-wishers—Theron surrounded by his supporters from the Umbra pack, me by my father and other Elios members. Aria pushes through to my side, linking her arm through mine.

"Look at you," she whispers excitedly. "Already changing the world."

"Terrifying, isn't it?" I say, fingering the pendant at my throat.

"Gloriously so," she agrees.

The next hour passes in a blur of congratulations and hushed conversations. Members from both packs approach me—some genuinely supportive, others clearly there to assess the threat I now pose.

My father remains close, fielding questions from Elios elders who seem torn between pride and concern. "Of course I have reservations," I overhear him saying to a particularly persistent elder. "But my daughter has proven herself worthy of this mantle. The time for blind prejudice is in the past."

"Lyra Mooncrest," a voice calls me from behind, and I

twist around to find a man in a robe with the hood covering his head. "Your presence is requested for the Onyx Covenant final offering. The ceremony awaits you." Their voice is low.

I scan the crowd quickly, searching for Theron's tall figure among the mingling guests. The sea of faces blurs together—some familiar, some strangers—but he's nowhere to be seen.

"He must have already been called," I murmur, suddenly nervous. My fingers instinctively touch the tender skin where the manacle had been just hours ago as if I somehow miss the thing.

Aria squeezes my arm, her touch grounding me. "Go be brilliant. I'll save you some of the good wine for after." She gives me a playful shove forward. "This is it—your moment. The one you've earned."

As I move to follow the robed figure, Kieran appears, making his way toward Aria through the crowd. I don't miss the way Aria's posture straightens, how her fingers instinctively smooth her hair, and the slight quickening of her breath.

"Go," I whisper to her with a knowing smile. "Talk to him."

She bites her lip, then nods. "Fine. But only because it serves the greater political good," she quips, though her eyes are already fixed on Kieran.

I watch them for a brief moment—my best friend approaching the man who would once have been considered forbidden by both our packs' laws. His smile as he sees her is genuine, unguarded in a way I've rarely seen from him. If Theron hadn't chosen me as his Harvest Ritual partner, if we hadn't challenged those ancient boundaries together, this simple interaction would have been impossible.

As I follow the robed figure through the crowd, I catch Selene's venomous glare from across the gathering. The hatred in her eyes is unmistakable, burning bright despite everything that's happened. Some things never change— she will always despise me for taking what she believed was rightfully hers.

I meet her stare evenly. Let her hate. Let her seethe. After her trying to kill me, she should be grateful she's even allowed to attend. If she wants forgiveness, she'll have to grovel for it—and even then, I'm not inclined to make it easy.

The robed figure leads me away from the main celebration, around the perimeter of the Covenant building. The sounds of conversation and laughter grow fainter as we move deeper into the shadows. The stones beneath my feet change from polished marble to rough-hewn granite.

"Where is Theron?" I ask, unease prickling at the back of my neck. "Isn't the offering held in the main chamber?"

The figure doesn't answer, just nods ahead and continues walking. We round the rear of the building where the stone walls rise blank and forbidding, unmarked by windows or decoration. Moss creeps between the stones, suggesting this section rarely sees visitors. A small, unremarkable door is set into the wall—one I've never noticed before despite my years of observing the Covenant from afar.

"This doesn't seem right," I say, slowing my steps. "I don't think—"

The figure moves with unexpected speed, pushing the door open and shoving me roughly inside. I stumble forward into darkness, the door slamming shut behind me with a heavy, final sound.

The darkness is absolute, disorienting. The air hangs thick with the scent of damp stone and something else, something metallic and vaguely sickening.

"Hello?" My voice echoes in the space. "What is this? What's going—"

A hand closes around my throat, slamming me back against the cold stone wall with crushing force. I claw at the fingers cutting off my air, panic surging through me as my feet barely touch the ground.

A faint light flickers to life, just enough to illuminate the face inches from mine—Theron's father, his features twisted with hatred and rage. This close, I can see the family resemblance—the same strong jawline, the same intense eyes—but where Theron's gaze holds warmth, his father's burns with cold malice.

"You filthy scavenger," he snarls, spittle hitting my cheek as his grip tightens. "You think you can come in here and take over? Eradicate decades of Umbra leadership?"

I kick wildly, fingers scratching at his hand, but his

grip is like iron. Dark spots begin to dance at the edges of my vision.

"You may have tricked my son," he hisses, "but I see through you. Your little performance in the maze might have fooled everyone else, but I know what you are—vermin from a lesser pack, clawing your way to power you don't deserve."

His other hand rises, striking me hard across the face. The blow snaps my head to the side, the taste of copper flooding my mouth where my teeth cut into my cheek.

"Did you really think I would allow this?" His voice drops to a deadly whisper. "Allow my bloodline to be tainted by your kind? Allow my legacy to be dismantled by a female who should be groveling at our feet?"

I manage to twist my face back toward him, blood trickling from the corner of my mouth. "Your legacy," I rasp through his chokehold. "It's cruelty and division. It deserves to be dismantled."

He releases my throat only to grab me by the shoulders and throw me bodily across the room. I crash into what feels like wooden crates, splintering through them as pain explodes across my back.

"You know nothing of leadership," he says, stalking toward me as I struggle to rise from the debris. "Nothing of what it takes to keep order among beasts who would tear each other apart without a firm hand."

I push myself up, ignoring the sharp pain in my ribs and the warm trickle of blood from a cut on my arm. "Is that what you tell yourself? That your tyranny is necessary?"

"Tyranny?" He laughs, the sound devoid of any humor. "I created peace. I maintained balance. What do you think will happen when the old barriers fall? Chaos. Bloodshed. The very fabric of our society will unravel."

"Or maybe," I say, backing away from his advance, searching desperately for anything I might use as a weapon, "we'll finally heal wounds that never should have existed in the first place."

His hand lashes out again, catching me across my cheekbone, sending me staggering back against another wall. Before I can recover, he's on me, one hand pinning me by the throat again, the other raining blows to my stomach and my ribs.

"You're nothing," he growls between strikes, each word punctuated by another blow. "A nobody. A mistake my son will soon regret."

I try to block his attacks, but he's too strong, too fast. Pain blossoms everywhere his fists connect. I manage to land a strike of my own, my knuckles connecting with his jaw, but he barely seems to notice.

"When I'm done with you," he continues, grabbing a fistful of my hair and slamming my head back against the stone. "No one will even remember your name. I'll tell them all how you rejected Theron, how you hated everything he stood for. How you ran like the coward you are."

Through the haze of pain, I see him reach into his coat

and withdraw something that glints in the dim light—a blade, its edge wickedly sharp.

"Do you know where we are?" he asks, almost conversationally as he traces the tip of the blade along my jawline, not quite breaking the skin. "The old punishment chambers. No one comes here anymore. No one will hear you scream."

My heart hammers against my ribs, death flashing in his eyes. "They'll know it was you," I manage to say. "Theron will know."

"My son," he spits the word like it tastes foul. "Has been blinded by you, but he'll see reason once you're gone. Or perhaps I'll tell them you attacked me, threatened the Onyx Covenant itself. A tragic case of self-defense." His lips curl into a horrible smile. "Who would question the High Alpha's word?"

The blade presses harder, drawing a thin line of blood across my collarbone. I try to twist away, but his grip on my hair keeps me pinned.

"I've waited a long time to purge our bloodline of weakness," he says, his breath hot against my face. "My son almost had me believing he could be strong. Until you. Until he chose compassion over power." He shakes his head in disgust. "The greatest mistake I ever made was not crushing that tendency in him when he was a child."

Something snaps inside me at his words—not fear, but pure, molten rage. This man, this monster who calls himself a leader, who calls himself a father—he's everything wrong with our world.

I gather my strength and slam my forehead into his nose. The crunch of cartilage is immensely satisfying, as is his howl of pain and the momentary loosening of his grip. I twist free and drive my knee up into his stomach.

He staggers back, blood pouring from his nose, but recovers quickly. With a roar, he charges me, blade slashing wildly. I dodge the first swipe, but the second catches my arm, slicing a burning path across my flesh.

"I'm going to enjoy watching you bleed out," he snarls, circling me now. "Slowly. Painfully. As all traitors deserve."

I press my hand against the cut, feeling warm blood seep between my fingers. "The only traitor here is you," I retort, matching his movements, looking for an opening. "Betraying your own son. Your own pack."

He lunges again, but this time, I'm not fast enough. The blade sinks into my side—not deep, but enough to make me cry out. He grins, that ugly, triumphant grin, as he twists the knife before pulling it free.

"That's just the beginning," he promises, watching me press my hand to the new wound. "By the time I'm done, you'll be begging me to finish it."

I back away, my vision swimming from the pain. My back hits a wall—there's nowhere left to retreat. He advances slowly, savoring my fear, my pain.

"Any last words, bitch?" he asks, raising the blade.

Theron

I scan the crowd, tension building in my chest with each passing moment. The celebration continues around me—laughter, conversation, the clinking of glasses—but Lyra is nowhere to be seen. I'd expected to find her with her family or perhaps with Aria, but she's absent from both groups.

Something feels wrong. I can't explain it, but a cold unease has settled in my gut, growing more insistent by the minute.

I spot Aria across the gathering, deep in conversation with Kieran. The sight would normally please me—evidence that the barriers between packs are already beginning to dissolve—but now I move toward them with a singular purpose.

"Aria," I interrupt, not bothering with pleasantries. "Where's Lyra?"

She looks surprised by my tone. "She was summoned for the Covenant final offering," she says. "I assumed you'd be there, too. Wasn't that the whole point of tonight?"

The cold feeling intensifies. "What? There's no final offering scheduled tonight."

Aria's smile falters. "But... someone came for her. Wearing the official Onyx Covenant robes. Said she was needed for the ceremony."

"Who?" I demand, scanning the area again. "When?"

"I don't know who. They wore a hood. It wasn't long ago." Her expression shifts from confusion to concern. "Is she in trouble?"

Something sharp and terrible travels up my spine. My father has been absent as well.

"Which way did they go?" I ask, my voice dripping with venom.

Aria points toward the east side of the building. "That way, around the—"

I don't wait for her to finish. I'm already moving, slicing through the crowd with single-minded intensity. People dart out of my path, conversations faltering as I pass. I feel the stares and hear the whispers, but none of it matters.

All that matters is finding Lyra.

I circle the building, my pace quickening with each step. The main entrance yields nothing—the ceremonial hall is empty, silent. I continue around, checking every door, every pathway, fear building into a terrible certainty.

My father would never accept this union. Never accept sharing power, especially not with a wolf from the rival pack. Never accept his son choosing love over tradition.

As I round the back of the building, the oldest section of the Onyx Covenant grounds, I find nothing. No sign of Lyra, no sign of my father. Just ancient stone walls, indifferent to my growing panic.

I'm about to turn back, to raise the alarm with the others, when I hear it, faint but unmistakable—a cry of pain from somewhere beyond the wall.

Something primal awakens in me—not thought, not strategy, but pure, devastating instinct. I follow the sound to a small, weathered door set deep into the stone. Without hesitation, I slam my shoulder against it. The ancient wood splinters but holds. I back up and charge again, putting all my strength, all my rage into the impact.

The door explodes inward, and the scene that greets me stops my heart—Lyra, bloodied and cornered, my father looming over her with a blade raised high.

Time slows and narrows to a single point of clarity. There is no hesitation, no internal debate. Only action.

My hand finds my own blade, and I launch myself forward with a roar that seems to shake the very stones. My father turns, surprise flashing across his face for a split second before my body slams into him, driving him away from Lyra.

We crash to the ground together, rolling in a tangle of limbs and blades. My father is strong—has always been strong—but I fight with something beyond strength. Pure, unfiltered rage guides my movements, making me faster, deadlier.

"You," my father spits, managing to throw me off and scramble to his feet. I do the same. "Of course you'd come for your little whore."

"Don't you dare speak of her," I growl, circling my father, blade at the ready. Blood drips from a cut above my eye, but I barely notice. "What have you done?"

My father laughs, the sound chilling in its emptiness. "What should have been done weeks ago. Removing a disease before it spreads."

We clash again, blades meeting with a metallic screech.

"You've always been weak," my father taunts. "Always been a disappointment. I should have killed your mother when she was pregnant with you... saved myself years of watching you squander our legacy."

The words sting, but I don't falter.

"I knew you killed her," I roar.

My father's smile is a terrible thing, devoid of anything human. "Might as well have. By the time I was finished with her, there wasn't much left."

Something snaps in me—the last thread of restraint, the final barrier between man and beast. With a growl that doesn't sound human, I lunge forward, feinting left before driving my blade upward, under his ribs, angled toward his heart.

My father's eyes widen in shock, then narrow in hatred. "You'll never be—" he begins, but I twist the blade deeper, silencing him.

"You fucking bastard," I snarl, driving the blade deeper still, feeling warm blood coat my hand. "You goddamn fucking monster. You're nothing. NOTHING."

I pull the blade free, then plunge it in again and again, each strike punctuated by another curse, another roar of pain, rage, and grief.

Finally, I step back, chest heaving with exertion. My father collapses to the ground, blood pooling beneath him, his eyes already growing dim.

"You were... never... worthy..." he manages to whisper, blood bubbling at his lips. Then he's gone, his final breath escaping in a last, hateful sigh.

I stand frozen for one heartbeat, two, the reality of what I've done washing over me like ice water. I killed my father. The High Alpha. My own blood.

But as my gaze shifts to Lyra, slumped against the wall, blood seeping through her fingers as she presses against her wounds, regret vanishes like morning mist. I cross to her in three strides, gathering her gently into my arms.

"Lyra," I whisper, my voice breaking. "I'm here. I've got you."

Movement at the shattered doorway makes me tense, ready to fight again, but it's only Tarek and Melian, the senior Covenant members. They take in the scene—the dead Alpha, the wounded Omega, the blood-soaked son.

I straighten, Lyra cradled against my chest. "I have nothing to hide," I say, voice steady despite the storm of emotions within. "He deserved to die a long time ago."

To my surprise, both elders nod solemnly.

"We have nothing to add here," Tarek says, his usually

stern face softened with what might be relief. "You did what you deemed fit, as you are now the Onyx Covenant."

"We've served the Umbra for decades," Melian adds, her eyes lingering on the fallen Alpha. "But not all service comes with pride. Some come with shame that we could not act sooner."

"You knew?" I ask, disbelief coloring my words. "You knew what he was doing, what he was capable of?"

"We suspected," Tarek admits. "But our hands were tied without proof."

My jaw tightens. "I will find the evidence. I will expose every cruelty, every horrible thing he's done to destroy our packs." I glance between them, suspicion creeping in. "You had access to the Covenant records. You must have seen something."

"Perhaps we didn't know where to look," Melian says carefully. "Or perhaps we were too afraid to see what was in front of us."

"Cowards," I bark, feeling Lyra stir against my chest. "I'm going to care for my Omega, my partner, my mate. Then we are moving into the Covenant building, and you are both moving out immediately."

I step past them without waiting for a response, carrying Lyra through the shattered doorway and into the cool night air. The sounds of the celebration seem distant now, belonging to another world.

"Thank you," Lyra whispers against my neck, her voice weak but steady. "I thought I was going to die. He just... ambushed me."

I tighten my hold on her, careful to avoid her wounds. "It's all right," I murmur into her hair. "Nothing is ever going to harm you again. I swear it on my life."

She nestles closer, despite her injuries. "With us now overseeing both packs," she says, a hint of wonder in her voice, "nothing will ever be the same again."

"In the best possible way," I agree, pausing to look down at her. Despite the blood, despite the bruises forming on her beautiful face, her eyes still burn with the same fire that first captivated me. The same determination that kept her fighting in that maze, that kept her standing up to my father until the very end.

She wraps her arms around my neck and leans up, pressing her lips to mine. I lose myself in the kiss, in the miracle of her—alive, here, mine. My heart breaks anew at the sight of her injuries, but the breaking makes room for something else to grow. Something fiercer, more protective, more devoted than anything I've felt before.

When we finally part, I whisper against her lips, "I have loved you for a long time, Lyra. Longer than I even understood. And I love you more deeply with each passing day."

A smile breaks through her pain, radiant even now. "And I love you so much," she whispers back. "Through every battle, every trial. Beyond every ending, into every new beginning."

As I carry her away from the shadows and back toward the light, I think about how I feel nothing for my father's death. How I know I made the right decision.

With Lyra in my arms and the future stretching before us, the world we are going to build together will be worth every sacrifice, every scar, and every drop of blood it took to reach this moment.

And nothing—no force, no threat, no ancient hatred—will ever tear us apart again.

TWENTY

LYRA

Morning light slices through the tall windows of the Onyx Covenant building, casting silver-blue streaks across the polished obsidian floor. I nudge a stray book out of my path with my foot, still not used to the eerie way it sounds when something scrapes against the stone here—hollow, like disturbing a tomb.

It's been a week since the Harvest Ritual, a week since Theron drove a blade into his father to save my life, and a week since we marched into this huge monument to power as the new Onyx Covenant council. A week since everything changed.

From the outside, this place is intimidating as hell—a fortress of black stone. But inside? That's where the real surprise hit me. The outer walls contain some crystalline substance that turns nearly transparent from the inside, giving us views that stretch for miles while keeping prying eyes out. It's like living inside a one-way mirror—we see everything, but no one sees us.

I pause at the window overlooking the eastern forests, watching a hawk circle lazily above the trees. Somewhere down there, wolves from both our packs are hunting. My wolf stirs on the inside to join them, but my path has shifted for now. Theron and I have changes to implement across our two packs, but until then, we can't be seen joining normal hunting routines. Though, I had no idea how much I'd miss it...

I continue my exploration of the Onyx Covenant building, climbing the spiral staircase to the third level. The steps hover without visible support, carved from some material that resembles black glass but feels warm beneath my bare feet. Ancient runes flicker to life with each step I take, acknowledging my right to be here.

Still freaks me out a little.

The main hall on the first floor spans nearly the entire building, with ceilings so high it feels like standing in a cathedral. The council chamber sits at the center, a circular room with seats arranged around a table formed from a single piece of polished moonstone. The surface ripples when touched—actually fucking ripples like water—responding to the emotions of whoever touches it.

The second floor houses the library. The shelves stretch forever, some books so old they'd crumble to dust if not for the preservation spells holding them together.

Then there's the third floor—our private sanctuary.

Spacious rooms are connected by arching hallways, with balconies overlooking the sacred groves. It's more luxury than I've ever known, and sometimes, I still expect someone to appear and throw me out for trespassing.

I pause at the top of the stairs, listening. Theron disappeared after our morning meal, muttering something about exploring the east wing. Living together has been easier than I expected, his presence somehow both thrilling and comforting.

Following the sound of shuffling papers, I make my way down the eastern corridor, past rooms we haven't fully explored yet. For the next decade, this entire structure is ours alone. The previous Covenant members, Tarek and Melian, relocated to the Umbra pack after the ceremony, while the guards and trainees who serve the Covenant live in the barracks outside. No one enters without our explicit permission—a boundary that's given us precious privacy during this transition.

I find Theron in what appears to be an old study, methodically pulling books from shelves and examining the walls behind them. He's got on fitted black pants and a simple shirt that stretches across his broad shoulders, defining every muscle as he moves. His dark hair falls across his forehead as he concentrates, jaw set in that determined way that still makes my stomach flip. Gods, I still find him so handsome, maybe more so with each passing day.

For a moment, I simply watch him, remembering how

impossible this once seemed—an Elios priestess and an Umbra Alpha heir together as equals.

"You planning to stand there all day, or are you going to help?" he asks without lifting his gaze to me.

"Depends," I reply, leaning against the doorframe. "The view from here is pretty damn appealing."

Now, he does glance at me, eyes glinting with that predatory light that never fails to send a thrill down my spine. "Is that right?"

"Don't let it go to your head." I push off from the door and move into the room. "Why are you destroying the library, anyway?"

He runs a hand through his hair, leaving it even more appealingly disheveled. "I'm looking for something."

"Obviously. Care to be more specific?"

He straightens, setting aside the thick leather book he'd been examining. "It's about time I start to find the things my mother mentioned in her journals…" He pauses, jaw tightening.

The sudden darkness in his voice draws me closer.

"According to what she wrote, there's a secret area in this building that previous Onyx Covenant members may not have known about… or perhaps just chose to ignore. Ignorance is bliss, they say." He moves to another shelf, fingers tracing the spines of ancient texts. "She heard from her grandmother that when the Elios ruled, they hid historical information here out of fear that when Umbra took over, certain documents might be destroyed."

"By your family," I say, not bothering to soften the truth.

His shoulders tense, then relax. "Yes. They would have happily erased anything that didn't support their version of history." He shakes his head, his expression grim. "I assumed most Covenant members were too weak to stand against him, but seeing Tarek and Melian at the ceremony..."

"When they finally grew spines?" I interject.

A ghost of a smile touches his lips. "Something like that."

"Only took them a decade," I mutter, running my fingers along the shelves. "They seemed all too happy to abandon their posts once we took over."

"Ten years trapped between warring packs would drain anyone's courage," Theron says, though there's little sympathy in his tone. "Especially with someone like my father watching their every move."

I retrieve a chair from behind the desk, dragging it to the wall and climbing up to examine the higher shelves. "So, what exactly are we looking for? Secret lever? Hidden door? Ancient chest full of forbidden knowledge?"

"I don't know exactly," he admits, glancing up at me. "My mother wasn't specific in her journals. Just look for anything unusual."

"This entire building is unusual," I grumble but continue my search.

For several minutes, we work in companionable silence. I test loose stones, pull random books, and tap on suspicious-looking panels. Occasionally, I steal glances at Theron, admiring every inch of him.

"If you keep looking at me like that," he says suddenly, "we're never going to find anything useful."

"Like what?" I ask with feigned innocence.

"Like you're imagining me doing things that have nothing to do with secret passages." He abandons his search, crossing the space between us in three long strides.

Before I can formulate a sarcastic response, he's there, one hand closing around my wrist and tugging me down from the chair. In seconds, I find myself trapped between the solid wall and his harder body.

"You were saying?" I manage, heart already racing.

His arms cage me in, palms flat against the wall on either side of my head. "You're mine now," he admits, voice dropping to that dangerous register that vibrates through my chest. "No escape routes. No rescue coming."

Instead of fear, heat floods my veins. I tilt my chin up defiantly. "I don't need rescuing. I'm exactly where I want to be."

"And where's that?" His eyes darken, pupils expanding until only a thin ring of gray remains.

"With you," I say simply. "Where else would I be?"

Something shifts in his expression—the playful dominance giving way to something rawer, more primal.

"Say it again," he commands, his voice rough.

I hold his gaze steadily. "I'm yours."

His thumb traces my lower lip, pressing just hard enough to sting. "I've wanted you since we first met in the woods, Lyra. I burned when I lost you, and I watched you from afar, knowing I couldn't have you but desperately ached for you."

"And now?" I ask, sliding my hands up his chest, feeling the rapid thud of his heart.

"Now, nothing stands in my way." A savage satisfaction colors his words. "And you're mine."

"Yours," I agree, then dig my nails into the fabric of his shirt, pulling him closer. "But don't forget... you're also mine. The most feared wolf in the territory, brought to heel by an Elios priestess. Imagine what they'd say."

A growl rumbles deep in his chest. "Is that what you think? That you've tamed me?"

I smile, slow and deliberate. "I think I like having a dangerous predator wrapped around my finger."

His other hand tangles in my hair, tilting my head back to expose my throat. "Dangerous is right," he murmurs against my pulse point. Suddenly, he claims my mouth in a bruising kiss. There's nothing gentle about it —this is possession. His teeth catch my lower lip, biting just hard enough to send sparks of pleasure-pain racing along my nerves.

I gasp as his tongue invades, taking immediate control. My body responds instantly, melting against him like it was made for this alone. I claw at his shoulders, seeking purchase, needing him closer still. He tastes of wild berries and mint leaves from our morning meal, and beneath that, something darker and uniquely his—like pine needles and smoky amber.

His hands are everywhere—in my hair, gripping my waist, sliding beneath the hem of my shirt to find bare skin. Each touch leaves a trail of fire in its wake, and I arch into him, wanting more, needing more.

"I thought..." I manage when he finally releases my mouth to attack my neck. "I thought you were searching for something important."

"I am," he growls against my throat, teeth scraping sensitive skin. "But I'm finding myself thoroughly distracted." His fingers trace the edge of my waistband. "I should probably return to my search," he murmurs, pulling back slightly.

I grab his wrist, keeping his hand in place. "Don't you dare."

The smile he gives me is pure predator. "As my lady commands." In one swift motion, he spins me around to face the wall, his chest pressed hard against my back. "Though I don't think ladies usually beg quite so prettily for corruption."

His breath is hot against my ear, his body a solid wall of heat behind me. One arm wraps around my waist, pulling me tight against him, letting me feel exactly how much he wants this—wants me. The thickness in his pants presses hard against my rear.

"How many times do you think I've imagined this?" he whispers, his free hand sliding up my side to cup my breast through my shirt. "Having you exactly like this, at my mercy whenever I want?"

I push back against him, grinding deliberately, and am rewarded with a sharp intake of breath.

"At your mercy?" I challenge, glancing back over my shoulder. "Are you sure about that? Because it seems to me you're the one who's desperate."

His hand tightens in warning, then slips beneath my shirt, fingers tracing up my ribs to find bare skin.

"You have no idea what desperate feels like," he promises, his voice dark with intent. "But you will."

His mouth latches onto the side of my neck, sucking hard enough that I know it will leave a mark, while his fingers find my nipple through the thin fabric of my breast band. He rolls it between his fingers, alternating between gentle teasing and sharper pressure that draws gasps from my lips.

My head falls back against his shoulder, my body surrendering even as my mind maintains the challenge.

"Prove it," I demand. "Show me exactly how desperate you can make me."

A low chuckle vibrates against my skin. "Such a demanding little thing." His hand slides lower, deftly undoing the laces of my pants. "Always giving orders, even when you're the one pinned and helpless."

"I'm never helpless," I retort, though my voice shakes.

"No?" His teeth graze my earlobe. "Then stop me."

Instead, I reach behind me, my hand finding the hard

ridge of his cock through his pants. Gods, he's so hard, so beautifully big.

"Why would I want to do that?" I ask innocently. "Especially when I can feel how much you need this, too?"

He hisses at my touch, hips jerking forward instinctively. "Need you," he corrects, his voice rough with desire. "Only you."

His admission sends a fresh wave of heat through me. I turn my head, seeking his mouth, needing to taste him again. He obliges, kissing me deeply while he's already tugging on my pants and underwear. He finally pulls from my kiss and crouches down as he draws them along my legs. I step out of them, feeling so vulnerable, so sexy and hot for him.

Back on his feet, he grins sinfully and kisses me once more, keeping me still facing the wall.

I moan into his mouth as he explores, touches, and learns exactly what makes me tremble. His other hand yanks impatiently at my shirt, pushing it up to expose me completely.

"Say it," he demands against my lips. "Tell me who you belong to."

"You," I gasp as his hand slides over my hips, across my lower stomach, and falls between my thighs. I moan loudly as his fingers slip between my folds, where I'm burning up and soaking. "I'm yours, Theron."

He growls his approval, his touch teasing my clit so rapidly I'm left breathless. Hands pressed to the wall, I tremble as I spread my legs for him when he pushes two fingers into me.

I cry out as he licks my neck, then sucks down on my earlobe. His hot breath washes across my skin, making me shake against him.

Releasing me, he spins me to face him. His eyes are almost entirely black now, with only the thinnest ring of silver remaining.

"And I'm yours," he says, the words sounding as if they've been torn from him. "Body and soul. The last thought in my mind will be of you."

There's something devastating about the raw honesty in his voice. I reach for his pants, pulling at his belt and buttons, then tug them down, revealing that he's wearing nothing underneath. His throbbing cock springs free, alert and pointing at me. Drawing his mouth down to mine again, I pour everything into the kiss. His hands grip my thighs, lifting me effortlessly, and I wrap my legs around his waist as he presses me back against the wall.

We don't bother with removing our clothes entirely—too urgent, too desperate. He positions himself at my entrance, and I moan as the tip pushes into me, my pulse racing in my veins.

"Look at me," he commands, waiting until my gaze locks with his before pushing forward in one powerful thrust.

I cry out at his thickness, the way he stretches me, my nails digging into his shoulders through his shirt. The sensation is overwhelming—perfect, too much and not enough all at once. He gives me only seconds to adjust before he begins to move, setting a rhythm that has me gasping with each thrust.

"Your sweet, tight pussy is mine," he growls, one hand gripping my hip hard enough to bruise while the other tangles in my hair. "Say it."

"Yours," I manage, my voice breaking as he hits a spot inside me that makes my vision blur. "Fuck, Theron..."

His pace increases, thrusting faster, driving me to lose control. I cling to him, my back scraping against the wall, the slight pain only enhancing the pleasure building in my core. His mouth finds my neck again, biting and sucking as if he can't get enough of my taste.

"Fuck, you smell and taste so addictive." His words are a dark vow against my skin. "I'll kill anyone who tries to take you from me."

The possessive declaration shouldn't send another wave of heat through me, but it does. There's something raw and right about being claimed so completely by him, about knowing he'd tear the world apart to keep me safe.

"No one would dare," I gasp, my head falling back against the wall as arousal coils tighter in my belly. "Everyone knows I'm yours."

He shifts his angle slightly, and suddenly, the pressure intensifies, threatening to shatter me completely.

"Come for me," he demands, his voice strained with his own approaching release. "Let me feel you come all over my cock, squeezing me."

His fingers slide down between us, adding pressure on

my clit where I need it most, and I'm lost. The world fragments around me, pleasure crashing through my body in waves so intense that I cry out his name, my voice echoing off the stone walls. My pussy clenches around him, pulling him deeper, and I feel rather than hear his answering groan as he follows me over the edge.

At the height of my crescendo, my hand slams back against the wall, searching for something, anything, to anchor me as sensation threatens to sweep me away completely. My palm connects with a section of stone that gives slightly under the pressure, different from the rest. There's a soft clicking sound, barely audible over our ragged breathing, then the wall behind me begins to move.

Theron reacts instantly, his arms wrapping securely around me as he stumbles backward, pulling us both away from the opening panel. We stagger, still intimately connected, as a section of the wall swings silently inward to reveal a darkened passage beyond.

For a moment, we simply stare at the opening in stunned silence, him still buried deep inside me. Then I start to laugh, the sound bubbling up from my chest uncontrollably.

"Of course," I gasp between fits of giggles. "Of fucking course that's how we find a secret compartment."

Theron's expression shifts from confusion to amusement, and soon he's laughing, too, the sound deep and rich against my neck. "Well, that's certainly a new method of exploration."

I can't help but join him, the absurdity of the moment too perfect. "Only we would literally stumble upon a secret door while fucking."

With reluctance, we disentangle ourselves, our bodies separating, though my skin still hums from his touch. Theron disappears briefly, returning with a damp cloth. He kneels before me, and it makes my heart clench. With surprising gentleness, he tends to me, wiping me clean with careful strokes.

"You don't have to do this," I tell him, suddenly self-conscious under his intent stare.

His gaze lifts to mine, one eyebrow raised. "I want to." His hand stills momentarily. "Unless you'd prefer I didn't?"

"No, it's just—" I struggle to find the words. "Most Alphas wouldn't consider this their responsibility."

A small smile plays at the corner of his mouth. "I'm not most Alphas. And you're not most Omegas."

His brow furrows in concentration, as if this simple act of care requires the same focus he brings to battle strategy.

"Too much?" he asks softly.

I shake my head, strangely moved by his consideration. "Perfect."

"Good." He presses a kiss to my inner thigh, casual and affectionate. "I should hope I know what you can handle by now."

"Arrogant," I accuse without heat.

"Accurate," he counters.

Once done, he cleans himself efficiently and quickly. There's something profoundly moving about this fierce, dangerous man being so attentive, so gentle in these private moments.

After we hastily rearrange our clothing, Theron moves first into the hidden compartment, and a soft blue glow automatically illuminates a narrow corridor beyond the hidden door.

"Shall we?" he asks.

I approach cautiously, running my fingers along the edge of the opening. The mechanism is completely invisible—no handle, no obvious latch, nothing to indicate that a door exists at all.

"How did no one discover this before? The Covenant members lived here for years."

"Maybe they weren't looking, or maybe they knew?" Theron says. We follow the narrow passage extending about twenty feet before ending at what appears to be another door.

The air is stale but not unpleasant, suggesting the space has remained sealed for some time. Unlike the hidden entrance, the iron door we find makes no attempt to disguise its nature. It's clearly a barrier meant to keep people out.

"No handle," I observe, running my hands over the cold metal surface. "And no obvious way to open it."

Theron examines the door carefully, seeing no engravings or markings.

"Wait," he says suddenly, pointing to the far left of the door. "Look at this."

I lean closer to see what he's found. It's a circular depression about two inches in diameter, deep enough that the bottom disappears into shadow.

"A keyhole?" I suggest, frowning. "But it's not like any I've seen before."

"It's not for a conventional key," Theron agrees, tracing the opening with his finger.

I touch the medallion hanging from my ceremonial chain—the one that grants us access to the Covenant building. "Do you think it could be this?"

He considers it, then shakes his head while I contemplate if I've seen any keys in the building since arriving but come up short.

"We had to use a key in the maze," he blurts out and glances at me. My eyes widen as it all comes back to me.

A thought strikes me suddenly. "The Bloodstone Key!"

"You still have it, right?" he asks urgently.

"Yes, I brought it with me after the maze. It's in our bedroom, in the carved box on the shelf."

"I'll get it," he states, already turning back toward the passage. "Stay here and see if you can find anything else."

While he's gone, I examine the door more carefully, noting how the hallway has no markings either and how this whole section doesn't fit the same design as the Onyx Covenant building—as though someone built this secretly.

Theron returns moments later, slightly breathless

from hurrying. The Bloodstone Key gleams dully in his palm and is small enough to fit comfortably in the hand, with strange symbols etched into its surface.

"Let's see if this works," he says, holding it up to the depression in the door.

The Bloodstone Key fits perfectly into the hole. For a moment, nothing happens. Then Theron gives it a slight turn, and we hear a series of clicks from within the door.

Slowly, silently, the heavy door swings inward, revealing the darkness beyond.

I take his free hand and squeeze it, then we step through the doorway into the unknown.

The chamber is larger than I expected, perhaps twenty square feet, with a vaulted ceiling. Dust motes dance in the beam of our blue light, swirling in the disturbed air. The room is lined with shelves from floor to ceiling, packed with books, scrolls, and what appear to be wooden filing boxes. A large table sits in the center, surrounded by cushioned chairs.

"By the moons," Theron breathes, stepping inside. "This is it. This must be what my mother was referring to."

I follow him in, running my fingers along the spines of books whose titles have faded with time. "There's so much here. Records going back... centuries, by the look of it."

"We need to read all of it," Theron says, already pulling volumes from shelves. "Everything. There could be crucial information about both our packs, about the Covenant itself."

"This will take months," I observe, opening one of the wooden boxes to find neatly filed parchments.

Theron glances up, a half smile playing on his lips despite the seriousness of the moment. "Good thing we have ten years, then."

We spend hours examining the contents of the hidden chamber, carefully placing items onto the table for closer inspection. Some documents are so fragile they threaten to crumble at a touch, while others are better preserved.

As daylight fades outside, neither of us suggests stopping. At some point, Theron drags the cushions from the chairs to provide more comfort on the floor.

The last thing I remember is resting my head on his shoulder, just for a moment, as I struggle to decipher a particularly faded text...

I wake to pale morning light filtering through the hidden doorway. Theron is no longer beside me, and for a moment, I feel a pang of disorientation. Then I spot him by the window in the study beyond, surrounded by stacks of books and folders, his expression grave as he reads from a leather-bound journal.

Stretching the stiffness from my limbs, I rise and make my way to him.

"Find anything?" I ask, my voice still husky from sleep.

He looks up, and the raw emotion in his eyes stops me cold. They glisten with what might be unshed tears, something I've never seen from him before.

"So much," he says quietly. "Too much."

I kneel beside him, taking his hand. "Tell me."

He draws in a deep breath, gesturing to the documents spread around him. "Evidence of Umbra corruption going back to my father's grandfather—patterns my father simply continued and expanded upon." His jaw tightens. "And worse, records kept by previous Onyx Covenant members over the earlier decades when they started documenting everything but doing nothing to stop it."

"They just... hid the evidence here?" I ask, anger stirring in my chest.

"They knew," he confirms, his voice laced with fury. "They fucking knew, and they chose to be neutral observers rather than mediators. They betrayed their sacred duty."

I pick up one of the journals, scanning entries that detail systematic advantages given to Umbra during supposed fair territory divisions.

"The Onyx Covenant members choose what laws to enforce," I say slowly. "And they were wrong to ignore this."

"Criminally wrong," Theron blurts. His hand clenches around a particular document, wrinkling the ancient paper. "There are records here of hunts where the Elios pack was given maybe ten percent of catches, deliberately keeping your people on the edge of starvation during harsh winters."

I swallow hard, remembering the lean years of my childhood. "We always suspected but could never prove it."

"I haven't found anything on my mother yet, but I doubt they would have recorded her death here. And after what my father said before I killed him, I know he took her life." His voice shakes, and I lean in closer to him, embracing him, my heart hurting for him.

"But why keep these other records at all? If they were complicit, why not destroy the evidence?"

"From what I've seen, all the records here are at least thirty to forty years old, nothing recent. So someone back then wanted the truth to come out but must have been too afraid to expose it," Theron states, gesturing to the shelves of damning evidence. "Why else maintain the secret room, organizing everything so meticulously? Why else would they add the key in the maze that resets itself every ten years? They wanted someone to eventually discover this room and the information."

"They could have used the Onyx Warriors," I say, sighing. "They had the means to stand against your family."

"But what happens after their ten years of service?" he

answers. "They'd have to return to their packs, where my father could eliminate them. Or he could kill their families while the Covenant members were still in here, protected."

We're silent for a long moment. Finally, he nods slowly.

"Fear is a powerful motivator, but cowardice is no excuse for enabling a tyrant."

I press my hand over his. "What do we do with all this now?"

He reaches for an ancient leather-bound journal, its pages yellowed with age. "There's something else I found. Something that changes everything we thought we knew and what I think my mother was hinting at in her journal." His fingers trace the faded symbol on the cover— two crescent moons, one silver, one black, forming a perfect circle together.

"What is it?" I ask, leaning closer.

"The original Covenant," Theron says. "Written in the hand of an Alpha who led both our packs."

My breath catches. "Both?"

We'd suspected it. The carvings in the maze hinted at unity—at something older than the split we were raised to believe in. But this... this is different.

He opens the journal carefully, revealing intricate drawings and text in an ancient script.

"Elios and Umbra weren't just once united," he says. "They were never meant to be divided. One pack. One strong, unified pack that worshipped both moons together."

His eyes meet mine, alive with the weight of truth. "The silver moon of light and the black moon of shadow... they were always two halves of the same whole."

I shake my head, trying to absorb it. "That goes beyond anything we saw in the maze... even what I was taught in priestess training."

"Exactly."

Theron flips through more pages, revealing detailed illustrations of wolves gathered beneath both moons, dancing, howling, living as one.

"The division wasn't some divine order," he says. "It was a choice. A betrayal. Power-hungry Alphas twisted the original teachings to serve themselves."

He points to a passage, tracing the words with his fingertip.

"As the moons find balance in the night sky, so too must the children of silver light and obsidian shadow find balance within one pack. Neither can exist without the other; together, they create harmony."

I feel dizzy with the implications. "So, all this fighting, all this hatred between our packs..."

"Was based on a lie," he finishes. "Or at the very least, a terrible misinterpretation that maybe became dogma."

"This changes everything," I whisper, tracing the symbol of the joined moons. "We haven't just been doing it wrong—we've been working against our very nature."

Theron nods, then gestures to the hundreds of documents still waiting to be examined. "There's so much more here to uncover. Secrets buried for generations."

I look up at him, a new resolve burning within me. "We need to let everyone know. Not just about your father's crimes, but about this—our true heritage. We need to bring the packs back together the way they were always meant to be."

He leans closer to me. "We do what the Onyx Covenant was always meant to do. We bring balance. We expose the corruption, make restitution to those who suffered, and create new laws that can't be so easily manipulated." His eyes shine with determination. "And yes, we reunite our people, step by step."

"We'll do it slowly, without war," I say firmly.

"Good thing we have the Onyx Warriors at our command if things don't go smoothly," he adds with a grim smile.

I press my forehead to his, and we stare into each other's eyes.

His hand comes up to cup my cheek, his touch infinitely gentle despite the storm of emotions I know are raging within him.

"I never thought I'd say this, but I'm almost grateful for my father's final act of cruelty. If he hadn't tried to kill you, I might never have found the courage to end him. To free our packs from his poison."

"And now we have the evidence to show everyone exactly who he was," I say.

"No one will be able to paint him as a martyr."

"Then we'd better get to work." I rise to my feet and extend my hand to him. "We have a lot to accomplish in ten years."

He takes my hand, standing to his full height. In the morning light, with determination hardening his features, he looks every inch the leader our packs need.

"No," he says softly. "We have a legacy to build that will last far beyond our ten years. Starting now."

As he pulls me to him for a kiss that feels like a promise, I hold the ancient journal between us—a physical reminder of the truth we've discovered. For the first time, I can envision a future where our packs aren't just at peace but truly unified, as they were always meant to be. Two aspects of the same whole, like the dual moons overhead.

EPILOGUE

LYRA

Three Months Later

I've never seen this many wolves gathered peacefully in one place—at least fifteen hundred from both packs, spread around dozens of cooking fires, their faces illuminated by dancing flames as they share stories, food, and strong berry wine. Three months ago, this scene would have been unimaginable. Now, it feels like the first breath after being underwater too long.

"One more speech and I'm throwing myself into the nearest ravine," I mutter to Theron, my fingers toying with the heavy medallion hanging from my ceremonial robes. The damn things weigh more than armor and have about as much grace as a bear wearing stockings.

"No ravines for at least another hour," Theron replies,

his voice pitched low enough that only I can hear. His own robe—identical to mine, with its midnight-black fabric and intricate silver embroidery depicting both pack symbols—somehow looks regal rather than ridiculous on his imposing frame. Bastard. "You promised the elders you'd participate in the moon blessing after the feast."

"I lied," I say cheerfully. "First rule of leadership: Tell people what they want to hear, then do whatever the hell you want."

A smile plays at the corners of his mouth. "Is that what they taught you in priestess training? No wonder the Elios rituals were always so chaotic."

"Like the Umbra ones were any better?" I scoff.

"Fair point," he concedes, his hand finding the small of my back. "Though I think we've improved things considerably."

He's not wrong. The platform we're standing on—constructed at the center of the massive clearing specifically for this celebration—gives us a perfect view of what we've accomplished. Across the field, cooking spits turn with the day's hunt—deer, boar, and wildfowl harvested by joint hunting parties of Umbra and Elios. For the first time in generations, the meat is being divided equally and shared without suspicion or fear of poisoning.

Children from both packs race through the gathering, playing games that would have been forbidden just months ago. A group of youngsters has set up an elaborate obstacle course using logs and stones, competing to see who can navigate it fastest while carrying a wooden ball in their mouth. Others play a game involving a leather sphere stuffed with dried beans that they kick back and forth between goals made of bent willow branches.

Near the eastern edge of the clearing, a group of teenage wolves tests their skills at archery, the targets illuminated by hanging lanterns. I spot my cousin Noah among them, laughing as he shows an Umbra girl how to correct her stance. Three months ago, he would have been more likely to shoot her than help her.

"We should mingle," Theron says, nodding toward the crowd below. "Let them see us up close, not just looming over them like judgmental deities."

"Speak for yourself," I say. "I make an excellent judgmental deity."

He laughs, the sound still rare enough to make my heart skip. "You're terrible at looking intimidating. Everyone can see right through you."

"That's patently untrue," I protest. "I scared that messenger from the southern territories so badly yesterday that he practically fell over himself backing away."

"Because you threw a book at his head when he suggested women couldn't understand border treaties."

"A small book," I clarify. "And I missed. Intentionally."

Theron's hand slides down to intertwine with mine. "Come on. Your father's been trying to catch your eye for the last ten minutes."

Sure enough, when I scan the crowd, I spot my

father standing near one of the larger cooking fires, deep in conversation with Elder Maren from the Umbra pack.

"Fine," I sigh, feigning reluctance. "But if one more person tries to feed me their *special* family recipe for blessing bread, I might actually scream."

We descend the platform steps together, our movements automatically syncing after months of living in each other's space. The crowd parts respectfully as we move through it, wolves from both packs offering quick bows or the traditional heart-touch of greeting.

A small girl—no more than six or seven—darts in front of us suddenly, her eyes wide with wonder. She's clearly Elios with her blonde-toned hair, but the intricate beads woven into her braids are distinctly Umbra craftsmanship.

"Are you really her?" she asks, staring up at me. "The wolf-who-walks-with-moonstone?"

I crouch down to her level, ignoring how my ceremonial robes pool ridiculously around me. "That's what some call me," I say, smiling. "But my friends call me Lyra."

She nods solemnly. "My mama says you killed three monsters in the maze and took their hearts as trophies."

Behind me, Theron makes a sound that might be a hastily suppressed laugh. I shoot him a warning glance before turning back to the girl.

"Your mama's stories sound much more exciting than what actually happened," I tell her. "Though there was definitely a maze, and it was plenty scary without adding heart-stealing to the mix."

The girl looks vaguely disappointed. "Oh." Then she brightens. "What about him?" She points at Theron. "Did he really turn into a giant wolf and eat his father whole?"

This time Theron does laugh, a sharp bark of genuine amusement. "Not quite," he says, kneeling beside me. "Though that's a much more interesting story than the truth."

The girl's mother appears, face flushed with embarrassment. "Nessa! I told you not to bother the Covenant leaders." She grabs her daughter's hand, offering us a flustered bow. "I'm so sorry. She's been obsessed with the stories since the Harvest Ritual."

"No bother at all," I assure her.

We continue through the gathering, stopping frequently to speak with members of both packs. I'm surprised to find how many names I now know, how many faces have become familiar through our work at the Covenant. There's Eldon, an Umbra blacksmith who's teaching metalworking techniques to Elios apprentices, and Jera, an Elios healer who saved an Umbra child from a wasting sickness last month.

Small victories, building one atop another.

As we near my father, a familiar voice cuts through the murmur of the crowd.

"Well, look who finally decided to join the commoners!" Aria appears in front of us, hands on her hips, wearing a dress of such deep blue that it looks almost black in the firelight. Silver bracelets jangle on her wrists, and her chestnut hair has been elaborately braided with azure ribbons. She is beautiful like always.

"Who are you, and what have you done with my best friend?" I ask, eyeing her outfit. "The Aria I know wouldn't be caught dead in something that couldn't double as combat wear."

"Special occasion," she says with a dismissive wave. "Don't get used to it. This thing is torture—I can barely breathe."

"Worth it," says Kieran, materializing at her side with two cups of what smells like berry juice. He's dressed more formally than I've ever seen him, in fitted leather pants and a tunic embroidered with his family's traditional hunting pattern. His eyes never leave Aria as he hands her one of the cups.

"You clean up surprisingly well," I tell him, hiding my smile as his gaze finally tears away from Aria to acknowledge me. "Almost didn't recognize you without mud and blood splatter."

"Funny," he deadpans. "You should see the pile of weapons I had to leave behind to fit into these clothes. I feel naked."

"You're still carrying at least three knives," Theron observes. "I can see the outlines."

Kieran grins, unabashed. "Five, actually. But who's counting?"

Aria rolls her eyes. "You're all impossible. Come on, my father's been saving the good wine for you two." She links her arm through mine, dragging me toward a group of Elios elders while Theron and Kieran follow behind.

"So," she whispers once we're out of the men's earshot. "Tell me, how's the country's most powerful couple handling their first major inter-pack celebration? Ready to run screaming into the forest yet?"

"Only about six times so far," I admit. "But the night's still young."

"It's going well," she says, her tone shifting to something more serious. "Better than anyone expected. Did you see Selene actually laughing with Elios warriors earlier? The same ones she would have gladly gutted a few months ago."

I follow her gaze to where Selene stands with a group of mixed-pack hunters, describing something with animated gestures. The transformation in her is remarkable. Since her humiliation at the Harvest Ritual, I'd expected nothing but continued hostility, perhaps even sabotage. Instead, after several weeks of sullen avoidance, she'd approached the Covenant with an unexpected proposal—a joint training program for young hunters from both packs.

"People can surprise you," I say. "Sometimes, even pleasantly."

"Speaking of surprises..." Aria glances back at the men, who are now deep in conversation about hunting techniques, judging by Kieran's enthusiastic arm movements. "There's something I need to tell you."

The intensity in her voice makes me stop walking. "What's wrong?"

"Nothing's wrong," she says quickly. "It's just... unexpected."

A group of dancers swirls past us, moving to the rhythm of drums and bone flutes played by musicians from both packs. The music they create is strange but beautiful—Umbra percussion underlying the haunting melodies of Elios wind instruments, producing something entirely new.

Aria pulls me farther from the crowd, behind one of the massive oak trees that edge the clearing. In the relative privacy, she takes a deep breath.

"I'm pregnant," she blurts out, her eyes wide as if she's still shocked by the words herself.

My jaw drops. "You're WHAT?"

Several nearby wolves turn to look at us. Aria winces, slapping a hand over my mouth. "Gods, Lyra, why don't you just announce it to the entire gathering?"

"Sorry," I mumble against her palm. When she removes her hand, I hiss, "How? When? I mean, I know how, but—"

"About two months," she says, a blush creeping up her neck. "It wasn't exactly planned."

"You and Kieran?" I clarify, though the answer is obvious from the way she can't quite suppress her smile when she glances in his direction.

"No, the baker's son," she says sarcastically. "Of course, Kieran."

A thousand questions flood my mind. "Does he know? How did he react? Are you happy about this? What about your families?"

"Yes, surprisingly well, terrified but yes, and we haven't told them yet," she answers in rapid succession. "You're the first to know, besides us."

I'm momentarily speechless—a rare occurrence that Aria never fails to point out. "A baby," I finally manage. "A child of both packs."

"The first in generations, as far as anyone knows," she says, her hand unconsciously moving to rest on her still-flat stomach.

I throw my arms around her, squeezing tight before remembering her condition and jumping back. "Sorry! Did I hurt you? Gods, I don't know anything about pregnancies."

She laughs. "I'm pregnant, not made of glass. Though you wouldn't know it from how Kieran's been acting. Won't let me lift anything heavier than a dinner plate, insists I rest every hour..." She rolls her eyes, but there's undeniable affection in her voice.

"I can't believe it," I say, still processing. "You're going to be a mother."

"And you're going to be an aunt," she says firmly. "The best aunt any child could have, whether we share blood or not."

Emotion tightens my throat. "Damn right I am."

"We're telling Theron tonight," she adds. "But I wanted you to know first."

"He'll be thrilled," I assure her. "Especially since it means Kieran has something to focus on besides antagonizing the training recruits."

We rejoin the men, and I struggle to keep my expression neutral as Kieran immediately fusses over Aria, making sure she isn't too cold, too warm, or too tired. Theron catches my eye, one eyebrow raised in silent question. I shake my head slightly—not my news to share.

My father approaches, clasping forearms with Theron in the traditional Elios greeting before pulling me into a tight hug. "There's my girl," he says warmly. "Finally decided to join the celebration properly?"

"Had to make a dramatic entrance," I say, returning his embrace. "How are you finding the festivities?"

"Better than I could have imagined," he admits, glancing around at the mingling packs. "When I was your age, the idea of breaking bread with Umbra wolves would have been unthinkable. Now look at us."

"Change comes whether we're ready or not," Theron observes. "Better to guide it than be drowned by it."

My father nods thoughtfully. "Wise words from one so young. Your mother would be proud."

A shadow crosses Theron's face at the mention of his mother, but he inclines his head in acknowledgment. "I hope so."

"Lyra!" a voice calls from nearby. "We need you for the blessing ceremony!"

I groan. "Duty calls, apparently."

"Go," my father says, squeezing my shoulder. "I'll save

you some of the blackberry wine for when you're done playing high priestess."

The next hour passes in a blur of ritual and ceremony. Despite my earlier complaints, there's something deeply satisfying about leading the Blood Moon blessing, especially with elements from both pack traditions woven together. Theron stands beside me throughout, his steady presence an anchor as I guide the gathering through ancient words of thanks and renewal.

When the formal portion of the celebration concludes, smaller groups form around individual fires. Communal plates of food circulate—rich venison stew, roasted root vegetables seasoned with mountain herbs, flatbreads topped with wild honey and berries. The air fills with the sounds of laughter and conversation, the occasional burst of song rising above the general din.

Aria finds us again as we're sampling food from the eastern firepit. She pulls Kieran forward, her expression a mixture of nervousness and excitement.

"We have something to tell you," she announces, her fingers intertwining with Kieran's.

Theron pauses with a piece of bread halfway to his mouth. "You're moving to the southern territories?"

"What? No." Kieran looks confused. "Why would you think that?"

"Because you've been declining every hunting expedition for the past month," Theron says. "I assumed you were planning some kind of major change."

Kieran and Aria exchange a look that contains an

entire private conversation. Finally, Aria clears her throat. "You're not entirely wrong about the major change part."

I bite my lip to keep from giving away that I already know. Theron sets down his plate, giving them his full attention.

"I'm pregnant," Aria says, her voice steady despite the slight tremble in her hands.

Theron's eyes widen fractionally—the equivalent of a shocked gasp from anyone else. Kieran stands straighter, as if bracing for judgment but determined to face it head-on. The silence stretches for one heartbeat, two, and then Theron's face breaks into a rare, genuine smile.

"Well done, brother," he says, clapping Kieran on the shoulder hard enough to make him stagger slightly. "I had no idea you were capable of creating anything besides chaos and training injuries."

Relief washes over Kieran's face, followed by indignation. "I'm capable of plenty," he protests. "In fact—"

"Please don't finish that sentence," Aria interrupts, though she's smiling, too. "Some details should remain private."

"A child of both packs," Theron muses, his expression turning thoughtful. "The living embodiment of the future we're building."

"Poor kid," Kieran groans. "Already carrying the weight of symbolic importance before they're even born."

"They'll be strong," Theron assures him. "With parents like you two, how could they not be?"

Aria preens slightly at the compliment. "I'm going to

be an excellent mother. Firm but fair. Just the right balance of structure and freedom."

"She's been researching," Kieran stage-whispers. "Every book on child-rearing has mysteriously disappeared into our quarters."

"Better than your approach," she retorts. "Which consists entirely of panicking and sharpening increasingly tiny training knives for an infant who won't be able to hold them for years."

"I'm not panicking," he insists. "I'm preparing. There's a difference."

I laugh, leaning against Theron's side. "You're both going to be wonderful parents," I tell them sincerely. "And you'll have all the support you need."

The conversation flows from pregnancy to training programs to the latest political developments with the southern territories. Eventually, Aria and Kieran drift away to speak with her parents, leaving Theron and me alone by the fire.

"They seem happy," I observe, watching them go. "Never would have predicted those two ending up together."

"And now they're having a baby," he says, then his arm slides around my waist, pulling me closer against the night's growing chill.

We watch the celebration continue around us. Nearby, a group of elders plays a traditional strategy game using carved stones on a wooden board while children chase each other through the clearing, their shrieks of laughter carrying on the night air. In the distance, several couples dance to the soft music still playing near the central fire.

After a comfortable silence, Theron's lips brush against my ear, his voice pitched low for me alone. "The challenge has been set," he murmurs. "Get ready because we start tonight."

I turn to face him, confused. "What challenge?"

His eyes gleam with predatory intent in the firelight. "Getting you pregnant, of course. I'm not about to let Kieran outdo me in this."

I nearly choke on my wine. "Excuse me?"

"You heard me." His hand slides around to my stomach, splaying possessively across it. "Imagine it, Lyra—a child with your fire and my strength. A true heir to the new world we're building."

I stare at him, trying to determine if he's serious. The intensity in his gaze leaves little doubt. "You're actually serious."

"Entirely." His expression softens slightly. "Unless you don't want—"

"I didn't say that," I interrupt, surprised by how much the idea appeals to me now that it's been voiced. "I just wasn't expecting this particular conversation tonight."

His smile turns wolfish. "I've been thinking about it for weeks. Watching you lead the Covenant, seeing how naturally you handle both packs..." His thumb traces circles on my hip, sending warmth spreading through my core. "The thought of you carrying my child—our child— is becoming rather... distracting."

"Everything's a competition with you," I observe, though I can't keep the fondness from my voice. "First the maze, then the Covenant leadership, now fatherhood?"

"Only the things worth winning," he says, completely unapologetic. "And this would be the greatest prize of all."

Despite my initial surprise, I find myself imagining it—a child with Theron's eyes and perhaps my blonde hair, running through the Covenant halls, learning from both our traditions.

"A baby," I say softly. "Our baby."

"The first of many," he promises, and the certainty in his voice sends a shiver down my spine.

I turn in his arms to face him fully. "You're being crazy now."

"And yet you love me anyway," he counters, brushing a strand of hair from my face with unexpected tenderness.

"Fates have mercy—I do." The admission comes easier now, after months of shared struggles and victories. "Fine. Challenge accepted."

His eyes darken, pupils expanding until only a thin ring of gray remains. "You'll make a magnificent mother."

"And you'll be a terrifying father," I counter. "The poor child will have the most intimidating protection detail in history."

"I prefer vigilantly protective," he corrects, pressing a kiss to my temple. "Someone needs to balance out your tendency toward reckless bravery."

"It's not reckless if it works," I argue automatically, then we make our way closer to where Aria and Kieran stand.

Aria's voice cuts through our moment. "What are you two whispering about so intensely? You look like you're plotting something."

I feel heat rising to my cheeks, but Theron just smiles.

"Just discussing future projects."

Kieran narrows his eyes suspiciously. "What kind?"

I hesitate, then decide there's no point in hiding it from our closest friends.

"The kind that might result in your child having a cousin of sorts."

Aria's eyes widen comically. "Are you saying—"

"That we've decided to start our own family," Theron confirms, his arm tightening around my waist. "Sometime in the near future."

Aria squeals with delight, throwing her arms around me. "Our babies can grow up together! They'll be the closest of friends. We'll have joint naming ceremonies and shared first moon celebrations, and—"

"Breathe, love," Kieran interrupts gently, though he's grinning, too. "Let them actually conceive the child before you plan its entire life."

"Details," she says dismissively, still clutching my hands. "This is perfect! The two highest-ranking families in both packs raising the next generation together. It's like something from the ancient prophecies."

"Wolf, help us all," Kieran mutters, exchanging a look

with Theron. "Can you imagine the chaos? Four of us and two of them?"

"I'm counting on it," Theron replies, a rare lightness in his expression.

The moon climbs higher in the night sky, its blood-red glow touching every face in the clearing—Umbra and Elios alike. Around us, the celebration continues, but at this moment, it feels like we've carved out a pocket of possibility, a glimpse into a future that once seemed impossible.

As the night deepens, more families gather their drowsy children, though many wolves remain, settling in for long conversations around the fires. The musicians play softer melodies now, suited to the quieter mood. Theron's hand remains at my waist, a warm presence that grounds me amid the swirl of activity.

"Do you think it will last?" I ask him quietly, watching an Umbra elder teach an Elios child a traditional knot-tying technique. "This peace we're building?"

He considers the question with characteristic thoughtfulness. "Not without effort," he finally says. "Nothing worthwhile ever comes easily. But yes, I believe it will last and grow stronger with each generation that doesn't learn to hate first and question later."

"Starting with them," I nod toward Aria and Kieran, who are now seated by a nearby fire, his arm draped protectively around her shoulders.

"And continuing with our children," Theron adds, his voice holding such certainty that I can almost see them—

strong, proud wolves who will never know the divisions that scarred their parents' lives.

I lean into him, suddenly overwhelmed by gratitude for this moment, this night, this man. "Who would have thought the Harvest Ritual would lead us here?"

"I did," he says simply.

I look up at him in surprise. "You expected all this? The joint leadership, the merger of the packs, us?"

His expression turns serious, eyes reflecting the firelight. "From the moment I chose you, I knew everything would change. I just didn't know how completely." His hand traces the curve of my jaw. "But I hoped. Gods, how I hoped."

The honesty in his voice steals my breath. I rise on tiptoes to press my lips against his, not caring who might see. His arm tightens around me as he returns the kiss.

When we part, I'm aware of several approving glances from nearby wolves. Times have indeed changed— months ago, such a public display between an Umbra and an Elios would have caused outrage. Now, it draws knowing smiles.

"Take me home," I whisper against his lips. "If we're starting this challenge tonight, I'd prefer not to have an audience."

His eyes darken further, a growl too low for others to hear rumbling in his chest. "As you wish."

We make our excuses to the gathering, transferring ceremonial responsibilities to the elders, who are more than happy to oversee the rest of the celebration. Aria gives me a knowing smirk as we leave, while my father and mother simply nod.

The walk back to the Covenant building is quiet, the night air cool against my skin after the warmth of the celebration fires. Theron's hand remains firmly in mine, his thumb occasionally brushing across my knuckles in a gesture that's become familiar yet never fails to send warmth through me.

The Onyx Covenant building rises before us, its black stone gleaming silver in the moonlight. What once seemed an intimidating fortress now feels like home— our home, where we've begun to build something neither of us could have imagined before the Harvest Ritual.

As we climb the steps to the massive front doors, Theron pauses, turning to face me. The Blood Moon bathes his features in crimson light, highlighting the sharp planes of his face and the intensity in his eyes.

"What?" I ask, suddenly self-conscious under his scrutiny.

"Just memorizing this moment," he says softly. "You here, with the dual moons behind you and the future ahead of us."

I reach up to touch his face, my fingers tracing his cheek. "Pretty words from a wolf once known for his silence."

"You changed that," he says simply. "You changed everything."

As he pulls me into another kiss, more heated this time, I think about the journey that brought us here: the maze, the trials, the bloodshed, and the sacrifice. The ancient prophecies spoke of union between the packs, of peace following centuries of strife, but they never mentioned this—the simple, transformative power of choosing love over hatred, of building something new from the ashes of the old.

They never told us in the stories that the most defiant act wouldn't be baring fangs or drawing blood, but this— loving so fiercely that generations of hatred simply couldn't stand against it. That in choosing Theron, I wouldn't just find my mate but my strength, my purpose. My home.

BONUS SCENE
ARIA & KIERAN SEPARATED AT THE RIVER

Aria

The current tugs at my limbs with greedy fingers, trying to drag me back into the churning depths. I dig my nails into the muddy bank, fighting for purchase as I haul myself from the river's furious grasp. Water streams from my hair, my body—Gods, I'm soaked to the bone, and the night air already pricks at my skin with its chill.

"Everyone alive?" I call out, pushing wet strands of hair from my face.

A few yards downstream, Kieran pulls himself onto the bank with far more grace than should be possible for someone who just got tossed around by rapids. Fucking Umbra and their river-swimming skills. His reddish hair is plastered to his skull, water running in rivulets down his neck and bare shoulders. He's already shifted back to human form, completely unconcerned about his nakedness.

I avert my eyes. Or at least, I try to. Muscles, so many...

"I'm good," he replies, shaking himself like a dog. "Orion? Rachel?"

Rachel emerges from the water next, coughing and sputtering. "Present," she manages between gasps. The Umbra woman looks half drowned, her dark hair in tangled clumps around her face.

Orion follows shortly, dragging himself out of the water with a dramatic groan. "Someone remind me why we thought jumping off the cliff was a good idea?"

I scan the opposite bank, squinting against the fading light. "Where's Lyra? And Theron?"

Kieran follows my gaze, his expression suddenly tense. "Not sure. Current might have taken them in a different direction."

"They'll be fine," Orion interrupts, wringing water from his clothes as he pulls them out of his bag he'd been wearing on his back. His handsome face is set in that dismissive expression I once found authoritative but now just find irritating. "Theron's practically part fish, and your friend has survived worse."

I glare at him. "We should look for them."

"Not in this dark night," Rachel adds. "And not in these temperatures. We need to get dry and warm, or we'll all end up as wolf-sicles by morning."

Kieran nods, though his eyes still scan the opposite shore. "Rachel's right. Theron can handle himself, and I've seen Lyra fight in her training. They'll be fine."

Something in his tone makes me look at him more closely. There's concern there, yes, but also a genuine respect when he mentions Lyra. Unusual for an Umbra warrior to acknowledge the skills of an Elios priestess.

"We should move," Orion states, already dragging on his wet clothes. "Get to higher ground."

I retrieve my own pack, grateful for the oilskin I used to keep my spare clothes partially dry. From the corner of my eye, I catch Kieran watching me, a half smile playing on his lips. When I glare at him, he just winks and turns around.

Cocky bastard.

Once dressed in somewhat dry clothes, we begin our trek through the woods, while I keep glancing back to the river in the hopes of spotting Lyra. The twilight deepens around us, shadows stretching between the ancient trees like spilled ink. I find myself oddly aware of Kieran's presence beside me, the way he moves with casual confidence through terrain that should be unfamiliar to him.

"They're probably already making camp," he explains after we've been walking for about an hour, his voice pitched low so only I can hear. "Theron's good at finding defensible positions."

"And Lyra's good at spotting resources," I reply. "If they're together, they'll be fine, I'm sure."

He nods, his gaze flicking to mine. "They make a surprisingly good team."

"Surprising because she's Elios and he's Umbra?"

A ghost of a smile touches his lips. "Surprising because they're both stubborn as hell and used to getting their own way."

Despite myself, I laugh. "Fair point."

We continue in companionable silence for a while. The night grows colder, the wind picking up and cutting through my damp clothes. I suppress a shiver.

"We should stop soon," he says, just as Rachel stumbles over a root.

"Agreed," she mutters, rubbing her ankle. "I can barely see my hand in front of my face, let alone where I'm stepping."

Orion, who's been leading our little group, turns back with a frown. "We need to put more distance between us and the river. These banks flood easily."

"And we need to not break our necks walking in the dark," I

counter. "There's a small clearing up ahead—I can smell the different vegetation. Should be enough space for a fire, at least."

Kieran nods his approval. "Good eye."

"Good nose," I correct, tapping the side of it.

He grins, and something warm uncurls in my stomach that has nothing to do with the prospect of a fire.

The clearing is perfect—a small open space surrounded by sheltering pines, with a fallen log that will make a decent windbreak. Rachel immediately sets about gathering smaller branches for kindling, while Orion surveys the perimeter. Kieran drops his pack and stretches, his shirt riding up to reveal a strip of toned abdomen that I definitely don't notice.

"Orion, get us some real firewood," he announces. "Something substantial enough to last the night."

Orion groans under his breath, while Rachel gives him a death glare. "Fine, I'll set up a basic camp," he says.

I hesitate to butt in, then make a decision. "I'll check the river for fish. We could all use a hot meal."

"I'll join you," Kieran says quickly. "Better to hunt in pairs."

Orion raises an eyebrow but says nothing. Rachel is too busy arranging stones for a firepit to notice the exchange.

We head back toward the river, now little more than a darker shadow at night. The moon provides just enough light to navigate by, silvering the edges of leaves and the curve of Kieran's jaw as he walks alongside me.

"You're quite good at this," I observe, breaking the silence.

"At what?"

"Moving silently." I gesture to the forest floor. "Most Umbra wolves I've tracked sound like drunk bears crashing through the underbrush."

He laughs, the sound startlingly genuine. "Most Elios I've tracked move like frightened mice—too light, too cautious. Makes it easy to predict where they'll go next."

"Tracked many Elios, have you?"

His pace slows slightly, allowing me to draw even with him. "A few. Never caught any worth keeping, though."

There's a challenge in his voice that makes my pulse quicken. "Maybe you weren't fast enough."

"Or maybe I was waiting for one that would give me a proper chase."

Our gazes clash in the darkness, and something electric passes between us. I look away first, suddenly fascinated by a nearby tree trunk.

We reach the river's edge, where the water has calmed somewhat from the raging torrent that separated us from Lyra and Theron. Kieran kneels by the bank, studying the flowing water with an expert eye.

"There," he says, pointing to a deeper pool where the current slows. "Perfect spot for fish to rest."

I nod, shrugging off my outer jacket. "I'll get them if you spot them."

"You're going in?" He sounds surprised. "The water's freezing."

"I'm still half wet anyway," I reply with a shrug. "And I'm quick with my hands."

His grin turns wicked. "I bet you are."

I roll my eyes, though a flush of heat touches my cheeks. "Just tell me when you see movement."

I wade carefully into the shallows, wincing at the icy bite of the water. Kieran points out the shadowy forms of fish, and I strike, spearing two decent-sized trout within minutes. Then I catch two more. By the time I emerge from the river, my legs are numb with cold, but I'm holding our dinner triumphantly aloft.

"Impressive," Kieran admits, helping me back onto the bank. His hand lingers on my arm a moment longer than necessary. "I've got a surprise of my own."

From his pocket, he produces a handful of small, pale mushrooms. "Found these by the bank while you were creating a fish massacre. They'll make a good tea—warm us up from the inside."

I peer at them suspiciously. "You sure they're not poisonous?"

"Would I poison myself?" he asks, looking offended.

"Maybe, if it meant taking out a few Elios with you."

He laughs again, that same genuine sound that makes something loosen in my chest. "Fair point. But no, these are frost caps. Perfectly safe, and they have... interesting properties."

"Interesting how?"

His smile turns mysterious. "You'll see."

We return to camp to find the fire already crackling, casting an orange glow over our makeshift shelter. Rachel has constructed a decent wind barrier with branches and leaves, while Orion has laid out the bedrolls in a neat semicircle around the flames.

"Fish!" Rachel exclaims when she sees our catch. "Gods bless you, Aria."

"And mushrooms," Kieran adds, displaying his find.

Orion eyes them suspiciously. "What kind?"

"Frost caps," Kieran replies, already setting water to boil in a small pot. "Good for warming the blood."

"And clouding the mind," Orion mutters but doesn't object further.

We prepare the fish simply, gutting them and spearing them on green sticks to roast over the flames. The aroma of cooking flesh soon fills our little camp, making my stomach growl audibly. Kieran, meanwhile, brews his mushroom tea in a small hollowed gourd he found nearby in the woods, the pale fungi steeping in the hot water until it turns a milky blue color.

"Drink up," he says, passing around crude cups fashioned from folded bark. "Best while it's hot."

I sniff the concoction warily before taking a small sip. It tastes better than expected—earthy with a hint of sweetness, and a warmth that spreads through my chest immediately.

"Not bad," I admit, taking another, deeper drink.

Orion sips cautiously. "My tongue feels strange."

"That's because you're a lightweight," Kieran teases. "One little frost cap and you're ready to see the moon spirits dance."

Rachel giggles, a sound I've never heard from the typically stoic Umbra woman. "It does make your mouth tingle, though."

We eat our fish and drink our tea. The fire crackles merrily, sparks dancing upward to join the stars, and the wind's bite seems less harsh now.

"—so there we were," Kieran continues his story, gesturing dramatically with his makeshift cup, "surrounded by three senior warriors with training spears while Theron's bleeding from the shoulder. Looks like we're finished, right?"

He leans forward, firelight dancing across his features. "But they didn't know I'd spent weeks studying that training ground. I grab Theron, pull him behind this massive oak, and before the seniors can follow, I've cut the hidden trip wire I'd set up days before."

"You did not," Rachel says, rolling her eyes.

"Did too," Kieran insists, grinning widely. "All three of them face down in the mud pit I'd dug. And who gets credited with the most innovative tactical thinking that month? This guy." He points both thumbs at his chest. "Theron never lets me forget I used him as bait, though."

Despite myself, I'm laughing along with everyone else. There's something infectious about the way he tells it—even if I suspect the story grows more heroic with each retelling.

I find myself watching him more than I should—the way the firelight plays across his features, highlighting the sharp angle of his jaw, the curve of his lips when he smiles. There's a vibrancy to him that draws the eye, an energy that seems barely contained within his skin.

Orion is speaking now, some dull tale about border patrols that I would normally find fascinating but tonight seems painfully boring. I realize with a start how long I've been infatuated with him—years of pining after his handsome face and serious demeanor, his perfect form and perfect technique. And yet, sitting here now, I can't remember what I found so captivating. He barely looks at me, barely acknowledges my existence beyond my usefulness.

My gaze drifts back to Kieran. He catches me looking and raises an eyebrow, the corner of his mouth quirking upward in that infuriating, attractive way. I should look away. I don't.

Later, as the fire burns lower and the tea's warmth spreads through my limbs with languid heat, Rachel and Orion curl into their bedrolls, their breathing soon evening into sleep. Kieran rises, stretching his arms above his head.

"Going to get more firewood," he announces quietly. "This won't last the night."

Without really thinking about it, I stand, too. "I'll help."

He doesn't question it, simply nods and leads the way into the darkness beyond our camp. We don't go far—just enough to still see the fire's glow through the trees, but far enough for privacy.

"You're not really looking for firewood, are you?" I ask as he stops beside a massive oak.

He turns to me, moonlight silvering his hair and catching in his eyes. "Not particularly, no."

"Then why am I out here freezing my ass off?"

"Because you wanted to be," he replies simply. "With me."

I should deny it. I should scoff and turn away, go back to the fire and the safety of familiar hatred. Instead, I step closer.

"You're very sure of yourself."

"I'm sure of what I see in front of me." His voice has dropped lower, rougher. "And I see the way you look at me when you think no one notices."

"And how's that?" I challenge, though my heart hammers against my ribs.

"Like you're wondering what it would be like to touch the enemy." His hand lifts, fingers hovering near my cheek without quite making contact. "Like you're wondering if I taste as dangerous as I look."

"That's ridiculous," I breathe, even as I sway slightly toward him.

"Is it?"

And then it happens—I'm not sure who moves first, but suddenly his mouth is on mine, hot and insistent. His hands grip my waist, pulling me against him as if he can press us into a single being. I match his hunger with my own, fingers tangling in his hair, tugging sharply enough to draw a growl from deep in his chest.

It's nothing like I imagined kissing him would be—not gentle or sweet or tentative. This is devouring, consuming, a battle neither of us wants to lose. His teeth catch my lower lip, biting just hard enough to send a shock of pleasure-pain down my spine.

"Fuck," I gasp against his mouth.

He laughs, the sound vibrating through me. "That's the general idea, yes."

Before I can retort, he's spinning us around, pressing me back against the rough bark of the oak. His mouth trails from my lips to my jaw, then down the column of my throat, finding a pulse point that makes my knees weaken when he sucks at it.

"Kieran," I manage, my voice embarrassingly breathless.

"Say it again," he murmurs against my skin. "I like how my name sounds on your tongue."

"Insufferable," I accuse, even as my hands slip under his shirt, exploring the hard planes of his chest, the ridges of muscle along his abdomen.

"Irresistible," he counters, his own hands busy with the laces of my shirt.

His fingers work at the ties of my leather vest while mine tug impatiently at his belt. We're a tangle of urgent hands and desperate breaths, neither of us willing to break apart long enough to make this easy.

"Shit—wait," I gasp as my back presses against a knot in the tree trunk.

Kieran pauses immediately, his pupils blown wide in the darkness. "What's wrong?"

"Nothing," I murmur, repositioning myself. "Just—"

I shift my weight, and my knee connects with something soft. Kieran makes a strangled sound, doubling over slightly.

"Sorry!" I bite my lip, fighting back a laugh. "Did I just—"

"Almost ended this before it began," he confirms, wincing dramatically but already pulling me back to him. "Dangerous in more ways than one, aren't you?"

I press my lips to his jaw, feeling the rough stubble against my mouth. "You have no idea."

His hand slips beneath my loosened shirt, palm hot against my ribs, fingers tracing upward with tantalizing slowness. When he cups my breast, his thumb circling the sensitive peak, I arch into his touch with a gasp that seems to echo through the silent forest.

"Gods, you're responsive," he breathes against my neck.

I want to make some cutting remark about Umbra arrogance, but then his other hand slides down my stomach, dipping below my waistband, and coherent thought scatters like leaves in a storm. His fingers find me slick and ready, and the first touch draws a moan from deep in my throat that I barely recognize as my own voice.

The cold air raises goose bumps on my exposed skin where he's pushed my shirt up, but everywhere Kieran touches blazes like wildfire. Heat spirals outward from his fingertips, pooling low in my belly, making me tremble with need.

"More," I demand, rocking against his hand.

He obliges, capturing my mouth in another bruising kiss as one finger slips inside me, then another, his thumb circling in rhythm with his tongue. The rough bark scrapes against my shoulders through my thin shirt, the slight sting a counterpoint to the pleasure building with each skilled stroke of his fingers.

For a moment, I remember who we are—Elios and Umbra, hereditary enemies tangled together in the moonlight—and the forbidden nature of it all only intensifies the sensations cascading through me. I'm panting now, my head falling back against the tree, my hips moving instinctively against his hand.

"Look at you," Kieran murmurs, pulling back to stare at me in the moonlight. "So beautiful like this."

"Less looking, more doing," I command, drawing him back to me.

His laugh vibrates against my lips as I draw him closer. My hands slide to the waistband of his pants, fumbling with the ties in my eagerness.

"Wait," he murmurs, his fingers catching mine. "Let me."

He steps back just enough to shed his own pants, kicking them aside before kneeling in front of me. His hands slide up my legs, fingers hooking into my waistband, looking up at me with a question in his eyes.

"Yes," I breathe, and he slowly draws my pants down my legs, his lips following the path of newly exposed skin. I step out of them, shivering more from anticipation than the cold night air.

"Tell me you want this," he says, voice husky as he rises to his feet. "Tell me you want me."

The vulnerability in his question catches me off guard. This isn't the cocky, self-assured Kieran I'm used to sparring with. I reach for his face, my palm against his cheek.

"I want this," I tell him, holding his gaze. "And you."

He guides me down onto his discarded jacket and pants, laying them across the forest floor before lowering me onto my back. The moonlight filters through the branches above, casting dappled shadows across our skin as he spreads my legs and lowers himself over me.

"You're so beautiful," he whispers, tracing the curve of my hip.

I pull him down to me, impatient for his touch. "Don't make me wait."

A wolfish grin spreads across his face. "Anything you want."

When he finally pushes inside me, the sensation is overwhelming—a delicious stretch that has me arching beneath him, my legs wrapping around his hips to draw him deeper. He stills for a moment, giving me time to adjust, his breathing ragged against my neck.

"Gods, Aria," he groans, sounding almost pained with pleasure. "You feel incredible."

I rock my hips, urging him on. "Show me what an Umbra warrior is capable of," I challenge.

His eyes flash with competitive fire. He begins to move with deliberate, measured thrusts. I clutch at his shoulders as he pumps into me, rapidly.

There's nothing gentle about the way we come together—it's all desperate need and primal hunger. His mouth finds mine again, swallowing my moans as he drives deeper, harder.

"Look at me," he demands, one hand tangling in my hair to tilt my face to his. "I want to see you come undone for me, Elios."

I should be offended by the tribal designation, but somehow, in this moment, it only heightens the forbidden thrill of what we're doing. I open my eyes, meeting his gaze as he thrusts particularly deep, when suddenly, I'm losing all control and stars are exploding behind my eyelids.

"Fuck, Kieran—"

"That's it," he encourages, his movement growing more erratic as he chases his own pleasure. "Let go for me, Aria."

The use of my name, spoken with such hunger, pushes me completely over the edge. I come with a muffled cry against his shoulder, my body clenching around him in waves that seem to go on forever. He follows moments later, his face buried in my neck as he groans my name like a prayer.

For several heartbeats, we lie there on his clothes, my legs still wrapped around him like I've forgotten how our bodies work. I can't remember the last time I felt so... undone.

Kieran pulls out and rolls to his side, looking down at me with this annoyingly satisfied expression. "You alive there, Aria?"

"Barely," I mutter, shoving his shoulder. "Don't look so smug. It's unbecoming."

"Can't help it." He grins, reaching for his pants. "Not every day you render an elite Elios scout speechless."

"I wasn't speechless," I argue, sitting up and wincing slightly. "I was... conserving energy."

He chuckles and tosses my shirt at me, and I catch it in midair.

As I tug my clothes back on, I think about what I've just done. Holy shit. I had sex with Kieran Stormfang. Our enemy. On the forest floor. Less than fifty yards from sleeping pack mates. Including Orion, who'd probably challenge Kieran to a death match if he knew.

What in the twin moons was I thinking?

"We shouldn't have done that," I blurt out, smoothing my hair with shaking hands.

Kieran looks up from fastening his pants, his expression unreadable in the moonlight. Then, slowly, a smile spreads across his face—not his usual cocky grin, but something more genuine, almost tender.

"Yes, we should have," he says quietly. "And we're going to do it again."

I open my mouth to protest, but he closes the distance between us, one hand cupping my cheek with surprising gentleness.

"I'm going to make you mine, Elios wolf," he murmurs, his thumb tracing my lower lip. "Whether either of us planned for it or not."

And stars curse me, but I believe him.

About Mila Young

**Find all Mila Young books at
www.milayoungbooks.com**

Best-selling author, Mila Young tackles everything with the zeal and bravado of the fairytale heroes she grew up reading about. She slays monsters, real and imaginary, like there's no tomorrow. By day she rocks a keyboard as a marketing extraordinaire. At night she battles with her mighty pen-sword, creating fairytale retellings, and sexy ever after tales.

Ready to read more and more from Mila Young?
www.subscribepage.com/milayoung

Join Mila's **Wicked Readers group** for exclusive content, latest news, and giveaway.
www.facebook.com/groups/milayoungwickedreaders

For more information...
mila@milayoungbooks.com